The Proof of My Innocence

Praise for Jonathan Coe

'Few contemporary writers can make a success of the state-of-the-nation novel: Jonathan Coe is one of them' *New Statesman*

'The funniest serious novelist practising in this country' *Independent*

'Coe far outranks many Booker winners in his talent for characterization and captivating narrative' *Literary Review*

'Coe's particular gift is to understand how nostalgia, regret and an apprehension of what the future will bring might make us more, not less, empathetic to the frailties of those around us' *Financial Times*

'A sweeping and multilayered portrait of a country bent on self-immolation . . . While we want everything we read at the moment to speak with the voice of our own particular echo chamber, Coe – a writer of uncommon decency – reminds us that the way out of this mess is through moderation, through compromise, through that age-old English ability to laugh at ourselves' *Observer* on *Middle England*

'Coe is an extraordinarily deft plotter . . . the book zips along . . . he tackles big ambitious themes, in this case the effect of politics on people's lives, and political opinions on personal relations' *Mail on Sunday* on *Middle England*

'Recaptures the witty juggling of genres that was the hallmark of *What a Carve Up!*, creating a new hybrid form melding fiction, memoir, screenplay, and criticism while still embracing the pleasure of narrative' *LA Review of Books* on *Mr Wilder and Me*

'*Bournville* is a wickedly funny, clever, but also tender and lyrical novel about Britain and Britishness, and what we have become. Told over a series of seven historical occasions – witnessed on different models of television set – it offers both a big picture window that opens out on the social changes between VE Day and the end of lockdown, and a small intimate window that reveals one family's struggle through three generations, their differences and secrets, and attempts or refusals to overcome them. Told with compassion, steadiness, decency and always a glint in the eye, this is a novel that both challenges and delights. For anyone who has felt lost in the past six years, it is like meeting an ally' Rachel Joyce, bestselling author of *The Unlikely Pilgrimage of Harold Fry*

'*Bournville* is a beautiful, and often very funny, tribute to an under-examined place, and also a truly moving story of how a country discovered tolerance' Sathnam Sanghera, bestselling author of *Empireland*

'For all the novel's satirical tang and historical sweep, *Bournville* is at root a tender portrait of apparently simple folk trying to fathom the mystery of their own personalities' *Spectator*

'At heart *Bournville* is a novel designed to make you think by making you laugh, and the seriousness of the subject matter is tempered throughout by the author's piercing eye for the more ludicrous elements of human nature' *New Statesman*

'This is another eminently readable Coe, full of believable characters and fizzing dialogue. And it couldn't be more timely' *Big Issue* on *Bournville*

'Coe has the great gift of combining engaging human stories with a deeper structural pattern that gives the book its heft' *Guardian* on *Bournville*

'*Bournville* is one of the most warm-hearted, brilliant and beguiling of Coe's state-of-the-nation novels. To show three generations of an ordinary Midlands family, their paths taken and not taken, their friends, lovers, jobs, achievements and losses; to interweave this with seventy-five years of national history – and to do so with such a lightness of touch – is a tremendous achievement. All the absurdities of our nation wrapped up in something as bitter, sweet and addictive as a bar of the best Bournville chocolate' Amanda Craig, author of *The Golden Rule*

By the same author

FICTION

The Accidental Woman

A Touch of Love

The Dwarves of Death

What a Carve Up!

The House of Sleep

The Rotters' Club

The Closed Circle

The Rain Before It Falls

The Terrible Privacy of Maxwell Sim

Expo 58

Number 11

Middle England

Mr Wilder and Me

Bournville

NON-FICTION

Like a Fiery Elephant: The Story of B. S. Johnson

FOR CHILDREN

The Broken Mirror

The Proof of My Innocence

JONATHAN COE

PENGUIN
VIKING

VIKING

UK | USA | Canada | Ireland | Australia
India | New Zealand | South Africa

Viking is part of the Penguin Random House group of companies
whose addresses can be found at global.penguinrandomhouse.com

Penguin Random House UK,
One Embassy Gardens, 8 Viaduct Gardens, London SW11 7BW

penguin.co.uk
global.penguinrandomhouse.com

Penguin
Random House
UK

First published 2024
001

Set in 12/14.75pt Dante MT Std
Typeset by Jouve (UK), Milton Keynes
Printed and bound in Great Britain by Clays Ltd, Elcograf S.p.A.

The authorized representative in the EEA is Penguin Random House Ireland,
Morrison Chambers, 32 Nassau Street, Dublin D02 YH68

A CIP catalogue record for this book is available from the British Library

HARDBACK ISBN: 978–0–241–67841–1
TRADE PAPERBACK ISBN: 978–0–241–67842–8

www.greenpenguin.co.uk

FSC
www.fsc.org
MIX
Paper | Supporting responsible forestry
FSC® C018179

Penguin Random House is committed to a sustainable future for our business, our readers and our planet. This book is made from Forest Stewardship Council® certified paper.

Contents

PROLOGUE
2nd–5th September 2022
5

PART ONE
See It
43

PART TWO
Say It
149

PART THREE
Sorted
229

EPILOGUE
27th February 2024
323

The detective soon picked out her suspect in the midst of the crowd at Paddington station, even though it was a busy Tuesday morning and the concourse was thronged with passengers. She watched the scuttling, furtive figure cutting a path towards Platform 5 and boarding a train to Worcester.

Joining the train herself, she found a seat that was close to the suspect, but not too close. One carriage away. She could remain unseen here, and still have a good view of her quarry, if she leaned forward and peered through the glass doors between the two carriages.

The train eased itself into motion exactly on time. As it picked up speed and moved through London's western suburbs, an announcement came over the speaker system:

If you see something that doesn't look right, speak to staff, or text British Transport Police on 61016.

We'll sort it.

See it. Say it. Sorted.

There was something profoundly annoying about the announcement, although the detective couldn't have said exactly what it was. She knew that the suspect would be getting out at Moreton-in-Marsh station – a journey of about ninety minutes – and she had been hoping to use that time to organize her notes on the case. But every few minutes her thought processes would be interrupted by this infuriating message.

If you see something that doesn't look right, speak to staff, or text British Transport Police on 61016.

We'll sort it.

See it. Say it. Sorted.

It was the word 'sorted' that was so irritating, she decided. The faux-demotic of it. Did anybody really use the word like that? In their attempt to strike an inclusive, non-elitist note, did the person who had composed that message really have to make it sound like something out of a mockney gangster movie?

She tried to stop thinking about it. She tried to focus her mind on the case and to put her finger on the one element – whatever it was – that had still not fallen into place. She was ninety-nine per cent convinced that the person she was tailing was the guilty party. But she would not feel truly comfortable until that one per cent of doubt had been removed.

If you see something that doesn't look right, speak to staff, or text British Transport Police on 61016.

We'll sort it.

See it. Say it. Sorted.

The stations flashed by. Reading. Oxford. Hanborough. Charlbury. Kingham. And it was at this point, with only five minutes to go before they reached their destination, that the clouds suddenly cleared, and the detective realized that she had found the thing she had been looking for. She picked up her phone and a few seconds' clicking and scrolling took her to a page which confirmed her suspicions. Confirmed them exactly. The one per cent of doubt had disappeared. The moment had come to put caution aside, and to take decisive action.

The white-haired detective, dressed entirely in black, got out of her seat and made her way into the next carriage. Her body swayed with the motion of the train. Soon she was standing over the suspect, who was bent over the screen of a smartphone. It was showing a live broadcast from the steps of Number 10 Downing Street. As the detective's shadow fell across the screen, two wary, questioning eyes were slowly raised to meet hers, and she saw the flame of recognition start to burn in them. She spoke the suspect's full name and said, 'I am arresting you for the murder of—' before once again being interrupted.

If you see something that doesn't look right, speak to staff, or text British Transport Police on 61016.

We'll sort it.

See it. Say it. Sorted.

PROLOGUE

2nd–5th September 2022

Phyl leaned forward on the garden bench and felt a shiver run through her body. It was twenty to eight, the sun was already setting and the evenings were starting to feel colder. The privet hedge, tall and perfectly trimmed, was casting its long shadow across the lawn which her father had mown into neat stripes a few days earlier. From the depths of the lily pond, Gregory the ancient and alliterative goldfish rose occasionally to the surface and blew indifferent kisses in her direction with his bulbous lips. Birds she could not have identified were singing their sunset songs from the branches of trees she could not have named. Clouds punctuated the reddening sky and between them in the distance she could make out the silver glint of an aeroplane making its slow descent to Heathrow. It was a scene of lovely tranquillity, which left her completely cold. She had solved today's Wordle in three guesses and, checking her stats, discovered that she now had a streak of sixty-eight. That meant that today, Friday 2nd September, marked sixty-eight days since she had left university. Sixty-eight days since her father had driven up to Newcastle in the new Toyota of which he was so proud, crammed her possessions into the back and carried her away for good from the filthy, mouldering, rat-infested house where she had spent the happiest year of her life. Away from the six friends whose annoying attitudes, banal conversation and gross personal habits she missed more than she could ever have imagined. Away from all that and back home to the comfort, quietude and stultifying affluence of her ageing parents' daily existence. She shivered again.

Seventeen minutes to eight. Time seemed to pass so slowly when she wasn't at work. For the last three weeks, Phyl had been working nine-hour shifts at a branch of a highly successful chain specializing in Japanese food. The branch was located in Heathrow Terminal 5, about fifteen miles from her parents' house. This chain's USP was the novelty of having miniature trays of sushi winding between the customers' tables on little conveyor belts. Most of the dishes were put together on the premises so Phyl spent her days chopping up vegetables and covering tiny briquettes of rice with thin layers of smoked salmon. She had started to learn the difference between the various Japanese kitchen knives: the wide-bladed *usuba*, which was used for vegetables; the *yanagiba*, best suited for slicing raw fish into sashimi strips; the heavier, thicker *deba* knife, used for cutting through bones. It was hard work, and after nine hours (with a twenty-minute lunch break) she would finish up with glazed eyes, an aching back and legs, and fingers smelling indelibly of fish. However, the mindless boredom of this job helped her temporarily to forget the mindless boredom of her home life, and the long, complicated bus journey from the airport back to her parents' town gave her time to think about her plans for the future, or rather lack of them: because she had no idea what kind of jobs to apply for next, or what she wanted to do with the rest of her life. Apart, that is, from one thought which had implanted itself recently, but which was so private, and so . . . audacious, that she didn't dare share it with anyone, least of all her mother and father.

She was thinking of writing a book.

What kind of book? A novel? A memoir? Something in the hinterland between the two? She didn't know. Phyl had never written anything before, even though she was an avid reader. All she knew was that since coming back from university – no, before that: she'd first noticed it in those few long, languid weeks after her finals – she had felt a growing impulse, a growing *need* (the word was not too strong) to create something, to put words on a screen, to try carving something shapely and full of meaning from the dull block of marble that made up her inert and formless experience.

She didn't know what it would be. But today, she had decided upon one episode that would definitely form a part of it. It was something that had happened to her a few hours earlier. A small incident, but one that she knew was going to stay with her.

When her shift had ended at three o'clock, Phyl had made her way to the lifts and waited for one to arrive. Terminal 5 was quiet. The lift had to come from four floors below and then you had to wait a while for the doors to open. There was a button to call the lift and a button to open the doors but Phyl had realized by now that these were only for show and everything was done automatically. There was literally no point in touching them. Shortly before the lift arrived on her floor, a man of about her own age approached and stood beside her. He was carrying a sports bag and wearing shorts which showed off his tanned, muscular, hairy legs. (Since working at Heathrow, Phyl had been surprised by the number of men who wore shorts when travelling by plane.) He stood next to her and jiggled his leg impatiently as the lift arrived. Phyl was standing closer to the buttons, but she didn't touch them. She knew that the lift doors would open automatically after ten seconds. She had been through this every day. After nine seconds, though, the man's impatience got the better of him. He wasn't going to have his journey delayed by this passive, helpless female. He leaned across her and pushed the button and, sure enough, one second later, the doors opened. They both stepped inside.

As their descent to ground level began, Phyl knew exactly what this man was thinking. He had saved the day. Without his swift, decisive action, they would still be standing on the fourth floor waiting for the doors to open. The self-satisfied vibe coming off him was so strong, it was almost as if he was waiting to be congratulated. But she wasn't going to congratulate him. Instead, by the time they had descended one floor, her feeling of irritation was so strong that she had to say:

'They were going to open anyway, you know.'

He looked up from his phone. 'Uh?'

'The doors. They would have opened anyway.'

He looked at her blankly.

'You didn't have to push the button.'

'Well I did,' he answered.

'But you didn't have to.'

'I pushed it,' he said, 'and they opened. Seems a weird coincidence.'

'But they would have opened anyway.'

'Yeah, but you don't get lift doors to open by just standing there.'

'As a matter of fact you do,' said Phyl. 'With these doors, that's exactly what you do.'

He shrugged and went back to his phone.

'I use these lifts every day,' she continued.

'Good for you,' he answered, without looking up. And after a pause: 'That's a lot of flying. Think of the carbon footprint.'

'Hilarious,' said Phyl. 'I work here, actually.'

'Look,' said the man, reluctantly glancing up from his phone and clearly intending to put a stop to this conversation with a deranged woman. 'If it wasn't for me, we'd both still be standing up there. Just admit it.'

The lift came to a halt and the doors opened.

'Well, what do you know?' said Phyl. 'They opened. Without either of us having to touch a button.'

'Get a life,' he said, storming off in the direction of the taxi rank. 'Fucking loser.'

She stood motionless, watching his receding back. She was stunned – stunned and paralysed, and for the next few hours she could not get the man's last two words out of her head. She had thought about them on the bus journey home, and she was still thinking about them even now. In fact there was a danger that, unless she did something decisive, she would carry on thinking about them all evening and all night, until she went to sleep, whenever that was likely to be. (Insomnia being one of her many problems at the moment.) So she did what she so often did at moments of stress. Skirting the garage where her father was looking for cardboard boxes, and the study where her mother was working, she made her way briskly upstairs to her bedroom and lay full length on the bed. EarPods in place, holding her phone in the air above her, Phyl went onto Netflix and scrolled down, looking for an episode of *Friends* to watch. This, for her, was a regular televisual comfort blanket, one of the most reliable ways of beating a temporary retreat from the world. She had already seen every episode more than a dozen times, so these days it was really just a question of spinning the wheel. Today she hit on Season 1, Episode 21: *The One with the Fake Monica*, in which one of the characters had her identity stolen by a credit card thief. It was a strong episode, Phyl thought, not least because the fraudster herself turned out to be so engaging. At the end of the show she went to prison and Phyl was always sorry that she never reappeared in any further episodes. She would have liked to know more about her: what was so bad about her own life that made her want to steal someone else's identity and reinvent herself? Such a tempting idea, in so many ways. To disappear, to vanish into thin air, leaving behind a lifetime's worth of mistakes and embarrassments, and then to re-emerge in an entirely different guise. Reborn . . .

Of course, there were the other subplots to enjoy as well: Ross's quest to find a new home for his pet monkey, Joey's attempts to decide on a new stage name. For Phyl, the whole appeal of the *Friends* universe was the charming predictability sustained throughout every one of its 236 episodes. When this one was finished she felt (as she always did) much calmer. The hurtful tang of her encounter at the lifts was wearing off, leaving just a lingering sense of fury at the man's arrogance. She was more certain than ever, though, that to write about it would prove cleansing, and cathartic. She just had no idea how to begin. Perhaps she should simply dive in and tell the story, start putting it into words, and see where that process took her. Was that how writers did it?

She decided to look in her father's library for inspiration.

The vicarage at Rookthorne was a late-Victorian building, like the church, and – like the church – it was defiantly unattractive, but what it lacked in charm it more than made up for in size. The ground floor alone comprised an enormous vaulted kitchen, a dining room, two reception rooms, the study where Phyl's mother worked on what her daughter referred to as her 'vicar stuff' and one further sitting room which had been given over to her father's ridiculous collection of books. 'The library', her parents called it, and it was testament to a bibliomania that had long since spiralled out of control, with shelves running the length of all four walls and filled from floor to ceiling with many thousands of books, most of them eighteenth- or nineteenth-century volumes bound in leather, interspersed with a few thousand more recent works of history and biography and a smattering of modern firsts. There were also three comfortable armchairs, with their backs turned towards the light admitted by the sash windows, and it was in one of these chairs that Phyl's father, Andrew, was sitting now, straining his eyes over the tiny print of some forgotten Victorian novel or other. He was surrounded by cardboard boxes, and also by piles of books, stacked up in a number of precarious towers, which he seemed to be sorting according to some system of his own. Looking up when his daughter came in, he said:

'Everything OK, love?'

'Yeah, I'm fine,' she answered. She took in the organized chaos of her father's situation. 'What are you doing?'

'Having a clear-out. We've got an overflow problem.' He looked around him and sighed, seemingly daunted by the work still to be done. 'Difficult process, actually. I've got to choose fifteen feet's worth of books and pack them all up.'

Phyl took a paperback from one of the piles and glanced at it mechanically, without real interest.

'Then what will you do with them?' she asked.

'Take them to Victor, I suppose, and sell them, very reluctantly.'

She could not think who 'Victor' was, at first: then remembered that he was one of her father's London friends, an antiquarian bookseller he sometimes did business with.

Andrew was craning to see the cover of the novel she'd selected. 'What's that?'

Phyl looked at it properly for the first time. It was a hefty volume, more than five or six hundred pages long. The title was *Lilliput Rising* and the author was called Piers Capon. Both the cover design and the typeface seemed to belong to a far-off era. She checked the publication date and saw that it was 1993.

'Can't say I have any recollection of buying that,' her father said.

Phyl was reading the publisher's blurb. 'Wow. Listen to this. "*Lilliput Rising* is an epic satire on the madness of modern life, spanning continents and generations, which shows one of our most brilliant young novelists working at the height of his powers. It is without doubt destined to become a future classic."'

Her father gave a dry laugh. 'Well, that didn't work out too well, did it? If even someone like me can't remember who this guy . . . Piers Capon . . . was. Put it on the pile for the charity shop, will you?'

Phyl took the book over to where he was pointing, placed it on top of the pile, and then stood looking down at it for a moment, lost in thought. A weird, inexplicable sadness came over her at the realization that once, almost thirty years ago, an author had been assured by his publisher and by reviewers that he had written a classic novel which would be admired for generations to come, and now he was quite forgotten, completely unread. He might as well not have bothered writing at all.

On top of the next pile was a book she did recognize, although she had never read it: *Money*, by Martin Amis. Despite the fact that her father was constantly telling her it was a masterpiece, the idea of it had somehow never appealed to her. She opened it at the title page and noticed that it bore the subtitle 'A Suicide Note'. That was intriguing, in a way. She was also struck by the plain, pale blue cover of this paperback copy, which bore no adornment apart from the title, the author's name, and the words 'Uncorrected proof copy. Not for quotation or for resale.'

'What does this mean?' she asked. '"Uncorrected proof copy"?'

'Oh, that's an industry thing,' said her father. 'When the first proofs come in, the publisher will sometimes bind them up and send them out to magazines and reviewers and so on. The thinking is that editors are more likely to read them if they look like a real book.'

'But won't they have mistakes in?'

'Sometimes,' said Andrew. 'That's why they can be valuable on the collectors' market. I'll take that to Victor next week. He can tell me whether it's worth anything.'

Phyl replaced the book and picked up a nice hardback first edition of *Titus Groan* by Mervyn Peake instead. This one brought back some good memories. She remembered reading it when she was about sixteen or seventeen, getting happily lost in its maze of Gothic narratives and identifying fiercely with the character of wilful, solitary Fuchsia. Expecting to get a delicious nostalgic rush from the opening page, she sat down in one of the armchairs and started reading, but found that even here she couldn't concentrate. This mood of aimlessness, of dissatisfaction, could not be shaken off. She put this book to one side as well, and found herself staring glumly into space.

Before long the question recurred, more insistent and more unanswerable than ever. She sighed heavily.

What was she going to do with the rest of her life?

'Can you remember what it felt like when you left university?' she asked her father.

'I can indeed,' he said, still sorting and stacking. 'It felt horrible. Totally anticlimactic. Three years gone by in the twinkling of an eye and then back living with my parents. I was miserable – just like you are now.'

'I'm not miserable,' Phyl insisted. 'Just a bit . . . restless. I don't really know what to do next.'

'Well, you've got plenty of time to think about it,' her father said. 'Give yourself a break. You're only twenty-three.'

'True,' said Phyl. 'But what about . . . I mean, when you were my age, did you have any plans? Did you know that you wanted to be a . . .' Her mind went suddenly blank. '. . . What was it you did again?'

'I was a chartered surveyor,' said her father. 'For more than thirty years.'

'Yes,' said Phyl. 'Sorry. I don't know why that's never stuck in my mind.'

'And no,' said Andrew. 'That was never my plan. Certainly never my childhood dream. I just sort of drifted into it. Nothing wrong with that. Lots of people drift into things.' He glanced at the discarded copy of *Titus Groan* by Phyl's side. 'You used to love that,' he said. 'What's the matter, not in the mood?'

'Not right now. I want something more contemporary. Something that's going to explain the world to me. I don't know . . . something political, maybe.'

'Since when have you been interested in politics?'

'You don't know what I'm interested in,' said Phyl, her indignation rising. 'In three days' time we're going to have a new Prime Minister. That's interesting, isn't it?'

Andrew shrugged and stared for a long time at the cover of Samuel Johnson's *Rasselas*. He seemed undecided as to its fate, and in the end all he said was, 'Prime Ministers come and go.'

The easy fatalism of this statement momentarily enraged Phyl. 'How can I have a conversation with you when you say things like that? What does it even mean?'

'If you want to talk about politics,' Andrew said, 'your mother's friend Christopher is coming to stay tomorrow, and he'll be more than happy to oblige. In the meantime, you could always read his blog. I'm told it's very political.'

Recognizing an unaccustomed sharpness in his voice (and her father was not an easy man to provoke), Phyl beat a strategic retreat from the library. She had forgotten that Joanna's friend would be visiting. Her father hadn't sounded too happy about it, she thought.

Drifting into the kitchen and finding it empty, she began to wonder whether she should offer to make dinner, as there seemed precious little sign of that happening at the moment. But inertia was gripping her too tightly, and after taking three black olives from a bowl in the fridge and popping them into her mouth, she went to look for someone else to talk to.

Her mother, Joanna, was in the study, tapping away at her computer. Radio 3 was on in the background. Phyl looked over her shoulder to see what she was typing. It seemed to be an amendment to a resolution of the church council, specifying the exact size and shape of the typeface to be used for a health warning which would be put up in the church, regarding the allergenic properties of the flower displays. Phyl sat down on the little sofa behind her mother's desk, depressed to think how forcibly the exact meaning of the word 'parochial' had been brought home to her during these last two months.

The music on the radio was strange. Strange, but rather beautiful. A high male voice (a countertenor? Was that the name for this kind of voice?) was singing a melancholy tune, accompanied by a spare, gentle, barely audible guitar. There was a lot of echo on the recording.

'This is nice,' said Phyl. 'What is it?'

Her mother didn't look up from her typing. 'I wasn't really listening.'

'What's the point of having it on, if you don't listen to it?'

Her mother's fingers continued to click on the keyboard. Realizing that she was not going to get any conversation here, Phyl was on the point of standing up and leaving again when the song detained her. It had an eerie melody: haunting and wistful, but with a slightly sinister undertone. As for the words, she was not sure, at first, that she was hearing them correctly.

Oh, you have been poisoned, oh Randall, my son
You have been poisoned, my handsome young one
'Tis truth you've spoken, Mother
'Tis truth you've spoken, Mother
Please make my bed soon, for I'm sick to the heart
And fain would lie down

'So this is a song about someone being poisoned, is it?'

'Hold on, love, I've nearly finished here.'

Phyl closed her eyes and tried to concentrate on the words. The clicking of the keyboard was distracting.

Oh, what will you leave your sweetheart, my son?
What will you leave her, my handsome young one?
A rope from hell to hang her
A rope from hell to hang her
Oh, make my bed soon, for I'm sick to the heart
And fain would lie down

'And now he's going to hang his sweetheart, is that right? After he's died from the poisoning.'

Joanna pressed the Delete key on her keyboard repeatedly. 'Why does it keep *doing* that?' she asked. 'It keeps trying to reformat the whole document.'

The song came to an end, fading away with a last sorrowful cadence. There was a short silence before a female voice announced that it was an old folk song from England – or perhaps Scotland, or perhaps the border country between the two – entitled 'Lord Randall'. Phyl made a mental note of the name.

Then she watched, with increasing frustration, as her mother continued to be thwarted by the vagaries of Microsoft Word.

'Can I help you with anything?' she asked.

'No, I'll work it out,' Joanna snapped. 'Just let me get on with it for a few minutes, will you?'

Phyl stood up and made for the door, but turned before leaving.

'What's your friend's name?' she asked.

'Mm?'

'Your friend, who's coming to stay tomorrow.'

'Oh. Christopher.'

'Christopher what?'

'Swann. A-double-n.'

'OK. Thanks. Do you want me to make dinner?'

'Your father will probably do it.'

And so Phyl went back upstairs to her bedroom, lay full length on the bed again – this time with her feet on the pillows – and flipped open her laptop. She put 'christopher swann blog' into Google and found it in no time. The page was headed by a youthful photograph of a face that was familiar – vaguely – from a few years back when her mother's friend had last visited: dark brown hair flecked with grey; a high, intellectual forehead; wire-rimmed spectacles; an enquiring, steely glint in the eyes. Yes, she remembered him now. A bit pompous, she had found him. Quite cold and offhand. Prone to mansplaining.

The photograph sat awkwardly atop a banner headline that read, *USING THE POWER OF TRUTH TO TELL TRUTH TO POWER*, which was lame in the extreme, Phyl thought. However, the content of the latest post (written just three days earlier) was quite interesting.

> *A luxury hotel on the outskirts of an idyllic Cotswold village* [she read] *will play a minor role in British political history next week, when delegates gather for the first of what we are promised will become an annual event – the British TrueCon conference on the future of conservatism.*
>
> *Regular readers of this blog will be familiar with the nature of TrueCon. Originally an American foundation, it has now opened a British wing and has strong links both to the most Trumpian extremes of the Republican Party and our own dear Conservative Party's lunatic fringe. Indeed there will be several Tory cabinet ministers in attendance during the three-day shindig, along with a good number of predictable names from the usual rabble of right-wing columnists, academics and online culture warriors. Among the enticing topics to be debated are 'The Woke War against National*

Belonging' and 'Family, Flag, Freedom and the Need to Restore our Common Life'.

Two names we should certainly not be surprised to see among the advertised speakers are those of Emeric Coutts and Roger Wagstaff. (See this blog, passim.) The now rather elderly Coutts has, of course, been regarded as one of the country's leading conservative thinkers ever since the establishment of his famous Cambridge Seminars in the late 1970s. It was there, as an undergraduate, that Wagstaff fell under his spell, although he has since taken Coutts's teachings in a direction which the Master himself could surely never endorse. These last few years, nonetheless, have been good for Wagstaff. His think tank, the Processus Group, was officially founded in the mid-1990s (although it had existed in embryonic form ever since his Cambridge days), and was trailed as a vehicle for keeping the Thatcherite torch aflame following her dethronement by traitors in her own cabinet. It languished in the political wilderness for more than twenty years, but since 2016, when the Brexit vote triggered a decisive shift to the right in the Tory Party, he and his colleagues have been much in demand: not just popping up on every TV channel and radio station, being invited to broadcast their frankly crackpot views in the spurious name of 'balance', but even being taken on as unofficial or sometimes even paid advisors to several of the more unhinged cabinet ministers. By the beginning of next week, if (as all the polls seem to suggest) Liz Truss becomes our new Prime Minister, their influence will no doubt increase still further. Processus is a sinister organization, with a specific but hidden agenda which I have been promising to reveal for some time. Rest assured that I now have decisive proof of their real intentions, and will be blogging about it in some detail in a matter of weeks or even days . . .

Phyl's curiosity was very much piqued by this hint. When they did all finally sit down to dinner at ten o'clock (her father having done the decent thing and thrown together some pasta and pesto sauce) she mentioned it to her parents but received a dampening response.

'Oh dear,' her mother said. 'You haven't been reading Christopher's blog, have you? I do wish he'd give up on that.'

Seeing his daughter's surprise at this remark, Andrew merely said:

'The thing you have to remember about him is that he *can* be –' he searched around for the right word – 'something of a fantasist.'

Thinking about it in bed that night, Phyl guessed that it was at least five years since she had last seen Christopher Swann. Even now she couldn't recall what he did for a living or indeed anything else about him, except that she seemed to remember he'd married an American and lived over there on the East Coast for a while before getting divorced and returning to the UK. She had forgotten to ask how long he would be staying for. No more than a day or two, she hoped.

She missed his arrival on Saturday morning, her day having started early, being driven by her mother to the airport through the near-dark of the Berkshire countryside in time for her 6 a.m. shift. The first she saw of their visitor, then, was when she arrived home in the afternoon. Another day spent watching bowls of sushi slowly winding their way around the tables occupied by excited travellers had once again left her feeling dazed and confused, and she was too tired to attempt the journey home by public transport: a journey of only fifteen miles which nonetheless could take anything up to three hours, owing to the withdrawal of most local bus services during the last few years. So instead she took a taxi, wiping out the earnings of half her nine-hour shift, and was home by a quarter to four. Christopher and her mother were in the library, looking through an old photograph album and chuckling over the pictures in an intimate, rather exclusive way. Her father was in the sitting room, watching an old British comedy film set in a boarding school called *The Happiest Days of Your Life*. Just from seeing a few minutes Phyl could tell that it wasn't for her, but she knew why her father liked this kind of film. There was something quaintly reassuring about the world it portrayed: black-and-white Britain in the 1950s, with its familiar cast of character actors and the series of harmlessly farcical situations they found themselves in. She supposed it was his version of re-watching old *Friends* episodes: nostalgia for a time he was too young to remember himself. Phyl enjoyed the sight of his smiling, quietly contented face, then left him to it and went upstairs to have a shower and snatch a couple of hours' sleep.

Later that evening, over dinner, she had a chance to study the dynamics between her father, her mother and her mother's friend.

She was aware that Joanna had known Christopher for longer than she had known her husband. They had been students together at Cambridge, some years before Joanna and Andrew had met. As a result, there was a special, long-lasting intimacy between the two university friends from which her father must have felt excluded. In conversation, Joanna and Christopher kept coming back to their Cambridge days and Andrew, who had been to a more humble university, had nothing to contribute. Like Phyl, he could only sit and listen, and ask for the occasional clarification.

'So I read Brian's memoir a few weeks ago,' Joanna was saying. 'And it all came flooding back. So many things that I'd forgotten.'

Her husband looked puzzled already. 'Who was Brian?'

'Brian Collier. You've heard us talk about him, loads of times. We were best friends, the three of us, ever since we met in the first week.'

'Oh, yes – the chap who died last year.'

'That's right. Well, he managed to enjoy one year of retirement before the cancer got him, poor thing, and in that time he wrote this little memoir.'

'I'd love to see it,' said Christopher. 'Do you have a copy? Could I read it while I'm here?'

'Yes, of course. Jackie sent me a copy of the manuscript. It's in my study somewhere. Actually I haven't been able to find it for a few weeks but it's definitely in there.'

'Joanna, you *have* to be more organized . . .' Andrew said.

She ignored the rebuke, and continued: 'I'd forgotten that I'd taken him to so many of Emeric's salons. They obviously made a big impression on him.'

'Hold on – who was Emeric?'

'Oh, come on, love – I've told you about him so often.'

'Was he the history don you were all a bit scared of?'

'Philosophy don,' Joanna corrected, patting his arm.

'The one with a glamorous daughter, who played the harpsichord – Virginia, wasn't it?'

'Lavinia,' Joanna said. 'And it was a clavichord. And she didn't play it – she sang songs while somebody else was playing it.'

'OK, so . . . whatever. Emeric was famous for his literary salons, I think you told me.'

'Not really literary,' Christopher demurred. 'Sometimes he invited writers, but politics was always the main focus.'

'I've told you all about this, dozens of times,' said Joanna.

'I'll actually be seeing Emeric next week,' Christopher went on hastily, before a marital argument could break out. 'I don't think he had much to do with organizing this conference, but he's going to be there, as its sort of . . . presiding spirit.'

'Gosh – how old would he be now?'

'Late eighties, I should think. In fact the whole thing is going to be quite a Cambridge reunion. Wagstaff will be there too, of course.'

For a moment it seemed that Andrew wasn't going to bother to ask who Wagstaff was. He seemed to have given up trying to follow the streams of reminiscence. But eventually a sense of duty got the better of him, and he said:

'Another of your friends?'

'Hardly a friend,' said Joanna. 'Horrid man. Even I hated him.'

'Not very Christian of you,' her husband observed, in a tone of dry mischief.

'Nobody liked Roger Wagstaff.'

'Apart from Rebecca,' Christopher pointed out.

'Rebecca! My God, I'd forgotten all about her. What a sad case she was!'

At this mention of yet another unfamiliar figure from the past, Andrew's patience finally ran out.

'*Who the hell was Rebecca?*' he said. 'Why was she a sad case?'

'No need to get angry, dear,' Joanna said, looking at him with wounded surprise. 'She was a girl who lived on the same staircase as me, that's all. She was . . . oh, I don't know, how would you describe her?'

'Bit of a wallflower,' Christopher suggested.

'Yes, I suppose that's right. Nothing wrong with her at all – quite sweet, in a way – but no sex appeal, so of course none of the men would so much as glance at her, even though women weren't exactly thick on the ground in Cambridge back in those days. Anyway, they would all have been wasting their time with her, because she only ever had eyes for Roger.'

'You know, it always amazes me,' said Christopher, 'that you've found your calling as a sort of shepherdess of human souls, when you seem to have no understanding of human nature whatsoever. Either that, or you're just wilfully inclined to see the best in people. By no stretch of the imagination could Rebecca Wood be described as "quite sweet". She had a core of absolute steel, that woman, and the reason she fell for Roger was that they were kindred spirits. She was a nasty piece of work.'

'I've no idea what makes you say that.'

'You know she still works as his PA, forty years later? What sort of person would you have to be to make *that* your life's mission? There's nothing that woman wouldn't do for Roger Wagstaff.'

'Oh, for goodness' sake,' Joanna said, irritated now. 'You're not going to bring up that poor young man again, are you? The one who fell down the stairs? *Accidentally*.'

'Rebecca was in the same building at the time. And no one has ever been able to explain why.'

Andrew's wandering attention seemed to refocus at this point. 'OK, *that* sounds more interesting. Did this happen at Cambridge too?'

'No,' said Christopher. 'This was years later.'

'Nothing was *ever* proved,' Joanna reminded him.

'I know nothing was ever proved. But it certainly did Roger no harm to have that man safely out of the way. Removed what could have been a serious obstacle to his progress. Which remains unstoppable, by the way. He's heading for the House of Lords in a few months' time, if my sources are to be believed.'

Joanna tutted. 'Well, that *is* shameful. Although I suppose we shouldn't really be surprised.'

'Oh yes, it was bound to happen sooner or later,' said Christopher. 'Ennobled for services to making the rich even richer, making the poor even poorer, and generally fucking up the country to the best of his ability.'

Joanna frowned at his use of the swear word, and said: 'I wonder what Emeric thinks about the success of his protégé.'

'I imagine he has mixed feelings. Probably feels rather used by him. After all, it was *Emeric* who always had Mrs Thatcher's ear, back in the eighties. I'm pretty sure he advised her on policy. John Major too, I think. But in the last ten years or so I get the impression he's been frozen out. Now it's Wagstaff who has half the cabinet on speed dial. Hence his invitation to join the Lords. And when the Tories continue their lurch to the right and choose their new leader on Monday, no doubt he'll become more influential than ever.'

Phyl thought about this while sipping from her wine glass, then sat upright and said: 'I'm sorry, but it's just crazy to me that we live in a modern, developed country, in 2022, and people are still calling each other Lord and Baron and Dame or whatever and they're all getting these puffed-up titles for services rendered, without even making any secret of it. I mean, does this sort of thing happen in other parts of the world, or are we uniquely corrupt and peculiar?'

Christopher gave a rueful smile. 'Britain is a unique country in all sorts of ways.'

'Which is probably,' Joanna said, 'what makes it so colourful.'

No doubt it was intended as a light-hearted remark, but it annoyed Phyl intensely. Passivity, emollient humour, shoulder-shrugging acquiescence: these were the tools her mother seemed to use to navigate every kind of situation, these days. They were beginning to get on her nerves.

Andrew, it seemed, had also had enough of this conversation.

'How about watching a film?' he said.

After some discussion, they made a choice. Joanna asked for something 'a bit more modern than usual', which turned out to mean a film that was in colour, and preferably no more than sixty years old. Phyl herself vetoed *Don't Look Now* (a thriller about a grieving couple who encounter a murderous figure in red while staying in Venice) on the grounds that she'd already been made to watch it too many times. Instead they settled for Ken Russell's adaptation of *Women in Love*. To her surprise, Phyl found that she was rather enjoying it – especially the scene of nude homoerotic wrestling – but she was also very tired after her long shift at work, and she fell asleep on the sofa long before it was over.

*

The next morning she woke up late, to the pleasant realization that she had the day off. She came downstairs at about eleven to find Christopher alone in the kitchen, drinking tea and reading the Sunday papers. He didn't notice her come in at first, since he was listening to music on a set of noise-cancelling headphones. When he did become aware of her presence and took the headphones off, Phyl was surprised to find that he seemed to have been listening to 1970s jazz-funk, of all things.

Her mother was out, taking the morning service, and her father was bound to be at the church with her, offering moral support (despite his atheism). She made herself some coffee and ate a bowl of cereal. After which, Christopher suggested that they went for a walk together.

They crossed the bleak stretch of parkland between the vicarage and the town centre, and were soon strolling along Rookthorne's high street. Never very alluring, it had changed for the worse in the time that Phyl had been away at university. The two main pubs, the Bell and the White Horse, had both closed down and were boarded up. Abelman's the butcher's – a staple of her family world for almost two decades – had closed earlier in the year, as had the post office, the one high street bank and a once-thriving independent bookshop. The only new business to have arrived in the last few months was a pizza delivery company which now operated out of the old post office, its windows still covered with newspaper and a temporary sign nailed to the frontage. About a mile and a half away, however, on the far outskirts of the town, a new trading estate had recently sprung up, featuring two supermarkets, a home furnishings warehouse, a discount store and a coffee shop, all of them part of large national chains. And it was to this location that the residents of Rookthorne flocked every day, leaving their cars in its enormous car park, trawling the shops for affordable items but nevertheless considering £5 a small price to pay for a coffee when it also entitled you to free Wi-Fi and a warm refuge for as long as you wanted it. Meanwhile the high street lay forlorn and deserted.

'Look at the way it's changed,' said Christopher. 'It was nothing like this when I last visited.' He stopped and frowned in concentration, trying to recall some words. Then declaimed: '"Sweet smiling village, loveliest of the lawn / Thy sports are fled, and all thy charms withdrawn." ' He looked at Phyl, apparently expecting her to recognize the quotation. 'Come on,' he prompted. 'You did English, didn't you? You must know where that comes from.'

She shook her head.

' "Ill fares the land, to hastening ills a prey / Where wealth accumulates, and men decay." No? Doesn't ring a bell?'

'Afraid not.'

He sighed. 'Just shows how old I'm getting, I suppose. I kind of assumed that poems like "The Deserted Village" would still be on the curriculum. Oliver Goldsmith – you've heard of him? *The Vicar of Wakefield*?'

Phyl hadn't.

'You're making me feel very ignorant,' she said.

'Ah well.' He smiled. 'Things are different since I was a student, I realize that. You read all sorts of interesting stuff now that wouldn't have got a look-in at Cambridge in the 1980s. Still, it's a good poem, if you ever feel like looking at it. I'm sure your dad's got a copy of Goldsmith lying around somewhere. It's about how capitalism breaks up communities, essentially.'

'He's never mentioned it,' Phyl said. 'But then Dad doesn't talk about his books much. Or politics. Or . . . well, anything, really.'

As they walked on past a barber's, a nail bar and a beauty salon, Christopher said: 'I suppose it's quite tough for you, being back here with your parents, after three years at uni?'

Phyl shrugged. 'It was OK at first. It's beginning to get to me a bit now.'

'You've got a job anyway.'

'Oh yes, I've got my zero-hours, minimum-wage job. Doing my bit to keep the capitalist machine ticking over.'

Christopher took this in, and thought back to the conversation at dinner last night.

'You sound pretty cynical,' he said.

'Not really. It's just that my generation has no illusions about the situation we've been left with.'

'I know.' They had stopped outside the former bank, and Christopher was contemplating the hole in the wall where the cashpoint machine used to be. 'It's a crying shame. I've blogged about this quite a few times, as it happens.'

'Ah yes,' Phyl said, as they walked on, 'I think I read a couple of those posts.'

'Oh!' said Christopher, not troubling to conceal either his surprise or his pleasure. 'You've visited the blog?'

Annoyed with herself for having admitted it, Phyl said, 'Once or twice.'

She said no more, at this point. It would have been tactless, probably, to tell him that what he had written was obviously well intentioned, but that there was still something patronizing about a man in his early sixties parading his sympathy for the plight of young adults just starting to make their way in the world. So she moved the subject swiftly on to his more recent posts.

'I saw what you wrote about the conference next week.'

'Ah yes. TrueCon. What a strange gathering that promises to be.'

'You're going to be there too?'

'I am. I'll be about as welcome as a dose of the clap, of course, but it's open to the public. I've registered and paid like everyone else. So they can't stop me turning up.'

'Who are these people?' Phyl wanted to know.

'Well, they're a mixed bunch. Some of them are relatively harmless cranks. Some of them are out-and-out racists and sadists. Personally, the ones that I like the least are Roger Wagstaff and his followers. You heard us talking about him last night – your mother and I were in the same year as him at Cambridge. Disciple of Emeric Coutts. I've been following his trajectory for quite a while now.' Despite the fact that they had the high street more or less to themselves, Christopher lowered his voice. 'They really are dangerous. I don't just mean that they're quite fanatical in their politics, and have gone mainstream in the last few years. That's worrying enough. I mean that they're . . .' He lowered his voice still further. 'Literally dangerous.'

Phyl wasn't sure what he was getting at. For some reason she felt a sudden compulsion to giggle, which she did her best to suppress.

'You mean . . . ?'

He nodded. 'Yes, I've had a number of threats. And a couple of months ago I nearly got run over in the street. A motorbike.'

'How awful,' said Phyl. But couldn't help adding: 'Maybe that was just an accident, though . . .'

Christopher shook his head. 'I don't think so. What they're planning to do to the NHS they've been planning to do for years. And a lot of very big American business interests are waiting for them to pull it off. Big money's at stake. Huge amounts of money.'

'Murder, though?' said Phyl, still incredulous. 'Isn't that a bit . . . far-fetched?'

Christopher said nothing at first. He stopped in front of a shop. He stood with his back to the shop window, narrowed his eyes against the sunlight and seemed to be gazing warily into the distance, as if looking out for potential assassins. Phyl remembered again how her father had described him: 'something of a fantasist'.

But what he said after a few moments was: 'Murder –' and then he paused for effect – 'is deeply embedded in the British way of life.'

With these words, he turned around to indicate the contents of the shop window. They were standing in front of a charity outlet, another of the few places which still appeared to thrive on Rookthorne's high street. In among the board games, the DVDs, the tacky jewellery and scuffed kitchenware, someone had arranged a display of books. There were about a dozen of them, all paperbacks, all slightly dog-eared and careworn, and all displaying a remarkable consistency of theme. Prompted by Christopher's last words, Phyl took notice of the titles: *The Rectory Poisonings*, *The Village Green Murders*, *Death on the Eighteenth Hole*, *Murder at the Bowling Club*, *The Clotted Cream Killer* (this last one, the cover informed her, being 'Book Seven in the Devonshire Detective Series' and 'A Cosy Murder Mystery for Long Winter Evenings').

'I see what you mean,' she said, fascinated by this display.

'Bizarre, isn't it?' said Christopher. 'The "cosy crime" phenomenon. I don't think there's another country in the world that would take the subject of violent homicide and rebrand it as "cosy". It's very British, in some indefinable way.'

'Do people read this stuff?' Phyl asked, looking at the titles more closely.

'I imagine so. The market seems to be pretty flooded.'

A thought crossed her mind. Surely she could write a book like this? If she wasn't quite ready, just yet (and she had a feeling that she wasn't quite ready) to bare her soul on the printed page – to write something serious, something that truly reflected her outlook on life – what was to stop her dashing off something like this and making some quick bucks? It had to be better than making sushi all day, and how hard could it be? Take an idyllic rural setting, 'quintessentially English', whatever that meant, throw in a cast of clergymen and pub landlords and cricket umpires, devise a cursory murder plot. There would have to be a detective, she supposed, someone quirky and unusual – maybe give them a wooden leg or a weird hobby like collecting butterflies or riding a penny-farthing. It would be like writing a student essay: all you had to do was to make sure that you structured it properly and followed the agreed formula, and you'd get a decent 2:1. Worth a try, surely?

'Well,' she said, as they resumed their walk. 'Judging by those books you should be fine, as long as you stay away from vicarages and garden centres and Olde English Tea Rooms.'

'You say that,' said Christopher, 'but I suspect that the setting for this conference is going to be *exactly* the kind of place where one of these murders would happen.'

Later that afternoon, Phyl found her mother on her knees in the utility room: not praying, on this occasion, but transferring clothes from the washing machine to the dryer.

'Where is everybody?' she asked.

'Your father's gone to the supermarket. Chris has gone to Heathrow to pick up his daughter.'

'To pick up *who*?'

Joanna rose to her feet, holding a stray sock in one hand. 'Didn't we tell you? Rashida, she's called. She's coming to stay for a couple of nights.' And then, noticing that her daughter seemed distressed by this information: 'I thought you'd be pleased.'

'Why would I be pleased?'

'I don't know – she's your age – we thought you might hit it off.'

'Mum,' said Phyl, 'when I was about seven, it might have made sense to introduce me to another seven-year-old at a party and say,

"You two will get on famously – you're both seven." But it doesn't work that way when you're in your early twenties. People need a bit more in common than that.'

'She's not his real daughter, she's adopted,' said Joanna, as if this made any difference. 'He and Elspeth couldn't have children of their own.' And then, equally bizarrely, she added, 'She's from Ethiopia,' as if this was the final selling point.

Phyl understood the underlying assumption only too well: this would surely clinch it, her mother believed, for someone of her generation, with its oh-so-eager embrace of multiculturalism. But instead of rising to the bait, she just said:

'Well, surely you could have given me a bit more warning.'

Exasperated, her mother said: 'I just don't understand you. You're always complaining how lonely you feel, stuck here with your father and me.'

'Yes, but I *like* being lonely. I find social situations stressful. Have you really not noticed that by now?'

She wandered off to the sitting room in a bad mood, and spent a few minutes on her phone playing a card game called Pyramid until she was disturbed by the sound of Christopher's car pulling up in the driveway with a scrunch of gravel. Phyl withdrew to one of the window bays and watched as a tall, graceful woman of her own age – but completely different in demeanour, far more composed and assured – got out of the passenger seat and unloaded her mauve cabin bag from the boot. She heard the woman complaining loudly about something to her father as they entered the house through the unlocked front door, and then realized with some alarm that the voices were coming ever closer. A few seconds later, father and daughter had entered the sitting room, and Rashida was still talking:

'So the thing is, you didn't *have* to press the button, because the elevators are automatic. There was even a sign that *told* you they were automatic.'

Phyl was surprised to hear that she had a marked American accent. Her voice was deep and musical.

'Right, right,' Christopher was saying. He didn't really seem to be listening. He was looking at something on his phone. 'But this guy took no notice, is that what you're saying?'

'No notice *whatsoever*,' she said; and then became aware of Phyl standing by the window.

'Hello.' Her lips spread into a confident half-smile. 'I didn't see you hiding there.'

'Well . . . Hi. I'm Phyl,' said Phyl, stepping forward, and waving her hand in an awkward gesture.

'I know who you are,' said Rashida, returning the wave. 'And I'm—'

'I know who you are,' said Phyl, by now managing to return the half-smile. And then: 'Are you talking about what I think you're talking about?'

'I don't know – what do you think I'm talking about?'

'The lifts at Terminal Five.'

Rashida's eyes widened and she smiled in eager agreement. '*Yes*,' she said, with tremendous emphasis. '*Yes. Exactly*.'

'They're automatic,' said Phyl to Christopher, who had finished with his phone and was now looking from one of them to the other, trying to understand their shared grievance. 'They have buttons, but it makes no difference whether you push them or not. But there's always some guy –' she glanced at Rashida – 'it was a guy, right?'

'Of course.'

'– Always some guy who steps up at the last minute.'

'He steps up at the last minute and presses the button and then the doors open and he looks *so fucking pleased with himself*.' She turned to Phyl. 'So this happened to you, right?'

'Just the other day.'

'Well it happened to me just now. It couldn't be the same guy, could it?'

'Mine was tall, with blonde hair, and shorts.'

'Oh. Mine was short, with dark hair, and skinny jeans.'

'Different man, same attitude.'

'Sounds about right. I mean, I know we shouldn't obsess about this, it's such a small thing, but it's driving me mad, I've been thinking about it for the last half-hour. The *arrogance*, the *entitlement* . . .'

'Is your mother around?' said Christopher to Phyl, butting in. 'I just wondered which room Rash was being put in.'

'Oh, don't worry,' said Phyl, picking up the mauve cabin bag. 'I know where you'll be. Come on, follow me.'

And together they went upstairs.

Phyl wasn't sure why she had BBC News notifications enabled on her phone. The stories popped up far too often and the annoying little sample of the television news tune became maddening after a while. This, anyway, was how she learned that Conservative Party members had chosen Liz Truss as their leader – and so, by default, as Britain's new Prime Minister. The announcement came at around midday on Monday 5th September, during the twenty-minute break in her nine-hour marathon of vegetable-chopping and fish-slicing. She shared the information with a couple of her co-workers but neither of them seemed very interested. For Phyl, it was all part of the drip-drip effect of bad news that leaked out of her phone every day: small items like this, jostling for space in her brain with stories about the oppression of Palestine, the war in Ukraine, the recent flooding in Pakistan, climate change generally . . . It all amounted to the steady construction, brick by brick, of a wall of despair that seemed to block off every glimpse of a viable future.

Surely, with all of that in mind, the promise of a slightly more right-wing British Prime Minister wasn't such a big deal? Maybe. But it was one more little brick in that wall, and it was still bothering her at the end of her long and complex journey home. Christopher and his daughter were talking to her mother in the sitting room, but Phyl hurried past without saying hello, feeling oddly resentful of the guests' presence in her house. Upstairs, she sat on the bed with her back to the wall, clicked on her phone's Netflix tab (which was permanently open) and began watching a *Friends* episode at random. It was Season 3, Episode 3, as it happened. She had just got to the scene where Ross was explaining to Chandler how to disentangle himself from a bedtime hug with his girlfriend when she became aware that Rashida was standing in the doorway. Phyl started guiltily and put down the phone, as if she had been interrupted watching porn. But all that Rashida said, in a friendly tone of voice, was:

'*The One with the Jam*, right?'

Phyl nodded. It was amazing how many people – the most

unexpected people, sometimes – seemed to know these episodes off by heart.

'That's it.'

'Can't remember much about it, to be honest.'

'It isn't one of the best. But Joey does look especially hot in this one.'

'Ah.' Rashida sat down on the bed beside her. 'Well, I wouldn't know about that.'

'Not your type?'

She smiled. 'I don't really have a type.'

After making this slightly enigmatic remark, Rashida lay back on the bed, resting on her elbow. Phyl was struck by her confidence in assuming this languorous pose in a stranger's bedroom, and felt suddenly very conscious of her physical proximity.

'How often do you watch it?' Rashida continued. 'How bad's your habit?'

'Couple of episodes a day,' said Phyl. 'Three or four, sometimes, if I'm feeling rough?'

'Well, don't worry. I'm not a judgy person. And it's good that they bring us something nice, occasionally, isn't it, as well as all the horror they let in?'

'What do you mean?'

Rashida held up her phone. 'These. Our generation's great blessing. And greatest curse.'

Phyl didn't answer. She didn't really know what to say.

Rashida looked down at her phone and said, quietly, 'Don't you ever feel like just getting rid of it, sometimes? I mean, going to a lake or a canal or something and just tossing it in? Maybe we should do that. Maybe we should make a pact. I mean, I just dread what I'm going to find on here sometimes.'

Phyl felt a strange kind of burden being lifted when she heard this. She had thought the same thing so many times, but had never felt able to say it.

'When did you start feeling that way?' she asked.

'I don't know . . . Years ago, I suppose.' Rashida stared into space, thinking. 'There was a time when it was really bad. I started getting these emails, telling me I had a voice message, and when I listened to them . . . wow, they were really creepy. I never found out who it was. Some guy at college, I think.'

'You didn't report them or anything?'

'Maybe I should've done. I just stopped clicking on them. Haven't had one for about a year, anyway. But for a while, you know . . . my stomach just used to turn over whenever I saw a new one had arrived.'

Neither of them spoke for a while. Then Phyl said:

'They don't have them, of course.'

'Who don't?'

'The characters in *Friends*. I read an article by someone who reckoned that's why people our age like the show. Nostalgia for a time before we were born.'

'They don't have mobile phones?'

'Not smartphones. Just these things that look like bricks and have radio aerials sticking out of them. I don't think any of them ever sends a text. Not in the whole ten seasons.'

'Is that right? Well, Chris would know. I might ask him.'

'Your dad?'

'I don't call him my dad,' Rashida said, sitting up again. 'Just Chris. But yes – him. He knows everything about that show. Surprising, huh?'

'Yeah, that is pretty surprising. How come?'

Rashida thought about this for a few moments before answering.

'Well, for one thing he has an amazing memory. Very retentive. He remembers everything he ever learns, basically. But as for the *Friends* thing . . . I suppose it goes back to when I was about eleven or twelve. My parents had split up and Chris had come back to live in the UK. I was sent over here to spend one summer with him, and it was really awkward. I guess since he'd last seen me I'd gone from being a kid to a teenager and we didn't really know how to relate to each other any more. So we spent pretty much the whole time watching *Friends* together. And even now, when we're driving in the car or something, and we've run out of things to say – which happens *a lot* – we'll play a game where we test each other on the minor characters and the names of the episodes and stuff.'

Rashida seemed to be in a talkative mood, so Phyl decided to make the most of this and find out more about her.

'What are you doing over here at the moment?' she asked.

'I'm in the middle of a Master's,' Rashida said. 'Just about to start my second year.'

'In London?'

'Yes. Chris thought it might expand my horizons to live here for a while. And it's a good excuse to get away from Elspeth. I just spent the summer with her and it . . . didn't go well. The two of us haven't really got on for years. Pity, in a way, because where she lives is pretty idyllic, I'm not going to lie. Upstate New York.'

'Is that where you grew up?'

'Yes. I lived there most of my life. Well, I was born in a place called Mekele, up in the north of Ethiopia, but I don't remember any of that. Both my parents were killed when the Eritreans bombed it during the war. I was put in an orphanage and then Chris and Elspeth adopted me when I was two. It was the kind of thing a lot of good American liberals were doing at the time.'

Phyl nodded but didn't enquire any further about this, being afraid that her questions might sound foolish, and would simply offer the proof of her innocence, her unworldliness. She decided to move the conversation on to more comfortable ground instead.

'Where do you live in London, these days?'

'I've got a house share in Wanstead.' Restless, now, Rashida stood up, and began to walk around the bedroom. Phyl was reminded again of her height, and her casual elegance. 'It's not very handy for college, and it's not very nice, and I don't get on too well with the people I'm sharing with, but still, for some weird reason . . . for some reason I really like it.'

Phyl thought again about her student house in Newcastle, which could hardly have been more unsanitary or inconvenient in most respects, and once more felt a powerful, dampening wave of nostalgia for her time there. She was envious of Rashida for having a year of university left, and was also beginning to feel slightly envious of the people who had this striking, charismatic woman as their housemate.

'What are you studying?' she asked.

'Business and management.'

It was a disappointing answer. She couldn't picture Rashida wearing office clothes, or bent over a computer, punching figures into a spreadsheet.

'I'd like to run my own business one day,' she went on. 'Nothing too big – maybe a restaurant or two, something like that. The important thing is that it belongs to you. Otherwise, you're just making money for someone else, aren't you? Who wants to do that?'

She had wandered over to Phyl's desk by now, and was peering with unashamed curiosity at the photos pinned to the wall all around it. 'Anyway. That was my thinking. Maybe it would have been more fun to do something like . . . I don't know, English, but a degree like that's pretty useless in the end, don't you think?' She turned around. 'What about you? What did you do?'

'English,' Phyl answered.

'Oh.' She laughed. 'Sorry.'

'It's OK. You're quite right, in a way. Here I am, back home, with no idea what I want to do with my life.' She noticed, with a sudden rush of panic, that Rashida was now looking at one of the pages of her open notebook. 'Oh – look – take no notice of those, they're just . . . Well, I don't know what they are.'

'*Death in a Thatched Cottage*?' Rashida read aloud. '*The Beach Hut Murders*? *The Flapjack Poisonings*? These sound like . . . book titles?'

'Yeah, I had this crazy idea that . . .' Well, she might as well come out with it. '. . . that I'd try writing a book.'

Rashida let out a small laugh before she could help herself. 'I'm sorry – I think that's a great idea. I mean, why not? But – this is what you're going to call it?'

Briefly, and with some difficulty, Phyl told her about the window display she'd seen with Christopher the day before, and how he had introduced her to the concept of 'cosy crime'. It was not an idiom that Rashida had heard before, and it took a little bit of explaining.

'I know it sounds kind of cynical, just picking a genre like that, and writing to a formula, but . . . I don't know, I've never written anything before. I thought it might be a good way to start – to learn the basics, kind of thing.'

Rashida nodded. 'I suppose that makes sense. But maybe start with a kind of book that you actually like yourself? I mean, what do *you* enjoy reading?'

Without much hesitation, Phyl said: 'Dark academia.'

'Which is . . . what, exactly?'

'Oh, you know . . . novels about university students – outsiders – forming themselves into friendship groups and getting involved with secret societies and murder and stuff.'

'And this is a thing?'

'Sure. Haven't you read *The Secret History*?'

Rashida shook her head. 'I've heard of it.'

'There've been lots of others since then, obviously.' Feeling the germ of an idea coming on, Phyl reached across for her notebook, turned to a fresh page and wrote down the first two items in a list. When she had done this, she raised her eyes to see that Rashida was looking at her – for the first time, it seemed – with something approaching interest. She felt absurdly flattered.

'I love creative people,' Rashida said. 'The sad fact is I don't have a creative bone in my body. Where does it come from, the creativity? What makes you want to write?'

'Look, I haven't actually written anything yet . . .'

'No, but – where does the impulse come from? Is it because you want to leave something behind? A kind of . . . push for immortality?'

Phyl smiled at this idea. 'I think these days, if you want to be remembered, writing a book isn't the way to go about it.' By way of explanation, she added: 'I was looking in my father's library the other day, and there was this *massive* novel someone had written in the nineties, and you wouldn't believe the things people were saying on the cover – a masterpiece, a future classic, all that sort of thing – and you know what? Nobody remembers this guy any more. Even my dad didn't recognize his name. Gone. Forgotten.'

Rashida took a no-nonsense approach to this story. 'Well then, he probably deserved to be forgotten. Christ, when I think back to some of the writers we were made to read in high school. Nobody would have been reading *them* if our teachers hadn't been forcing them on us.'

'Maybe you're right,' said Phyl, laughing, And then, more thoughtfully: 'Anyway, I don't think there's anything special about creativity. There's no magic formula to it. Anyone can write. Have you tried? Maybe *you* should give it a go.'

Rashida shook her head.

'I've never been able to make up stories. Not even when I was a little kid. Whenever we had to write something like that for homework, I couldn't bring myself to do it. There was always something about it that felt . . . fake, to me. Fake, and kind of embarrassing.'

'So what did you use to do? Hand in a blank sheet of paper?'

'No, I could *write*. I could write *something*, obviously. But I just ended up writing . . . real stuff. Stuff that had happened to me. I just told the truth about myself.'

'Well, nowadays people call that autofiction. It's very fashionable, actually.'

'Really? That's a thing too?'

'Sure. Also known as life writing, creative memoir . . . Basically you're writing about your own life but not in a "This happened, then that happened" kind of way. You're taking a particular bit of experience and writing about it as if you were writing a novel.'

'Hmm. Maybe *you* should try something like that. Sounds much more honest than making up some murder story.'

Phyl chewed on her pencil and thought about it. She couldn't tell whether or not Rashida was being entirely serious. But she added a third item to the list in her notebook anyway, so that her options as a fledgling writer now consisted of:

1. *COSY CRIME*
2. *DARK ACADEMIA*
3. *AUTOFICTION*

At which point, they heard Andrew calling them down to dinner.

They found him waiting impatiently for them in a kitchen that was otherwise empty. He had cooked an elaborate Greek meal with a moussaka centrepiece, laid the table for five people and even poured five glasses of wine, but at the moment there was nobody there to eat any of it. Rashida sat down at her designated place and unfolded her napkin carefully. Phyl went off in search of her mother and Christopher.

They were in the study, talking in murmurous voices. She had been on the point of interrupting them, but something about their tone made her pause at the threshold, take a step backwards, and listen to what they were saying.

They were discussing Brian.

Brian, as Phyl had learned the other evening, had been their mutual best friend at Cambridge forty years earlier. For a while, the three of them had been inseparable. A trio of provincial, state-educated teenagers turning up at one of the wealthiest and most elite of the Cambridge colleges and immediately finding each other and clutching on to each other for support. Despite some ups and downs, their friendship had endured throughout their three years at Cambridge and the decades that followed.

A man of wide-ranging interests, Brian had studied medicine at university but had spent much of his time there attending lectures in other subjects. His subsequent career as a psychiatrist had been stellar, but it had recently been cut short: at the age of sixty-one he had been diagnosed with liver cancer, with a prognosis of only six months; and even that had turned out to be optimistic. He had died ten months ago, in November 2021.

Now Joanna and Christopher were talking about him. She was showing him a blue ring binder full of papers and saying:

'Look, I found the memoir! It was buried under four years' worth of newsletters.'

'Wonderful! Is it all right if I take it to the conference with me?'

Joanna hesitated. 'I think it might be better if I keep it here and get someone in the office to make a copy. Do you mind?'

'No, of course. That's fine.'

'I'll send it to you as soon as I can. There's lots about you in it.'

'Really?' Christopher flicked through the pages. 'What about Roger Wagstaff – does he rate a mention?'

'Oh yes. And there's some fascinating stuff about the salons. When that writer came to visit, and so on.'

'In that case,' said Christopher, handing it back to her solemnly, 'you'd better look after this carefully. Do you have a safe or anything?'

'Of course not! Why?'

'Because this is a historical document.'

She looked at him, a sceptical laugh in her eyes. 'What do you mean?'

'We witnessed something, while we were there. We witnessed the start of something.'

'We did?'

'With Emeric, yes. And Roger Wagstaff. We were there when he set out on his path.'

'Oh, Chris, I do think you exaggerate his importance. You always have.'

'He's dangerous, I tell you. The conference is going to prove that, once and for all.'

There was an undertone of nervousness and anxiety in his voice that surprised both Joanna and her listening daughter.

'What do you mean?'

Christopher looked embarrassed, and had to admit: 'I don't know. I just feel that . . . Well, frankly, I feel that anything could happen to me in the next few days.'

The expression of a particularly exasperated and affectionate sigh from her mother at this point made it seem like a good moment for Phyl to step forward. Both Christopher and Joanna looked around at her guiltily. It was as if she had interrupted a conversation between two lovers.

'Dinner's ready,' she said, after a suitable pause.

Her mother took back the manuscript and locked it in one of her desk drawers.

For Phyl, there was something special about that final dinner with Christopher and his adopted daughter: some sense of momentousness.

She had been reading a lot more of Christopher's blog, over the last day or two, and had found it fascinating. She felt that she understood, now, a little more about the project to which he'd been devoting himself for so long: tracking the evolution of conservative politics over the last forty years, since the days of Thatcher in the United Kingdom and Reagan in the United States. Phyl had never given the slightest thought to this subject before, but she was beginning to see why Christopher was so exercised by Liz Truss's appointment as Prime Minister; beginning to see what a significant staging post it must appear, to him, on the political path that Britain was hurtling down.

It was true that she still hadn't warmed to him, as a person. She still found him verbose; too sure of himself; condescending, at times. But besides having concluded that he was more interesting than she'd first imagined, she had decided that on the whole she liked having guests in the house again, after more than two months of living in isolation with her parents; and more than that, she felt that this dinner somehow marked the end of one era in her life and the beginning of another. In part this was because she'd decided to begin her attempts at writing the very next day, after completing her early shift at Heathrow. But it also had to do with other, less tangible elements that she sensed around the dinner table that evening, elements which gave her an indefinable sense of fullness and possibility: the way the light fell onto the scene from the lamp above them, giving the room an almost spectral atmosphere, a kind of numinous glow; the obvious pleasure her mother was taking in seeing Christopher again, the sense of an old friendship being rekindled; and, perhaps more than anything else, the strong, vibrant presence of Rashida, who seemed to fill the whole room with her energy and her poised, careless beauty.

She was certainly on impressive form this evening. Inevitably, the conversation turned more than once to the new Prime Minister. If for no other reason than to provoke Phyl and Rashida into a reaction, Christopher insisted on reciting (from memory) a tweet posted by Liz Truss four years earlier, in which she had sung the praises of their generation as 'Uber-riding, Airbnb-ing, Deliveroo-eating freedom fighters' (adding the hashtags #freecountry #livefree #choice and #destiny for good measure). Neither of them having heard this pronouncement before, they both reacted by making vomiting noises and putting their fingers down their throats, but it was Rashida who went on to say: 'Seriously? This woman thinks that being able to book taxi rides and takeaways online compensates for being left with a fucked political system and a fucked planet?'

'Apparently, yes,' said Christopher. 'That's exactly what she thinks.'

'She thinks that we feel *free* because we know it'll be fifteen years before we can afford to buy a shitty little apartment?'

'Sounds like it.'

'And we're spoilt for choice because once every five years we get to decide between two political parties, one of them a tiny bit less right-wing than the other?'

'Hey,' said Christopher, holding up his hands in a gesture of mock-surrender. 'Don't blame me for any of this.'

'Well, you're the one that's here, Chris. Someone has to take the blame. I think it's really about time the Boomers realized exactly what Gen Z thinks of them.'

'And what do you think that is?' Joanna asked, with her usual quiet intensity.

'OK – of course I'm not talking about you guys personally,' Rashida said. 'But what it is . . . Basically what it is, is that we don't *understand*. We don't understand why your generation hates us so much. What have we done to annoy you? The people who voted for this woman are all in their sixties and seventies, right? Ageing Tories with two or three houses and no mortgage and nice fat pensions to live off. So why have they done it? Is it just to punish younger people? Wasn't it enough to give them Brexit and take away their chance of living all over Europe? Yeah, go on, crush that dream, baby. Or in the States, give them Trump to suck on for four years. That'll teach them to know their place, with their lives full of possibility and their good looks and their good health and their fantastic sex lives.' She noticed the surprise on everyone's faces. 'Yes, come on, *that's* what they envy. *That's* what they're so pissed about. They've lived these miserable joyless lives and none of the money they've made can make up for that sense of . . . disappointment. The anticlimax of it.'

A long silence followed this impassioned monologue. Phyl felt awestruck by her new friend's eloquence, by her fearlessness in addressing these remarks to the very audience that stood condemned by them. Joanna looked embarrassed, and stared down at her plate. Andrew seemed amused more than anything else, but didn't venture an opinion of his own. Instead he turned to Christopher and said:

'Well, what do you make of that? She has a point, maybe?'

Their guest answered with his characteristic practised smile. Nothing ever seemed to perturb him too deeply. 'As always,' he said, 'my daughter has a strong opinion, and puts it forward in her inimitable style. If that's how her generation feels, what can we do? It's a bit early to say whether Liz Truss is actually an instrument of torture that the old have decided to use against the young. One thing's certain, though. Tomorrow she becomes Prime Minister, which means that tomorrow –' and this would be the phrase that Phyl would remember, and be haunted by, in the weeks to come – 'tomorrow will mark Britain's final severance from reality. Tomorrow is when real life stops, and fantasy begins.'

PART ONE

See It

50p
Murder at Wetherby Pond
A Cosy Crime Mystery
Murder at Wetherby Pond

1.

Christopher Swann carefully steered his car between the yellowing drystone walls of the quaint old bridge that carried the road over the brook. There was only room for one car to pass between the walls, but on a quiet Tuesday morning like this, there was little chance of encountering another vehicle. Just a few hundred yards after crossing the brook, he entered the village of Wetherby Pond itself. At the sound of his engine (even though he was driving a quiet, hybrid model) the ducks on the eponymous body of water took flight with a volley of complaining quacks. Christopher followed the road around the edge of the pond, his eyes taking in every unlikely detail of the old post office, the red telephone box standing outside the village shop, the row of trimly thatched cottages and an elderly resident reading a copy of *The Times* while sitting on a weathered oak bench. Although Wetherby Pond had the reputation of being pretty and unspoilt, he could not quite believe what he was seeing: it felt as though he had stumbled upon a forgotten corner of England that evoked the set of a 1950s film more than it resembled contemporary reality. He steered his car further down the village street and pulled up smoothly in one of the parking bays outside the well-preserved seventeenth-century inn which still bore its original name: the Fresh Lettuce.

He remained in his car for a few moments, wanting to settle himself, because his journey this morning had not been without drama. In fact on his way to Wetherby Pond he had nearly been involved in a nasty accident. It had happened on the steep incline known as Fish Hill, just outside Broadway in the Vale of Evesham. Christopher had been negotiating one of the two or three hairpin bends that led to the summit when another car had overtaken him so narrowly, and cut in front of him so sharply, that he had come close to being forced off the road at the very point where there was a sheer drop of several hundred feet on the left-hand side. Christopher had been quite shaken up, and had then pulled over to the hard shoulder where a white-van driver – who had been following close behind him and had witnessed the whole incident – kept him company for ten minutes or so while he recovered his composure. People could be very kind; but people could also be recklessly clumsy. Neither of these realizations was new, but they had both struck him with unusual force that morning, and he reflected on them again now as he felt himself being gradually calmed by the limpid, soothing atmosphere of this lovely old English village. Soon he felt ready to try his luck in the pub.

'Does that television work?' Christopher asked, as the landlord methodically pulled him a pint of the dark, coppery local bitter, Thruxton's Old Undrinkable. He nodded towards the set fixed to the wall above the shove ha'penny table.

'It does,' the landlord said, 'but we don't usually have it on at this time of day.'

'Well, do you mind if I watch the news?' said Christopher. The landlord seemed taken aback by this request, so he added: 'After all, it is something of a special day.'

'It is?' said the landlord, reaching for the remote control on a shelf behind the bar. He clearly had no idea what Christopher was talking about. 'What's special about it?'

He turned on the television set and a few seconds later an image of the doorstep of Number 10 Downing Street appeared on the screen.

'We have a new Prime Minister, of course,' Christopher explained.

'We do? Who's that, then?'

'You really don't know?'

'Don't know,' said the landlord, picking up a cloth and wiping the counter, 'and don't care, frankly.'

'But surely,' said Christopher, 'whether we like it or not, we're all affected by who's leading the government?'

'I couldn't even tell you who the government *is* right now,' said the landlord. 'And do you know why? Because . . .' Putting his hand close to Christopher's face while still holding the cloth, he made an emphatic gesture with it, sending droplets of water flying into his face. 'Because *I . . . GOVERN . . . MYSELF.*'

With which words, he turned and disappeared through a doorway, leaving Christopher to ponder this remarkable declaration alone in the bar.

He was not alone for long, because a minute or two later Liz Truss herself appeared in the doorway of Number 10, stepped forward to the lectern and began to address the nation in her usual unpolished style.

I have just accepted, she said, *Her Majesty the Queen's kind invitation to form a new government. Let me pay tribute to my predecessor. Boris Johnson delivered Brexit, the Covid vaccine, and stood up to Russian aggression. History will see him as a hugely consequential Prime Minister.*

'True, that,' said a voice behind Christopher.

He turned round to see that two more men had entered the pub. One of them was glancing over the food menu at the bar while the other was sitting on a stool next to his friend, gazing up at the television screen with an expression of moderate interest.

I'm honoured to take on this responsibility at a vital time for our country, the new Prime Minister was saying.

'What do you think, Tom?' said the man looking at the menu. 'Starters and mains?'

What makes the United Kingdom great, the Prime Minister continued, *is our fundamental belief in freedom, in enterprise, and in fair play. Our people have shown grit, courage and determination time and time again. We now face severe global headwinds caused by Russia's appalling war in Ukraine and the aftermath of Covid. Now is the time to tackle the issues that are holding Britain back. We need to build roads, homes and broadband faster. We need more investment and great jobs in every town and city across our country. We need to reduce the burden on families and help people get on in life. I know that we have what it takes to tackle those challenges.*

Of course, it won't be easy. But we can do it.

'She's got a bit of spirit, anyway,' Tom was saying. 'I like a woman with a can-do attitude.'

'Vote for her then, did you?'

'I did indeed. Best of a bad bunch.'

'They should never have got rid of Boris in the first place. There was no need.'

'None whatsoever.'

We will transform Britain into an aspiration nation . . . with high-paying jobs, safe streets and where everyone everywhere has the opportunities they deserve.

'You been up the Hall this morning, I gather?' the man with the menu now said to Tom.

'That's right. Doing a bit of a recce for His Lordship. He wants the whole place rewiring.'

Christopher's curiosity was suddenly aroused. He did his best to divide his attention between the speech on screen and the conversation at the bar.

I will take action this day, and action every day, to make it happen.

'Rumour has it that he has a few financial problems.'

'That's an understatement if ever I heard one.'

United with our allies, we will stand up for freedom and democracy around the world – recognizing that we can't have security at home without having security abroad.

'What's his plan for the hotel, then?'

'It'll be closed before the end of the year, if you ask me.'

This, Christopher thought, was an especially interesting nugget of information.

As Prime Minister, I will pursue three early priorities.

Firstly, I will get Britain working again. I have a bold plan to grow the economy through tax cuts and reform. I will cut taxes to reward hard work and boost business-led growth and investment. I will drive reform in my mission to get the United Kingdom working, building and growing.

'Closed?'

'He just hasn't been getting the guests.'

'What about the big conference this week?'

'That's not going to save it.'

We will get spades in the ground to make sure people are not facing unaffordable energy bills and we will also make sure that we are building hospitals, schools, roads and broadband.

'So what's his plan?'

'Close down the hotel. Do a total refurbishment. Reopen as a stately home. Garden centre, tea rooms. Boating lake, rides for the kids. Anything that'll bring in a bit of money.'

Secondly, I will deal hands-on with the energy crisis caused by Putin's war. I will take action this week to deal with energy bills and to secure our future energy supply.

'How's he going to pay for all that, then, if he's run out of cash?'

Thirdly, I will make sure that people can get doctors' appointments and the NHS services they need. We will put our health service on a firm footing. By delivering on the economy, on energy, and on the NHS, we will put our nation on the path to long-term success.

'Reckon he'll be applying for grants. English Heritage, National Trust . . . Anyone he can think of.'

We shouldn't be daunted by the challenges we face. As strong as the storm may be, I know that the British people are stronger. Our country was built by people who get things done. We have huge reserves of talent, of energy and determination.

'Sounds like a bit of a long shot.'

'I dare say. But what else is he going to do? If this plan doesn't come off, he'll have to sell up. He'll lose the lot.'

'Lose Wetherby Hall? But it's been in the family for centuries.'

I am confident that together we can ride out the storm, we can rebuild our economy and we can become the modern brilliant Britain that I know we can be.

Digesting these stirring words and, at the same time, the contents of the conversation he had just overheard, Christopher finished his pint and left his glass on the bar. He nodded goodbye to the two men, neither of whom responded, and made to leave the Fresh Lettuce just as Liz Truss was concluding her speech.

This is our vital mission to ensure opportunity and prosperity for all people and future generations. I am determined to deliver. Thank you.

The two men at the bar nodded approval and made a silent toast to her. Christopher left the pub and drove on to Wetherby Hall.

2.

Christopher drove out of the village, along a quietly winding B-road, until after about three-quarters of a mile he reached the massive wrought-iron gates of Wetherby Hall on his left. There were no signs indicating that the TrueCon conference was to be held here over the next three days, but he had not expected there to be. It was not exactly a secret, but neither were the organizers or the delegates courting publicity.

The hotel was approached by a long avenue lined with beech trees. At the end of the avenue was a semicircular forecourt in which a number of SUVs, Teslas and other expensive vehicles were already parked. Christopher followed the sign to Overflow Parking, which was to the right of the Hall's imposing main building. Retrieving his suitcase, laptop and dinner suit from the boot, and locking the car as he walked away from it, he made his way to the front entrance and for the first time took in the full grandeur of Wetherby Hall in the early-afternoon sunshine.

It was a mixture of Palladian and vernacular design, built of fine old Cotswold stone in the early years of the eighteenth century. The facade was perfectly symmetrical, with ivy and wisteria climbing up towards the twelve mullioned windows on the first floor. Six wide steps led towards the arched doorway with its rusticated surround. At the centre of the arch, the keystone bore a simple inscription, recording the day on which the building of the house had been completed: 8th February 1724. The slate roof was punctuated by high-pitched gables in honey-coloured brick with tall chimney stacks, around which rooks were wheeling and circling, cawing hoarsely as they sought out their nests. As Christopher paused outside the entrance, he could not help noticing that the Corinthian columns on either side of the front doorway were in a woeful state of repair, their stone all cracked, chipped and streaked with three centuries' worth of rain damage. As he was in the process of turning the handle of the heavy oak door, a small chunk of masonry detached itself from the facade somewhere above him and landed on the flagstones, shattering into pieces.

He joined a queue of four people at reception, and took in the details of the entrance hall while he was waiting to check in. It looked to him as though Wetherby Hall was having an identity crisis. This vestibule was cluttered with generic olde-worlde artefacts of every description and from every historical period. The fabric of the building may have dated from the early eighteenth century, but the four suits of armour ranged against the walls were much older, while the oversized chess set and ponderous grandfather clock (stopped at ten past seven) seemed to be Victorian. The decor generally smacked of desperation. Damp had established itself around the skirting boards and the cornicing. Sections of plaster had come away, leaving gaps which had been hastily filled in and painted over. Nonetheless, there was still something magnificent about the place. Christopher always found himself being impressed, against his better judgement, by these unabashed monuments to wealth, power and prestige. And he was quite disappointed when the receptionist told him, after ten minutes waiting in line, that his allotted room was not in the main building after all, but in the modern annexe which lay towards the rear of the grounds.

This building had been put up in the 1980s, although its lemony Cotswold stone still gave it a pleasing congruity with the main house. It was here, in its eighty rather basic and compact rooms – more like student accommodation than a luxury hotel – that many of the visitors to the TrueCon conference would be housed. The rest would be staying at other hotels, scattered further afield.

As it happened, Christopher arrived outside the door of his room at exactly the same time as another of the guests: a short, balding man with thick black spectacles which framed a pair of restless and somehow unnerving green eyes. He appeared to be staying in the room opposite. Both he and Christopher had difficulty getting their keycards to work at first.

'Never straightforward, these things, are they?' said the man, waving his card repeatedly over the sensor.

'I'm sure there's a knack,' said Christopher. 'I just don't know what it is.'

'Ah! There we go,' the man said in a tone of quiet satisfaction, as his lock clicked open at last. Before pulling his suitcase through the doorway, he held out his hand. 'I'm Howard, by the way.'

'Christopher. Pleased to meet you.'

The handshake was brief. Christopher did not anticipate striking up a friendship with this person.

Entering his room now, he found that it had a pleasant view towards a meadow where cattle were grazing contentedly between clumps of thistle and dandelion. It also offered a glimpse of Wetherby Hall's small ornamental lake, at the edge of which a solitary fisherman was sitting on a little canvas chair, staring out across the water in an attitude of absolute stillness. Christopher put down his luggage, laid his dinner suit out on the bed and then sat down to read the conference programme that was waiting for him on the bedside table. It was a glossy affair, thirty-two pages long, which gave full background detail on the speakers who were scheduled to appear in the next three days. Most of the names were familiar to him, of course. Columnists for the *Mail*, the *Spectator* and *UnHerd*. People who had begun their careers as journalists for the magazine *Living Marxism* in the 1980s and had since embraced libertarianism and free-market economics. Members of opaquely funded think tanks such as the Taxpayers' Alliance and the Institute of Economic Affairs, as well as the Processus Group itself. There was also a sprinkling of Conservative MPs, one of them being the Right Honourable Kwasi Kwarteng: a speaker who might now, Christopher thought, be unable to fulfil his commitment on Thursday afternoon, given that Liz Truss had just made him Chancellor of the Exchequer.

Soon he began to feel restless again, and decided that it was time to explore the main building more thoroughly.

Re-entering the hotel by the front entrance, he skirted the reception desk – which was busier than ever – and set off in a direction which seemed to lead away from the crowds. It quickly became apparent that the ground floor of Wetherby Hall presented a maze of corridors, punctuated by staircases which all seemed to lead off in different directions to different floors of the house, winding and twisting at unpredictable angles so that it was impossible to guess where they would take you. Gloomy family portraits and morbid landscapes lined the walls of the corridors. Strange little alcoves would appear at unexpected moments, often containing suits of armour or glass display cases filled with tatty relics – including, in one case, a rather dangerous-looking collection of oriental knives. Another such recess played host to an enormous stuffed grizzly bear rearing up on its hind legs with a startled expression on its face. There seemed to be no bedrooms on this floor: glancing through some of the open doorways, Christopher saw reception rooms furnished with chintz sofas and low coffee tables, an oak-panelled dining space complete with three long trestle tables and a minstrels' gallery, two bars (one of which also seemed to serve as the breakfast area) and, finally, the library. This was a room towards the rear of the house, its sole window offering a view across the kitchen garden towards the annexe and the stables. Very little light was admitted by this window, so the library created an immediately crepuscular impression which was reinforced by the uniformly dark, sombre spines of the books lining its shelves: Victorian, mainly, and consisting largely of bound collections of forgotten nineteenth-century periodicals, along with the inevitable collected works of Dickens and Scott. The only pools of light came from the antique lamps standing on three desks placed at intervals around the room. And at one of these desks, someone was tapping away on a laptop, beside which were stacked numerous piles of paper in an impressive state of disorder. From behind, at first, it was not easy to tell whether this person was male or female. But it was definitely a middle-aged woman who, upon hearing Christopher's footsteps behind her, turned around and gave him a brief, enquiring glance before returning to her work. She didn't seem to recognize him, but that glimpse of her face – combined with her distinctive short-back-and-sides haircut – was enough to convince Christopher that they were, in fact, acquainted, even though it was almost forty years since they had last met. He walked around to the front of the desk and approached her directly.

'Excuse me – it's Rebecca, isn't it? Rebecca Wood?'

The woman looked up, and took off her reading glasses. There was a glint of curiosity in her grey eyes.

'Christopher Swann,' said Christopher. 'From St Stephen's. Do you remember?'

It took Miss Wood a few moments to react to this introduction. Then she sat back, folded her arms, and a combative smile appeared on her face.

'Christopher Swann,' she repeated. 'Well, I never. I wouldn't have thought that you, of all people, would have the nerve, the *audacity* to turn up here this week.'

'What on earth do you mean?' said Christopher. He sat down in a leather-backed armchair and inched it slightly closer to her desk. 'This is a public conference. I paid for my pass like everyone else. I'm here as a disinterested observer, nothing more and nothing less.' He looked down at the piles of documents on her desk, and saw that most of them were printed on notepaper headed with the Processus Group logo. 'Still fighting the good fight on behalf of Roger, I see.'

Rebecca did not reply.

'Four decades of loyal service,' he continued. 'I hope you get more than a gold watch on retirement day.'

Again, no response at first. Rebecca turned over some pages and typed a few more words on her laptop. 'The work itself is its own reward,' she said finally. 'There are few things more satisfying than devoting yourself to a cause you believe in. But I don't suppose a cynic like you would ever understand that.'

'A cynic?'

'Exactly. That's how people saw you at Cambridge, and nothing seems to have changed since then, if your . . . online outpourings are anything to go by.'

Instead of answering this, Christopher mused: 'I imagine it can't be easy, working for a man with such a . . . well, such a complicated life. He's on to wife number three now, isn't he? Or is it four?'

Rebecca flashed him another look of contempt, and carried on typing.

'I hope he treats you well, that's all,' he added. 'I hope he doesn't take you for granted.'

'I have no idea what you're talking about,' she said.

'I just think,' Christopher ventured, 'that if you're going to sell your soul for someone—'

Rebecca slammed her laptop shut. 'You know nothing about my *soul*. Nothing at all.' Standing up and leaning forward on her desk, she continued: 'The fact that, in the very distant past, you and I studied together at Cambridge, does not mean we have to talk to each other forty years later. I disliked you then, and I like you even less now. Roger is a good man, whose motives and actions you consistently misrepresent to your readership, such as it is. If you try to obstruct his work in any way, with your stupid attempts at so-called, self-published journalism, the indifference I feel towards you will turn to something very different. It will turn to hate. Roger happens to be the focus of my life. I make no apology for that, and you may interpret it however you wish. I really don't care what you think of me. What I do know is that I don't have to feel ashamed for anything I've ever done, either for him or for the Processus Group.'

Christopher listened to the words impassively, absorbing them, letting them sink in, before saying: 'Really?' And then: 'What a shame Paul Daintry is no longer alive to share his views on that.'

Rebecca glared at him, furious, unable to believe what she had just heard.

'Get out,' was all she said.

Christopher met her gaze for a moment or two, then rose to his feet and left the library. She watched him go with an unwavering stare. The expression in her eyes could only be described as murderous.

3.

Christopher spent the next two hours writing up notes in his room, then changed into his suit and strolled back towards the main house for dinner.

Once again, the entrance hall seemed to be crowded. Almost immediately he recognized the figure of the hotel's owner, Randolph Wetherby, standing at the centre of a group of six or seven. A short, self-important man, whose shock of dark curly hair looked suspiciously like a toupee, Randolph (Christopher could never bring himself to think of him as Lord Wetherby) was holding forth to this circle of guests, pointing out some of the distinctive features of the hall while diverting their attention away from the patches of damp and the crumbling plasterwork. It appeared that a small, unofficial tour was in progress. Christopher suspected that attendance was by invitation only. Nonetheless, by lurking on the outskirts of the group he was able to discreetly attach himself to it, and when they all set off down the East Corridor, with Randolph in the lead, he sauntered along with them and nobody seemed to notice that they now had an additional recruit.

Randolph proved to be an enthusiastic guide. He paused in front of every family portrait and gave lengthy biographies of his ancestors for the benefit of the guests. Here, for instance, was Tarquin, the 7th Earl of Wetherby, surrounded by his children, all of whom, it subsequently transpired, had been fathered by James the stable boy during the Earl's many absences in India to oversee the running of his tea plantation. Here was a photograph of Jolyon, the 9th Earl of Wetherby, posing with two African lions he had just slaughtered, the photograph being taken seconds before a third lion, hiding in the undergrowth behind him, leapt out of the bushes and bit his head off. Here was Julietta, the 6th Countess of Wetherby, posing with the parrot to which, in a fiercely contested will, her deranged husband later bequeathed the entire estate. And here, in a glass display case, was the collection of Japanese kitchen knives filched from their rightful owners by Florian, the 8th Earl of Wetherby, during his fifteen-year sojourn in that country: a beautiful but also deadly assembly of razor-sharp instruments designed for slicing, peeling and filleting, one of which had turned out to be very useful when he decided, in 1893, to commit ritual *hara-kiri* following a humiliating defeat on the croquet lawn. In short it became more and more evident, as the tour progressed, that the Wetherby family history was little more than a series of regrettable episodes characterized above all by violence, mental illness, and an unswerving commitment to the exploitation of anyone less powerful than themselves.

It turned out, however, that the present Earl was not completely indifferent to modern sensitivities. Passing a small empty display case at a point where the corridor turned a sharp corner, he said:

'Now this case used to house an Australian artefact which the Ninth Earl brought back with him from New South Wales. A small boomerang. We decided that it was quite unacceptable for us to retain possession of an object which belonged, by rights, to the Aboriginal people. And so, earlier this year, we returned it.'

He did not mention how great had been the rejoicing at Wetherby Hall when this small object, of no great financial value, had been discovered in a little-used storage cupboard by one of the cleaning staff. At a time when the owners of houses such as this were coming under ever-closer scrutiny for their dubious roles in Britain's colonial history, it had provided a perfect opportunity to make a media-friendly gesture of public reparation. The boomerang had been posted back to elders of the Wiradjuri people at a carefully staged photo-opportunity by Randoph Wetherby in person.

If the Earl believed that he could be fairly relaxed about his family's historical record, however, this complacency did not survive a somewhat tetchy exchange with Christopher towards the end of the tour.

The group was gathered in front of a large painting which showed a galleon docked at the quayside of a bustling harbour. The painting was hidden away in a shadowy corner at the bottom of one of the Hall's many forbidding staircases. It must have been an impressive work at one time, but the centuries had not been kind to it: the colours were faded, sky and sea both being reduced to the same near-identical shade of grey, and much of the original fine detail was impossible to make out. Of some features, however, Randolph was certain.

'The man standing on the poop deck there,' he said, 'is Septimus Wetherby – so called because he was the Fifth Earl.' (Neither Latin nor maths, it seemed, having been among the family's strong points.) 'There can be no doubt of this, because we can still make out the Wetherby coat of arms embroidered on his waistcoat. The harbour has been identified as Bristol, and the era is probably the late seventeenth century, or the early years of the eighteenth. It seems the ship is soon about to embark on its latest voyage. The Earl is shown looking through his telescope in a south-westerly direction, and all the cargo has been safely stowed away in readiness for the voyage. Unfortunately, the name of the ship, once visible on the prow, has become difficult to read. But we can be fairly sure from the remaining legible letters that it was a vessel called the *Horatia*.'

At this point Christopher, his curiosity aroused, stepped forward and said: 'Do you mind if I take a closer look at that?'

'Of course,' said Randolph.

Christopher peered intently at the name painted on the ship's prow, then took out his phone and shone its torch onto the same area. After a few seconds' careful inspection, he stood back and said: 'Well, I may be wrong, but that doesn't look like *Horatia* to me.'

'Really?'

'It looks more like *Henrietta*.'

He shone the torch on the painting again, so that Randolph himself could take a closer look.

'Yes,' the 11th Earl conceded. 'Yes, it could be *Henrietta*. Well, not that it makes any difference . . .'

'But it does,' said Christopher. 'It makes a great deal of difference. May I?' And without asking further permission, he began taking a number of photographs of the painting, concentrating in particular on the ship's prow.

'How does it make a difference?' Randolph asked.

'Because the *Henrietta*,' said Christopher, still clicking away, 'was one of the most notorious slave ships of the late seventeenth century.' He took three more photographs and then stood up straight, addressing Randolph without noticing that his face had turned white. 'It sank off the coast of Jamaica in 1705, but not before it had made almost a dozen enslaving voyages. Until now, we didn't know who was behind the trading company that operated it. Well, I think that mystery can be declared solved.'

Lost for words at first, Randolph finally recovered some of his powers of speech, but not his capacity for stringing a sentence together.

'I . . . But – but . . . But I – I'm sure you've made a . . . I mean, you must be mistaken . . . My family – the Wetherbys – we never . . . I believe your eyesight must . . .' He peered once again at the relevant area of the painting, while his whole body shook with agitation. Meanwhile one of the other guests came forward and said:

'I say, Randy, who *is* this fellow anyway? There were only six of us when we met up in the hallway. This chap just seemed to appear from nowhere.'

'Yes,' one of his friends agreed. 'He just sort of tagged along. One minute he wasn't there, and the next minute . . . he was.'

'Exactly,' said Randolph, standing upright and wheeling around. 'Who the hell are you anyway?'

'My name is Christopher. Christopher Swann. I'm here for the conference – like the rest of you, I imagine.'

Turning to the small circle of onlookers, Randolph said: 'Would you allow me to have a few moments in private with this gentleman?' And, when the others had gone, he faced up to Christopher, saying: 'Look, quite frankly I think you've got the wrong end of the stick, here. The wrong end entirely.'

Christopher smiled his most emollient smile. 'I don't think so. In fact if you look at this picture –' he held his phone up for Randolph's inspection – 'the name can be read even more clearly. I can see that it's embarrassing for you. Nobody wants to be reminded that their family fortune is based on that sort of thing. If it's any consolation you're hardly alone. I think a lot of people are starting to wake up to the idea that most of our stately homes were built on the backs of slaves.'

'Exactly!' said Randolph, trying to strike a pally, man-of-the-world sort of tone, and falling some way short. 'So . . . look, be a decent chap and wipe those pictures from your phone, eh?'

Christopher thought about this for a moment or two. 'Why would I want to do that?'

'It's just that . . . Between you and me, I'm in the process of applying for funds, to do this place up a bit, and . . . Well, you know what the current climate's like. Everybody's gone so bloody *woke* recently. They only have to get a whiff of this sort of thing – anything to do with the slave trade – and they have a fit of the vapours.'

'Hmm.' Christopher smiled again. 'I do sympathize, of course. But . . . Well, I can't help thinking that my readers would be interested in these pictures.'

Randolph turned, if possible, an even whiter shade of pale. 'Readers? You're not a journalist, are you?'

Christopher nodded. 'Online, these days, mainly. Still, with a couple of hundred thousand hits a month, I must be doing something right.' He slid the phone into his jacket pocket. 'Thanks for the tour, anyway. Most informative. Wouldn't like those Japanese knives to get into the wrong hands, would you?'

It was at dinner that evening that Christopher got his first glimpse of Emeric Coutts and Roger Wagstaff. They were sitting at the top table, with Lord Wetherby between them, and there came a point during the main course when Christopher was sure, from their air of conspiratorial intimacy, and from the occasional glances they threw in his direction, that they had noticed him, and that he was the subject of their conversation. No doubt they all considered him troublesome, in their different ways.

After breakfast the next morning, he received a surprise. He was walking past the reception desk, on his way to the opening session of the conference (which was to be held in the stables theatre) when a voice called out:

'Oh, Mr Swann?'

He turned around to see the receptionist beckoning him.

'Yes?'

'Just to say that your new room is ready for you.'

She held out a key, attached to a heavy tasselled brass weight.

Christopher stepped forward and took the key uncertainly. 'My . . . new room?'

'Yes. Number nine. It's on the first floor. You can get into it now if you want.'

'But – was there a problem with my other room?'

'No. It's just that Lord Wetherby said . . .'

At this point the Earl himself appeared, emerging smoothly from the office which lay somewhere behind the reception desk.

'Good morning, Mr Swann. I simply thought you'd much prefer to stay in the main building. Where the action is, so to speak. Number nine is a beautiful old room. You'll be very comfortable there. And since we had an unexpected cancellation . . .'

'Well . . .' Christopher found himself nonplussed. 'That's very kind, but I'm quite settled in the annexe.'

'Your things have already been moved over,' said the Earl.

'Really?'

'Yes. I took the liberty of getting someone to do it while you were having breakfast.'

Christopher said nothing, not knowing what to make of any of this.

'No need to return your keycard for the annexe,' said Lord Wetherby. 'It's already been cancelled.'

His tone was perfectly polite, even obsequious. But as he turned back towards the office, and nodded goodbye to Christopher, his eyes told a different story. There was a cold inscrutability there, which hinted not at politeness, but at something else altogether. Something very much more dangerous. Something lethal.

4.

At ten o'clock that morning the conference began in the only way it could begin: with a keynote address by Sir Emeric Coutts. Although he was somewhat elderly now, and long since retired from his academic post at St Stephen's, the old philosopher's powers of rhetoric had not faded. Much of his speech was taken from one of his most famous books, *How I Became a Conservative.* Christopher was familiar with it, but he suspected that many of the people in the theatre – being quite a bit younger than him, for the most part – had never actually read this seminal text by one of the figureheads of their movement. They listened in rapt silence, all the same, as Professor Coutts rehearsed his familiar narrative. The disaster of the 1945 election, and the elevation to power of a Labour government determined to establish a powerful, wide-ranging welfare state, the bedrock of which would be the National Health Service: the beginning, in other words, of Britain's 'dependency culture'. The catastrophic moment of Suez in 1956, with its fatal blow to British self-confidence. The disastrous decision to join the EEC in 1973. The inexorable rise of union power, which by the end of the 1970s held the country in a stranglehold. Most of this had been observed by Emeric at first hand. He had read Adam Smith and Edmund Burke at an early age, and had soon concluded that in an ideal society the duty of the politician was simply to stand back and interfere as little as possible in the equitable, harmonious workings of the free market. By 1979, however, Great Britain was far from being an ideal society. Having ceded its sovereignty first to the unions, and then to the European bureaucrats, the country was in a weak, desperate state. A great crisis called for a great political figure: and sure enough, she stepped forward. 'I was not an unqualified admirer of Mrs Thatcher,' Professor Coutts told his audience (some of whom booed the statement half-jokingly). 'But during the next ten years we became very close. She frequently summoned me to Number Ten for policy advice and I had the opportunity to see how her mind worked at close quarters. She was lacking in imagination, perhaps even lacking in empathy. Certain areas of life – for example the world of culture, of books, music and art – were of no interest to her. (Incidentally this is the real reason why so many artists – and writers in particular – hated her.) But in most respects she was unflinching: unflinching in her devotion to her country, unflinching in her determination to serve the British people; and above all, unflinching in her love of freedom. Never forget what her tireless efforts achieved for the people of Eastern Europe and the Soviet Union.

'Freedom,' Professor Coutts continued, 'is at the very heart of what it means to be a conservative. That means freedom within the law, of course. But if people make laws that are unfair, that are not suited to the British way of life, we must also have the freedom to vote them out of power. That is why our decision to leave the European Union in 2016 was the single most decisive blow struck for British freedom since Magna Carta.' (Applause.) 'Twentieth-century history has given us terrible lessons in what can happen when that freedom is taken away from us in the name of socialist idealism. But not everybody has learned those lessons. The modern Left is continually looking for new and ever more insidious ways of limiting the freedom of the sovereign individual. Today, it seems that their aim is to wield absolute control over what we say and even what we think. Cancel culture. Political correctness. The insidious advance of "wokeness". If you hold the wrong opinions, you must be silenced and punished. But this is *not the British way*. The British people believe in freedom of thought, and freedom of speech. The British people speak their minds, and they will have no truck with anybody who tries to stop them.'

These sentiments, and others like them, were received by the audience with approval rather than outright rapture. Emeric Coutts was clearly a respected figure among these delegates, even if not all of them were exactly sure who he was. But there was a good deal more recognition, as well as enthusiasm, for the next speaker: Coutts's disciple, the founder and leader of the Processus Group, Roger Wagstaff, who stepped forward to the podium to a prolonged round of cheers and applause.

He made just a few opening remarks, concerning the political events of the last two days.

'Ladies and gentlemen,' he said, 'we didn't plan it this way, but it turns out that this conference is taking place at an amazing moment in Britain's recent history. For the first time in many years, we have a *genuine* conservative as our new Prime Minister.' (Applause.) 'A Prime Minister who is not afraid to commit herself to low taxes, to minimal government, and to curbing the interference of the state in our lives and in our businesses. A Prime Minister who is going to *get Britain back on track*!'

After these words, which were received, again, with wild applause and cries of 'Go for it, Liz!', Wagstaff proceeded to introduce the first panel discussion of the conference: a four-way debate on the subject, 'Britain's NHS – Does It Have a Future?'

The panel consisted of a Tory MP, a *Telegraph* journalist, a maverick doctor who had built up a lucrative sideline in media appearances, and Roger himself. Christopher listened to the discussion carefully, and took detailed notes, but when the hour was over, he did not feel that he'd learned anything new. He had been curious to see whether, in this setting, Roger would feel emboldened to come clean about the full scale of his vision for Britain's health service. To which the answer appeared to be: not just yet. Today's discussion featured the usual denigration of the NHS as a 'sacred cow' which was 'fetishized' by the British Left. There had been talk of the impossibly long waiting lists, the inefficient bureaucracy, the chronic shortage of medical staff. Most of these problems, Christopher suspected, were the deliberate result of policy decisions designed to prepare the Health Service for its inevitable fate: full-scale privatization. This objective was not spelt out during the panel discussion, but Christopher knew that Processus were pushing for it hard behind the scenes. He had seen the proposals, examined the secret spreadsheets, identified the American pharma companies who were ready to step in as soon as the green light appeared. But he also knew that Processus were holding their fire for now; that they were keeping a close eye on the public mood, and were fully aware that the British people still weren't quite ready for such a radical and irreversible step. And that, in Christopher's view, was what made his own position so powerful: because he had proof of their intentions, and could do untold damage to their project by revealing it early.

Rather than listen to the second debate of the morning (a plenary session entitled 'What Does Post-Brexit Conservatism Stand For?'), Christopher decided to walk back to the main building. He was curious, by now, to see the new room which he had been mysteriously allocated. He took a longer route to the house than before, following the path beside the ornamental lake and once again noticing the figure of the lone fisherman, sitting in contemplative silence and gazing out across the water which, like him, seemed to be infinitely calm and infinitely patient. Christopher wondered if he came to fish there every day.

Passing swiftly through the hotel's reception area, he climbed the impressive oak staircase which stood at the centre of the building, leading to the first floor. There he found himself in a wide, gloomy and forbidding corridor, with doorways leading off on either side. His room, number 9, was at the far end of the corridor, at the back of the house. The two doors preceding it, he noticed, were marked 8/1 and 8/2. Connecting rooms, no doubt. The key for his new room was amazingly heavy, and fitted rather awkwardly in the lock. But after struggling with it for almost a minute, he managed to get inside.

His first impression was merely of size. It was an enormous room, about four or five times bigger than the ones in the annexe. It was also swathed in darkness, even at this hour of the day. The windows, which allowed a restricted view of the kitchen garden, were small and leaded, with the result that they admitted very little light. A large four-poster bed dominated the space. Leading off in one direction was a long, thin bathroom; there was also a third room – or so Christopher thought at first, since it was big enough to accommodate a small bed or at least a sofa. However, the absence of windows and the presence of coat hangers made him realize that it was, in fact, a gigantic walk-in wardrobe. His dinner suit was already hanging there. All of his belongings, he noticed, had been laid out meticulously around the bedroom, and his toiletries had been arranged in a neat row on the shelf above the capacious bathroom washbasin. All of the items of furniture in the main room were ancient and heavy: none more so than the huge winged armchair which sat in front of the empty stone-flagged fireplace. He flopped down into this chair and sat brooding for a few minutes. It was a luxurious and comfortable room, for sure, if not exactly cheerful. On balance it was preferable to the one he had been allocated yesterday. And yet he couldn't for the life of him see why he had been moved so abruptly.

There was something strange about it. What was going on?

Wetherby Hall had two bars. One, the Dunciad Room, was busy and rowdy. The other, the Addison Lounge, was much more pleasant but for some reason seemed to be shunned by most of the guests. When Christopher arrived there after dinner that evening, at about ten o'clock, he found that, apart from a presenter from GB News and a *Spiked* columnist snogging vigorously in a quiet corner, the only other occupant was Sir Emeric Coutts, sitting at a table by himself and squinting over his mobile phone. Christopher approached his table and coughed discreetly.

'Sir Emeric?' he said, when the philosopher looked up. 'Would you allow me to buy you another drink?'

Before answering this question, Emeric said: 'Do we know each other?'

'Yes, we do, after a fashion,' said Christopher. 'I'll explain in a moment. The same again?'

Emeric looked at his glass, as if he had forgotten what was in it, and replied: 'Very well. Brandy and soda.'

Christopher bought the same for himself, and when he returned to Emeric's corner of the lounge, he placed both drinks on the table and sat down beside him, saying, 'I hope you don't mind if I join you?' when it was already a fait accompli.

'Not at all, not at all,' said Emeric, without much enthusiasm. He raised his glass to Christopher in a wary and uncertain movement. 'Well, cheers. And thank you very much.'

'I hope you don't think,' Christopher said, 'that you're being accosted by a perfect stranger. As it happens, we have met, several times. But it was a good many years ago. I was an undergraduate at St Stephen's in the early eighties.'

'The early eighties! Good God, that is delving back into ancient history.'

'I used to attend your salons, now and again.'

Emeric did not respond, so Christopher added, by way of reminder:

'You used to hold salons, in your rooms in Kite's Court.'

When Emeric did not respond again, Christopher wondered whether the old man's memory might be failing. But finally an answer came: '"Salons" is rather a grand way of putting it, I think.'

'But they *were* grand,' Christopher insisted. 'Amazingly grand, to a twenty-year-old boy fresh out of grammar school in Somerset.' Laying a little trap, he said: 'You even had a harpsichord in there, for heaven's sake.'

'It was a clavichord,' Emeric corrected him. (So the old duffer's memory was still pretty sharp, after all.) 'Usually one of the music scholars would perform something. And occasionally my daughter would sing. She had rather a fine voice.'

'And how is Lavinia?' Christopher asked. 'Keeping well, I hope?'

'So far as I know,' said Emeric, somewhat drily. 'We don't see each other very often. She's taken her own route.'

'To America, I believe.'

'Exactly. You've been well informed.'

Christopher held out his hand. 'The name's Christopher, by the way. Christopher Swann. In case you were having any trouble putting your finger on it.'

'Christopher Swann . . .' Emeric leaned back in his chair and, with an effort, retrieved something from his memory. 'Are you the man with the blog?'

'I suppose that's one way of putting it,' said Christopher.

'Hmm. I've glanced at it once or twice. Given your own politics, I can only assume that you've come here to spy on the opposition, have you, and write something sarcastic about the proceedings?'

'I'm simply a historian of the conservative movement,' said Christopher, 'and whatever my personal—'

'Ah, Emeric!' They were joined at the table now by Roger Wagstaff, who had rushed into the bar looking flustered. 'I'm sorry I'm late. There are just too many people here who want to talk to me.'

He sat down, and suddenly realized who he was sitting next to. 'Oh Christ, it's you, Swann. I thought I got a glimpse of you across a crowded room earlier. What the bloody hell have you turned up for?'

'To cause trouble, I think,' said Emeric.

'Well I hope he isn't causing you any.'

'No, not at all. We were having a perfectly civilized little jousting match.'

'Can I get you a drink, Roger?' Christopher asked.

'No thanks. Emeric and I have some private business to discuss.'

'Well then, I'll just drink up, and leave you to it.'

He took a small sip of his own brandy and soda, roughly three-quarters of which remained in the glass, and then sat back in his chair with a relaxed smile.

Roger stared at him frostily, but it was clear that he wasn't going to move.

'Fine,' he said. 'This isn't exactly top secret, anyhow. Kwasi's had to pull out, of course.'

'I assumed he would,' said Christopher. 'Our new Prime Minister has saddled him with rather a daunting task – finding room for tax cuts in the middle of an economic crisis. Enough to keep any Chancellor busy for the next few days. Who have you got to replace him?'

Roger turned to Emeric. 'How did you get on with your Venetian friend?'

'Very well. He was delighted to accept. He's getting an early flight and should be here by lunchtime.'

'Excellent. Can you make an announcement ahead of tomorrow's first session?'

'Of course.'

'You've got a speaker coming in from Venice?' Christopher said.

'Something that you on the Left find it hard to understand,' said Emeric, 'is that turning your back on the European Union is not the same as turning your back on Europe.'

'Quite,' said Roger. 'Personally I love Europe.'

'Of course you do,' said Christopher. 'The far Right is thriving there as well. In France, in Italy, in Spain . . .'

'Oh, for God's sake, Swann, spare us the student politics. We've moved on from St Stephen's now. At least most of us have.'

'In any case,' Emeric said, 'the speaker I approached is not a politician. One of my reservations about this conference was that no one had been invited to talk on a cultural theme.'

'Well, you could see our difficulty,' said Roger. 'Every writer, actor and musician in the country is a lefty.'

'It's true that conservative voices are not well represented in the arts,' said Emeric. 'That's why it's very important to give a platform to those who are. Or were.'

'So who's flying in from Venice, then? Jeffrey Archer? Andrew Lloyd Webber?'

'Tell me,' said Emeric, calmly passing over this provocation, 'have you heard of a writer called Peter Cockerill?'

Christopher hesitated. The name rang a very, very faint bell, but he couldn't remember where he had heard it before.

'I'm afraid not,' he said. 'You'll have to enlighten me.'

'Well, I just wondered,' said Professor Coutts. 'He was rather an interesting novelist, active in the 1980s. You mentioned the, um, "salons", and since he was once one of the invited speakers, I wondered if you might have been in the audience.'

'Ah – no. I wasn't present, on that occasion.' Christopher frowned. 'Possibly one of my friends was, though. Now that I think of it, I do recall him mentioning that name at the time.'

Emeric gave a rueful sigh. 'I wasn't able to be there either, as it happens. Most unfortunately, I was . . . severely indisposed that evening. Something I've always regretted. You've never read him, then?'

Christopher shook his head.

'Well, I recommend that you do. Most people consider *A Rope from Hell* to be his best. But his final novel is remarkable, too. A change of direction, and a significant artistic experiment. But not a comfortable read, by any means.'

'Well, I look forward to hearing him speak,' said Christopher. 'I suppose he must be getting on a bit now.'

'Alas, he won't be coming in person. Peter Cockerill died a long time ago. Just a few years after his visit to St Stephen's. He committed suicide.'

'I see. How tragic.' Christopher didn't know how else to react to this decades-old piece of news. 'So – I don't understand – who will be addressing us tomorrow afternoon?'

'Professor Richard Wilkes. The world's leading authority on Cockerill. He lectures at Ca' Foscari University. He will be giving a talk entitled –' he looked at his phone screen and tapped on it a few times – '"Master of Reinvention: Themes of Renewal in the Novels of Peter Cockerill, and Their Importance to the Conservative Movement".'

'Well, that should raise the tone, at least,' said Christopher, privately wondering how such an address would be received by the audience of passionate economic libertarians who seemed to dominate this conference. (Talking of passion, the GB News presenter and the *Spiked* columnist had by now vacated the bar and headed off to take their business elsewhere.) 'Do you happen to know the reason for his suicide?'

Emeric smiled at the naivety of this question. 'As I'm sure you understand, it's a very complicated phenomenon, which rarely admits of one interpretation. There are several theories in his case. We know that he was very, very bitter about the lack of recognition for his work. I'm pleased to say there has been a remarkable rebirth of interest in him over the last few years – not least because of the efforts of Professor Wilkes. But back in the mid-1980s, it was an entirely different cohort of young writers – Rushdie, Ishiguro, McEwan and so on – who were getting all the attention. Cockerill felt that he deserved the same, and was being punished for his politics. He refused to toe the fashionable anti-Thatcher line, you see. Which is precisely why you should read him. If you've not been convinced by anything that I've written, perhaps his novels might persuade you. The world view which I've tried to articulate in my essays, he also expressed in narrative form. The importance of family, of God; a sense of national cohesion and belonging. He was that rarest of beasts: a real writer, and a real conservative. In many ways I see us as kindred spirits.'

'What about you?' Christopher asked, turning to Roger Wagstaff. 'Are you a fan too?'

'Can't say that I've read him, to be honest.'

'Why doesn't that surprise me?'

This was spoken flatly, and sotto voce, as if to himself. Nonetheless, Roger heard it and – rather to Christopher's surprise – he rose to the bait.

'I don't know, Christopher. Why *doesn't* it surprise you?'

'Well, it hardly sounds like your thing, does it?'

'My thing?'

'It doesn't bear much resemblance to your own political philosophy.'

'*My* political philosophy? You don't have the faintest idea what you're talking about. I'm a conservative just like Emeric. Conservatism is a broad church.'

'What you guys are up to these days has nothing to do with conservatism.'

'"You guys"?'

'Processus. Which seems to be more or less driving the policies of the British government right now.'

'Oh, you're a fantasist, Swann. Always have been.'

'I'm just struggling to find much of a connection between what Emeric said to the audience this morning and what you've all been talking about for the rest of the day.'

'If I may make a little contribution in this war of words,' Emeric interposed, 'can I just say that I'm perfectly happy with the way my legacy is being carried forward by Roger and his colleagues?'

'Really?' said Christopher, turning towards him. '*Really*? Proroguing Parliament? Lying to the Queen? Trashing the Good Friday Agreement? Tearing up international treaties left, right and centre? Sending refugees to Rwanda? Setting up freeports? Even your beloved Mrs Thatcher would baulk at most of that.'

'Can I just remind you,' Roger said, 'that the government has a democratic mandate for these things, from the British people?'

'Bollocks. The British people would be out on the streets if they knew what was being discussed in here. Privatizing the NHS, for Christ's sake . . .'

'Another of your fantasies. Nobody said a word about privatization this morning.'

'Of course not. Even now you're scared to come right out and announce it. The service has to be driven even further into the ground before that can happen.'

'Have you ever considered writing a novel yourself? Fiction seems to be right up your street.'

Christopher paused, as if aware that he was about to take an irrevocable step. Then he said: 'I have read it, you know.'

'Read it? Read what?'

'The Second of August Report.'

The effect of these words upon Roger was electric. His whole body froze. He stared at Christopher in horror. He was stupefied. For several excruciating moments he remained quite motionless, and quite silent.

'That is how you refer to it, I think?' Christopher continued. 'I believe because that was the day it was completed, and circulated.'

Once he had recovered his powers of speech, Roger said: 'I have literally no idea what you're talking about.'

'Really? Well then, perhaps I should try asking Rebecca instead. I imagine she was the one who typed it all up, and inputted all the data?'

'Kindly leave her out of this. That woman has served me loyally for almost forty years.'

'In a professional capacity, or a personal one? I notice that the two of you have connecting rooms upstairs. Eight/one and eight/two, isn't it?'

Roger's face was puce with fury. In a tone of preternatural calm, he said: 'OK, Christopher, you will leave me and Emeric alone now. We have business to discuss, and this conversation is at an end.'

'Ah, there it is – your catchphrase!'

'My catchphrase?'

'Even at Cambridge, that was what you used to say to people when you'd just lost an argument. Which was most of the time. You haven't changed a bit.'

'Neither have you. A complete failure in life, just as I always knew you'd turn out to be. And just as deluded as ever – because I can tell you categorically that there is *no such thing as the Second of August Report*.'

Christopher took out a flash drive from his inside jacket pocket and laid it on the table between them.

'Well, that's very odd,' he said. 'Because I have a copy of it right here.'

For a long time the two men, Roger and Christopher, stared at the little portable storage device on the table between them. Was Christopher bluffing? Could he really have laid his hands on such sensitive information? There was no way of knowing.

They spoke no more words to each other that evening, at any rate. Christopher said goodbye to Emeric and headed off to his room. Roger watched him leave the bar. His lips were tightly shut and he offered no parting insult, no final threat, but there was fire in his eyes. Sir Emeric Coutts noticed it and, when he spoke to his friend and protégé, there was a complex note in his voice: concern mixed with twinkling amusement.

'Why, Roger, I don't think I've ever seen you give a look quite like that to anybody before.'

Putting up a poor display of bravado and insouciance, Roger asked: 'What sort of a look?'

Emeric thought for a moment, and eventually hit upon *le mot juste*.

'Well, to be honest, I would have to describe it as . . . *homicidal*,' he said.

5.

The next day was marked by three significant events: Professor Richard Wilkes arrived at Wetherby Pond from Venice; Her Majesty Queen Elizabeth II passed away at the age of ninety-six; and Christopher discovered that he had lost his flash drive.

His argument with Roger had, in fact, discomposed him far more than he had been willing to show. He had been shaking when he left the bar, and was still highly agitated when he reached room 9. When he got inside, he slumped in front of the fireplace in the lumpen winged armchair, and drank some whisky from one of the tiny bottles in the minibar. Before taking his jacket off and hanging it in the wardrobe, he could have sworn that he had patted the inside pocket to check that the flash drive was still there, and had felt its reassuring hard outline. But in the morning, when he discovered that it was gone, he was not so certain. Thinking back, the last time he could actually remember seeing it was when it lay on the table in the bar between him and Roger, at the climax of their argument. He washed and dressed and hurried back down to the Addison Lounge, but of course the gadget was no longer there. The bar was closed and there was no one to ask if it been handed in or discovered by the barman.

It was all rather worrying. It was not that this drive contained his only copy of the sensitive file. Christopher never uploaded anything to the Cloud, because he didn't trust it, but in the case of this file he had backups on his laptop and on his desktop computer at home. Even so, he didn't like the fact that the drive itself had disappeared without explanation – didn't like it at all – and resolved to continue his enquiries during the lunch break.

The first session of Thursday morning was very well attended, the speaker being something of a celebrity and indeed an icon in these circles. She had a high-profile column in a national newspaper, her name was Josephine Winshaw (daughter of the legendary journalist and media mogul Hilary Winshaw) and her theme today might have been predicted by anyone familiar with her output over the last year or so. It was, 'Britain's Real Pandemic: The Woke Mind-Virus'.

Josephine was introduced on stage by Sir Emeric, who prefaced her appearance with the following announcement:

'As you may have heard, ladies and gentlemen – or indeed, as you may have expected, even if you hadn't heard it – one of our guests this afternoon has had to withdraw from the conference. The speaker who has agreed, at very short notice, to take his place, could hardly be more different. But what he has to say is, in my view, just as important as anything the new Chancellor might have told us. His name is Professor Richard Wilkes and at this very moment he is flying in from Venice, where he teaches English Literature at the University of Ca' Foscari.

'I do hope you won't be put off by the fact that the theme of Professor Wilkes's talk will not be directly political. He will be speaking about the life and work of the novelist Peter Cockerill. If that name is not familiar to you, might I recommend that any of our delegates who find themselves with a few minutes on their hands take a look at the visitors' books of this hotel, which are on display in the library? They date back to the early 1920s and provide a marvellous roll-call of twentieth-century historical names. Winston Churchill stayed here, as did Edward VIII and Wallis Simpson. Evelyn Waugh was a guest, and so were Benjamin Britten and Peter Pears.' (These last three names, Christopher thought, did not seem to be ringing many bells with some of the audience.) 'And, for two nights, the thirteenth and fourteenth of May 1985, another distinguished writer, Peter Cockerill, was a visitor. "What a privilege," he wrote in the book, "to be able to stay as a guest in what used to be one of the great country houses of England. Lord Wetherby –" that is the current Earl's father – "was generous enough to welcome me personally, and gave me a long and comprehensive tour of the house, including some of its most fascinating secret nooks and crannies." For some people, perhaps, Peter Cockerill himself belongs among the "secret nooks and crannies" of modern English literature. However, for many of us – especially those of us working within the great tradition of British conservatism – his work is rather more important than that. So, please, I do urge you to come and hear what Professor Wilkes has to say. It promises to be a most stimulating and unusual talk.'

Sir Emeric followed this announcement with a few sentences about Josephine Winshaw, but there was no need to say very much, since the audience – including those who were standing in the aisles or watching on television screens in the overflow room – were already fully primed for her appearance.

Josephine, who was thirty-two years old now, took to the stage in a dress of cobalt blue, complete with pearl necklace and interlocking crystal brooch (by Gucci, for those who knew about such things). Once the anticipated ovation had subsided, she launched straight into her polemic. The first half of her title was provocative enough, but she spent only a few minutes on it: her thesis being that the dangers of the Covid pandemic in 2020 had been exaggerated, that lockdown had delivered an unacceptable hit to the British economy, and the whole thing could have been avoided if people had been a bit less squeamish about the deaths of a few thousand pensioners who would all have died anyway, a few months later.

But then she got to the heart of the matter. The problem with British society, the thing that was really crippling it and holding it back, was wokeness. She did not actually say what wokeness was. She didn't have to, because her audience understood it. Rather, she adopted an approach to the word that Lewis Carroll's Humpty Dumpty would have been proud of: words were her servants, and she could use them to mean whatever she wanted them to mean. And so, everything was woke. Or at least, everything that Britain's elite said and did was woke, even though this elite, too, could not really be defined. Anyway, she was in no mood to let niceties of terminology hold her back. The BBC was woke. That was blindingly obvious. The Church of England was woke. That much was clear. The judiciary was woke. That went without saying. Nearly all of the print media were woke, nearly all of the online media were woke, and obviously (in fact it was almost too obvious to need saying) the whole of academia was deeply, fatally, irredeemably woke. Paying your TV licence was woke. Getting vaccinated was woke. Wanting to rejoin the European Union was woke. Putting out your rubbish in different-coloured bins was woke. Saving the planet was woke. Giving money to homeless people, welcoming immigrants and wanting to pay care workers a living wage were all woke, woke and woke respectively. Taking the knee was woke, taking the train was woke – especially when the alternative was travelling by plane – eating vegetables was woke, buying avocados was woke, and reading novels was woke.

Christopher's mind began to wander at this stage and he found himself taking out his phone and writing a quick email to Joanna:

> *I don't suppose* [he wrote] *that Brian's manuscript makes any reference to a writer called Peter Cockerill? I believe he was a guest speaker at one of Emeric's salons during our time at St Stephen's. If so, could you send me, as a matter of urgency, some JPEGS of any of the pages that mention him?*

There was no let-up from the podium. Listening to experts was woke. Believing in science was woke. Oxford and Cambridge were woke. North London was woke. Chai lattes were woke. Lentils were woke. Not having a car was woke. Riding a bicycle to work was woke. Working from home was exceptionally woke, about the wokest thing you could do, according to Josephine.

Joanna's reply came swiftly.

> *Yes, it does, as a matter of fact. And of course – I'll send you the pages later this morning. You do realize that email is considered an antiquated mode of communication these days? (So Phyl tells me.) In any case the parish website will be down for maintenance starting at midnight tonight, after which my email address won't be working again until next week.*

The National Trust was woke. The Ramblers' Association was woke. The RSPCA, the RSPB and the NSPCC were all woke. Channel 4 was woke. Radio 4 was woke. Radio 3 was woke. Every national treasure you could think of, from Richard Attenborough to Judi Dench, from Maggie Smith to Stephen Fry, was woke, woke,

woke and woke. Prince Charles was as woke as they came. Prince Harry was woker than they came. Meghan Markle's wokeness was simply off the scale. Biden was woke. The Democrats were woke. Hollywood was woke. Bollywood was woke . . .

By now Christopher had got the gist and was feeling the need for a few breaths of fresh air. Getting up and pushing past the other delegates in his row, all of whom were listening with rapt attention and nodding along furiously, he left the stables theatre by the rear door and once again decided to take some exercise by walking beside the ornamental lake. It was such a tranquil spot, perfect for quiet reflection, and once again there was no one to interrupt his thoughts apart from the lone fisherman sitting on his canvas stool. Christopher nodded hello as he walked past, but then, on an impulse, he stopped, turned, and went to have a few words with him.

'Any luck this morning?' he said.

The man shook his head. 'Nope. No luck today.'

'I'm sorry to hear that. What are you hoping for? Pike, perch, trout?'

'Hard to say.'

'Well, how many would you expect to catch, on a typical day?'

'None.'

'None at all?'

'Nope. Never seen one, never caught one.'

'Oh.' Christopher was quite dampened by this confession. 'Tell me, how long have you been coming here?'

'Near on five year, I suppose.'

'And not a bite?'

'Not a nibble.'

'Dear me. It seems something of a . . . futile exercise.'

The man thought about this, and then gave a shrug. 'Whole of life's futile, really, isn't it, when you think about it?'

Christopher pondered this unanswerable piece of personal philosophy as he completed his walk back to the main building. Then, as he stopped by the reception desk to see if there were any messages for him, the receptionist said:

'Get any sense out of him?'

'Who?' Christopher asked.

'Old Bob Hopkins. Saw you talking to him out of the window.'

'Ah. Well . . . yes, a little bit of sense, I suppose. Something to think about, anyway.'

'Poor man's simple,' the receptionist said. 'That's the problem.'

'Simple?'

'Yes, and I'll tell you what's so funny about it: there are no fish in that lake. Not one. Never have been. It's never been stocked, see? And yet he comes here day in and day out, in all weathers. Lord Wetherby lets him do it. Very kind that way, His Lordship. Sees no harm in Old Bob, so why shouldn't he be allowed to sit by the lake all day?'

'Why not indeed?' said Christopher. And repeated, more musingly: 'Why not indeed . . . ?' The conversation seemed to be at an end, so he climbed the staircase to the first floor.

At two o'clock that afternoon, Christopher decided to take a bath. His flash drive was still missing, but a distraction from this puzzle had arrived in the form of Joanna's email, to which were attached high-res images of all the pages from Brian's manuscript which related to Peter Cockerill. He was surprised to see that there were so many of them. Christopher positioned his laptop somewhat precariously on the antique brass-plated bath rack with which his bathroom was helpfully equipped, and settled down in the hot soapy water to read, occasionally wiping steam away from the computer screen with his hand towel.

On a first reading, he was impressed by how much ground seemed to be covered in Brian's memoir. He hadn't realized that his late friend would remember their student days in such detail, or with such clarity. As soon as Christopher began to read, he was transported back to Emeric Coutts's rooms at St Stephen's College in the early 1980s, and the strange, febrile atmosphere of those salons which he had sometimes (though not on this occasion) attended himself.

Peter Cockerill [he read] *was a long, slender, angular man, with delicate features and a face that would have suggested melancholy at the best of times. He was currently sitting alone on one of Emeric's four-seater sofas, with a copy of his newly published novel open on his lap. Occasionally he would take a sip of white wine from the glass at his side, but mostly he was concentrating on the book and making some pencilled notes in the margins.*

There followed a short digression about Cockerill in general: how his reputation had been revived in the twenty-first century (largely thanks to the efforts of Professor Richard Wilkes) and the place occupied by his novel *A Rope from Hell* within his work as a whole. The account resumed with a description of Cockerill reciting an old folk song, entitled 'Lord Randall', which had served as an epigraph to this book.

He put the book aside, having no need of it for the time being. Clearly he knew the song by heart, and as he began to recite it, the atmosphere in the room – which had consisted up until now of bored or uncomprehending silence – was transformed into something more attentive, more charged. Cockerill closed his eyes in concentration, and his voice was calm, measured. He drew out the rhythm of the verse with expert emphasis, and spoke slowly, with long, expressive pauses between verses.

At this point Christopher was distracted by a sound coming from his bedroom: at least, it seemed that it was coming from there. It was the sound of a door opening softly and then, about thirty seconds later, gently closing. At once he sat up in the tepid bathwater, straining to listen. There were no further noises. However, the situation still warranted investigation. He climbed out of the bath, pulled on his white fluffy bathrobe and made his way into the bedroom with cautious steps.

'Hello?' he called out.

There was no one there.

The only explanation Christopher could think of was that a maid or bellboy must have come into the room, perhaps with clean towels or a couple of those silly little chocolates that hotel managers liked to have placed on your pillows. But then he remembered that he had put the chain lock on the door before running the bath, and it was still securely in place. So nobody could have come in that way. He must, surely, have imagined the noise. The internal walls of the house were pretty thick, but it was still possible that it came from a door opening and closing in another nearby room. Now that he thought about it, the sound had definitely had a muffled quality.

He dismissed the episode and, despite feeling slightly uneasy, sat down in the armchair to resume his reading of Brian's pages. He read them to the very end, with increasing fascination. The final scene was especially remarkable – revealing, as it did, a quirk of Peter Cockerill's behaviour which struck Christopher as most unusual. Perhaps even unique.

At four-thirty he made his way over to the stables theatre again. He was curious to hear the presentation by Professor Richard Wilkes, and was disappointed – but not surprised – to find that it was by far the most thinly attended event of the conference so far. The auditorium was half-empty.

Roger Wagstaff himself introduced the speaker, and began by apologizing for the change of programme.

'In today's closing session we were going to hear from the Right Honourable Kwasi Kwarteng, MP. However, as you will all know, on Tuesday, Kwasi was appointed Chancellor of the Exchequer by our new Prime Minister.' Roger paused for effect. 'Let that piece of information sink in, ladies and gentlemen. When Liz and Kwasi helped to co-author the book *Britannia Unchained* in 2013 – their manifesto for a low-tax, low-regulation economy – they were dismissed as mavericks and fringe thinkers. Look at them now! Our two great offices of state, occupied *at last* by people who actually get it, who actually understand what it means to be a conservative in Britain in 2022. We've made it, ladies and gentlemen! The citadel has been stormed, and we're finally inside!'

A huge round of applause followed these words, and continued until Roger raised his hands to quell it.

'Well, tonight we can all drink a few glasses of champagne to mark this moment. I shall certainly be doing so. Meanwhile, our understanding is that Kwasi intends to deliver a new mini-budget about two weeks from now, so you can imagine that his time is currently very precious. He sends his deepest and most sincere regrets for not being here.

'But fear not, ladies and gentlemen! For we have a brave soul who has agreed to step into the breach at the last moment. And what a . . . what a very different, and challenging, perspective he proposes to offer us, on the meaning of modern conservatism. "Master of Reinvention: Themes of Renewal in the Novels of Peter Cockerill, and Their Importance to the Conservative Movement". Who is there among us who hasn't, at some point, wished to hear a paper on precisely that topic? Well, ladies and gentlemen, we need wait no longer. It is now my very great pleasure to offer the floor to Professor Richard Wilkes, straight off the plane from Italy, who will tell us more about this most fascinating and – for reasons which I'm sure we will all understand in the end – important subject.'

There was a smattering of polite applause as Professor Wilkes climbed with an air of diffidence onto the stage, clutching what seemed to be an intimidatingly large sheaf of papers. His appearance was very much what Christopher would have expected from a professor of the humanities who was by now past normal retirement age. (According to Wikipedia he was sixty-nine, but he looked about five years older.) Fraying grey-flannel suit, navy blue tie, grey hair worn rather too long, fussily trimmed beard, signs of incipient stoop from too many years spent hunched over books and computer screens. The only slightly incongruous feature – with which he was hoping, possibly, to strike something of a rakish note – was his V-necked sweater, which was a positively lurid shade of bright red. A shade of red so dazzling, in fact, that Christopher found himself quite distracted by it at first.

The Professor stood at his lectern, and took stock of the rows of faces trained upon him, awaiting his first utterance. He seemed in no hurry to begin. No doubt several decades of speaking to a captive audience of students had given him the habit of expecting to be listened to. And then:

'*The past,*' he declaimed loudly and unexpectedly, '*is the only dead thing that smells sweet.*'

This declaration was followed by a long and pregnant hiatus. Until at last the Professor continued:

'You will recognize these words, I'm sure, as being a quotation from the great British poet Edward Thomas. As conservatives, we look to the past, we learn from the past, we take our inspiration from the past. To us, it certainly "smells sweet". But should the main focus of our attention really be a "dead thing"? In fact, was Edward Thomas even right about that? *Is* the past really "dead" at all? Sometimes, a thing which *appears* to be dead can be more alive, more brim full of life and possibility, than we ever suspected. Sometimes the *illusion* of death can be a manifestation of something else entirely. A portent of renewal, and rebirth. Today, I want to explain how this paradoxical idea is expressed, and indeed enacted, in the work and in the short – much too short – life of the novelist Peter Cockerill.

'Let me begin,' the Professor continued, having stunned his audience into silence with this overture, 'with some biographical detail. Peter Cockerill was born in 1948, in the Gloucestershire village of Bradbourne. He was the only child of a working-class couple, whose marriage broke up when he was very young, when his father, George, an engineer in the tool room of the Bristol Aeroplane Company a few miles away, left his wife, Betty, for another woman and moved with her to London. Since George had been a churchwarden and a pillar of the local community, the scandal rocked the village and had a long-lasting effect on Cockerill himself. He was an only child and from then on, his relationship with his mother became exceptionally close. Peter was a precocious boy, with interests unusual for someone of his age and class. He won a place at the local grammar school and, in his mid-teens, discovered a taste for modernist fiction, immersing himself in the novels of James Joyce and Samuel Beckett. At the same time, he developed a passion for local history, for church architecture, for the recovery and preservation of rural traditions and folklore. He was awarded a scholarship to Balliol College, Oxford, where he began to write in earnest. His first novel, *O Tempora!*, was published when he was still in his twenties. It was followed by the experimental *Motet in Four Parts*, and then three years later came *A Rope from Hell*, the book which, by general agreement, represents his aesthetic breakthrough. Regarded as a masterful romantic tragedy by some, cited by others as evidence of a cruel and misogynist streak in his work, it concludes with what the author describes as an "almighty aposiopesis", in which he appears to renounce fiction altogether and promises that in future he is going to tell only "the truth in the form of a novel". Cockerill can therefore be seen as a pioneer in the literary genre that is today popularly known as autofiction, and his first excursion in this form was the autobiographical novel *My Innocence*, published in 1987. However, this was to be his last book, and is now famous for a reason which has little to do with its considerable literary merit. On its final page, the narrator announces his intention to commit suicide, and indeed, a few months before the novel was published, Cockerill had already taken this terrible step.

'But why talk about this writer at all, at a political conference? Because his novels, taken collectively, offer a very rare expression of the conservative vision in imaginative form. Cockerill was neglected in his lifetime. He was dismissed as a "young fogey". He refused to follow the anti-Thatcher line that in the 1980s seemed to be an essential prerequisite for being taken seriously as an artist. And yet—'

But Professor Wilkes, who had flown all the way from Venice to deliver this talk, had been speaking for less than four minutes when he was interrupted in the most dramatic way. Someone hurried into the theatre and handed Roger Wagstaff a slip of paper. A few seconds later, Roger ran up to the stage and, after apologizing to the speaker for breaking in upon his lecture, he turned to the audience and said:

'Ladies and gentlemen, I think we shall have to bring a premature end to today's proceedings. It is with great regret – the deepest regret – that I find myself bringing you the most terrible, shocking news: at two-thirty this afternoon, Her Majesty, Queen Elizabeth the Second, passed away.'

There followed one of the profoundest silences that Christopher had ever heard. Even he, a staunch anti-royalist, appreciated the gravity of the moment. The Queen had been on the throne for exactly seventy years. Through seven decades of political change – none more turbulent than the last decade or so – she had provided continuity, of sorts. An emblem of continuity, at any rate. Badly governed and riven by political division, Britain was already going through a difficult time. This could only make it more difficult, in the short term.

From that moment on, a mood of solemnity draped itself over Wetherby Hall, and was never more palpable than when everyone gathered in the great dining room for the final dinner of the conference. It fell to Lord Wetherby himself to propose two toasts, the first one to the memory of Queen Elizabeth, the second to the long life and good health of His Majesty King Charles III: a designation which came with some difficulty to the lips of many of the diners, who had all been slagging off the new King for being too woke during the last two days. The Earl then added these concluding words:

'Allow me to propose one more toast, ladies and gentlemen, because before today's tragic event was announced, I had already been planning to share with you some more personal and more positive news.

'As you can imagine, we host a great many conferences here at Wetherby Hall, but it has been a particular pleasure to welcome this one. By offering a home for TrueCon 2022, I really feel that I am doing my own little bit to help a worthy cause. I want to offer my personal thanks both to Roger Wagstaff, first of all, not just for organizing the conference but for being an inspiration to us all, and of course to the great Sir Emeric, who has stood up for everything that is good and true in political life over the course of his long lifetime.

'It is because of this sense of being among kindred spirits that I now feel able to make an announcement to you. Some of you may have noticed, when you stand at the main door to this house, that on the keystone of the arch above the door, a date has been engraved – the eighth of February 1724. This was the day upon which the final stone was laid in the construction of Wetherby Hall, and my ancestral family took up residence. I am proud to say that this magnificent building has survived more or less intact for almost three centuries. For one of those centuries, it has been in use as a hotel. But now, that era is coming to an end. In fact, you will be the last guests ever to stay at Wetherby Hall. This weekend, the hotel will close down, and eighteen months of reconstruction will start. It will not be easy. It will not be cheap. We will be relying on grants from such bodies as English Heritage and the National Trust, and in the current climate, you cannot always rely on them to do the right or the sensible thing. The "woke mind-virus", as Miss Josephine Winshaw so beautifully put it, has infected every institution in this country, and to be sure of getting their support, one must pass every sort of test of bogus ideological purity. However, unless something goes seriously awry –' and was it Christopher's imagination, or did Lord Wetherby look pointedly at him while speaking these words? – 'I am confident that our cause will be successful. Wetherby Hall will reopen to the public, who will be able to enjoy it as the great family home that it once was. So confident are we of success, in fact, that we are setting a date for the grand reopening. And that date will be the three hundredth anniversary of the laying of that very final stone. The eighth of February 2024.'

The listening diners spontaneously rose to their feet and applauded.

'Thank you, thank you,' the Earl said, holding up his hands to quell their enthusiasm. 'All I would ask you to do now, my friends and fellow travellers, is to drink one more toast. To the eighth of February!'

'*The eighth of February!*' everybody echoed, draining their glasses.

At which point the waiters entered, bearing the first item on that evening's five-course menu: a mosaic of pan-seared *foie gras* with apple, celeriac and truffle *beignets*.

After dinner, Christopher once again repaired to the Addison Lounge, as he had noticed Professor Wilkes heading off in that direction a few minutes earlier. The forlorn Professor did not seem to have struck up many friendships among the delegates, and was sitting alone at the same corner table at which Christopher had argued with Roger Wagstaff the night before. Occupying another table, also alone, was the diminutive Howard, the man who had briefly been Christopher's neighbour in the annexe. But Christopher had, for some reason, taken an instinctive dislike to this furtive-looking little man, and in response to his smile and his hopeful wave of greeting merely offered a polite nod, before walking straight over to Professor Wilkes and introducing himself.

The Professor was drinking a large whisky and willingly accepted Christopher's offer to buy him another.

'So sorry that you weren't able to deliver your talk this afternoon,' Christopher said, after they had clinked glasses. 'I was looking forward to it. I must admit, Professor, that the more I learn about Cockerill, the more intriguing he sounds.'

'Do call me Richard. And that's most kind of you to say. I have the text of the talk here, if you want to look at it.'

He fished the folded sheets of paper out of his jacket pocket and passed them over to Christopher. But he was clearly in the mood for conversation, and rather than allowing him to read them, went on:

'It is somewhat deflating to have travelled all this way for nothing. But of course, this is a momentous day. It was a decision that had to be taken, out of respect to Her Majesty.'

'Is that how Cockerill himself would have seen it?'

'Of course. He understood how important the monarchy was to the constitutional fabric.'

'I found some of your first pieces of journalism in an online archive last night,' said Christopher. 'From the *Guardian* in the early eighties. You didn't seem to be quite such a monarchist yourself back then.'

Richard glanced at him sharply; then smiled. 'Really? That stuff is still floating around? I don't think I could bear to look at it myself. Such callow nonsense one comes out with at that age.'

'Some of it was rather good, I thought. A detailed profile of Rushdie. A perceptive review of Amis Junior.'

Richard laughed. 'Well, I haven't read a word by those two in the last thirty years, I shouldn't think. The fact is, we were all looking for the wrong thing, in the wrong place.'

'And the right place would have been . . . ?'

'Cockerill, of course.' He took what seemed (to Christopher) rather a large slug of whisky. 'I hadn't even bothered to read him before then – I just dismissed him, like everyone else did, as a silly old-fashioned Tory twit. Then one year, some time in the mid-eighties, I wrote one of those typical pieces that arrogant young critics like to write – the English novel is dead, none of our writers have a clue, we should look to America, we should look to Europe, blah blah blah. And in response to that, Cockerill actually wrote to me, and sent me a copy of *A Rope from Hell*, and said, "Look, as it happens, I think we are in agreement with one another." So I read the book, and . . . well, it turned out he was right. It was an absolute revelation. Then I read all of his novels and realized that what he was doing made the books that everyone else was churning out feel shallow and irrelevant.'

'So a book really can change your life? He changed your political viewpoint as well?'

'He made me see that up until then I didn't *have* a political viewpoint. Just knee-jerk anti-Thatcherism, like all my contemporaries.'

'Well, you've certainly done his posthumous reputation a favour. You've written two books about him now, I think?'

'Three. Though my proudest achievement has been getting one of his novels reissued in Penguin Modern Classics.'

'That's *A Rope from Hell*, right?'

'Correct.'

'Did you ever meet him?'

'No, we never met.'

'What a pity. A friend of mine did, as it happens.'

This information had a startling effect on Richard. He was suddenly very curious. He took the next in his ongoing series of generous slugs of whisky and said:

'Really? In what context?'

'It was when we were undergraduates at Cambridge. Cockerill came to give a reading at one of Emeric's salons.'

'Ah, yes. Sir Emeric did tell me about that. He was very keen to invite him, being one of his few public admirers at the time.' Richard had by now emptied his own glass and had begun – apparently by mistake – drinking from Christopher's instead. 'He regretted very much being indisposed on that occasion, and not being able to attend. Appendicitis was the problem, I think.'

'Quite. Well, my friend seems to have been very struck by him. Spent a couple of hours in his company, actually, and among other things, he did mention one unusual detail, which was that—'

But just then, they were interrupted by the arrival of Roger Wagstaff, with the faithful Rebecca in tow, carrying her usual armfuls of files and documents. Neither of them looked happy that Christopher was there, but they sat down anyway. It seemed that they were going to take advantage of Richard's present (though rapidly dissipating) sobriety in order to get him to complete some paperwork.

'I'm so sorry to trouble you about this, Professor Wilkes,' Rebecca said, laying a long and complicated form in front of him. 'Processus –' (she glanced pointedly at Christopher) – 'is very much a stickler for making sure that everything is above board, payment-wise. You have to fill out three copies of this, I'm afraid, giving all your bank account details and so on. Do you mind doing it now? Best to get these things out of the way, I always think.'

'Of course, of course,' Richard mumbled. He furrowed his brow and set to work.

While Richard was squinting over the small print of the form, Rebecca went to the bar for more drinks: whisky for Professor Wilkes, gin and tonics for herself and Roger, nothing for Christopher. He registered the snub and occupied himself instead by looking at the beginning of the lecture. He had been hoping to re-read the opening remarks about death and renewal, but they seemed to have been an afterthought: there was no sign of them in the printed text apart from a handwritten reminder:

Master of Reinvention: Themes of Renewal in the Novels of Peter Cockerill, and Their Importance to the Conservative Movement

[Insert quotation from Edward Thomas, etc.

Peter Cockerill was born in 1948, in the Gloucestershire village of Bradbourne. He was the only child of a working-class couple, whose marriage broke up when he was very young, when his father, George, an engineer in the tool room of the Bristol Aeroplane Company a few miles away, left his wife, Betty, for another woman and moved

So instead, Christopher focused his attention on the main body of the lecture, and began to absorb the information contained in the first few, biographical paragraphs. He had just reached the top of the third page when the barman came over to speak to him.

'By the way, sir, I'm very sorry to say there's been no sign of your memory stick. Are you sure that you left it here last night?'

'No, I'm not sure at all,' said Christopher. 'But I can't think what else I might have done with it.'

'Oh, yes,' said Roger. 'I heard about that. Most unfortunate.'

'Just after we'd been talking about it, as well,' said Christopher, with a sarcastic emphasis.

'Which pocket did you have it in?' Roger asked. 'Out of interest.'

'This one,' said Christopher. 'Inside left.' He put his hand against the outside of the pocket – the first time he'd done so for several hours – and felt, to his surprise, a familiar hard shape. Reaching into the pocket, his fingers closed on the object. He drew it out slowly, and stared at it in amazement. Here was his flash drive after all, safe and sound, just where he always kept it.

'Good God,' said Christopher. He couldn't take his eyes off it. 'But that makes no sense . . .'

Roger laughed cruelly, and exchanged a smirk with Rebecca.

'Mystery solved,' he said. 'I should lay off the whisky tonight if I were you, old chap. Good job Rebecca didn't get you one, really.'

Christopher had no answer to this. He searched his memory furiously, wondering how this could possibly have happened. Had he been skilfully pickpocketed, and had the stolen item been returned with equal dexterity? That seemed to be the only possible explanation. The only other thing that occurred to him . . . Well, there was the sound of that door opening and closing this afternoon, while he was in the bath . . . Could that have anything to do with it?

Once Richard had – with some difficulty, and after a number of false starts – filled in all three copies of his payment form, Roger and his assistant left the Addison Lounge without troubling themselves to say goodbye. At Richard's insistence, and very much against his better judgement, Christopher ordered two more large whiskies. Their conversation resumed, growing gradually louder, then more convoluted, and then more incoherent. His hand on

Christopher's shoulder, as though they were lifelong friends, Richard complained to him about the difficulties of being a conservative thinker in the current academic climate. 'Scruton got it right, you know,' he slurred. 'Slodger Cruton. I mean, Roger Scruton. He said that conservative academics . . . we were like homosexuals in Proust. We don't dare to announce ourselves, so we have to recognize each other by certain signs. Secret signs. Have you read him, by any chance? Not Proust. Scrodger Luton. I mean, Lodger Scrotum. Brilliant man. Absolutely brilliant. What would you say to another couple of large whiskies, by the way? Must be my round by now, surely . . .'

Christopher could not be sure how much longer they stayed in the bar together. He did notice that Richard's diction became more and more erratic. It was when his efforts to pronounce the name Kwasi Kwarteng failed after seven attempts that Christopher decided enough was enough. He helped the now almost incapacitated scholar to his feet and gave him back the text of his lecture, which Richard stuffed into his jacket pocket.

'Very good of you,' came the mumbled response. 'Very decent. Think I may have overdone it a bit.'

With Richard clutching on to him for support, Christopher stumbled out of the bar and took a right turn down the corridor. It was well after one o'clock in the morning now, and the ground floor of the hotel seemed to be deserted. He was making for the reception area and the main staircase, but before they reached it, Richard tugged on his arm and pulled him towards one of the small alcoves that led off from the corridor on either side. It was the same alcove that had featured the painting of the slave ship *Henrietta*. Christopher noticed that the painting had been removed now, leaving a rectangular patch of wall that was cleaner and whiter than its surroundings. Next to where the painting had hung was a small oak door. Richard pulled the door open. It led on to a steep, narrow staircase which he immediately began to climb, although on the third step he tripped and fell.

'Are you all right?' Christopher asked, helping him to his feet.

'Fine, fine, perfectly fine,' said Richard.

'Do you know where you're going?'

'Taking a short-cut,' said Richard. 'Full of little surprises, this house.'

And it turned out, remarkably, that he was right: after a few twists and turns, the staircase brought them out on the first floor, midway between Richard's room (number 7) and Roger Wagstaff's (8/1). It was when Richard took out his room key and attempted to unlock the door that Christopher realized quite how drunk he was. He couldn't even get the key in the lock, let alone turn it, and dropped it on the floor three times during the attempt. Eventually Christopher took the key from his hand and unlocked the door himself. When it was open, Richard stood in the doorway for a number of seconds, swaying from side to side, apparently unsure whether to enter or not. Christopher placed his hand in the small of his back and gave him a gentle push. Richard tottered forward three steps and then came to a halt again. Christopher sighed. These were going to be a difficult few minutes.

Eventually, Richard was in bed. He had not managed to wash his face or clean his teeth. The smell of whisky on his breath was overwhelming. With Christopher's help, some of his clothes had been removed – his trousers and jacket, at least. He was already somewhere between waking and sleep. He was brokenly muttering to himself – or perhaps to Christopher – although not many of the words could be made out.

'Siddown, why don't you . . . Siddown by the fireplace . . .'

Not sure why he was being instructed to do this, Christopher eased himself cautiously into the armchair by the hearth.

'Don't go just yet . . . Keep me company for a bit, there's a good chap . . . Not feeling too . . . Feeling a bit . . . May have drunk too much . . . Don't go just yet . . .'

And so Christopher remained in the room for another five minutes or so. During this time, something strange happened. Richard's drunken mutterings faded away. Instead, Christopher heard another noise coming from the direction of the bed. At first he wasn't sure what it was, or what it signified. When he realized – or rather, when the suspicion that he understood what was happening began to creep over him – he was paralysed, at first, by amazement and indecision. But this did not last for long. Soon he knew exactly what he had to do. He took out his phone, opened the Voice Memos app, and pressed Record.

The last person to see Christopher alive was Rebecca Wood. From her usual vantage point in the library, she saw him at about 9.45 on Friday morning, striding out towards the kitchen garden where Richard Wilkes was squatting down and examining the iceberg lettuces. The garden was some distance away, but Rebecca recognized Professor Wilkes on account of his distinctive bright red sweater. The two men, she said, had a 'very animated' conversation which lasted for a minute or two, and she then saw Christopher walking back towards the hotel, alone. Shortly afterwards, the Professor came into the library. Rebecca was asked to describe his demeanour at that moment, and after pondering this question, she replied that a familiar expression occurred to her.

'And that expression would be?' she was asked.

To which Rebecca answered:

'The expression would be, "If looks could kill . . . "'

6.

The body of Christopher Swann was discovered in room 9, on the first floor of Wetherby Hall, at 11.17 on Friday morning by a maid who had noticed blood seeping out from beneath the door. In a frenzied attack, he had been stabbed eleven times with a *yanāgiba* knife, a long, thin-bladed instrument which had been taken from the collection of Japanese kitchen utensils on the ground floor. The door of his room had been locked from the inside, and all the windows were also closed and locked on the inside. There was, at first glance, no explanation for how the murderer had made his or her entrance or exit. Despite the violence of the attack, however, there was some evidence that Christopher had remained alive for a short time after it was over: because he had somehow managed to drag himself over to the desk, picked up his pen, and scrawled the following message on a piece of notepaper.

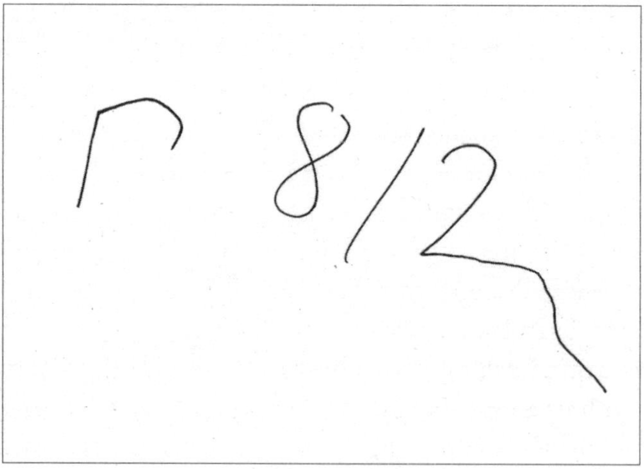

And so, for the second time during this unfortunate week, the proceedings of the TrueCon conference were interrupted. An absorbing discussion entitled 'Why Free Markets and Nationhood

Go Hand in Hand' had to be curtailed, the audience members were sent back to their rooms, the stables theatre was closed, and everyone was told that they would be unable to leave Wetherby Hall until the police had arrived and given their instructions.

Inspector Prudence Freeborne, who was sixty-four years and three hundred and sixty-three days old on the morning that Christopher was murdered, was on her way to her own retirement party when news of the crime came in. Her friends and colleagues, already waiting for her in the hospitality room of the Oxfordshire constabulary headquarters with champagne glasses filled and canapés in hand, were obliged to mark the event without the presence of the guest of honour. Instead, DI Freeborne hurried outdoors to the car park. She was surprisingly agile for a woman of her age and build: she was short and rotund, with a figure which owed itself to a lifetime's enjoyment of good food and even better wine, but carried herself with a grace and cheerfulness which impressed everyone who met her. These qualities, combined with her penchant for black clothing and her shock of thick and brilliant white hair, gave her something of the aura of an eccentric lawyer from a Dickens novel. Waiting for her in the car park was her loyal assistant, Detective Sergeant Jakes. Together they jumped into her vintage black Lamborghini, which she drove at considerable speed in the direction of Wetherby Pond while DS Jakes gave her such details of the case as he had already managed to gather.

'There's been some controversy about the conference,' he told her. 'A few articles about it in the press. We're talking about the extreme right wing of the Tory Party here. And a lot of people who are even more extreme than that.'

'All very harmless, I'm sure,' said DI Freeborne, and sniffed. 'Let's not go around calling people fascists just because they might disagree with us about some things.'

'The murder victim,' DS Jakes said, ignoring the rebuke, 'had already posted some very critical remarks about the conference on his blog.'

'I see. So he would have had plenty of enemies there. Political enemies.'

'Exactly.'

'And how many people attended this conference?'

'There are –' DS Jakes consulted his notes – 'two hundred and seventeen registered guests.'

DI Freeborne gave a mirthless chuckle as she careered around a sharp bend in the country road.

'Whoopee,' she said. 'One victim, two hundred and seventeen suspects.'

In the event, the case turned out to be – on first inspection, at least – considerably less complex than that.

Dr Schumacher, the forensic pathologist, was already in attendance, and efficiently going about her business. She put the time of death at between ten o'clock and ten-thirty. Meanwhile a police constable directed DI Freeborne towards the note on the desk which Christopher had scrawled in the seconds before he died. She scrutinized it quickly and then, turning to DS Jakes, she said:

'Find out who was staying in room eight/two, will you? It's the one next door. And whoever it is, don't let them go anywhere. And find the owner, Lord Wetherby, and send him up here.'

While her colleague was engaged upon this errand, DI Freeborne carried out a brief inspection of the room. She noted the position of the body and the arrangement of the furniture, and checked the locks on the windows and the doors, all of which were secure, and none of which, it was clear, had been tampered with or forced recently. In less than five minutes, the reliable Sergeant Jakes had returned with the relevant information as to the occupant of room 8/2. He handed his superior a note with a name written on it. She glanced at the name, nodded, and folded the note away in her pocket-book.

'His Lordship will be here in a moment,' DS Jakes assured her.

'Good.'

She took the sergeant to one side and informed him, in an undertone:

'We find ourselves confronted here, Bernard, by what theorists of detective fiction refer to as a "locked room mystery". No visible means of entry, or of exit. And yet a murder has been committed, and the murderer must have got in and out somehow.'

Lord Wetherby entered the room. He at once saw the gruesome cadaver which lay sprawled and twisted on the bloodstained carpet, and turned deathly pale. DI Freeborne nodded at him before resuming her whispered conversation with the sergeant.

'Now, a mediocre writer of such mysteries,' she said, 'will invent some unlikely contrivance such as a secret passage. Obviously, we must approach the problem without resorting to fantasies like that.'

'Of course.'

DI Freeborne turned to the Earl, who had been given a glass of water by the constable, and was now looking a little better.

'Your Lordship,' she said. 'As the proprietor of this hotel, you must be familiar with its layout. Our murderer, it seems, entered this room neither by the door nor by the windows. Can you think of any explanation?'

Lord Wetherby blew out his cheeks. 'Well, I would imagine,' he said, 'that they must have used the secret passage.'

DI Freeborne and DS Jakes glanced at one another.

'I see,' said the former. 'Perhaps you could elaborate?'

Lord Wetherby led them towards the walk-in wardrobe in the corner of the room.

'It actually used to be the passage for servants to use, when they were bringing food upstairs from the kitchens,' he explained. 'It leads from my office downstairs – which used to be the butler's pantry – and comes out here.' Reaching towards the panelling at the back of the wardrobe (a space which could easily accommodate the three of them) he found a groove in the woodwork, pushed at it, and thereby opened a lightweight door which swung smoothly outwards on to a dark corridor. Flicking a switch, Lord Wetherby turned on a single naked light bulb bright enough to reveal the full extent of the passage. To the left, it ended in a narrow staircase leading downwards: to the right, there were two more doors leading off on either side.

'Where would those take you?' DI Freeborne asked, immediately curious.

'That one takes you to the shared sitting room between rooms eight/one and eight/two. The other takes you into room seven, emerging through the fireplace.'

DI Freeborne was checking the flagstones for footprints, but there didn't appear to be any.

'I suppose that makes your job a good deal easier,' said the Earl.

'How so?' she asked, still preoccupied.

'Well, because that narrows it down to three suspects. Only three people had access to this passage from their rooms.'

DI Freeborne rose from her stooping position and gave him a piercing glance.

'Three, Lord Wetherby? I thought you told me that the starting point of the passage was your own office downstairs, which used to be the butler's pantry?'

'Erm . . .' His Lordship seemed suddenly confused, and huffed and puffed a great deal. 'Well, yes, I suppose that is the case.'

'In fact,' the detective said, 'I think it would be a good idea if you took us there right now.'

The three of them trooped down the narrow staircase, at the bottom of which a door led off to the left. Opening it, Lord Wetherby was about to show DI Freeborne into his office, but she stopped him.

'This does not appear to be the end of the passage,' she said. Indeed, it continued some way into the distance, then turned a corner, and disappeared out of sight.

'No,' said Lord Wetherby. 'It carries on for another few hundred yards. There's a little door which brings you right out by the side of the lake.'

'Something to investigate further,' said DI Freeborne, half to herself, and followed the Earl into his office, with DS Jakes bringing up the rear. She took in the details of the room, which was sparely furnished, its desk almost empty apart from a laptop, its shelves filled with box files, and three grey filing cabinets ranged against one wall. 'This, I think, will make a good base for my activities this afternoon. I'll need to speak to all the principal suspects – including yourself. And first of all, I'd like to have a word with your chef.'

'My chef?' Lord Wetherby echoed. 'Really, I think that would be a waste of your time. He's been busy all morning, and couldn't possibly have got into room nine.'

'That's as maybe,' said DI Freeborne. 'But I need to talk to him about lunch. I noticed on my way in that pheasant is on the menu, and Sergeant Jakes will tell you that I'm very particular about how it should be cooked.'

DI Freeborne and DS Jakes took their lunch in a private room which was located next to the Addison Lounge. The pheasant was good, and it was accompanied by a bottle of excellent burgundy which DI Freeborne drank in its entirety.

'On the day of my retirement,' she said, 'I don't see why I should worry about drinking on duty. Anyway –' she was speaking between mouthfuls of bread, which she was using to mop up the gravy on her plate – 'I don't think this will prove to be a very complicated case. Already everything points to one person in particular. Take the note, for instance, that the victim managed to write shortly before he died. What do you make of it?'

'I'm not sure,' said DS Jakes. 'The first symbol is . . . what? The beginnings of a letter? P, I suppose – or D, or R.'

'R, I think.'

'But why didn't he finish writing it?'

'Well,' said Prudence Freeborne, dabbing at her lips with a napkin. 'Let's assume that there are four suspects – the people who had access to the passage which led into the victim's room. The occupants, in other words, of room seven, and rooms eight/one and eight/two. Plus Lord Wetherby himself, of course. Now, imagine, if you can, that you have just been stabbed by one of these people, they have left the room, and you still have a few moments of life left in you. Just enough to drag yourself to your desk, pick up a pen, and scrawl something. You don't have the time or the energy to write the murderer's name, so what do you write instead?'

'His initials, perhaps. Or hers.'

'Exactly! And here we come up against one of the unique features in this case. What do our four suspects have in common? Rooms eight/one and eight/two, and the sitting room between them, are shared by Roger Wagstaff and Rebecca Wood. A rather intimate arrangement, I must say, for two professional colleagues. Room seven is occupied by one Richard Wilkes, an elderly academic who flew here all the way from Venice yesterday, to give a lecture which was abandoned after four minutes owing to the death of the

Queen. And downstairs in his office we have the owner of the hotel, Randolph Wetherby. Four suspects. All of them – unfortunately for our victim – with exactly the same initials.'

'Ah! Of course. So he gets halfway through writing the R, realizes that it's not going to help anybody identify the killer, and quickly has to think of another clue to write.'

'Exactly. A clue which points – rather unambiguously, it seems to me – to one suspect in particular. Rebecca Wood.'

DS Jakes thought about this. 'Hardly enough to convict her in front of a jury, though.'

'Well, there's another thing that counts against her. Forensics have been very efficient this morning. The handle of the door that leads from the passage to the victim's room has already been dusted for fingerprints. And the four principal suspects have already had their prints taken. There's a clear match.'

'Rebecca?'

DI Freeborne nodded.

'Hmm. That is damning,' said DS Jakes. But he added, after thinking for a moment: 'Or at least it would be, if there had been any fingerprints on the handle of the knife. But as I understand it, there weren't. Why would you take care not to leave your fingerprints on the murder weapon, and yet leave them all over a door handle?'

'You don't necessarily think straight when you're committing a murder.'

'True.'

Over dessert (banoffee pie with salted caramel chocolate sauce), DS Jakes outlined the other salient details he had uncovered so far. There was the curious fact, for instance, that Christopher Swann had been moved, without consultation, from his room in the annexe to a bigger and more expensive room in the main building. There was the additional fact that his mobile phone seemed to have disappeared from the scene of the crime. There was also the interesting story (told by the bar staff in the Addison Lounge) of his lost flash drive, and its sudden and inexplicable rediscovery. And DS Jakes had, additionally, spoken to Old Bob Hopkins, the fisherman who came and sat every day, in all weathers, by the side of the ornamental lake, and had found him in a state of high excitement: because today he had, for the very first time in 'near on five year', not actually *caught* a fish, but distinctly *heard* one jumping in the water just a few yards away. Something which might well be irrelevant, but was certainly unusual, given that it was widely known there were no fish in the lake at all. Was the old man simply losing his wits?

'I suspect there is a very good explanation for that,' said Prudence. 'Let's go and explore.'

She swiftly downed a balloon of brandy and then, with lunch completed, she and DS Jakes returned to Lord Wetherby's office, which the Earl had somewhat grudgingly turned over to them as the room in which they would conduct their interviews. They began by opening the door to the hidden passage and turning not to the right, this time – which would have led them upstairs – but to the left. This took them down a corridor which became ever narrower and darker, especially once they had turned a sharp right-angled corner. Bent almost double, by the light of the torches on their mobile phones they stumbled on for two hundred yards or more, with cobwebs brushing their hair and spiders scuttling away at their feet. The black brickwork on either side started to glisten with damp. Finally a small wooden door, consisting of four ancient planks which had almost rotted away, was all that stood between them and the outside world. Bright daylight could be glimpsed at its ragged edges. Prudence pushed it outwards and found that it opened easily enough – almost as if someone else had recently done the same thing. The passage had brought them to the very shore of the ornamental lake, and the two or three yards of long grass which lay between the doorway and the water were visibly trampled. She turned to DS Jakes and said:

'Well, I don't think any fish have been jumping here this morning, do you? But I do think that if a diver were to search the floor of this lake, he would probably find the murder victim's mobile phone. That's my hunch, anyway. And now I think it's time to have a proper conversation with our first suspect.'

7.

Interview Number One: Rebecca Wood

When conducting their first informal interview that afternoon, DI Freeborne and DS Jakes adopted their usual procedure. She sat behind the desk (Lord Wetherby's desk, in this case) and the object of her questioning sat opposite her. At the far end of the desk, meanwhile, DS Jakes positioned himself with his laptop open, listening carefully, sometimes intervening, sometimes carrying out quiet searches online which were prompted by the direction the interview had taken.

Prudence began with a routine question.

'Miss Wood, can you tell me, please, whether you were acquainted with Christopher Swann before he came here to attend the conference this week?'

'Distantly acquainted, yes,' she answered.

'In what capacity did you know him?'

'We were at Cambridge together, back in the early 1980s.'

'Did you know each other well, at that time?'

'No.'

'Did you keep in touch subsequently?'

'No.'

'This was the first time you had seen him, since your time at Cambridge together?'

'Yes.'

'Did you like each other, back then?'

'I have no idea whether he liked me or not. On a personal level, my feelings towards him were entirely neutral.'

'On a personal level.'

'Yes.'

'There was another level?'

'Later on, Christopher became an outspoken critic of our movement. To tell you the truth, I found his politics abhorrent.'

Prudence gave a tight smile and said: 'Well, since you have brought that up, let's talk about your "movement", as you call it. How long you have been in your current employment with the Processus Group?'

'Twenty-six years and three months,' Rebecca replied without hesitation.

'Since its foundation, in other words,' DS Jakes interposed.

Rebecca glanced at him, as if unaware of his presence up until now. 'Yes.'

'And how long have you known Roger Wagstaff?' Prudence asked.

'About forty years.'

'You also met at Cambridge, is that correct?'

'Quite correct.'

'And in that time, has your relationship been purely professional, or has it been personal as well?'

Rebecca's face turned a bright shade of crimson.

'I have no idea what you're implying, or what the relevance of that question might be.'

'The relevance is clear. Because of your closeness with Mr Wagstaff, you seem to have been placed in one of the few rooms which had access to the passage leading to the murder victim's room.'

'I have no idea what you're talking about,' said Rebecca Wood stiffly. 'It's true, I think, that Roger and I are friends, as well as work colleagues.'

'You became friends at Cambridge?'

'I would say so, yes.'

'Would he?'

'I'm sure you will be asking him that yourself, in due course.'

'You were never lovers?'

'Never,' said Rebecca: and if there was any overtone of regret in that statement, she kept it well hidden.

'Who booked the rooms for you at this hotel?'

'I made the bookings.'

'And why did you book the rooms that you did – adjacent bedrooms, with a shared sitting room?'

'It seemed the most practical business arrangement, given that we were going to be doing a lot of work together.'

'Did Roger raise any objections?'

'No.'

'Did his wife hear of the arrangement?'

'I have no idea. Roger and I never discuss his domestic affairs.'

'Of course. Now, I'm sure you recall, Miss Wood, that hanging in the sitting room which connects room eight / one with room eight / two, there is a full-length, life-size portrait of Percival, the Sixth Earl of Wetherby. Are you aware of what lies behind that portrait?'

'Behind it?'

'Yes. It comes away, on a hinge.'

'You amaze me. I am not in the habit of removing paintings from hotel room walls.'

'I agree, it would be an unusual hobby. However, if you were to do so, in this case, you would discover a door, which leads on to a passage.'

'I see. A servants' corridor, I assume. Not uncommon, in houses of this vintage.'

'Quite so. However, the point of interest here is that by means of this passage, the murderer could easily have gained entry into the victim's room.'

'How very useful for him.'

'Or for her.'

Rebecca sighed impatiently. 'I can see where this line of questioning is taking us, but I can assure you that, until you mentioned it just now, I had no knowledge of the existence of this passage.'

Prudence clicked her tongue, and fixed Rebecca with a solicitous gaze.

'I must advise you that it would be a very bad idea, in the situation in which you currently find yourself, not to tell the truth.'

'You don't have to state the obvious.'

'Perhaps I do.' After leaving a suitably weighty pause, Prudence explained: 'Our forensics team found just one set of fingerprints on the door which opened on to Mr Swann's room from the hidden passage. They were yours.'

A long silence ensued. Rebecca was clearly shaken by these words. She blushed, and bit her lip, and for some time seemed to be debating with herself which course of action to take next. Finally, with every appearance of exasperation, she shrugged her shoulders and said:

'Very well. I admit it. I did use that passage – and that door. I used them twice. But not this morning. And not with any violent intent.'

'How very reassuring,' said Prudence. 'Please explain.'

Rebecca took a breath.

'Mr Swann had obtained, apparently, some . . . sensitive information regarding the Processus Group.'

'Sensitive?'

'A lot of what they do – a lot of what *we* do, I should say – has to be formulated very carefully before being outlined to the public.'

'Such as privatizing the NHS, for instance,' DS Jakes suggested.

Rebecca turned to him and said: 'The Processus Group is a public-spirited body, and Roger Wagstaff is a philanthropist and a patriot. But the British public, sadly, is bound to certain institutions by a strong sentimental attachment, and does not always understand what will benefit them.'

'Obviously not,' said the sergeant. 'And incidentally, is it not wonderfully fortunate that the very things that you think will benefit them usually turn out, in addition, to make an enormous profit for someone?'

'Thank you, Bernard,' said Prudence, holding up her hand. 'We are not here to discuss politics. We are here to learn about Miss Wood's use of the secret passage. Please,' she added, turning to her interviewee, 'confine yourself to that, if you can.'

'Somehow or other – through his . . . *nefarious* network of contacts – Christopher had obtained a report that we had compiled. Or so he claimed.'

'Did it have a name, this document?'

'Within our organization, yes, it was known as the Second of August Report. Named after the day it was completed. And one evening this week – Wednesday evening, I believe it was – Christopher imposed himself – there is no other word for it – upon Roger and Sir Emeric in the bar, and boasted to them, quite openly, that he had obtained a copy of the report and was going to publish it, on that ridiculous blog of his. In the circumstances, Roger felt quite justified – and I must say that I agreed with him – in taking steps to find out whether he was telling the truth or not.'

'And these steps were . . . ?'

'Well – I had no idea, at the time, that there was a passage which connected Christopher's room to ours – I mean, to mine – to the sitting room which I shared with Mr Wagstaff. However, he did seem to know about it—'

'He?'

'Roger. I expect Lord Wetherby had given him a tour of the building at some point. So he asked me – or rather, he suggested – what I mean is, I *agreed* to . . . gain entry to Christopher's room, that night, to remove the flash drive which we knew to be in his jacket pocket, and to check its contents.'

'So, in the early hours of Thursday morning, you stole Mr Swann's flash drive?'

'No, I didn't steal it. I replaced it that same afternoon.'

'Using the secret passage both times?'

'Yes.'

'And Mr Swann didn't see you, on either occasion?'

'The first time, he was asleep. The second, he was in the bath. So I believe.'

'You believe?'

'I only had to enter his wardrobe. I didn't go into the room itself.' She looked at both Prudence and the sergeant, and didn't find much sympathy written on either face. 'I know that what I did might appear wrong . . .' she added.

DS Jakes snorted in a way which strongly implied agreement.

'It does occur to me,' he said, 'that your loyalty to the Processus Group in general, and to Roger Wagstaff in particular, is quite remarkable. Not many people would commit such a . . . *nefarious* act in the service of their employer.'

Rebecca did not reply.

'I suppose the name of –' he looked down at his computer screen – 'Paul Daintry is quite familiar to you?'

She reacted to this question at first with a start, and then with weary impatience.

'Really, Sergeant, do you have nothing better to do than to bring up that piece of ancient history?'

'Not a name *I've* ever heard before, at any rate,' said Prudence. 'Enlighten me, Bernard.'

'Of course. And I'm sure Miss Wood will correct me if I get anything wrong.'

(Rebecca said nothing.)

'Well, it seems that some time ago, back in the early 1990s, before devoting himself to politics full-time, Mr Wagstaff worked in the City of London. Ran his own hedge fund, in fact. Wagstaff and Henley, they were called. Miss Wood here was the secretary, is that correct?'

'Absolutely not. I was the office administrator.'

'Ah. My apologies. In 1994 they hired a young intern by the name of Paul Daintry. Bright lad, by all accounts. Straight out of Oxford. Knew quite a lot about the business already and didn't much like what he saw when he started working there. In fact he reported Mr Wagstaff to the Financial Ombudsman for insider dealing. A very serious charge, needless to say.'

'And totally fabricated,' said Rebecca.

'Well,' said DS Jakes, ignoring this interruption, 'the case would have come to court, but it hinged on Mr Daintry's testimony, and sadly, he met with an accident. He'd already found employment with another firm, and one evening he was leaving their offices, on the fourth floor of a block on Gresham Street, when he fell down the stairs. Died on the spot, poor lad. Broken neck.'

'And the relevance of this, Bernard?'

Rebecca shifted in her seat. 'Here it comes,' she said, in a tone of resignation.

'Probably no direct relevance,' he said. 'But our records contain a witness statement, in which the witness stated that he had observed an individual answering to Miss Wood's description leaving the scene of the accident.'

'And?' said Rebecca. 'Don't stop there. Tell your superior what happened next.'

DS Jakes swallowed. 'Well, an identity parade took place, at which . . .'

'Go on,' Rebecca insisted.

'At which the witness failed to identify Miss Wood.'

'Exactly,' said Rebecca, with a note of triumph. 'In fact the person he picked out of the parade wasn't even a woman. He didn't know what he was talking about. And this happened twenty-eight years ago, for heaven's sake. *Twenty-eight years.* And not a shred of evidence was found linking me or Roger to that poor boy's accident. So your bringing it up now is not just irrelevant, but deeply offensive. Inspector, do you have any useful questions to ask me? If not, I would like to leave.'

'Just one or two more things, Miss Wood,' Prudence said. 'Where were you between the hours of ten o'clock and ten-thirty this morning?'

'I was in the library, working.'

'Any witnesses?'

'Yes. A young woman came in and brought me a cup of coffee. And there was also that lecturer chap, Wilkes.'

'Ah! You saw Professor Wilkes during that half-hour, as well?'

'Yes. First of all I saw him outside, with Christopher Swann. They were in the kitchen garden. This would have been at about nine-forty-five.'

'He was talking to Mr Swann?'

'They were having . . . a very animated conversation, I would say.'

'But wait a moment,' DI Freeborne said. 'The kitchen garden is more than a hundred yards from the library window. Can you be sure it was Wilkes that Mr Swann was talking to?'

'Yes, I can,' Rebecca replied.

'How?'

'Because of his bright red sweater,' said Rebecca. 'No one else was wearing anything of that colour, or at all like it.'

'Very well,' said DI Freeborne. 'Continue. What happened next?'

'They separated,' said Rebecca. 'Christopher came back towards the hotel, and I assume entered it by a back door. Wilkes stayed in the kitchen garden for another few minutes. Then he too hurried back towards the hotel by the same route. He was looking for Christopher.'

'How do you know that?'

'Because shortly afterwards he came into the library, and asked me if I knew where Christopher was.'

'And how would you describe his demeanour, at that moment?'

Rebecca pursed her lips.

'A familiar expression occurs to me,' she answered.

DI Freeborne waited, and then asked: 'And that would be?'

'The expression would be, "If looks could kill . . . ".'

DI Freeborne and DS Jakes exchanged a brief glance. Rebecca's phrase seemed to have been chosen with some care; not to say calculation.

'Very well,' said Prudence. 'One more thing. In the moments before he died, Christopher Swann left a note. In it, he seems to have been trying to leave a clue to the identity of his killer. Do you know what he wrote?'

'Do tell.'

'He wrote the numbers eight/two.' When Rebecca offered no response, Prudence added, for clarity: 'That is the number of your room in this hotel.'

'I'm aware of that.'

'The clue, in other words, would appear to point in your direction.'

There was a long pause. Rebecca seemed unaffected by this turn of events.

'What conclusion would you draw?' Prudence asked her.

'I can only answer that,' Rebecca said, 'based on my knowledge of Christopher Swann's character. And my conclusion would be that his malice lives on, even from beyond the grave.'

End of interview

8.

Interview Number Two: Randolph, 11th Earl of Wetherby

'We will not detain you for long, Your Lordship,' said DI Freeborne.

'I'm glad to hear it.'

'And we would also like to thank you for the use of your office.'

'Not at all. It is always a pleasure, as well as a duty, to assist the forces of law and order.'

'Might I ask you, first of all, where you were between the hours of ten and ten-thirty this morning?'

'Mostly in here. Sometimes at the reception desk. There should be no shortage of people who can corroborate my movements.'

'Were you alone in this office at all?'

'Yes, but never for more than five minutes or so.'

'One minute to get up to room nine,' said DS Jakes, as if thinking aloud. 'One minute to commit the crime. Two minutes to get to the lake. One minute to get back here. Yes, it could be done.'

'Leaving aside your insulting inference,' said Lord Wetherby, 'what's this about the murderer going to the lake?'

'We believe that might be the case,' said Prudence. 'Tell me, is the door from the passage to the outside world used very often?'

'It hasn't been used for years.'

'Well, it was used this morning. Also, Old Bob Hopkins says that he heard a fish jumping in the lake today.'

'There are no fish in the lake.'

'So I understand. What, then, might he have heard?'

'Sounds as though somebody might have chucked something into the water.'

'My thoughts exactly. But before we come on to that, one of your receptionists told me a curious thing today. She said that Christopher Swann had originally been staying in the hotel annexe, but you moved him into the main building on Wednesday morning, without consulting him. Is there any truth in that?'

The 11th Earl shrugged. 'Obviously some wires have got crossed. My understanding was that he had requested to be moved.'

'Whatever the explanation, it certainly made life easier for the murderer, who was thereby able to gain access to the victim's room by a hidden route.'

'If someone is bent on murder, Inspector, I'm sure they would find a means to commit it, one way or another, whether they had the use of a secret passage or not.'

DI Freeborne tried a different line of approach.

'Were you acquainted with Roger Wagstaff, before this week?'

'We'd corresponded a few times, and run into each other at parties, that sort of thing.'

'You were friends?'

'Not really.'

'Political soulmates?'

'I like what he stands for, and the way he fights for it.'

'And what does he stand for, in your opinion?'

'Hard to sum up in a few words. Individual freedom, perhaps. Personal sovereignty.'

'You think that freedom is something that has to be fought for? In the United Kingdom, in 2022?'

'There's a nasty mood around at the moment. Censorious, puritanical. We're constantly being told what to do. Don't drive your car, don't take a plane. Don't complain when every other newsreader on the television is black, or a lesbian, or both. Don't be racist, don't be sexist. I don't care for it much, and neither do the British people. We don't like to be bossed around.'

'Bossed around? Rather an odd complaint to hear, from a hereditary peer and member of the House of Lords. Who's doing the bossing, if not people like yourself?'

Lord Wetherby laughed. 'Really, Inspector, if you think people like me are running things nowadays, you haven't being paying attention. Conservatives are the most embattled minority in the country at the moment.'

'Surely the party you support has been in charge for more than ten years now?'

'It has nothing to do with party. Real power lies somewhere else entirely. In the media, in the judiciary, in academia, in the major institutions.'

'And who runs those, would you say?'

'The liberal elite, obviously.'

'Of whom Christopher Swann, perhaps, was a typical member?'

'I must confess,' said Lord Wetherby airily, 'I'd never heard of the fellow until this week. I still don't know much about him. Apparently he had some sort of online outlet, which he used to disseminate his ideas. Bit of a fantasist, by all accounts. Seems he'd had it in for Roger for some time. Came here to cause trouble. Which he's certainly done, if not quite in the way he intended.'

'Did you speak to him directly, at any time this week?'

'Not that I recall, no.'

'That's odd,' DS Jakes interjected. 'Because I've already spoken to a witness who said that he joined an informal guided tour of the hotel that you were conducting early on Tuesday evening. Is that correct?'

'It's possible.'

'And I was told that you *did* speak directly to him. You had a conversation about a painting that was hanging in one of the corridors. Does this ring a bell?'

'It's coming back to me now, and . . . Yes, I believe something of that sort did take place.'

'Can you recall the artwork in question?' DI Freeborne asked.

'Yes, I can, now that you mention it.' Lord Wetherby was beginning to look uncomfortable. 'It was a painting of a ship that had belonged to one of my predecessors.'

'The Fifth Earl, I believe,' said DS Jakes, consulting a scribbled note on the desk in front of him.

'That's right.'

'It was the *Henrietta*, wasn't it? A notorious slave ship.'

'That was what Mr Swann alleged, yes. In my opinion it involved a large measure of conjecture on his part.'

'My witness said that he sounded rather confident about making the identification. Also, he seemed to imply that he might like to publish something on the subject.'

Lord Wetherby had little choice, at this point, but to come clean.

'Well, yes, he did say something along those lines, and I must say I found his attitude very objectionable. My family takes allegations of historical . . . impropriety like this very seriously, you know. You are aware, for instance, that this year we found an Aboriginal artefact on the premises, and we were at great pains to return it to its rightful owners as soon as possible?'

'Of course,' said DI Freeborne. 'We all read about that in the local newspapers.'

'Well then, there you are.'

'It was a boomerang,' she added. 'And since you failed to pay sufficient postage, it came straight back to you two weeks later.'

Lord Wetherby had received considerable ribbing on this subject over the last few months, and his response was silent and stony-faced.

'Returning to the subject of the disputed painting,' said DS Jakes. 'We were hoping to look at it ourselves, but we were told that it has been removed from display.'

'It needed cleaning,' said Lord Wetherby.

'Hmm. Well, it seems that Mr Swann took some pictures of it on his mobile phone, but – most oddly – his phone has disappeared.'

'Really?'

'Yes, it appears to be the one thing that the murderer removed from the scene of the crime.'

Lord Wetherby's mood seemed to have changed considerably during the last few exchanges, but he still managed to say, with an appearance of levity: 'You have rather a lot of loose ends to clear up still, don't you?'

DI Freeborne rose to her feet and held out her hand.

'Thank you for being so cooperative, Your Lordship.'

Lord Wetherby also rose, and shook her hand wanly.

'Not at all.'

'Good luck with your renovation work. Have all the necessary funds been secured?'

'Not quite. I'm still waiting to hear from one or two places.'

'Well, I'm sure everything will be fine. Here's to the magic date!'

'The magic date?'

'For the grand reopening. Eighth of February 2024, wasn't it?'

'That's right – the eighth of February.'

'Eight/two,' said DS Jakes, while typing something methodically on his laptop. He looked up to see that Lord Wetherby was staring at him in surprise. By way of explanation, he added: 'Eight/two – I suppose that would be the shortest way of writing that date, wouldn't it?'

'Yes,' said Lord Wetherby, backing out of his own office, and transferring his wary glance from the inspector, to the sergeant, and back again. 'Yes, I suppose it would.'

End of interview

9.

Before beginning the next interview, Prudence allowed herself a moment of stillness.

She wandered into the grounds of Wetherby Hall, took a quick look at the kitchen garden – from which she learned very little – and then strolled over to the ornamental lake, where she stood for some time beside the opaque, grey-green water, lost in thought.

She was not, generally, a woman given to introspection, but this afternoon it seemed inescapable. She found there was something intrinsically soothing about places like Wetherby Hall, these grand, somewhat complacent houses and gardens. Most of the conference delegates had left by now – there had been no reason to detain them – and the landscaped grounds were suffused with an atmosphere of heady late-afternoon, late-summer calm. It seemed hard to believe that an act of shocking violence had taken place in this setting just a few hours earlier. Of course, Prudence had seen many such acts during her forty-year career, but she had never become inured to them, and now she realized, for the first time, how much she had been looking forward to retirement, with how much relish she had been contemplating a future in which she would never again have to look at another murdered cadaver. To be able to enjoy a landscape again, to listen to birdsong, to catch the elusive scent of a meadow of wild flowers, without always experiencing these things as a mere backdrop to violence, bloodletting and evil. It was unfortunate, to say the least, that one final case should have landed on her desk on the very day she was supposed to walk away from all of this. A case, moreover, which felt somehow texturally different from all the ones she had handled before – although she could not really have explained why. Perhaps it was to do with the feeling of weirdness that seemed to have stolen over the whole country this week. How bizarre, for instance, that after seventy years on the throne, Queen

Elizabeth should have died only two days – *two days* – after meeting for the first time with a new, unfamiliar and untested Prime Minister. What had that meeting been like? Had Liz Truss failed to notice not just that Her Majesty was at death's door, but that the doorway was wide open and she had stepped most of the way through? What, after all, was going on at the top of British politics these days? Everything seemed to have become unmoored from reality. It was all very disconcerting. Discombobulating might be an even better word. (Prudence, an avid reader, was very fond of words, and enjoyed turning them over in her mind, rearranging them, looking at them from different angles – very much like the facts in a murder investigation.) To compound this feeling of nationwide unease, everyone had their own private anxieties to deal with. In Prudence's case, this meant fretting over her husband's health. Had he managed to speak to a doctor today, finally? Getting to speak on the telephone to anyone at their GP surgery was beginning to feel like an impossibility. She checked her mobile to see if Mark had texted. He had, but all the message said was, *I think we should pay tribute somehow*, which she didn't even understand.

Prudence put the phone in her pocket, sighed and turned slowly away from the lake. There was something timeless and reassuring about the placidity of its waters, which she was reluctant to leave behind. But there was a murder to solve. Perhaps, by solving it, she would bring a kind of order to things. Perhaps then she would be less dogged by this insistent, indefinite sense of anxiety, which seemed to pervade both national and personal life at the moment, making them both feel equally unstable.

She headed back towards Wetherby Hall.

Interview Number Three: Professor Richard Wilkes

'Professor Wilkes, thank you very much for your patience, and for giving us your time. I can assure you that this will only be a very brief interview.'

Professor Wilkes was flustered, and he was upset. He had already missed his flight back to Venice. He had not been able to book a replacement, because nobody seemed able to tell him what was going on. He did not see why it was necessary for DI Freeborne to interview him at all. Was he considered a suspect in this ghastly murder case?

'We wanted to speak to you for two reasons only. The first is that, although I'm sure you don't realize it, you happen to be one of the very few people staying in this hotel who had the opportunity to commit this crime.'

'Opportunity? What opportunity? What are you talking about?'

'Would it surprise you to learn that there is a secret passage in this house, connecting your room – room number seven – with room number nine?'

'Yes,' said Professor Wilkes, after taking a moment or two to digest this information. 'It would surprise me very much indeed.'

'You can hardly have failed to notice that your room is furnished with a most spectacular fireplace.'

'Indeed.'

'The height, in case you were wondering, is five feet and three inches. Tall enough for a man to walk into it, if he wanted to.'

'But why would he want to?'

'Because, if he were to walk into it, and turn right, he would find a narrow recess that leads to a door.'

'The secret passage, you mean.'

'Yes. You hadn't found this out for yourself?'

'No. I must say that it had never occurred to me to walk into the fireplace.'

'Of course not. Why should it?'

Since his superior seemed to have fallen silent following this question, DS Jakes took it upon himself to open the next line of inquiry.

'The other thing we wanted to ask you about, Mr – er, Professor Wilkes, is a report we received from a witness, who said that she saw you talking to Mr Swann shortly before the murder was committed. You were out in the kitchen garden, apparently, and she said that it looked as if you were having an argument.'

'An "animated conversation" was the phrase she used,' Prudence corrected. 'In addition to which, it seems you had another conversation with him – quite a long and intimate one, I'm told – in the bar last night.'

'Well, I'm not sure that I would describe it as "intimate",' Professor Wilkes demurred. 'We talked mainly about literature and politics. I'm afraid to say that I rather over-indulged in my favourite single-malt whisky – not very easy to obtain in Venice, you know – and, as far as I remember, Mr Swann was kind enough to help me up to my room. He really seemed a very amiable sort of person. Such a tragedy. Who could have wanted to do such a thing?'

'And yet this morning you argued with him,' DS Jakes prompted.

'Well . . . what can I tell you about that? First of all, you should know that I had a terrible hangover – quite dreadful – and was probably a little . . . irascible for that reason alone. He came out, I think, to ask me in a perfectly pleasant way if I had seen his mobile phone. He seemed to have lost it, and had some idea that perhaps he had left it in my room in the early hours of the morning, when we were both a bit the worse for wear. Anyway, I got hold of the wrong end of the stick, and thought that he was accusing me of taking it. That's why our conversation might – from a distance – have seemed rather . . . well, tetchy, shall we say?'

'Our witness,' said Prudence, 'says that you then came into the library looking for him.'

'I had calmed down by then, and wanted to apologize.'

'That wasn't her impression. Rather the reverse.'

Professor Wilkes shrugged his shoulders. 'Then she had the wrong impression,' he said.

DI Freeborne nodded, and said amicably: 'Well, these things can often be misconstrued. I gather that you weren't able to deliver much of your lecture yesterday?'

'Sadly, no. It was . . . well, elbowed aside, one might say, by national events.'

'Quite. Nonetheless, I would be interested to see it. Do you happen to have the text?'

'Upstairs in my room.'

'The paper copy – the one you were reading from?'

'Yes.'

'Would you be good enough to let me have it, before you leave?'

Professor Wilkes agreed to this request. After that, DI Freeborne took his Venetian contact details and, having received his assurance that he would not be leaving that city for the foreseeable future, told him that he was free to go.

End of interview

10.

Interview Number Four: Roger Wagstaff

It was the final interview of the afternoon. The energy levels of DS Jakes – who admitted that he had 'been looking forward to this one' – seemed to show no signs of flagging. DI Freeborne, on the other hand, was feeling tired, and already strangely disgusted by this whole case. She remembered that her husband, Mark, was cooking a special retirement dinner for her that evening – Beef Wellington with wild mushroom and Madeira gravy – and she felt a sudden pang of longing to be back home with him at their cottage in Stow-on-the-Wold, drinking her pre-dinner sherry with her feet up in front of some comforting TV quiz show. She hoped that this interview would not drag on for too long; but she was also determined, as always, to cover every angle.

'Mr Wagstaff,' she began, 'this murder is believed to have taken place between the hours of ten and ten-thirty this morning. Can you account for your movements during that time?'

'Of course. At ten o'clock, the first session of the day was just starting in the stables theatre. I introduced the speakers, and then listened to the debate.'

'This,' said DS Jakes, 'was the panel on "Why Free Markets and Nationhood Go Hand in Hand"?'

'Precisely.'

Roger sat back with his hands folded comfortably across his lap. He could not possibly have looked more smug at the production of this watertight alibi.

'I'm afraid,' Prudence said, however, 'that there is an inconsistency here, and your memory might not be entirely accurate. Several witnesses say that you *left* the stables theatre immediately after making your introduction, and didn't come back for about twenty-five minutes.'

Somewhat shaken by these words, Roger scratched his head nervously and at last admitted: 'Yes. Yes, you're right. I'd forgotten. Sir Emeric Coutts was leaving this morning, so I came back to the hotel to say goodbye and thank you to him.'

'That's right.' Prudence glanced at her notes. 'He checked out at four minutes past ten, and was driven away in a taxi at ten-thirteen.'

'Well, yes, so I was talking to him for most of that time. He will confirm that.'

'Most of that time?'

'Yes. I certainly didn't have time to murder anyone.'

'Two witnesses put your arrival back in the theatre at around ten-twenty-five.'

'Possibly.'

'So what did you do in the intervening twelve minutes, between Sir Emeric's departure and your return to the theatre?'

'I don't know. I think I . . . went to the loo, probably?' Meeting the impassive gaze of the two detectives, he added: 'Look, it's not exactly the sort of thing you want to share with people, but . . . since it appears to matter, I had to go for rather a long time. Last night's *foie gras*, I think. It seemed to go straight through me.'

'No witnesses, obviously,' said Prudence, writing a few words in her pocket-book. 'So I think we have, potentially, established opportunity. Let's move on. You had known Mr Swann for more than forty years, is that right?'

'Well, we met at Cambridge forty years ago, but we'd had very little contact since then.'

'I assume because you disliked each other so intensely.'

'I'm not sure that I *disliked* him, exactly.'

'You found him troublesome?'

'Well, it doesn't exactly endear someone to you if they spend half their time attacking you and your work. Luckily, nobody really read anything Christopher wrote, so he was never anything more than a . . . minor irritant.'

'Was he really so minor? He bothered you enough that you were prepared to steal something from him.'

Roger raised his eyebrows.

'You pilfered his flash drive, I believe.'

'I didn't do that.'

'I know. Miss Wood did it. On your instructions.'

'She also returned it on my instructions.'

'A risky and underhand endeavour, whichever way you look at it. Can you explain your motives?'

Roger Wagstaff hesitated, and when he began to speak, it was not in order to give a direct answer.

'The purpose of the Processus Group,' he began, 'is to think innovatively, outside the box. And the object is always the same: to work for the benefit of ordinary British people. The question that some of us have been asking, for several years now, is whether a model of universal healthcare that was devised more than seventy years ago, when life expectancy was shorter, the population faced very different health challenges, and the range of medicines and treatments at our disposal was much smaller than it is today – whether that model is still . . . well, fit for purpose. It doesn't seem to me to be an unreasonable question to ask. We've been asking it for some time, and producing a number of papers on the subject. The one that Christopher claimed to have got his hands on did contain some . . . well, some time-sensitive information. It was imperative that we found out whether he was bluffing or not.'

'And was he bluffing?'

Roger had no choice but to admit: 'No.'

'Did you delete the file from his flash drive, or interfere with it in any way?'

'No.'

'Of course not. There was no point. You knew that he would have backed it up somewhere.'

'Indeed,' said DS Jakes. 'Now, this document that Mr Swann had obtained was called the Second of August Report, is that right?'

'Yes,' said Roger, sounding none too pleased that the sergeant was already familiar with the title.

'And what was the nature of the "time-sensitive information" that it contained?'

Roger's answer, again, was on the oblique and long-winded side.

'There's nothing new about getting private companies involved in providing NHS services. It's been taking place under successive governments, Labour and Conservative. We believe that the process needs to be accelerated, but we're also aware that the public are nervous about seeing radical changes made to an institution which has been sentimentalized and turned into a sacred cow. This report did advocate reforms being made on a much bigger scale than before. Equipment, medicines, premises – health provision itself, for that matter – being turned over to competing companies from the private sector who could provide all of these things much more nimbly and efficiently than some lumbering centralized monolith. It all makes perfectly good practical and financial sense—'

'Financial, you say?' DS Jakes pounced on the word.

'Yes, of course. Everything comes down to money in the end. You'd have to be very naive to deny that.'

'Or idealistic,' said Prudence.

'Well, let's not split semantic hairs, shall we?'

'Did the report name any of the companies who might be involved in this, um . . . efficiency drive?' DS Jakes asked.

'Yes, it did.'

'Were any of them American companies?'

'Some of them, yes.'

'Were any of them among the funders of the Processus Group?'

'That, I'm not prepared to disclose.'

'Where *does* your funding come from, exactly?'

'It comes from many different sources. We have supporters all over the world.'

'Would it be accurate to describe this report,' said DS Jakes, 'as a proposal for the full-scale privatization of the National Health Service?'

Ignoring this question, Roger turned to Prudence – who seemed to him to be the more sympathetic of his two interrogators – and said: 'Is any of this actually relevant to your investigation? I thought you were trying to solve a murder case.'

'I think DS Jakes is trying to establish motive,' she replied. 'It sounds to me as though Mr Swann had obtained information which might at the very least embarrass your organization, and possibly have an impact on its finances.' She gave him a few seconds to digest this before moving to her next question, which was: 'Lord Wetherby is a friend of yours, I think?'

'An acquaintance, I would say.'

'You must have been in a good many meetings with him, in the run-up to this conference.'

'Quite a few, yes.'

'And these meetings were friendly?'

'Yes, they were.'

'Whose idea was it to move Mr Swann into room nine on Wednesday morning? Up until then he was staying in the annexe.'

'I couldn't say.'

'Were you the one who suggested it? I can see that it would be much easier to keep an eye on him when he was so close by.'

'Not at all. What a disgraceful suggestion.'

'And thanks to the passage, you effectively had access to his room.'

'So what? I told you I had nothing to do with it.' Roger's face was getting redder by the second.

'But you knew about the passage,' Prudence persisted. 'Because you instructed Miss Wood to use it, when stealing the flash drive.'

By now Roger's face was as red as Richard Wilkes's jumper and, having been caught out, he sounded more furious than ever.

'All right, so I knew about it. I still *deeply* resent your—'

'How did you know?'

'Because Lord Wetherby showed it to me. The first time I came to the hotel.'

'When was that?'

'About a year ago,' he shouted – impatience and embarrassment having wiped out all his reserves of politeness. He stood up. 'Look, I've had about enough of this. This conversation is at an end.'

'Well,' said Prudence, 'the decision's not really yours to make, but never mind.' She, too, rose to her feet. 'All right, Mr Wagstaff. You can go. And so, thankfully –' she offered him a handshake, which he returned most reluctantly – 'can we.'

End of interview

Before parting company, Prudence and her assistant had a few points to discuss and notes to compare. Rather than linger at Wetherby Hall, where the atmosphere, they felt, had become rather oppressive, they drove (with DS Jakes at the wheel) into the village of Wetherby Pond itself, and parked close to the yellow sandstone bridge that spanned the brook so gracefully on its outskirts. They crossed the bridge and strolled back along the lane that led away from the village. It was almost seven o'clock, and the evening sun bathed the fields and hedgerows in a warm and peaceful light. Prudence found herself distracted by the quiet beauty of the landscape, and her mind began to wander away from the morning's savage murder, the slippery, evasive answers of their four suspects, the dank odour of the secret passage and the grisly spectacle presented by room number nine. DS Jakes, on the other hand, could talk of nothing else, and already seemed to have reached a conclusion as to the guilty party, as he railed with particular hostility against Roger Wagstaff, the malign influence of the Processus Group, the opacity of their funding, the sinister ubiquity of their spokespeople on television and radio programmes, their close ties with rapacious American technology firms and healthcare providers. Prudence wasn't really listening, but she let him talk on while she enjoyed the familiar, cherished sounds and smells of the English countryside. It was only when he said something about 'big pharma' and she thought he was referring to the burly rustic who was driving his dawdling herd along the lane in front of them that she realized they were at absolute cross-purposes, and it was time to go home.

II.

The queue to file past the coffin of Queen Elizabeth while she lay in state at Westminster Hall opened at five o'clock in the afternoon on Wednesday 14th September. Prudence and Mark became part of it some sixteen hours later, on the morning of Thursday the 15th.

Joining the queue had been Mark's idea. *I think we should pay tribute somehow*, he had messaged his wife, on the day of the murder, and of course this was the obvious way of doing it. Prudence had fallen in with the proposal readily enough: while not quite such an ardent royalist as her husband, she had admired the Queen, and agreed with him that her moment of passing after seventy years on the throne should be marked in some way. Besides, by now the queue was, by all accounts, almost nine hours long, and that would give her plenty of time to think about the case. In the last few days she had been unable to focus her thoughts at all, and she was hoping that this paralysis might now be cured by a radical change of scene.

'First,' said Mark, as they stepped out of Tower Hill Tube station, 'we have to find the end of the queue.'

'You mean the beginning,' said Prudence. 'The end is when we get to her coffin, surely.'

They argued this point for some time, as a series of marshals directed them across Tower Bridge towards Potters Fields, which turned out to be a tiny park lying between the bridge and City Hall, on the south bank of the river. Here was the first sign that the British state, maligned as decrepit and dysfunctional by its critics over the last few years, could swing into efficient action when a royal occasion demanded. Steel barriers had been set up to form a winding corridor along which the mourners could shuffle in line, and everyone was given a pink wristband emblazoned with the letters 'LISQ'. Thanks to these, they were told, it would be possible to drop out of the queue at various points to go to the toilet or find something to eat.

'This is going to take a hell of a long time,' Prudence said, taking hold of the shooting stick her husband was offering her. 'I'm glad you decided to bring these.'

Mark had a shooting stick as well. The cupboard under their staircase at home was full of these rural accoutrements: sticks, Barbours, green wellies, flat caps, fishing rods, hip flasks, riding hats. They both enjoyed reading *Country Life* and even *Horse & Hound*, but that was where it stopped for Prudence: she suspected her husband of being secretly regretful that fox-hunting had been banned.

'Not to mention these,' said Mark triumphantly, producing one of said hip flasks from his jacket pocket.

'Ooh, well done. Brandy, or Lagavulin?'

'Brandy. I thought we might need fortifying at some point.'

'Lovely. Can I have a swig now?'

'Come on, Pru, it's nine o'clock in the morning.'

'Fair enough. I thought it might loosen up the brain cells a bit, that's all. I just can't seem to get any further with this business at the moment.'

'Well, we're going to have plenty of time to talk about it today. If you need a sounding board, just fire away.'

Over the last few years there had been many cases, in fact, which Prudence would have found it difficult to solve without the help of her husband. It was not that he had a brilliant mind, more that – like Holmes's faithful Dr Watson – he had the knack of making remarks and posing questions pitched at just the level of obtuseness where they became useful. As they started to make their way westwards along the Thames path – moving at quite a brisk pace so far, which was reassuring – he was happy to give his current opinion on the case, which Prudence had outlined to him in some detail.

'It seems to me,' he said, 'that it comes down to either Rebecca Wood or Lord Wetherby. They both have motive – which Professor Wilkes doesn't, so far as we know – and the victim's clue could point to either of them. It doesn't point to either Wilkes or Roger Wagstaff – and that should be enough, in my view, to rule both of them out.'

He stopped to pull his phone from his pocket and take a picture of St Paul's, looking especially fine today in the morning sunlight.

'As it happens,' said Prudence, 'Lord Wetherby has an even stronger motive than you might think. There's a reason for the dire state of the finances at that hotel, and it has nothing to do with the lacklustre tourist trade. I've been doing a bit of research into Randolph Wetherby. He has a nasty gambling habit. He's been siphoning money off the business and losing most of it at the casino in Monte Carlo. He goes there about once a month. As a result, the business doesn't just need an injection of funds – it's on the verge of bankruptcy.'

'Well, that's as maybe,' her husband said, 'but I can't help thinking that the clue itself leads us to Rebecca much more directly than it does to Wetherby. If it signifies her room number, then it points straight at her. Whereas in his case, it's just an oblique reference to a date that he mentioned in his speech the night before.'

'Not just any date,' Prudence countered. 'As I said, Lord Wetherby has a powerful motive, and that date sums it up nicely. If Christopher Swann *did* mean to direct people's attention towards him with that clue, it was rather a brilliant one. Gosh, what lovely flowers. Aren't people thoughtful?'

It had been a feature of the queue so far that, every few yards, gifts and tributes had been left by mourners at random spots on the pathway. Teddy bears and floral bouquets seemed to be the favoured options. The one that Prudence was drawing her husband's attention to was a particularly stunning arrangement of lilies, roses and hydrangeas. She picked the flowers up and took in their scent with a deep indrawn breath before replacing them reverently on the flagstones.

'Gorgeous,' she said.

Mark was keen to resume the discussion.

'That's as maybe,' he said, 'but everything you've told me about this Rebecca woman makes me suspect her. The story of the chap falling down the stairs just as he was about to blow the whistle, for instance. So, she was never formally identified – but it's a *hell* of a coincidence that someone looking just like her was spotted at the scene. And she never married, did she? Obviously she's been in love with Wagstaff since the day she met him. A forty-year, unrequited crush . . . Well, things like that can have a weird effect on the human spirit. She might be capable of anything, at this stage in her life.'

'Oh, really?' said Prudence, disappointed in her husband. 'Do I have to add middle-aged-woman-hatred to your flaws now? What you've just come out with is the purest misogynistic claptrap. Rebecca didn't strike me as in the least hysterical.'

'I never used that word.'

'You didn't have to.'

The looming bulk of a mock-Elizabethan building to her left made Prudence realize that they were walking past the Globe Theatre: or rather, half-walking and half-standing, because their initially rapid progress had been halted, and the queue was now coming to a standstill every couple of minutes, pausing for a few minutes more, and then inexplicably starting again, like traffic stacked up behind a lane closure on a busy motorway. For some reason this seemed much more tiring than walking at a slow but steady pace, and they were both relieved when they had shuffled past Tate Modern and beneath Blackfriars bridge, and the extra space as they approached the South Bank buildings allowed everyone to spread out and speed up.

'My gut feeling,' said Prudence, 'is that this will turn out to be a political crime rather than a personal one. I mean, I know in Rebecca's case the two things might be intertwined, but – I don't know, the fact that it happened at this conference . . . There were some pretty odd characters at Wetherby Hall this week, I'm telling you.'

Mark gave his wife a disapproving look. 'Not like you to describe someone as "odd" just because you don't like their politics.'

'It's a bit more than that,' Prudence said. 'I've been watching videos of all the debates, and these people strike me as being pretty extreme.'

'Extreme? What does that even mean, nowadays?'

'Well, my impression was that they all seem very angry, and rather obsessed. Obsessed with some sort of notion of . . . purity.' She paused for a moment to consider her own choice of word. 'Yes – purity. Everything has to be pure. No compromise. OK, so we've left the EU, but we have to be sure we've *completely* left the EU. We've got our sovereignty back, but we have to make sure it's *complete* sovereignty. We need free trade, but it can't just be free, it has to be *completely* free: no regulations, no restrictions whatsoever.

I think these people are almost anarchists, in a way. And then, yes, there's the anger. I suppose if your obsession is purity then you're always going to be angry and unhappy because nothing in life will ever be pure, things just don't work that way. If you can't accept compromise you're always going to be frustrated. But it did seem odd that they were so angry, given that the party they're all supposed to support has been in charge for the last twelve years.'

'Perhaps they regretted choosing Boris as their leader,' said Mark.

'Possibly. Some of them actually said he was too liberal for their liking. They were all very enthusiastic about Liz Truss, anyway. If she'd turned up I think she would have been treated like the Messiah.'

Two and a half hours had elapsed now since they had been given their wristbands at Potters Fields, and they were both beginning to tire. As soon as they reached Jubilee Gardens they unfolded their shooting sticks, implanted them in the turf and perched on them while Prudence opened their picnic bag and inspected the provisions her husband had prepared for the occasion. There was coffee, red and white wine, cold chicken, green salad, cherry tomatoes, crusty white bread, Ardennes pâté, celery sticks, crab paste and a selection of cheese.

'That looks nice,' said a voice beside them. 'Bit classier than what we've brought, anyway.'

'Did you want some?' said Prudence graciously.

'Oh no, not at all. I wasn't fishing.'

The speaker was a blonde woman in her fifties, dressed in smart pale blue jeans and a T-shirt emblazoned with a larger-than-life image of the late Queen's face. Next to her was a younger blonde woman – her daughter presumably – whose lightweight jacket sported a red, white and blue rosette bearing the slogan, *'Queen Of All Our Hearts'*. They were sitting on the grass and sharing a large packet of cheese-and-onion crisps. They both looked worn out.

'Don't worry,' said Prudence, 'we'll get there in the end.'

'I know,' said the woman. 'And it'll be worth it.'

'Have you travelled far?'

'Harrogate.'

'Quite an undertaking, then.'

'Well, we couldn't let this week go by without coming down and paying our respects, could we? She's been such a big part of our lives, over the years.'

Prudence pondered this remark. Had the Queen been a 'big part' of her own life? A presence, perhaps. A presence you were always aware of, but which hardly ever drew your attention, like wallpaper or background music: but she suspected the blonde woman would not be happy with this comparison.

'To tell you the truth,' she said, 'I was very much against the royal family, back in the day. My parents were hippies and I was brought up to think the whole thing was a complete waste of time and money, and a kind of blot on the constitutional landscape.' She sprinkled some salt onto a chicken leg and bit into it ruminatively.

'What changed your mind?' the woman asked.

'I'm not sure,' said Prudence, who had never really thought about it before. 'In my memory, it happened around the time of the Silver Jubilee. 1977. There was a big street party with all our neighbours and although my parents didn't want me to go, I went anyway, and copped off with the boy three doors along the street and had the most wonderful time. I was only nineteen and was a bit of a late developer and I suppose in a pathetic sort of way this was my version of rebelling against parental values.'

'Well,' the blonde woman said, 'luckily Lucinda and I have always been on the same page as far as the royals are concerned. Isn't that right, Looby-Loo?'

Her daughter offered up a terrified smile of acquiescence at this remark, and flashed Prudence a brief, imploring glance. She did not actually hold up a sign that said 'Rescue me', but she might as well have done.

Prudence laughed and said: 'Well, it got much worse as far as my parents were concerned. First of all I married the man who'd been running the Conservative group at my Oxford college, and then just to rub their noses in it I joined the police force. Are you sure you wouldn't like to nibble on a thigh?'

This time the blonde woman succumbed to temptation, and she and her daughter made short work of the pieces of chicken they were offered.

'My wife exaggerates,' Mark said. 'Her father was a Leftist, but a very respectable one. After the war his mother had helped to set up the National Health Service, and he went on to become a rather distinguished lawyer. Human rights and so on. He wasn't a hippie by any means. And his wife was a fine painter. Had a show at the Hayward, back in the day.'

'Well, she was *part* of a show. Now you're exaggerating.'

'I think human rights are a nuisance,' the blonde woman said. 'People are always kicking up a fuss about them.'

Neither Prudence nor Mark knew quite how to respond to this comment; and since the queue seemed to moving with surprising speed all of a sudden, they decided to pack up their meal and rejoin it beside the London Eye. On seeing their wristbands a Sikh family of five was happy to make way for them, and from there it took another twenty minutes or so to shuffle along to Westminster bridge. It was cheering, now, to be able to see the Palace of Westminster itself, and to think that their journey must almost be over: but from that point onwards, progress was slower than ever. They descended the steps from the bridge and found that the crowd of people on the Thames path had become noticeably denser. They were only able to walk for a few yards at a time before coming to a halt which might last for two minutes or more.

Shortly afterwards, the movement of the crowd slowed even further as people stopped to inspect the Covid Memorial Wall on their left. The wall, which consisted of more than two hundred thousand hand-painted red hearts, had begun life as an organic work of popular art during the first wave of the pandemic back in 2020, each heart representing one person who had died as a result of Covid. Mark himself drifted over to look at the hearts, and for a while he and Prudence became separated. They lost sight of each other for about five minutes, and when she managed to glimpse him again he had somehow got ahead of her, but she was stuck in the middle of a tight cluster of people and could not move in any direction. By the time she was able to shuffle forward again, Mark was even further ahead and now seemed to be in conversation with an elderly Black woman: they were walking side by side and examining the wall of painted hearts together.

Above and beyond the Covid wall, the view was dominated by the massive outline of St Thomas' hospital. It was here that Prudence's father had died, five years earlier. She refused to sentimentalize his death, knowing full well that confronting the mortality of your parents was just one of the routine horrors to be negotiated in late middle age, but still, there were some memories from his final days that she had not been able to get out of her mind: not least his twenty-two-hour wait on a trolley in the hospital corridor, when the only sustenance he'd been offered was a bottle of water and a pack of sandwiches. During those hours she had watched his fighting spirit ebbing away, but he never complained about the medical staff, who seemed to be doing the best they could in the face of extreme mismanagement. 'Your mum would be turning in her grave . . .' he managed to say, during one of their last conversations.

'There you are!' Mark cried out, pushing through the crowd to reunite with his wife. His new friend was still with him. Her name was Ellen Parker, and she was in London on vacation from Chicago: the first holiday she had taken by herself since her husband had died of Covid the previous year. Mark seemed to be feeling sorry for her, so they queued alongside her for the next couple of hours. During this time, even though they were now only a short distance from their goal, that goal itself began to feel almost unattainable. Having crossed the river at Lambeth bridge and entered Victoria Tower Gardens, they were less than half a mile from Westminster Hall where the Queen was lying in state. But the steel barriers had reappeared, dividing the gardens up into hundreds and hundreds of yards of makeshift corridor, and progress between them seemed to be non-existent. It was five o'clock in the afternoon and they had been queuing for eight hours. For a while Prudence nodded along with Ellen politely, listening with half her mind to what she was saying (her plans for the rest of her visit to the UK, speculations about what her late husband would have made of it all) while the other half attempted to refocus on elements of the murder case. More and more, though, she found herself triggered by that glimpse of St Thomas', and seething with repressed anger at the indignities of her father's final days and hours.

'You know, maybe I should be looking into Roger Wagstaff after all,' she said to Mark. They had wished a warm goodbye to Ellen, who had decided to press on ahead while they took their shooting sticks out once again, planted them in the grass and enjoyed fifteen minutes' much-needed rest. 'Perhaps there *is* a movement afoot to privatize the NHS, and Christopher Swann was about to publish the proof.'

Her husband patted her on the arm. 'Take a break from thinking about it. You said that today would help you look at things rationally. Not come up with crackpot conspiracy theories.'

He offered Prudence the hip flask and she took a sip of brandy. She looked chastened. 'You're right,' she admitted. 'What happened to my father shouldn't have anything to do with it.' The next words she addressed to herself, in a tone of sharp reprimand. '*Facts*, Pru, you idiot. Concentrate on the facts.'

She fell silent. A dozen or so mourners inched past them on their way to Westminster Hall. Then Mark said:

'All right, then – here's a fact for you.'

She looked at him expectantly.

'Well, maybe not a fact, but a new way of interpreting something. And actually, it *does* have a bearing on Roger Wagstaff.'

'Come on then, let's hear it.'

'It occurred to me while I was looking with Ellen at the hearts on that wall. Now, what was the name of the file that Swann was supposed to have laid his hands on?'

'The Second of August Report. What's that got to do with it?'

'On a lot of those hearts, you see, people had written dates. The dates when they lost their loved ones. We even saw one where somebody had lost *both* their parents. Ellen pointed it out to me, and said, "Just imagine, losing your mother *and* your father, within seven days of each other." '

'Horrible, but . . . So?'

'Well, the dates had been written like this: four / five / twenty-twenty and four / twelve / twenty-twenty. What does that say to you?'

'Fourth of May and fourth of December, obviously.'

'Exactly. Seven months apart. But she thought it meant the fifth of April and the twelfth of April.'

'Ah. Of course. Because of the way Americans write dates.' She considered this. 'Christopher Swann wasn't American, though.'

'No – but didn't you tell me that he'd had an American wife, and lived there for years? Maybe he still wrote dates the American way.'

'Maybe. In which case, eight/two would mean . . .'

'The second of August,' said Mark, at the very same moment that his wife did.

Afterwards, as they were driving along the M4 on their way back to Stow-on-the-Wold, Mark tried to express the complex blend of emotions he had experienced while standing in front of the Queen's coffin. It had been, he explained, a melange of grief, nostalgia for days gone by, admiration for everything she had achieved, and immense patriotic pride, all coalescing into what seemed, for him, to have been a profound and momentarily overwhelming spiritual experience. Prudence listened with every appearance of attention, and did not let on that for her own part she'd been wondering – during *her* allotted two minutes of silent tribute – how the mourners could be certain that it was really the Queen's body contained in that box, and what the exact circumstances of her death had been. At least this had put thoughts of Christopher Swann's murder out of her head for a while. But now these thoughts were back again, and back with a vengeance. Prudence's nine draining hours in the queue, she realized, had proved nowhere near as helpful as she'd hoped they would. No progress had been made, no clarity achieved. Still the same four suspects, three of them with a motive, and three of them (thanks to Mark's intervention) now the possible objects of Christopher's enigmatic clue. The only odd man out, in these respects, was Professor Richard Wilkes. But even there, there was a connection to the murder victim: because Richard Wilkes was the world's leading authority on the novelist Peter Cockerill, and just one day before the murder, Christopher Swann had emailed his old friend Joanna, and asked her to send him the pages of a manuscript describing Cockerill's visit to their Cambridge college back in the early 1980s. Why had he done that? What had he been hoping to discover? Prudence had examined the contents of Christopher's laptop and read these pages, now. They had been intriguing. They had made her want to read the whole manuscript. And interview Christopher's university friend, Joanna Maidstone. And maybe his adopted daughter, too. Perhaps the whole key to this affair was to be found not in room nine of Wetherby Hall, but in a story of student friendship that led all the way back to the 1980s.

It was probably time to pay a visit to Rookthorne.

12.

While Detective Inspector Freeborne was interviewing her mother and Rashida, Phyl remained upstairs in her bedroom. She curled up on the bed with her face to the wall and watched three episodes of *Friends*.

When she had learned of the murder one week earlier, Joanna's thoughts had almost immediately gone to Christopher's adopted daughter. His sister, Lydia, who lived in Edinburgh, had been his only close relative, and she and Rashida barely knew each other. Joanna felt that the right, and compassionate, thing to do was to invite Rashida to stay with them for as long as she wanted. Since then, as a unit of four they had all been trying to go about their daily tasks and to behave as though life still had a sheen of normality. Joanna attended to parish bureaucracy and Phyl kept putting in her shifts at Heathrow airport, working as a team member for Hey! Teriyaki, the Japanese fast-food chain. Rashida seldom left her bedroom. None of them really knew what she was doing in there, although once or twice, listening at the door, Phyl had overheard her talking to someone. Most likely it was Elspeth, who was due to fly over from America soon in time for the funeral. Meanwhile the days went by, and everyone waited for news.

The arrival of DI Freeborne, then, was a significant event. Phyl did not know what she had been expecting from it. She was relieved, at any rate, that this cheerful, friendly, bustling woman with the white hair and the rosy cheeks did not want to talk to her. And she imagined that when the interviews were over, the detective would drive off and leave them in peace. In the meantime she had *Friends* to console her, and while watching it she was able to sink again into that lovely fugue state, in which real life seemed to dissolve and be replaced by a reassuring world of coffee shops, stylish apartments, smart conversations and material well-being, in which the worst misfortune that could befall anyone was to go on a slightly awkward date or to miss out on a promotion at work. The first two episodes slipped by without Phyl even noticing (she knew them off by heart anyway) and she was midway through Season 5, Episode 21 – *The One with the Ball* – when Rashida came into the room and sat down beside her.

Phyl looked up and moved over to make space on the bed, but neither of them spoke. They just sat through the rest of the episode in silence. It was the one where Joey and Ross start throwing a ball back and forth across the apartment, and become so mesmerized by the activity that they can't bring themselves to stop. The quintessence of *Friends*, in a way. Television as anti-anxiety therapy.

The final beneath-the-credits sequence, a montage of Chandler having objects thrown towards him and dropping them all, would normally have made them laugh out loud. But Rashida seemed to be more subdued than ever this evening, and when the episode was over, Phyl looked into her friend's eyes for the first time and saw a terrible sadness there. She hadn't cried over Christopher's death, yet. Phyl and her parents had been discussing, in private, whether she might be in some sort of denial, putting up a veneer of composure, even indifference, in the face of her loss. If so, today the veneer was beginning to crack.

'You OK?' Phyl asked.

Rashida sighed and put her head in her hands.

'Shit, I don't know. This whole thing . . . this whole thing's really hit me all of a sudden. I suppose I've been keeping a lid on it, you know. Maybe not the best way to deal with things, but – well, that's what usually works for me, I guess. But today . . .' She rubbed her eyes. 'I don't know, you can never tell what's going to trigger you, can you? It can be anything, really. The smallest thing.'

'Has something happened?' Phyl asked.

Rashida sat forward and sniffed, trying to pull herself together.

'Do you remember me saying that I used to get these emails, telling me I had a voice message? And when I listened to them it was . . . Well, I don't really know how to describe it. The audio equivalent of dick pics, I suppose.'

'Yes, I remember. But I thought they'd stopped.'

'Well, I got another one. Looks like it came last week, but I only saw it this afternoon.'

'Oh no. The same guy?'

'I haven't opened it.'

'Oh, Rash, I'm so sorry.' Daringly, Phyl put her arms around her, and tried to give her a hug, but it wasn't returned. There was no reciprocal gesture. 'You really should tell the police.'

'I'm having plenty of dealings with the police at the moment, thank you. That's the last thing I need to do.'

Phyl put an end to the hug, such as it was, and leaned away slightly on the bed.

'Have you done your interview with the detective?'

'Yes, just now.'

'How was it?'

'It was fine.'

'What kind of things did she ask?'

'Oh, it was just routine stuff. Stuff about Chris's background.' She frowned, as though something had only just occurred to her. 'She seemed kind of fixated on one thing, though. The way he wrote dates.'

'Dates?'

'You know – how you write dates out in numbers. She wanted to know whether he did it the American way or the English way. Month first, or day first.'

'That's weird. What did you tell her?'

'I told her I couldn't really remember, but probably the American way, since he'd lived there so long.' They reflected on this, but neither of them was able to make much sense of it. Then Rashida stood up, more or less composed now: the brief spasm of emotion had passed, or was safely repressed. 'Anyway,' she said, 'I was told to fetch you down for dinner. Sounds like the policeman lady is going to be having it with us.'

Prudence hadn't been planning to stay for the whole evening, but once Joanna suggested it, she didn't hesitate: she had never been known to turn down a dinner invitation. Andrew had prepared the food, roasting a pork leg which was bathed in mustard sauce and garnished with rosemary and thyme. He served it with a choice of either Provençal rosé or a light and aromatic Muscadet, and between the five of them they got through seven bottles. Prudence, Joanna thought, must have drunk at least two of them herself, not to mention the three sherries she had polished off before dinner. Afterwards Joanna found it hard to remember what they had talked about, although she knew they had discussed the Queen's lying-in-state, which Prudence and her husband had queued to see the day before, and there had been some chat about what sort of Prime Minister Liz Truss was likely to make. For the most part they carefully avoided the topic of Christopher and the terrible events at Wetherby Hall. It was Joanna herself who inadvertently brought the subject up at one point, by mentioning the fact that the church website was down and her email address still wasn't working.

'It's been more than a week now,' she said.

'Really?' said Andrew. 'As long as that?'

'Yes. It happened the day before Christopher . . . Well, it was the day before. Because he sent me a message and asked me to email him those pages.'

Prudence was quick to pick up on this cue.

'Which reminds me,' she said. 'This writer, Peter Cockerill – didn't you mention that you have some of his books here?'

'Yes,' said Andrew. 'A couple, I think. I'll go and get them.'

He disappeared off to the library and reappeared a few minutes later with two books, the first of them being a slightly weathered hardback novel.

'*A Rope from Hell*,' Prudence read, taking it from him carefully. She glanced at both the front and back covers, then opened the book up to look at the title page.

'An inscribed copy, no less. Even if the inscription is a tad . . . perfunctory. Who was Thomas, do we know?'

'One of Joanna's university friends.'

'That's *Thomas*'s copy?' said Joanna, aghast. 'I thought I gave that back to him forty years ago.'

'Evidently not,' said her husband.

'But this is terrible! I should send it off at once. Do we have an address for him?'

A Rope from Hell

a novel by

Peter Cockerill

Oh, what will you leave your sweetheart, my son?
What will you leave her, my handsome young one?
A rope from hell to hang her
A rope from hell to hang her
Oh, make my bed soon, for I'm sick to the heart
And fain would lie down

For Thomas,

Best wishes,

Peter Cockerill.

Newman & Fox
London • 1982

'I think if he'd really missed it, he would have asked for it by now.'

'Is this worth reading, would you say?' Prudence asked.

'Rather depends on your taste,' said Andrew. 'Nasty book, in my opinion. The work of someone who clearly doesn't like women. The cover gives that away, I suppose. Very much of its time.'

'And this was his second novel, I think?'

'The third. After that he wrote just one more – this one.' He held up the other book, which was an altogether more modern and stylish paperback. Its title was *My Innocence*. 'This is a reissue from a few years ago,' he explained. 'Published by a small independent outfit. They did a good job, I think.'

'Can I have a look at that?' said Phyl, taking the book from her father and starting to read the back cover copy with some interest. 'Is he famous, this guy?'

'I wouldn't say he's famous. But he is one of the lucky ones, in a way. At least he's remembered. And in print.'

'I don't get it,' Rashida said. 'There's some connection between this writer and Chris's death?'

'Maybe,' said Andrew. 'A tenuous one. The day before he died, your father wrote to Joanna. He wanted to know – well, you explain, love.'

'Did your father ever mention a friend of ours called Brian?' Joanna asked.

'I don't remember, to be honest.'

'Well, he went to university with us. And last year, just before he died, he wrote a little book about his time at Cambridge. I've got the manuscript, and your father sent me an email from the conference, because he had an idea that this writer might be mentioned in it. Which he was, as it happens. So I sent him some scans of the relevant bits.'

Rashida digested this information and looked confused. 'That seems a strange thing for him to ask,' she said.

Prudence leaned across the table and took the paperback from Phyl's hands.

'And look – here's another connection,' she said. ' "With an introduction by Professor Richard Wilkes".'

'Who's that?' Phyl asked.

'He was another of the guests at Wetherby Hall.'

'Is he one of your suspects?' Rashida asked sharply, but Prudence didn't reply.

'By the way,' Andrew said, 'my friend Victor made a small fortune from that very novel last year.'

'Oh?' said Prudence. 'How so?'

'Well, something of a legend attaches to it, in the collectors' market. At the time of publication – 1987, I think – there was rumoured to have been a small run of bound proofs. About a hundred or so. But apparently they all disappeared.'

'Disappeared?'

'Over the years, some people claim to have seen one, but no one could ever actually produce a copy. "A proof of *My Innocence*" became a sort of byword in the business for something impossible, like the twelfth of never or once in a blue moon. But then last year Victor, who has a shop in Cecil Court, actually seems to have got his hands on one. God knows how. And I believe he sold it within a couple of days – for fifty grand.'

Prudence gave an appreciative whistle, and Phyl's eyes widened.

'Who has that kind of money to pay for a book?'

'Someone with no intention of reading it, I suspect. Victor won't tell me the names of his clients, of course, but it was probably some oligarch or Texan oil billionaire. Someone whose only concern is with the monetary value. He'll put it in a locked glass bookcase along with his Shakespeare first folio and never look at it again.'

After that the conversation drifted on to other topics. Andrew produced first some port, and then some brandy. Joanna kept putting her hand over the glass and saying, 'No, no, we've all had *way* too much.' Even Phyl and Rashida seemed to be taking it easy, but Prudence showed no such restraint, and had two or three glasses of each. They helped her to wash down the sticky toffee pudding which she was still serving herself in generous quantities long after everyone else had stopped eating. It was only when the time was getting on for midnight, and Andrew himself was beginning to feel the worse for drink, that he thought to say:

'Look, Pru, you're not going to drive home after all this, are you?'

Prudence looked perfectly alert, compos mentis and, in all

probability, capable of taking an advanced driving test at that very moment, but she chuckled and said, all the same: 'Ah. Very good point. Probably not a good idea to hit the road in this state.'

'That's all right,' said Joanna. 'We've got lots of spare rooms. You can bunk down here for the night.'

'Well, that's very kind of you,' said Prudence. 'Maybe that would be the best thing.'

The five of them stood up from the table and began to clear a few of the plates and glasses away. It wasn't a good idea: Rashida broke a sherry glass almost immediately, and Phyl sent a wooden salad bowl skimming across the kitchen with a careless sweep of her hand.

'Let's do this in the morning,' Joanna said. 'Come on, Pru, I'll show you to your room.'

'I think what I'm going to do,' said Prudence, resisting Joanna's attempt to take her arm, and heading for the corridor outside the kitchen, 'is to have a read of that manuscript before I turn in. Would that be all right? I'll just curl up with it in your library, if that's OK.'

'Are you sure? You must be very tired.'

'No, no, the night is young, as far as I'm concerned. If you could just make me a triple espresso, and bring it in when you're ready, that would be just the job. And maybe some of those delicious-looking chocolates I spotted on the dresser.'

The others were regarding her with something approaching awe. Both Phyl and Rashida were beginning to think that they might have found a new role model.

'Of course,' said Joanna, with a frankly disbelieving look. 'Coming right up.'

'It's just that . . . you know, my mind's racing, the game's afoot, strike while the iron's hot – all that sort of thing.'

'I'll put the coffee on,' said Phyl.

'And I'll make sure everything's set up for you,' said Andrew. He led Prudence into the book-lined room and before long she was installed in an armchair with the ring-bound manuscript in her lap and a good reading light positioned above her. The coffee, chocolates and what remained of the brandy were all sitting in readiness on the side table at her elbow.

'Goodnight, then,' said Andrew.

'Don't worry about me,' said Prudence. 'I shall be through this in a jiffy.'

He was just about to leave when she asked:

'By the way, you didn't get an email from Christopher, before he died? Nothing with an attachment, or anything like that?'

'No. I barely knew him, to be honest. I don't think he even had my address.'

'Of course. I just thought, with your wife's email being down, he might have tried to send something to you instead . . .'

'I very much doubt it.'

'Then to whom, I wonder?'

Andrew shrugged. 'I don't know. His daughter, maybe.'

'Ah, yes. Maybe. Well, goodnight.'

Andrew nodded, took one last look at their bright-eyed, wide-awake guest, and then went to join the rest of the family upstairs. Meanwhile, Detective Inspector Freeborne settled down and opened the ring binder on her lap. It looked as though there were about a hundred pages to get through.

In years to come, Brian Collier's memoir would be honed and polished by Joanna herself, glossed with some explanatory footnotes, and privately published as a slim hardback volume. The manuscript Prudence encountered that night, although it was raw and unedited, did not differ materially from that version.

She sipped her coffee and started to read.

PART TWO

Say It

The Shadow Chamber
The
Shadow
Chamber
A Dark Academia Story

I

The Situation

This is the situation I find myself in.

Bowel cancer was the original diagnosis, and it could have been operated on, but before they managed to catch the thing it had metastasized to the liver, and that, as everyone knows, is a death sentence. I don't have much longer. A few months, probably. And in that time I would like to create something that can be left behind, for my kids to read, and my grandkids if they want. And, indeed, anyone who happens to be interested.

I am in pain, but nobody wants to hear about that. It is not what I want to write about. I want to tell the story of some people I knew at Cambridge University forty years ago. I matriculated in 1980 and in March 2020, just before lockdown started, I went to a reunion dinner at my old college to mark the anniversary. This was what set me thinking about that time. I've led, I think, an interesting life: most of the last forty years have been spent working in psychiatry, and it would be true to say that pretty much every facet of human behaviour and human eccentricity has been offered up to me during that time. And yet, for some reason, nothing is stamped as vividly on my memory as the three years I spent at St Stephen's College, three years in which I almost never stepped outside the same one square mile of streets and buildings in the centre of Cambridge.

None of the people I'm going to write about in this little memoir attended that reunion. Most of the people I know are dismissive of that kind of thing, and in fact I surprised myself by wanting to be there. I suppose that, despite the way I chafed against the place, my time at Cambridge – which took me out of one world without really moving me into another – left a more lasting mark on me than it did on the people who had always felt that they belonged there as if by inalienable right. I grew used to it, of course.

You can grow used to almost anything. But that's not the same as feeling at home there. I never felt at home there. I never felt that I belonged. That was what made it special.

II
The Place

I was told that Cambridge is a chilly and cheerless place, the low-lying fens offering no protection against the icy winds blowing from the North Sea and, ultimately, from Eastern Europe and Russia. All I would say to that is, if you come from Middlesbrough, the climate is more likely to strike you as agreeably balmy.

Before arriving there as a student I had visited it just once, for my interview at St Stephen's College. A difficult journey of more than three hours, involving two changes of train. The first time that I had undertaken a journey like that by myself. I had been wearing an ill-fitting jacket and tie that I'd last worn for my brother's eighteenth birthday party three years earlier at our local snooker club. Strangely enough I can remember nothing about the interview itself – I was so nervous about it that I think I actually blacked out and entered some sort of fugue state – but I do remember emerging from it into the daylight, and standing on the periphery of Joseph's Court, trying to compose myself again. Gradually, the details of my surroundings came into focus, and they were astonishing. I was standing in a courtyard that could be described in many ways: ancient, intimidating, arrogant – but also undeniably beautiful. As I looked around me and took in the details of the mullioned windows, the ivy-covered walls, the quaint old wooden staircases, the tinkling fountain at the courtyard's centre and the college chapel rising austerely on the northern side, it slowly dawned on me that this could, in theory, be my living environment for the foreseeable future. And I suddenly realized that I wanted to be a student here. Wanted it more badly than anything I had ever wanted in my life.

Less than a year later, my mum and dad drove me down from home and helped me carry my stuff up one of those quaint old wooden staircases into my attic room. I was not being housed in Joseph's Court, as it turned out, but in one of a warren of rooms tucked away above a row of shops in Sidney Street. What did I care? I could walk around that courtyard whenever I wanted to, and in the meantime I had autonomy, independence, a place of my own. Mum and Dad left to drive home while it was still light: another difficult journey ahead of them, 200 miles up the A1, but that was OK by me, it was good that there was going to be some proper distance between us. I had my own little kingdom now. It was bounded by Grange Road on one side and Sidney Street on another; by two pubs to the north, on Bridge Street (the Mitre and the Baron of Beef), and to the south, by the Guildhall and Market Hill, at the far edge of the market square. For the next three years, whenever I was in Cambridge I almost never left this tiny quadrangle, which contained all the elements required to satisfy my simple young scholarly needs: libraries, lecture halls, dining halls, restaurants (not many of those in 1980), coffee shops (nor those), pubs, bars, bookshops, record shops, and . . . that was about it. Enough – more than enough – to keep me happy.

Was I happy, though? At times the story I'm about to tell you will probably seem like little more than a catalogue of social embarrassments. I was prepared for those, of course. I was naive, but not stupid, and I knew that I was not going to be a typical Cambridge student, and that I was not going to be welcomed by many of my peers as a kindred spirit. And there were times, many times, when I wished that my supervisors and teachers would try harder to make me feel comfortable. Then again: was it their job to make me feel comfortable? Did I do anything to make *them* feel comfortable? Confronted by an alien specimen like me they often seemed to be gauche and awkward, but my own gaucheness and awkwardness could be more than a match for theirs.

I suppose these things cut both ways.

Eating alone in the St Stephen's dining hall at the age of nineteen, I would constantly find myself surrounded by loud, confident people, certain of their own place in the world. Attending that reunion forty years later, at the age of fifty-nine, I still felt myself surrounded by loud, confident people, certain of their place in the world. I was retired – at the end of a long, successful professional career – and yet still I never seemed to have access to that certainty.

I don't suppose I ever will have access to it now. Well, I happen to regard that as a virtue, both in me and in my friends. The most dangerous people in the world are the ones who know exactly what they want, and are determined to get it.

I suppose this story is about some of those people. But now (unless I'm just getting sentimental as the end looms into view) I don't blame Cambridge for nurturing or accommodating them. The college was its own universe, and it contained multitudes. I myself could have taken much more from it, if I'd wanted to. But I was too young, too guarded: too frightened, more than anything else. For most of my time there I was a witness, not a participant. But some of what I witnessed was interesting. At least, I hope you find it so.

III
The Party

So I'll begin, if I may, with a short anecdote which will give you some sense of how very hopeless and very out of my depth I was when I arrived at St Stephen's College, Cambridge, in the autumn of 1980.

The story is true. My friends Joanna Reeves and Christopher Swann, among others, will be able to confirm it.

I was nineteen years old and had spent the last seven years at a state school in Middlesbrough, in the north-east of England. At the time it was rare for anyone from that school to go on to university at all: winning a place at Cambridge was unprecedented. Did I have a chip on my shoulder when I arrived? Not really. Mainly I was just nervous. True, I quickly made some friends but before I get on to that let me get this story out of the way. It's pretty embarrassing from my point of view. I still get hot flushes when I think about it.

Picture the scene. My first week at Cambridge, and in the pigeon-hole at the foot of my staircase I find an invitation to freshers' drinks in the Master's Lodge.

Already, there were three words in that sentence that were new to me. I had not realized that I was a 'fresher' (a student new to the college), that for the next three years I was to have a 'Master', or that my new Master lived in a 'Lodge'. This 'Lodge', it turned out, was not some kind of log cabin standing in the grass at the centre of Joseph's Court (although that was what the word suggested to me). No – it was an extended, self-contained suite of rooms which formed the whole of the eastern side of the sixteenth-century Kite's Court, adjacent to the river Cam. Bigger than many country houses, in fact, and entered by a massive, imposing arched doorway which, on the evening of the party, I stood outside for about five minutes before steeling myself to enter.

It was around six o'clock, on the second Thursday of the

Michaelmas term. I finally summoned the courage to get inside by tucking myself behind a group of much more confident freshers who had just arrived together. That way I managed to sidle in more or less unnoticed. We were directed up the stairs into a huge, oak-panelled reception room which was full of students, most of them looking perfectly confident in their gowns (I felt excruciatingly conspicuous in mine) and knocking back the sherry as if they owned the place.

After standing around in terrified silence for a while, I finally spotted somebody I knew, a young lad who lived on my staircase. However, he only deigned to speak to me for a minute or two, before being buttonholed by two people who'd gone to the same school as him (Westminster), whereupon he left me high and dry.

Now, I don't know what the criteria were for being invited to that party. Most of the people there were either freshers or dons. But somehow I managed to find myself talking to someone who wasn't a member of college at all. Maybe he was staying there as a guest of the Master or something. Anyway, he was about fifty (I realize now – at the time I thought he was probably eighty or more) and it turned out he was a C of E clergyman. Though not just any old clergyman, as I soon discovered.

'What are you here to study?' he asked me, in his outrageously patrician voice.

'Medicine,' I riposted. Then I fell silent, until I realized that I was probably expected to ask a question back. At which point I came out with the killer line: 'And what do you do?'

'Oh, I'm just visiting Cambridge,' he answered. 'Actually, I'm a bishop.'

A bishop! A fucking bishop, for Christ's sake! Here I was, just a young kid really, fresh from a council estate in Ormesby, who had never spoken to anyone posher than his own schoolteachers before. And now I was supposed to be making polite conversation with a bishop.

Well, the simple thing to have done would have been to ask him where he was bishop *of*. That was the obvious question to ask. And I did ask him that, after a fashion. But there was one thing I did know about bishops, and that was that the place they were bishops of was called a 'bishopric'. Don't ask me how I knew this, but it was a piece of information that had lodged in my brain, and I was determined to show it off. But I was also panicking, and I desperately wanted to look as though I belonged at that party, so somehow – God knows how my thought processes worked – I decided that bishops themselves probably didn't call it that, that they probably had a cool, slangy sort of term for it, and if I was also going to look cool and down-with-the-bishops, that was what I should use. So in the next second, I honestly heard myself saying not, 'Where are you bishop of?' like a normal person. But:

'Oh, a bishop, really?'

And then: 'So – do you have a nice pric?'

. . .

I don't remember how he answered: or indeed anything at all that happened after that, until I found myself outside in Kite's Court some time later, howling in fury at the autumn moon.

IV

The Friends

'Of course, you know what a psychiatrist would say if you told him that story?'

I gave Chris a weary stare. I knew exactly what he was thinking.

'Don't tell me – repressed homosexuality?'

Jo laughed and Chris said: 'Well, it's pretty obvious, isn't it?'

'I didn't want to sleep with this bishop, I promise you. He was three times my age, and he wasn't even good-looking.'

Chris shrugged. 'It just seems a very revealing thing to have said.'

'Well, thank you, Sigmund Freud. I'm quite capable of making my own diagnoses, as it happens.'

Obviously, I can't remember if those were the precise things we said: but I think they would have been fairly typical of the conversations I was having with Chris and Jo, just a couple of weeks after meeting them.

How was it that we had already discovered each other, so soon after arriving at college? Tempting to think that it was down to feral instinct, that we had just found ourselves irresistibly drawn to each other by some sort of kindred magnetism. Well, there is an element of truth in that. Jo and Chris were grammar-school kids, so one step higher on the strange British social/educational ladder than I was, but in St Stephen's terms that still made all three of us oiks, urchins, slum-dwellers. So we recognized that in each other, and it formed a large part of the bond between us. She was from Manchester, Chris was from Taunton. To my ears, Jo had all but lost her regional accent – many years earlier, I imagine. Chris, when he arrived at Cambridge, still had something of a Somerset burr, but he discarded it as soon as he could. He endured about one term's worth of jokes about mangelwurzels and cider-drinking, invariably accompanied by a chorus of 'I've Got a Brand New Combine Harvester', and after that it was gone. St Stephen's was a learning curve, for all of us.

So yes, there was that instinctual coming-together, certainly. But, on a more practical level: Jo and Chris had luckily managed to find each other at that freshers' party, while I was busy humiliating myself with the Bishop of wherever. That's how they became friends. As for Chris and me, we had been brought together by our mutual interest in avant-garde theatre. OK, that is not strictly true. In the second week of term, we had both attended a production by the Cambridge Avant-Garde Theatre Group in the unwelcoming atmosphere of the Leslie Stephen Room at Trinity Hall. It was a political piece called *May '68* and we had both been drawn there, I'm afraid to say, by a review in *Cam* magazine which promised that three female members of the cast would be naked throughout the performance. This would indeed have been the case, if we had gone there the evening before. But since then, unfortunately, the production had been closed down by Cambridge city council owing to alleged breaches of fire regulations. It seems highly unlikely that this was the real reason, in retrospect, but in our youthful naivety we took the blow on the chin, and instead sloped off together to the Arts cinema in Market Passage for a challenging double bill of *L'Avventura* and *L'Année dernière à Marienbad*. After that, since the pubs were closed, Chris invited me back to his room for a pint or two, and by three o'clock in the morning another tentative friendship had been formed.

The odd thing, I suppose, is that if Chris had for some reason visited Middlesbrough and found himself sitting next to me in a pub, he would have stood out a mile as a posh Southerner, and I would have had nothing to say to him. But at Cambridge we found ourselves on a very different playing field. Here it was enough that we dressed, if not in exactly the same way, at least not in the uniform of the public-school boys: no tweed jackets or yellow trousers for us. We wore jackets our mums had bought for us off the peg from the local department store, and jeans, and shirts from M&S and the same shoes we had been wearing to school for the last three years. And Chris, at least, could accept that he was talking to someone called 'Brian' without making fun of the name, without scratching his head and saying, 'You know what, I don't think I've ever met a Brian before. It's not really a name you encounter south of Watford, is it?' All enunciated, of course, in that ironic Home Counties drawl which is only ever used by people cushioned by so much privilege that nothing life throws at them can ever seem like more than a wryly amusing joke. And talking of regional dialect, can you imagine the fun those Etonians and Harrovians had with mine! All I had to do was step into the college bar and ask for a pint. That was enough for general hilarity to break out and for everyone to start shouting, 'Howay, lads!' and 'Canny neet tho but!' in accents that ranged from Brummie to Glaswegian and Welsh to Scouse. Oh, how I (didn't) laugh.

Jo was another one who saw no need to join in with this. Of the three of us, she was probably the most conventional. After all, years later she did become a vicar. Jo was the sort of person who attended her supervisions dutifully and handed in her essays on time but I can't say that I noticed she was very religious back then. Perhaps I was just unobservant, or didn't see what I didn't want to see. In retrospect, with her strong moral character and fierce loyalty, she was the bond that held the three of us together: it was no wonder that when she and I started going out with each other for a few months, beginning in our second term, it messed with the dynamics of our trio. After that, Chris and I drifted apart somewhat, although we never fell out or anything like that. But anyway, I'm getting ahead of myself . . .

Before moving on, there is somebody else I should mention, if only in passing. Another young man who lived on my corridor. Thomas Cope was his name, although we all called him Tommy. He came from the Midlands and he was studying English literature and he was another grammar-school boy, which means that he could, in theory, have made our threesome of misfits and lost souls into a quartet. But Tommy was too much of a loner for that. He was the quietest and shyest guy any of us had ever met, and unless you managed to catch him walking to the library or to a seminar, you never saw him at all. He passed through St Stephen's without leaving the slightest trace of his presence. None of us ever really knew what he was doing in his room. He did occasionally publish poetry in the college magazine, usually inspired by whichever female student he'd developed a passion for that week. (His romantic yearnings were transient, but intense while they lasted.) However, it turned out that he had also been writing short stories and even novels, which he began to publish in the years after we'd graduated. Much to the surprise of us all, some of them turned out to be mildly satirical in nature, and furthermore to suggest an interest in politics, something of which he'd never given any of us the least inkling when he was a student. I don't really follow these things, but I was told that one of them – a sophomore effort under the title *Quite the Mash-Up* – achieved what in literary circles is known as a 'modest success'. Who knew.

V
The Times

Now, when did the 1970s end, and the 1980s begin? I should warn you that there is a right answer and a wrong answer to this question. And one small clue: the right answer is not at midnight on 31st December 1979.

I was nineteen years old when I began my degree – and nineteen, in my opinion, is no age to go to university: certainly not Cambridge, and certainly not St Stephen's College. I think that possibly, just possibly, by the time I turned thirty I might have had the maturity to deal with the experiences that the next three years thrust on me. But for a start, who really knows what they want to do with their lives at the age of nineteen? Are you supposed to have decided, by then, how you want to spend the next five decades? It's absurd. I had enrolled at St Stephen's as a medical student. But I had no real desire to become a doctor, as I understood the job. Breaking terrible news to cancer patients and giving colonoscopies to old men was not my idea of an enticing future. I was more interested in the history and philosophy of medicine, at that stage, and I was more interested in studying the human mind than the human body. I'd chosen science subjects for A level because that was the direction my parents wanted me to go in, but my heart was still with Mr Gordon, my brilliant English teacher, and the radical writers he had encouraged me to read in the summer of '77, the summer after my O levels. He had introduced me to Orwell and Zola, Brecht and Céline. Writers like these remained my heroes, and during my years at Cambridge you were far more likely to see me carrying a copy of *Voyage au bout de la nuit* than *Gray's Anatomy.*

In short, I was in search of a counterculture. Well, good luck with that, in the United Kingdom in the autumn of 1980. In music, punk had been and gone, and now everyone had discovered synths and drum machines and was making awful robotic electro-pop. ('New romantics', indeed!) Our film industry was finished. As far as I could see (I was no expert), the British novel was an old white men's club revolving around the likes of Fowles, Golding, Amis and Burgess. Maybe I was just looking in the wrong places. Feminism had been kicking off for at least a decade and in a few years I would finally catch up, when I discovered the likes of Angela Carter and Kathy Acker. If I'd known a bit more about what had been happening in France I might have been reading Foucault and Lacan and Roland Barthes already. But even Britain's left-wing intelligentsia (such as it was) seemed mired in the past, as typified by the choice of the senescent Michael Foot as Labour leader. Which left me looking for a political home as much as an intellectual one.

I'm not sure that Jo and Chris shared these frustrations. Jo could never be persuaded to talk much about politics, and when she did, her views turned out to be pretty middle-of-the-road. Chris was a more complicated case. Whereas I'd voted Labour in the 1979 election so took no responsibility for the Thatcherite nightmare that was beginning to unfold, he had been just too young to have voted back then: but he did confide in me, one drunken evening, that he would probably have voted for Thatcher if he'd been able to. But he also said that, over the next three years, St Stephen's had somehow 'radicalized' him, which is a curious claim, since it wasn't exactly a hotbed of Marxist thought. What he meant, I'm guessing, is that the most politically engaged people at the college were all right wing and were all so horrible that you could hardly want anything other than to run as fast as you could in the opposite ideological direction. (I mention no names, of course. Well, apart from the obvious one: yes, I'm looking at you, Roger Wagstaff.)

Jo and Chris, in any case, were focused on their courses in a way that I simply wasn't. This was the first of my pre-clinical years, and hard as I tried to interest myself in the niceties of hormone activity, the allure of organelles or the fascinating intricacies of the integumentary system, my heart simply wasn't in it. People who didn't live through them assume that, whether you were a Thatcherite or not, the eighties were at the very least a dynamic era, but as I hinted, I don't believe the decade had really started yet, and when it came to the academic life my own energy levels were far more suited to the fag-end of the seventies, the torpor and paralysis of the Callaghan years. I spent my evenings nursing pints of Guinness in the college bar or, worse still, watching television in the Junior Common Room, where all the real losers and sad cases were to be found slumped in armchairs, staring either into space or at the jittery black-and-white TV screen. Daytimes were better, because I at least had enough intellectual curiosity to attend a few lectures.

Not medical lectures, though. I was not a very conscientious student in that regard (for which I paid the penalty in my first end-of-year exams). Instead, I would go with Jo to her philosophy lectures, or with Chris to his history ones. Sometimes, I would even take matters into my own hands and venture into the place which for a while became the favourite of all my Cambridge stamping grounds: the English faculty. This was a superficially unattractive, modern set of buildings on the Grange Road site not far from Gilbert Scott's imposing University Library, but to me it had an irresistible lustre. For a start there always seemed to be large numbers of female students here, and they were much prettier and more glamorous than the ones studying medicine. Furthermore they would all be carrying copies of *The Waves* and *Wuthering Heights* under their arms, so there was always the tantalizing prospect that you might get lost in an absorbing conversation with them about literature. (Not that this actually happened in my case, ever.) It felt like a rarefied and exotic environment to me, where the air seemed to be constantly buzzing with *ideas*, which were thin on the ground in my own faculty, to say the least. Sure, even here there was no shortage of crusty old dons whose lectures were guaranteed to put you in a coma, as they laboriously read out, for the thirtieth time, the same chapter from a book that they had published in 1949 and never revised since. (There was a certain lecturer, a specialist in one particular Elizabethan metaphysical poet, who was notorious for this: his book was popularly known as *Donne to Death.*) But there were also younger dons whose lectures had a flamboyant, theatrical quality, who were chipping away at the conventions, who were opening the doors to Marxism and Structuralism and popular culture, and who could fill a lecture theatre to overflowing, with disappointed punters turned away at the door.

One day in that first Michaelmas term, I attended just such a packed lecture by one of these modish figures, who was talking on the subject of 'Beckett and the Double Act'. I was reading *Malone Dies* at the time so this appeared to be right up my street. The lecture was mainly about *Waiting for Godot* and how Vladimir and Estragon were based on Laurel and Hardy, with all the business with the bowler hats and so on. However, the speaker also made a more general point which I thought was very interesting. Just as the hero of a play, he said – be it Oedipus or Hamlet or Arturo Ui – was often an archetype, standing for the individual consciousness of every human being, so the double act could be seen as the simplest representation of an entire society. Here, in the comic interplay between a Laurel and a Hardy, or an Abbott and Costello, you had a microcosm of how all people interacted with one another: frustration, misunderstanding, getting in each other's way, but also total interdependence and – in the case of the greatest double acts – real and unwavering love. Look at Vladimir and Estragon, he said – look at Laurel and Hardy; even look at Morecambe and Wise – and you see a pared-down image of a more-or-less functioning society. Human beings doing their best to get along together; unable to hide their impatience, sometimes, with the recalcitrant behaviour of their fellow earth-dwellers, but each one unable to do without the other.

Now, I found it interesting that he mentioned Morecambe and Wise. At this time, back in the early eighties, they were still on television (I had been watching them in the Junior Common Room just a few nights before) but they were beginning to look old, and the shows were past their best. It was hard to imagine how fondly they would be remembered forty years later. But if you look back at that time, now, I think you can see the reason why. Back in the 1970s, when television shows like theirs sometimes used to get more than twenty million viewers, I think people used to believe in a different kind of society. We had a model for it, back then: more or less organized, more or less functioning, held together by the belief that things should not be shared out too unequally. It was imperfect, of course, full of injustices and disagreements and bumps in the road, but above all it was cohesive: just like one of the great double acts.

In Britain, you could say that we started believing in that sort of society in 1945, and stopped believing in it about forty years later, when people began to be encouraged to think that individual happiness, individual success, individual rights were all that mattered. And now, in the 2020s, a lot of people are nostalgic for that brief post-war moment. For a time when our bowler hats may have got run over by steamrollers and our song-and-dance routines may have gone comically wrong but at least we could depend on each other, at least we had each other's backs.

I tend to think that one of the most powerful signifiers of the new individualism was the mobile phone, that improbable object which began life as a hilarious plastic brick with a radio antenna and has now become ubiquitous and indispensable, the centrepiece and cornerstone of our lives. Do you remember when it was publicly launched in the UK? New Year's Day, 1985. Do you remember who launched it? Ernie Wise, of course. Eric Morecambe had died the previous year, leaving Ernie alone, bereft: that perfect little microcosm of society with which he and his partner had entertained the nation for years had been permanently shattered. He was on his own, now: a fitting symbol of our new individualism which has turned out (why did no one think of this at the time?) to be just another word for loneliness.

So, don't let anyone tell you that the eighties began when the seventies ended. The eighties began on the 1st of January 1985, when Ernie Wise made the first public mobile call in the United Kingdom.

Meanwhile, back in Cambridge, back in the autumn of 1980, we were all still living in the hinterland.

VI
The Cult

It was amazing how quickly I took Cambridge for granted; became bored with it, even. It's true that I never really stopped being overawed by the beauty of the colleges, St Stephen's in particular: the arrogant scale of Joseph's Court, the severe beauty of the sixteenth-century Cygnet Library, even the college chapel which of course I never set foot in after taking a brief glance at it during the freshers' tour in my first week. The contrast with home was just too great and I could never quite get over it. However, I was also surprised that many of the students were so stupid and incurious, and that dullness seemed to be among the primary qualifications for becoming a Cambridge lecturer (especially in the medical faculty).

There were exceptions to this, of course. St Stephen's was not without its little pockets of academic glamour. Perhaps the most notable of these was to be found in the aura of prestige and mystique that surrounded Professor Emeric Coutts and his followers.

Coutts was a philosophy don in his late forties who had already been a fellow of the college for almost twenty years, and was one of the few fellows who had achieved a measure of fame outside the university itself. Besides intimidating his students with his rigorously traditional readings of Descartes, Hegel and the other pillars of the Western canon, he had surprised everybody by penning a rather successful popular guide to philosophy (*How Thinking Can Improve Your Life*) and following it with a long political essay which, even if it hadn't sold in the same numbers, was in its way even more influential. This was called *How I Became a Conservative*, and on publication in 1977 it quickly came to the attention of certain politicians who at that time were in opposition, namely Margaret Thatcher and her ideological guru Sir Keith Joseph. Invitations to lunch were rumoured to have followed, and before long Thatcher was namechecking Professor Coutts in interviews as 'my favourite philosopher'. He soon became a regular guest on the television discussion programmes which – to the general amazement, these days, of anyone under the age of about forty – were a regular feature of the schedules back then: grey, unhealthy-looking men in suits sitting around a table debating the thorny issues of the day in complete sentences and well-bred accents, before civilly agreeing to differ (within certain unspoken but well-defined parameters of acceptable opinion). Coutts became quite the fixture on these shows, and also began putting his name to the occasional column in the right-wing tabloid newspapers, although it was an open secret that these pieces were mainly written by his students, since the Professor himself wasn't fluent in the language of popular journalism.

Very soon after arriving at Cambridge, therefore, Jo discovered that she had been landed with a philosophy supervisor and director of studies who could, without too much exaggeration, be described as a celebrity. In fact – and this might be the very definition of a baptism by fire – Emeric Coutts was the first Cambridge don that she met, at the start of her second week, when he invited her to tea in his rooms to discuss that term's programme of study. The way she told it to Chris and me afterwards, it was a stressful experience. Once she had arrived and settled herself into an armchair, he asked her if she would like a cup of tea. She replied that yes, she would love a cup of tea. He asked her what kind of tea she would like. Jo did not know that there were different kinds of tea. She knew that there were different *brands* of tea – PG Tips, Brooke Bond, and so on – but not different *kinds*. Sensing her uncertainty, Professor Coutts made some suggestions, but words like 'Earl Grey' and 'lapsang souchong' were just meaningless assortments of letters to her. Finally she heard him mention jasmine tea and that sounded OK, she knew what jasmine was and, better still, she liked the smell of it. But when he brought her a bone-china cup filled with pale orange liquid she freaked out because she had never had tea without milk before and indeed she did not even know that sometimes people drank tea without milk and so she asked him to put some milk in it.

In Jo's version of events, Professor Coutts's reaction to this request took the form of amusement more than anything else. He made a great show of saying, 'Jasmine tea with milk? Are you quite sure about that?' in a way which already made her realize that she had made a mistake, but she couldn't go back on it now, and in fact she doubled down on it and said, 'That's how we always have it at home.' To which he replied, 'How extraordinary,' as he very slowly and carefully poured milk from a tiny silver jug into her tea, which turned a revolting colour ('It wasn't brown,' she said afterwards, 'it was a sort of . . . milky orange'). 'And is that how everybody takes their oolongs, in Wrexham?' he asked: a question which just made Jo more confused than ever, partly because she had never heard the word 'oolongs' before, but also because he somehow seemed to have got the idea that she was from Wrexham, and rather than allow him to persist in this illusion for the next three years, she decided to nip it in the bud by saying, 'Actually I come from Stockport,' to which Professor Coutts said, 'Ah! I do apologize,' and then, 'I didn't realize Stockport was in Wales,' another totally random comment, causing Jo yet more confusion, which she attempted to resolve by saying, 'Stockport is in Manchester,' to which he replied, in a tone of surprise, 'But you have a Welsh accent,' which she was about to deny, but then didn't, because she had never really thought about it before but maybe she *did* have a Welsh accent, and had never noticed it, although really, why would she have a Welsh accent, since she wasn't from Wales, but anyway, instead of either confirming or denying the Welshness of her accent she just muddied the waters even further, by saying, 'Well, I suppose Stockport isn't really *in* Manchester. It's part of the Greater Manchester area, I suppose, technically speaking.' To which Professor Coutts said, 'Ah! I see – so it's a suburb of Manchester,' obliging Jo to reflect on this and to insist, since she knew she was talking to someone for whom the precise use of language was crucially important, 'No, it's not really a suburb, it's a town in its own right,' and Professor Coutts pondered this and said, 'So – a town within a town, in other words?' 'Well, not exactly,' said Jo, 'because Manchester is a city, not a town.' 'Really?' he answered. 'But surely a city must have a cathedral, to be a *bona fide* city.' 'But Manchester has a cathedral,' Jo told him, to which he replied, 'Manchester has a cathedral? You astound me,' and then for the next half-minute or more he could be heard muttering to himself, 'Manchester has a cathedral! "Manchester Cathedral". How very surprising. I never heard the like . . .' until his voice tailed away, leaving an excruciating silence which Jo filled by taking her first tentative sip of the tea and finding its floral milkiness every bit as disgusting as she had feared.

Not the most promising start to a teacher–pupil relationship, on the whole, but things got better after that. Jo was an exceptionally bright and hard-working student, and over the next few weeks these qualities won her Professor Coutts's respect. By the middle of the Lent term she had risen so high in her august supervisor's estimation that she received a singular honour: she was invited to attend one of his Thursday-evening salons.

Now this was, without question, the hottest ticket at St Stephen's College. Nobody could remember when the tradition started, but Coutts had been hosting these events for at least five years. Their purpose, apparently, was to provide an informal setting in which political, cultural and philosophical discussion might take place, but everyone assumed there was more to the salons than simply that, and various outlandish rumours attached to them, usually circulated by people who had never attended one. There was talk of secret initiation ceremonies, involving a vellum-bound visitors' book which had to be signed in blood; oaths of allegiance which were sworn on a copy of *Atlas Shrugged* by Ayn Rand; a quartet of female undergraduates who entertained the guests by singing Renaissance madrigals while wearing see-through tabards. All of this, Jo assured me, after she had attended one of these meetings for the first time, was absolute nonsense. She told me that she'd had to listen to an exceptionally dry talk on US–Chinese trade agreements and the catering had consisted of nothing more exciting than one small glass of lukewarm Chardonnay and a bowl of peanuts. It was true that Coutts had a harpsichord in his room (or was it a clavichord?) upon which one of the college's music scholars had performed three or four of Bach's preludes and fugues: but he remained decently dressed throughout, much to Jo's (and no doubt everyone else's) relief.

This was all very disappointing to hear, but soon enough I would have a chance to learn the truth for myself. By the time the summer term's final salon was announced, Jo and I had embarked upon our brief, doomed attempt at going out together, and she had also ingratiated herself so thoroughly with her supervisor that she felt brave enough to ask if she could bring a guest.

'A guest?' he said, looking at her in a manner which (she told me) she prayed to God was not meant to be flirtatious. 'Do you mean a boyfriend?'

She nodded, and I was in.

It was a bright, warm evening in the middle of May, and I'd say there were about twenty-five or thirty of us crowded into the largest room of Professor Coutts's generous suite. Some were from St Stephen's; many had come from other colleges. There were dons, undergraduates and postgraduates. After the obligatory performance on the clavichord (or was it a harpsichord?) the guest speaker was introduced. He was a junior minister in the current government, whose overfed torso strained at the confines of a bespoke three-piece suit as he treated us to a lengthy disquisition on the subject of 'The Moral Case for Wealth Inequality'. His thesis, in a nutshell, was that the trade unions had to be defeated, not because they were militant and wanted to hold the country to ransom by striking, but because it was simply in a country's long-term economic interest to underpay its workers. Private profit should be maximized, he insisted; only in this way could management be offered a proper incentive to pursue efficiency and productivity. And if the people at the top were well remunerated, they would spend their money, and eventually it would spread throughout society; not by taxing the rich, but through the natural and immutable operation of the free market.

I realize now that I was listening to an early advocate of trickle-down economics. The term didn't exist at the time – or if it did, I wasn't familiar with it. Anyway, I thought he was talking the most ridiculous nonsense, but out of respect for Jo, I held my tongue. I didn't want to embarrass her and get stereotyped as the bolshie Northern boyfriend. So I sat and listened, good as gold, to the talk itself and then to the discussion that followed (the main thrust of which was that the speaker hadn't taken his argument far enough) and then rewarded myself afterwards by allowing the butler – yes, there was a butler, I don't know where he had appeared from – to refill my wine glass up to the brim.

Jo was talking to another first-year student sitting next to her, so I had nothing much to occupy me except for the wine and the chicken vol-au-vents which Coutts had laid on as a treat for this final session. I watched as most of the other guests said their farewells and made their exits. Finally the great man himself addressed a few words to me – probably as a way of hinting that I should leave – and said, 'Not a bad little Sauvignon, is it? I would offer you some more but that seems to have been the last bottle.' I'm ashamed to say that I held my glass up to the light as if I knew something about wine and said, in an effort to impress him, 'Very nice, very drinkable. Good year, that.' He nodded at me politely – being perfectly capable, I'm sure, of spotting a grade one bullshitter when he saw one – then made his excuses, said goodbye to Jo, and disappeared through a doorway at the back of the room.

'What did you make of that, then?' Jo asked me a couple of hours later. We were in bed together in her room in Leonard's Yard, and had been enjoying a moment of post-coital drowsiness. Her head was nestled against my shoulder, and I was stroking her hair with one hand, while the other rested on my . . . Well, perhaps I don't have to go into details.

'Bollocks,' I said, succinctly. 'Dangerous bollocks, if it comes to that. These people don't want a prosperous society. They just want more money for themselves and their mates.'

'You should have said something, then.'

'Really? You would have liked that?'

'Yes. I was waiting for you to do it. It would have livened things up. As it was, all you did was thank Emeric for giving you some nice wine, after everyone had gone.' I said nothing in response to this at first, stung by her criticism. Meanwhile Jo continued, thinking aloud: 'Where *did* everybody go, anyway? Did you notice at the end that the room was almost empty? But not many of them left by the front door.'

I didn't take much notice of this, being still preoccupied by how disappointed she had sounded in me. Was I being held back, even now, by social awkwardness, my ingrained sense of class inferiority, or was the truth even worse than that? Was Cambridge already getting to me, making me lose grip on my core beliefs?

I turned towards Jo and asked, with a note of urgency in my voice: 'Was it embarrassing when I said that thing about the wine? Be honest: did I make a fool of myself tonight?'

Jo pondered the question but didn't answer it. Instead she just smiled to herself and laughed and said: 'Well, at least you didn't ask him if he had a nice prick.'

As a postscript to this story, I might mention my parents' reaction, a few months later, when Emeric popped up on television one night. It was about halfway through the long, long summer holiday (my God, those holidays dragged), and Mum and Dad and I had been watching some comedy programme on TV together when a late-night chat show about books came on. Normally this would not have been tolerated for more than about five minutes in our household but when I saw that Emeric was taking part I pointed at the screen and said, 'I know that guy.'

My dad turned to me in amazement. 'What do you mean, you know him?'

'He teaches at Cambridge,' I said. 'He invited me to a party in his rooms.'

Yes, I believe I did actually put it like that, such was the desire to impress my parents. And it worked. They found it unbelievable that their own son should now be rubbing shoulders and quaffing Sauvignon with members of what would probably today be called the metropolitan elite. In our world, the people who appeared on television and the people who lived in Middlesbrough – our friends, our neighbours, our own family – could not possibly encounter each other: they belonged to different social and geographical galaxies. This was the natural order of things, as far as my parents were concerned, and this sudden exception was staggering to them. They couldn't get their heads around it. As for me, I quietly (and not so modestly) revelled in the fact that I had flabbergasted them in this way.

My comeuppance came the following morning in the form of a letter from Jo, telling me in fond but no uncertain terms that she had decided it would be for the best, on the whole, if we ended our relationship and went back to just being friends again. I didn't really understand – and still don't really understand – what had brought this on, but of course I respected her decision. It would be the cue for me to embark, on my return to Cambridge in October 1981, on a crusade of sexual adventuring through the somewhat limited pool of female undergraduates at St Stephen's, and while this was fun, in its way, it was a poor substitute for being with her. Our friendship throughout the next few months was rocky – these things always are, in the aftermath of a break-up – but we recovered, and in the decades since Cambridge we have kept in touch, and come to like each other more than ever (I hope). My feelings for her had run deep, deeper than I ever admitted, I think. For all her sometimes comical primness and sense of propriety, she was a special person: strong, loyal, admirable. A beautiful person, one might almost say. I wish I'd been better at expressing what I felt for her. I loved Joanna, after all: and I don't think I ever told her that. Not at the time, and never since. She was my first, too: the very first, for me. I don't think I ever told her that either.

VII
The Bear Pit

Another disaster that had befallen me during my first two weeks at Cambridge, in addition to my *faux pas* with the bishop, was the fact that I had allowed myself to be talked into acquiring life membership of the Cambridge Union. The current president had offered all St Stephen's freshers a tour of the Union building one morning, and had given us an hour-long, incredibly hard sell which had resulted in me foolishly parting with £40 – quite a substantial sum back then, or so it seemed to me. However, it soon turned out that belonging to this organization conferred none of the benefits of joining an actual union: it didn't stand up for students' rights, or campaign for more generous grants, or anything useful like that. Pretty much all you got for your money was use of the Union building just off Bridge Street, which included a bar (not very nice) and a library (pretty good). And then, of course, there was also the debating chamber, which to be fair seemed to be many people's main reason for joining.

The Cambridge Union has never had the prestige or pulling power of its brother organization at Oxford, which at that time routinely hosted Prime Ministers past and present, and during the second half of the eighties was a breeding ground for most of the post-Brexit Conservative government, from Boris Johnson downwards. Nonetheless, the debates at Cambridge were well attended, and offered the chance to be in the same room as a fair number of middle-ranking politicians or minor celebrities. In my first term I'd been to a couple of these events, but can't say that I enjoyed them very much. I had been expecting the cut-and-thrust of argument from the sharpest young minds in the country, but in fact the debating chamber was more like a bear pit, where the participants traded personal insults far more readily than finely honed discussion points, egged on by a rowdy, usually drunken audience, and culminating more often than not in the popular ceremony of 'de-bagging', where the speaker with the lowest approval rating would be set upon from all sides, pinned down to the floor and have his trousers removed and waved triumphantly aloft by the jubilant crowd. Not a very uplifting spectacle, in my opinion, although no doubt it was a good training for future debates in the Punch and Judy Show that is the British House of Commons, where many of the participants would ultimately find themselves.

I had resolved not to bother with any of these grisly occasions again, until some time midway through the Michaelmas term, 1981, when Chris asked me if I would take him along as my guest. Inevitably, during the time of my relationship with Jo, he and I had grown further apart; just as inevitably, as soon as we split up our friendship had been rekindled. The two provincial state-school boys could not remain distant for long: each needed the other as an ally in the unspoken, perpetual war against the Etonian and Harrovian hordes. So we quickly relaxed back into an easy-going friendship, and spent plenty of low-key evenings together in the college bar or the Eagle or the Blue Boar.

The theme of this particular debate was going to be – wait for it – 'This House Recommends the Abolition of the Welfare State'. As always, there were to be two speakers on each side. The custom was for one of them to be a student, and the other to be a public figure of some sort. Proposing the motion tonight was an economics student at St Stephen's called Roger Wagstaff. (I didn't know him, myself, but it seemed that he and Chris had one or two friends in common.) And alongside him was none other than Henry Winshaw, once a Labour MP, now a policy advisor to Mrs Thatcher and a hardline right-wing commentator for the *Daily Express*. A powerful combination, as it turned out. On the opposite side was the Right Honourable Roy Jenkins MP, another ex-Labour figure: but his defection had been less drastic than Winshaw's, because earlier that year he had been one of four Labour MPs to have left the party on the grounds that it had become too militant and extreme. This 'Gang of Four' had founded, in its stead, a new outfit called the Social Democratic Party, which some people (I think Chris might have been one of them) believed was going to break the mould of

British politics. As for the fourth speaker, that was the whole reason Chris wanted to go. It was a student on his history course, one Michael Harwood. This guy had been to school at Winchester so in theory he was in the enemy camp, but Chris thought that he was a good sort, and wanted to be there to support him. He was a quiet and reserved student, by all accounts, but sincere in his politics. Chris seemed a little anxious – not without reason – that he was going to be torn apart by the other speakers.

Shortly before the debate, we met for a couple of pints at the Eagle and then headed off to the Union at seven, in plenty of time to get good seats. There was already quite a crowd filing into the chamber. Just ahead of us was somebody else that Chris knew. Following behind, and seeing only a short-back-and-sides haircut, I thought it was a man at first, but when Chris tapped her on the shoulder and she turned around I soon realized my mistake.

'Hi, Rebecca,' he said.

'Oh, hello, Christopher.' She seemed far less enthusiastic about meeting in this way than he did. Her voice could hardly have been colder.

'Brian, this is Rebecca Wood. Rebecca, my friend Brian Collier.'

We exchanged nods and a flaccid handshake.

'Rebecca's doing English,' he explained. 'She's a friend of Tommy's.'

'"Friend" might be overdoing it a bit,' she said, and the temperature dropped another few degrees.

'I suppose you're here to support Michael,' Chris continued, undaunted. 'Somehow I think he's going to need all the help he can get.'

Now Rebecca laughed: and if you wanted an example of the famous 'mirthless laugh' beloved of novelists, you could hardly have wished for a better one than this.

'Oh dear, Christopher,' she said. 'Backing the losing side again, are you?'

'What do you mean?'

'I mean that I'm rooting for Roger.'

'Really? But surely you can't believe . . . surely you don't support the motion?'

Rebecca laughed again. We were inside the chamber by now, and as she took her seat next to Wagstaff, we both noticed that she was carrying with her a number of manila folders filled with paper. 'We have facts and figures to support our argument,' she said, tapping the folders complacently. 'Look at your chap! My God, this is going to be a bloodbath.'

It's true that Michael's demeanour at this point did not inspire confidence: his speech was written out on a couple of sheets of lined notepaper, and he was rehearsing it aloud to himself in a soft voice as the audience took their seats. His face was green and he was shaking with nerves. Roy Jenkins hadn't turned up yet. Meanwhile Roger Wagstaff and Henry Winshaw were chatting away like old friends.

A few years later, in his excellent book *A Pox on the Box* (which I recommend to anyone interested in the sorry decline of public service broadcasting in this country) the veteran television producer Alan Beamish described Henry Winshaw, in his later years, as a 'puffy, glowering old firebrand who stared at me across the table, thumping it with his fist and barking like a rabid dog'. That certainly squares with my memory of his performance that evening. He kicked off proceedings with a raucous broadside against 'bogus benefits claimants sucking on the teat of the nanny state', and was rewarded for his pains with numerous rounds of applause and a chorus of cheers. Towards the end, such was the force of his indignation, his neck started to bulge so much that I thought his spotted bow tie was going to ping off. Following this, Mr Jenkins had the floor, and had killed the atmosphere in the room stone dead within a few minutes, with a muted, rational, emollient speech setting out the achievements of the post-war Labour government but then undermining his case by wandering off on a tangent about how the unions were out of control and would have to be reined in. Muted applause greeted his contribution, after which Roger Wagstaff rose to his feet.

Now, there had been something comical in the spectacle of Henry Winshaw ranting until his voice was hoarse, his face getting redder and redder and the veins on his forehead standing out so vividly that it looked as though he might have been about to have an aneurysm. He was a fossil, a dinosaur, and it was quite easy to laugh him off on that basis. But this didn't apply in Wagstaff's case. There was something chilling in his calm, youthful rationality. His language was unemotional, and his statements were backed up with plausible statistics, occasionally taken from one sheet of paper or another handed over to him by Rebecca Wood, who seemed to be acting as some sort of unofficial assistant. Wagstaff's suit was so sharp, his haircut so smart, his accent so smooth, his tone so sweet and reasonable that it was easy to overlook, at times, the monstrosity of what he was proposing – which was, in essence, a society based entirely on the principle of the survival of the fittest. 'The poorest amongst us,' he argued, 'are poor for a reason. Not because some malevolent fate has dealt them a lousy hand, but because in a free society like this great country of ours, the same opportunities are available to everyone, and are there for the taking. So if you don't take them, I only have three words for you: *MORE . . . FOOL . . . YOU.*'

'Rubbish!' Chris shouted, unable to contain his indignation. His rewards were a condescending smile from Wagstaff, and one of Rebecca's signature frowns.

I noticed a figure sitting in the row behind them. Nodding along in agreement. Wincing a little, sometimes, at the rowdier moments, but on the whole observing these proceedings with benign, indulgent approval. Professor Emeric Coutts. I was surprised, I have to say. There was something happening in the chamber that night. A new kind of politics was making itself felt: tougher, nastier, more savage than the one we had been used to. Was Coutts happy about that? Did he really want to see his movement go down this road?

Whatever Furies we had been expecting to see unleashed upon the final speaker, they were nothing compared to the indignities he actually went through. He was only about thirty seconds into his speech before the jeering started. Cries of 'Pinko!', 'Lefty!', 'Trot!' and 'Wanker!' began to ricochet around the room. Then the missiles came: paper darts at first, shortly followed by a stink bomb, a squash racket, a roll of toilet paper, a slice of Victoria sponge, a wet flannel and a rancid tomato. To give him credit, Michael pressed on with his speech, but his well-chosen quotations from Nye Bevan and Tony Benn were submerged beneath the general howls of disapproval. Finally, before he had had a chance to sum up, and in response to a covert signal from Roger Wagstaff – nothing more than a nod and the raising of his index finger – four oversized members of the Sidney Sussex rugby First XV descended on the hapless orator, wrestled him to the ground and removed his trousers in a swift and ruthless movement. Roy Jenkins looked on in impotent horror, recoiling slightly in case there was a chance that he might be next. But he, at least, was to be spared that humiliation. It was only Michael who had to sit there in his Y-fronts while the votes were counted and the result announced.

The motion was carried by 183 votes to 27.

Chris and I went back to the Eagle and ordered another couple of pints. We were both a bit shell-shocked by what we had just witnessed. I had thought that some sort of private dinner would be laid on for all the speakers, but this didn't appear to be the case: Roy Jenkins was seen getting into a taxi and driving off to the station, while Michael Harwood had slipped off into the night, alone, probably heading to the college bar where he would no doubt start drinking heavily in order to ward off the first symptoms of PTSD. Meanwhile Roger Wagstaff, Emeric Coutts, Henry Winshaw and the President of the Union himself turned up at the pub a few minutes after we had seated ourselves, and were shown to a quiet corner table bearing a 'Reserved' sign. Rebecca Wood came in next, and we thought that she was going to join them, but apparently no place had been saved for her and she left by herself shortly afterwards, trying not to look disappointed. Meanwhile the VIPs were served steak, chips and red wine and embarked upon a convivial conversation conducted in low, animated voices.

I had not marked Chris down as the confrontational type, so what happened next surprised me. We drank up and were about to leave the pub, but in order to get to the exit we had to pass close by their table. Chris glared at Roger Wagstaff as he walked by, and since the glare was so direct and unavoidable, Wagstaff returned it. The two of them locked eyes for a few seconds, and then Chris had almost walked past the table when he suddenly stopped and turned.

I froze, and a wave of anxiety came over me. What was he going to do?

'That,' Chris said, after a somewhat dramatic pause, 'was one of the most disgraceful things I've ever seen.'

Wagstaff cut himself a morsel of steak and put it in his mouth before saying: 'Oh, come on, Swann. Spare us your grammar-school puritanism. They gave him his trousers back.'

'The atmosphere tonight did seem a little uncivilized, I must say,' Emeric remarked, sipping on his Merlot. 'I hope this isn't a portent of things to come.'

'Actually, I wasn't talking about that,' said Chris, focusing his ire solely on Wagstaff, it seemed. 'I was talking about *your* speech.'

'The one that carried the floor, you mean?'

'The creation of our welfare state,' said Chris, 'is one of post-war Britain's greatest achievements. And the National Health Service is its crowning glory.'

'Yawn,' said Roger, munching on a chip, and turned to Henry Winshaw. 'This,' he said – indicating Chris – 'is the sort of thing you're going to have to fight against.'

'Don't worry,' said Henry. 'Misplaced idealism is hardly an uncommon problem among British university students.' He laughed and slurped back some wine. 'Suffered from it myself once.'

'Mr Winshaw,' Roger explained (he'd had two or three glasses of wine, so his tongue had loosened by now), 'is currently advising the government on how the NHS can be streamlined.'

'Streamlined? And what does *that* mean, exactly?'

Roger was about to say more, when he noticed that Emeric was looking at him and shaking his head. He quickly took the hint.

'None of your business, Swann,' he said crisply. 'And by the way, you and your friend are interrupting a private dinner, so kindly go away and leave us alone.' He turned his back on us and finally, to drive the point home, pompously declared: 'This conversation is at an end.'

VIII
The Writer who Sang in his Sleep

Our story now moves forward one year, as I must describe the next time I attended one of Professor Coutts's famous salons.

There used to be a well-known tea shop in Cambridge called Auntie's. It was in St Mary's Passage, very close to the Market Square. A welcoming, old-fashioned sort of place. Exactly where you would take your parents for afternoon tea with scones and butter on a chilly November afternoon, when they came down to check up on you.

It was November 1982, in fact, when I was passing Auntie's late one afternoon and I glimpsed Jo sitting at a window table. The centre of Cambridge was suffused in that soft, dark blue, late-autumn light and I was walking along St Mary's Passage in a prematurely nostalgic frame of mind, realizing that I was going to miss this city when my brief time here came to an end. I saw Jo's silhouette outlined against the glowing amber lighting of the café and for a moment it pulled me up sharp. I was still a little bit in love with her, and things had never quite gone back to normal after our relationship ended. We didn't avoid each other, exactly, but there was still an awkwardness between us which I felt keenly, and suspect she did too. So I hesitated before going in to speak to her. But I was reassured by the fact that she wasn't alone. Tommy Cope, our mutual friend and would-be writer, was sitting with her, and so (to my surprise) was a third-year economics student called Nigel. I'd never spoken to this character before: he had lived on Chris's staircase in year one and we all used to make fun of him, so it was strange to see him sitting with her now. I decided to find out what was going on, and went inside to join them.

Poor young Tommy, I have to say, was looking even more wretched than usual. Needless to say, he was in the throes of one of his regular unrequited romantic obsessions, and when I heard the identity of his latest would-be *inamorata*, I realized that his situation was more desperate than ever. My first reaction on hearing the name was to laugh out loud. Luckily I stopped myself just in time, managed to adopt a concerned, friendly expression and merely said, in a sympathetic tone of voice:

'Rebecca? Rebecca Wood? Really?'

He nodded, his face a picture of misery. I looked down at the handwritten sheet of paper in front of him.

'Poem?'

He nodded again. With my eyes I asked if I could read it. He slid it wordlessly across the table.

Grey time, long petrified, hangs like a curse,
The ghost of deconstruction wages war;
My words align in strict formations, terse:
Obliquity shuts comprehension's door.
If 'meta' hides the meaning of my verse
It begs the question, what is 'meta' for?
My mind, that void . . . where nothing can replace
The logocentric emblem of your face.

There were a few more verses like this. I didn't really know what to say.

'What would your response be,' he asked me, 'if someone sent you that poem?'

'I think maybe Jo should answer that question.'

'I already have,' she said. 'I told him I wouldn't understand a word of it, and I'd much rather he just asked me out for a drink. Besides, he hasn't even shown it to her yet.'

Nigel let out a snigger. It was an unpleasant sound. I stared at him, then turned back to Tommy, who was insisting:

'But look, it's in *ottava rima*. One of the most demanding verse forms. That has to count for something, doesn't it?'

'I think Joanna's right,' Nigel chipped in.

'Well, I don't,' said Tommy. 'I still think poetry's the way to go.'

'OK,' I said. 'But how about something a bit more direct? Like . . . I don't know . . . "*Rebecca, Rebecca, please handle* my pecker"?'

This time Nigel laughed even more loudly than before, and scattered a few droplets of saliva over the table, some of which landed on my muffin. I quickly regretted the joke. Tommy was a sort of friend, after all, and I shouldn't have been making fun of him in front of this idiot, who I'd noticed by now was sitting just a tad too close to Jo, and kept looking at her just a tad too intently. To change the subject, I picked up the hardback novel Tommy had also brought with him.

'*A Rope from Hell*,' I read. 'What's this?'

'I made the mistake of buying that,' he said. 'I wanted to see what it was like.'

'This is the writer who's coming to read at Emeric's salon next week,' Jo explained. 'I thought Tommy might like to come as my guest.'

'Oh, yes? What did you think?' I asked him. 'Are you going?'

'Definitely not. I never read such a heap of meretricious garbage.'

This, I must say, was precisely the response I'd been anticipating. In fact I would have been disappointed if Tommy had given me any other. I had long since realized that complete, unequivocal and unshakeable contempt for all contemporary writers was an absolute prerequisite for being an English literature student at Cambridge. The fact that you might be an aspiring writer yourself was neither here nor there. Maybe you had plans to revive it, but the plain fact of the matter was, serious literature had come to an end in 1965, with the death of T. S. Eliot. (Tommy had once explained to me that there were only two exceptions to this rule: Samuel Beckett, whose insistence on remaining alive was increasingly starting to look like a personal insult aimed at his Cambridge admirers, and some don at another college, whose name I could never remember, who privately published the occasional very slim volume of poetry and could be claimed as an unsung genius with reasonable safety, given the ferocious incomprehensibility of his output.) So this poor guy – his name, I noticed now, was Peter Cockerill – had never stood a chance with Tommy: and it made perfect sense that his invitation to St Stephen's had not been issued by the English department.

'If you've got a spare place,' Nigel now said, fast as lightning, 'I'd be more than happy to come with you.'

'You?' said Jo, her eyes lit up by a twinkle of amusement that was just a little too affectionate for my liking. 'You've never read a novel in your life.'

'Of course not,' said Nigel. 'But it is happening at Emeric's, after all. And it might be amusing.'

I wasn't having this.

'I think this looks great,' I said, brandishing the book and offering this enthusiastic endorsement based on a quick skim of the cover and the title page. 'Can I borrow it, Tommy?'

'Sure,' he said.

'I'd love to come with you, please, Jo.'

'Really?' She looked first at me, then at Nigel, then back at me, trying to work out exactly what kind of power games were being played here.

'Come on,' I said, pressing home my advantage. 'I *read*. I read all the time. This sounds like it'll be a great evening.'

It worked. 'Oh well, you can come along next time,' Jo said to Nigel, with a sweet smile of apology.

'Fair enough,' he said; but he wasn't going to accept defeat gracefully. 'Far be it from me to cheat an English student out of a bit of innocent pleasure. An evening to look back on when you're serving Big Macs and fries to your customers in a few years' time.'

I favoured him with a laugh which was also a sneer at his tired old joke. 'Actually, I'm a medical student,' I said. 'I just happen to have a wide range of interests.'

'Even better,' he said. 'A few years from now, instead of just being an underpaid doctor, you can be an underpaid doctor who reads books.'

I sized him up for a few moments. I hadn't much liked this goon from the start, but now he was really beginning to annoy me.

'Not headed for one of the caring professions yourself then, Nige?'

'Maybe in my forties,' he said. 'When I'm retired.'

'Retired?'

He regarded me with a supercilious smile and asked: 'Were you close to your parents, Brian?'

'Yes,' I said, on my guard now.

'And did they ever give you . . . you know, *the talk*?'

'I don't follow. You mean the birds and the bees?'

'No, no, no,' he said, shaking his head and laughing. 'Not the birds and the bees.' He then proceeded to explain: 'On my fourteenth birthday, my father took me out for a meal and gave me a long talk about *money*. He said there were only two things you need to know about money: how to make it, and how to keep it. And those are the only two things you really need to know in life. In this country, you make money by going into the City of London, just like he did. Where are you from, again, Brian? Darlington, isn't it, or Hartlepool . . . one of those places.'

'Middlesbrough.'

'Do many people from Middlesbrough go to work in the City of London?'

'I somehow doubt it.'

'Well, they should. Once you're there, you get your hands on as much of other people's money as possible and you gamble with it and you speculate with it. You work bloody hard, every hour God sends, until by the time you're in your mid-thirties you've turned into one of these pale overweight men you see on the Waterloo and City line every day and your hair's falling out and your liver and your lungs are shot to pieces. But do you know what? You're worth a million quid. Give it another five or ten years and you're worth several million quid. And that's when you can pack it in. But the other thing is, *on no account* do you give any of this money to the government so they can splurge it on whatever they want. You take it as bonuses and dividends, not income, and you keep it offshore, you hide it in shell companies and so on. You do everything you can to make sure the Inland Revenue don't get their grubby little hands on it. And that's why, if I work hard and stick to my guns, in twenty-five years I'll be spending all my time on the golf course while you'll be knocking yourself out performing operations on sad old cases who didn't have the sense to take out private health insurance when they were younger.'

None of us knew how to respond to this speech. Or at least, Jo and I didn't know how to respond, and I don't think Tommy had been listening: he was still just staring into space with the misty eyes of the terminally lovelorn. Funny how Nigel's rant has stayed with me all these years, though. Odd, too, that he didn't really do it in a hostile or mocking way. I think he might actually have believed that he was giving me some useful information. Maybe he didn't see me as a rival, after all, and didn't bear me any ill will. As far as I know he didn't pursue Jo very seriously after that day.

This does raise the question of why he had been so keen to get invited to the salon with her. And the conclusion I reached, after thinking about it for a while, was that he had become interested in the salons for the same reason that half the male population of St Stephen's had suddenly become even more interested in them than they had been before: because they were all desperate to meet Emeric Coutts's daughter, Lavinia.

I had never given any thought to Coutts's personal life, so I hadn't known that he was a widower. He had married young, apparently, to a woman he had met at university in the fifties, and the couple had become parents while they were still young, too. After that, the story took a sadder turn. His wife – very accomplished and beautiful, by all accounts – had contracted sepsis following a routine operation in her early forties and, when it proved fatal, Emeric had been left with the sole responsibility of looking after their eighteen-year-old daughter. Nobody really seemed to know the details, but it was said that at some point she had been sent off to America to study, and had stayed there for four or five years. She had returned to England in the summer of 1982, having – as the cliché would have it – left as a girl and come home as a woman. A strikingly beautiful woman, too; or such, at least, was the claim of the few people who had ever seen her. She was extremely reclusive and seldom ventured outside her father's suite of rooms, in which she was said to have been allocated her own bedroom and sitting room with windows overlooking one of St Stephen's small inner courtyards.

Your best chance of catching a glimpse of Lavinia Coutts, it seemed, was by wangling an invitation to one of Emeric's salons. She had already been present at a couple of these, and had made quite an impression on the male guests. On both occasions, she had worn the same loose-fitting sleeveless black cocktail dress, offsetting the paleness of her skin. Her hair, too, was black, and she wore dark red lipstick and black eyeshadow which gave her something of the look (according to an over-excited friend of mine) of Morticia Addams – 'only much, *much* sexier'. At the second salon, she had caused an extra sensation by singing an aria by Purcell, accompanied by the inevitable harpsichord or clavichord or whatever it was. Some of the impressionable young men who had witnessed this episode said that there was something dreamlike and ethereal about Lavinia, some quality of other-worldliness. Even the people who had merely caught a rare glimpse of her walking in the shadows around the perimeter of Joseph's Court were inclined to this conclusion. I heard her described variously as 'elfin', as 'eldritch' (that one was Tommy Cope, always reaching for the slightly more recondite adjective) and once, less poetically, at a gathering of the rugby Second XV in the college bar, as 'fit as fuck'. Different vocabulary and different points of view, but it did seem that a consensus was building up.

Of course, my mind was on higher things, and as preparation for next week's event I began to immerse myself in the world of Peter Cockerill. I read *A Rope from Hell* in a couple of sittings and at the end of the process I had questions. A lot of questions. Whether I would have the nerve to put them to the author himself, in a room packed full of Emeric's acolytes, I didn't know.

'Well, at least you've done your homework,' said Jo, as we made our way across Kite's Court in the direction of Emeric's rooms on the night of the salon – a cold and cheerless Thursday. 'I haven't read a word by him. And I don't know if you'd heard, but Emeric's not even going to be here tonight.'

'Really? Why not?'

'He was rushed off to Addenbrooke's yesterday afternoon, apparently. Suspected appendicitis.'

I imagined that this would be rather disappointing news for our distinguished guest, and indeed, when we arrived in Emeric's rooms a few minutes later, I can't say that he was looking very cheerful. Peter Cockerill was a long, slender, angular man, with delicate features and a face that would have suggested melancholy at the best of times. He was currently sitting alone on one of Emeric's four-seater sofas, with a copy of his newly published novel open on his lap. Occasionally he would take a sip of white wine from the glass at his side, but mostly he was concentrating on the book and making some pencilled notes in the margins. He had a confident air about him and, given that the room was three-quarters full, perhaps didn't appreciate that the turnout was relatively poor for one of these salons, which were usually standing room only. I noticed that tonight, neither Roger Wagstaff nor Rebecca – his faithful sidekick – was present.

Sitting on the other sofa, opposite Cockerill, was Lavinia Coutts. She was flanked by two undergraduates who were busy trying to impress her: without much success, it seemed. Her gaze was drifting around the room and when she saw me our eyes met for a second or two. Her eyes were a very dark blue and there was an incredible energy in them. Hypnotic is the obvious word. Her cocktail dress was rather low-cut and I'm afraid I must have been staring because after a moment I felt Joanna jab me in the ribs. I turned in surprise.

'Stop gawping,' she said simply. 'And get me a glass of wine.'

We took our seats next to Cockerill on the sofa. After a few minutes there was a diffident cough to our left. It appeared to come from Dr Jonathan Glazeby, an English don who was famous for having a comically soft voice and also for not being able to keep control of a room even with only three students in it. It seemed that Dr Glazeby had been allotted the task of introducing the speaker in the absence of Professor Coutts himself. He rose to his feet with visible reluctance.

'Good evening, everybody,' he said, in his usual whispering manner. It took quite a while for people to realize that he had said anything, and to stop talking amongst themselves. 'It is my great pleasure . . . my *very* great pleasure, tonight . . . to introduce a special guest . . . a *very* special guest . . . to St Stephen's College. His name will be . . . oh, wait, I also just wanted to say . . . We are all sorry . . . *very* sorry indeed . . . that Professor Coutts is not able to be with us tonight . . . And I'm sure we wish him . . . and his, um, appendix . . . all the best for a full and quick recovery . . . Incidentally, his last book also had – in some people's opinion – rather a troublesome appendix, and . . . Oh dear, forget that I said that . . . That was a very poor attempt at humour . . . Most inappropriate . . . What was I thinking . . . Let's move on, as quickly as possible, to tonight's business, which is to extend our warmest welcome . . . our *very* warmest welcome . . . to our special guest . . . who really needs no introduction . . . no introduction at all . . . Although perhaps an appendix . . . No . . . no no no, I must stop making that joke . . . Or indeed any jokes . . . Not my forte, not my forte at all . . . Please forgive me, gentlemen . . . And ladies, of course . . . I keep forgetting there are ladies in the college now as well . . . Anyway, our special guest tonight . . . our very special guest . . . is the author of no fewer than . . . several novels . . . The latest of which . . . is also his most recent . . . Perhaps not all of us have read him . . . all of *you*, I should say, all of you . . . but we all know his name . . . and tonight, as a special treat for us . . . a *very* special treat . . . he will be reading from his brand new novel, no less . . . which, if it is anything like his others . . . if it is anything *at all* like his others . . . then it will . . . it will just go to show, I suppose . . . that the same man has written them . . . And this man, this very same man, gentlemen – and ladies . . . yes, I mustn't forget the ladies, especially Miss Coutts, whom I must say is looking . . . is looking . . . well, at the moment she is looking directly at me . . . which is rather off-putting, I must say . . . But anyway, let's move on, without further ado, and listen . . . *spellbound*, as I'm sure we soon will be . . . to our very special guest tonight, Mr Peter Cockerill!'

At which point Cockerill – who had half-risen from the sofa and sat down again about five times during the above discourse – finally stood up, cleared his throat, and began to read from the book clutched in his unshaking hand.

IX

The Writer who Sang in his Sleep (continued)

Another book is sitting on my desk in front of me as I type this. The title is *Oblivion and Rebirth: New Perspectives on the Novels of Peter Cockerill*. It's a recent volume, published by Cambridge University Press earlier this year, and the editor is one Professor Richard Wilkes of the University of Ca' Foscari in Venice, no less. I spotted it on the CUP website and ended up buying it out of curiosity, the absurd £120 cover price notwithstanding. Who would ever have guessed, after the evening I spent in the company of Peter Cockerill in November 1982, that almost forty years later his novels would still be in print and academics from around the world would be writing about them? I don't think I would.

Anyway, one essay in this collection caught my eye in particular. It alerted me to something else I would never have expected: that his novels, apparently, have become weirdly popular among Gen Z readers. This applies to the final one, *My Innocence*, in particular. (Although there is of course a lot of discussion about whether that one can really be counted as a 'novel' at all.) And it seems that the thing younger readers especially relate to in his books is the specific form of nostalgia they embody.

'The word "anemoia",' the author of this piece informed me, 'was invented a few years ago by the writer John Koenig, in his book *The Dictionary of Obscure Sorrows*. He coined it in order to provide a name for the feeling he described as "nostalgia for a time before you were born": a phenomenon he had increasingly observed among young people, whose longing for an idealized, anxiety-free and smartphone-less 1990s, for instance, has begun to manifest itself in obsessive watching of the American sitcom *Friends*. In the case of Cockerill, the focus of his nostalgia is the decade leading up to the Second World War, when his mother was still a child or a teenage girl. Of course, in this instance, Cockerill's nostalgia is intimately bound up with his strong – some would say obsessive – attachment to his mother, Betty. But that alone cannot account for the intensity with which he looks back at, and longs for, an era of which he could have no personal recollection: the 1930s, a decade which he idealizes as the last one in which the British people had any meaningful connection to a pre-industrial age, and the last one in which there could be said to exist an "authentic" British folk culture, before it was contaminated for ever by the incoming tide of American popular entertainment.'

Elsewhere in the book, several of the essays address *A Rope from Hell*, the novel which had only just been published when Cockerill came to talk to us at St Stephen's. There is nostalgia in this book, too – not for the decade before his birth, this time, but for one he could still scarcely have remembered: viz., the early 1950s. (Cockerill was born in 1948.) But *A Rope from Hell* is a complicated book, which mixes fictional and autobiographical elements. The outline of the story appears to have been based on fact: in the early fifties, Cockerill and his parents were living a seemingly contented life in a small Gloucestershire village. His father, George, a churchwarden and a keen local historian, was at the centre of the local community. George's wife had settled into the role of housewife and mother. Then, one day, a newcomer had arrived in the village: a young woman, single, attractive, a writer and journalist. Within a few weeks, George was having an affair with her; soon afterwards, they departed for London together. The situation seemed to have developed so quickly, nobody was sure exactly how it had happened. But the peaceful nuclear family was certainly shattered, destroyed, and from that time onwards, Peter was brought up by his mother alone. It seems that his father, meanwhile, almost immediately regretted his decision, and yet, being completely in thrall to his new lover, and allowing her much stronger personality to dominate his own, he became progressively more unhappy; until, a few years later, it was reported that he had died in London, in their squalid little one-bedroom flat in Bethnal Green; died of some unspecified wasting disease; which means that he died, in all probability, of remorse, and a broken heart.

In his novel, Cockerill recounts this story in unsparing detail. It is a painful and moving attempt to exorcize the family trauma that blighted his own childhood and adolescence. What seems to have made this particular book so attractive to Emeric and his acolytes, however, was its potency as a conservative allegory. The father (given a different name) represents tradition, continuity, the family, the Church. The lover (given her real name), who pens articles for the *New Statesman* and is writing a polemic on sexual freedom, stands for the forces of progression, modernity and consumerism: all the things that Cockerill himself hated. Her fate at the end of the story – unexpected and shocking – is what gives the novel its reputation for misogyny.

It was from this weird, anguished book, then, that Cockerill read to us in Emeric Coutts's rooms on that evening in November 1982. But he began by telling us, not the story of the novel itself, but of the song that had inspired it.

'"Lord Randall",' he began, 'is a traditional folk song, believed to have originated in the border country between England and Scotland some time in the seventeenth century. It takes the form of a dialogue between Lord Randall and his mother. Randall has been out to visit his lover. When he returns, he feels "sick to the heart" and realizes that his lover has poisoned him. We never learn her motives for doing so. The song exists in many different versions. The one I am going to read to you, and which you will later hear performed, goes like this.'

He put the book aside, having no need of it for the time being. Clearly he knew the song by heart, and as he began to recite it, the atmosphere in the room – which had consisted up until now of bored or uncomprehending silence – was transformed into something more attentive, more charged. Cockerill closed his eyes in concentration, and his voice was calm, measured. He drew out the rhythm of the verse with expert emphasis, and spoke slowly, with long, expressive pauses between verses.

Oh, where have you been, Lord Randall, my son?
Where have you been, my handsome young one?
I've been to my sweetheart, Mother

I've been to my sweetheart, Mother
Oh, make my bed soon, for I'm sick to the heart
And fain would lie down

Oh, what did you eat, oh Randall, my son?
What were you fed, my handsome young one?
Eels and eel broth, Mother
Speckled eel broth, Mother
Oh, make my bed soon, for I'm sick to the heart
And fain would lie down

Oh, you have been poisoned, oh Randall, my son
You have been poisoned, my handsome young one
'Tis truth you've spoken, Mother
'Tis truth you've spoken, Mother
Please make my bed soon, for I'm sick to the heart
And fain would lie down

Oh, what will you leave your mother, my son?
What will you leave her, my handsome young one?
My love to keep you, Mother
My love to keep you, Mother
Oh, make my bed soon, for I'm sick to the heart
And fain would lie down

Oh, what will you leave your sweetheart, my son?
What will you leave her, my handsome young one?
A rope from hell to hang her
A rope from hell to hang her
Oh, make my bed soon, for I'm sick to the heart
And fain would lie down

When he had finished, Cockerill hung his head and waited a long time before saying anything else to his audience. When he raised his head again, he looked beyond the sea of student faces towards the wall on the other side of the room, his eyes glistening with emotion.

'My mother,' he said finally, 'came from that same Scottish border country. She came down to the south of England with her family in the early 1930s. Her father – my grandfather – was looking for work, but he did not want to leave his family behind. So they all came with him, and they brought with them everything that they possessed – including the memory of that song. Her singing it to me when I was still in the cot – singing it to me as a lullaby – is my very earliest memory.'

He then went on to talk about his novel, and to read some pages from it. Then he announced that he would shortly be taking some questions from the audience, but before that, the song – as promised earlier – was going to be performed. At which point, the college organ scholar, Julian, took his place behind the clavichord (or maybe the harpsichord) and none other than Lavinia Coutts herself stepped forward and positioned herself next to him. An expectant hush fell over the room.

Now, I freely admit to being as susceptible to female beauty as the next heterosexual male. And no one could deny (well, Jo tried to deny it afterwards) that, if Lavinia had seemed beautiful before, when she was merely lounging on the sofa between admirers, while she was singing that song she looked simply . . . amazing. No other word for it. It wasn't to do with her looks, or what she was wearing: although it's true that the contrast between her fine, artfully disarrayed black hair and the pale skin that gleamed beneath the lamplight was striking, and somehow suited the moment. But no, that was only a small part of it. It was much more to do with her poise, her confidence. With the crystalline purity of her voice. With the fact that, standing there with her eyes closed, her hands by her sides, seemingly oblivious to her audience but in fact (I'm sure) supremely aware of it, she seemed possessed by an energy that transported her, so that it felt as though she was singing that song outside time and outside space. And what a song! What a melody! So beautiful, so eerie. The words by turns both heartbreaking and sinister. When she twice sang the phrase 'A rope from hell to hang her' in the final verse, investing it with a tenderness of expression which in no way seemed to temper the savagery of the sentiment, I felt goosepimples spring up all over my body.

The rest of the salon is a blur in my memory. I'm ashamed to say that, despite the fact that I was certainly the only person in the room to have read the novel, my nerve failed me and I never summoned the courage to ask Cockerill any of the questions about it that had been running through my head for days. Instead he had to be content with just one, immensely long, convoluted and irrelevant observation from Dr Glazeby, hingeing upon the ways in which – in Glazeby's opinion – Cockerill's work was marked by the deep and lasting influence of William Empson's seminal study *Seven Types of Ambiguity*; to which Cockerill's response – that he had not read the book in question – was short and to the point. Once that was over, I looked around for Lavinia. I wanted to say something to her, to congratulate her on her voice and her interpretation of the song. Of course, it would have mainly been a pretext to get into conversation with her, but I did genuinely want her to know how much it had moved me. But she seemed to have disappeared from the room almost immediately. Indeed, perhaps because Emeric himself wasn't present, there didn't seem to be any of the usual lingering and talking this time. I went over to a side table to refill my glass, and noticed that Cockerill's glass was also empty. No one seemed to be attending to him, so I went over to him with the bottle and, since he thanked me quite warmly for the top-up, I felt emboldened to sit down beside him and say:

'Thank you for that. Very interesting. Plenty to think about, there.'

Perhaps I had been expecting him to look grateful, given that no one else had offered him any feedback. But I could see at once that he was a man who regarded praise as being nothing more than his due, and having his work described as 'interesting' was probably a pretty lukewarm compliment as far as he was concerned.

'Thank you,' he said, somewhat stiffly. 'Always slightly nerve-racking, reading from a new book.'

'Lavinia's quite something, isn't she?'

'Lavinia?'

'Emeric's daughter.' He didn't seem to understand. 'The girl who sang the song.'

'Ah! That's his daughter, is it? Nobody told me. I merely asked if it might be possible to have the song performed, and they informed me that a female soprano would be made available. So that was his daughter! Well, well. I had no idea.'

He looked at me a little closer, and noticed that I was carrying Tommy's copy of *A Rope from Hell*. His eyes didn't light up, exactly, but he seemed quietly gratified.

'Ah well – one copy sold in Heffers this week, at any rate,' he said. 'Would you like that signed?'

It hadn't occurred to me. Was that what you did, when you met the author of a book?

'Why not?' I said.

'Is it for you?'

'Make it to my friend Tommy, if you would.'

'Tommy, or Thomas?'

'Maybe Thomas.' I watched as he wrote the name in tidy handwriting. 'He wants to be a writer himself, actually. Perhaps you could write something encouraging, like "Good luck with . . ."' Too late – he had already finished. 'Or "Best wishes",' I said. 'That'll do just fine.'

He handed me the book with a smile, and I decided that now, if ever, was the time to satisfy my curiosity. 'I did have a couple of questions, actually. The ending of the novel—'

I stopped when I heard a cough coming from above me. I looked up and saw that Jo was standing over me, looking impatient.

'Hey,' she said. 'Shall we go? We're the only ones still here.'

I looked around. Remarkably, this did seem to be the case.

'But there's all this wine left over.'

'Well, let's not let it go to waste.' She grabbed a bottle of Pinot Noir and headed for the door. I didn't move until she turned round to look at me and said, 'Are you coming or not?'

Suddenly it felt like I had no choice. I said a rapid, confused goodbye to Cockerill, and shook him by the hand. Then I followed Jo and together we clattered off down the staircase. Outside, in Kite's Court, the wind seemed to have dropped. There was a circle of grass in the middle of the courtyard, with an oak tree at its centre and a little wooden bench next to it. Strictly speaking, only fellows and dons were allowed to walk on this grass, but there was no one around, and anyway, we were third years by now, and quite blasé about college rules. We walked over to the bench, sat down, and began passing the bottle between us.

'So,' Jo said, 'did you notice anything weird about this evening?'

'The whole thing was pretty weird, to be honest,' I said. 'Let's not start normalizing this kind of stuff just because it's been our life for the last couple of years.'

'Do you remember how the last time we went to one of these, I pointed out to you that at the end, half the people seemed to disappear without us really noticing?'

I didn't remember this, as it happened, but I nodded anyway.

'Well, tonight was the same. Only they left even more quickly.'

'Surely that's because nobody had anything to say to that poor guy.'

'Yes, but hardly anyone left by the main door, the way they came in. Most of them went through a little door at the back. Didn't you notice?' I shook my head, and she sighed impatiently. 'No, of course you didn't. You were too busy hoping for another look down the front of Lavinia's dress.'

'What about it, anyway?'

She waited for me to have another sip from the wine bottle, then took it from me. She wiped the rim and had a long drink herself.

'For a while now, people have been telling me –' she looked around, as though there was a danger of being overheard – '. . . that there's *another salon.*'

'What do you mean?'

'After the main salon's over, some of the guests make their way to another of Emeric's rooms. A secret room. And then they have *another* meeting. They call it "the Shadow Chamber".'

I stared at her, not knowing what to make of this. Was she serious?

'The Shadow Chamber? What sort of thing goes on there?'

She shrugged. 'I don't know. Maybe they just have a big slap-up dinner. But most people reckon there's more to it than that.' She looked at me meaningfully. 'Lavinia goes.'

'Does she?'

'So they say.' She drank from the bottle again. 'Perhaps they have sex orgies. Who knows?' She shivered. 'Come on, let's go. I'm getting cold.'

My attention was elsewhere.

'Look!' I whispered.

She followed my line of vision and saw that Peter Cockerill had emerged from the staircase leading from Emeric's rooms, and was wandering around the courtyard looking lost. He had a bottle of wine in each hand – one red and one white. I got up and walked towards him, with Jo following a little way behind.

'Hello again,' I said. He looked at me without any obvious sign of recognition. 'Everything all right?'

Cockerill had made a circuit of most of the courtyard by now. He gazed around it in confusion.

'The strange thing is,' he said, 'that I've been given a guest room for the night, but for the life of me I can't remember where it is.'

'Ah. Is that the key?'

He handed me the wooden key fob, upon which was engraved the legend, 'FGR 2'.

'Fellows' Guest Room two,' I translated for him. 'That's on Botley Staircase, next to the bursar's office.'

'Um . . . Botley?' he said, looking around helplessly.

I tried giving him directions, but he didn't take them in, and I could see at once that he wasn't going to get there without assistance.

'Would you like me to show you?' I asked.

'That might be the best idea,' he said. 'Although I hate to put you to any trouble.'

'No trouble at all,' I assured him.

Meanwhile Jo was signalling at me frantically, waving her finger and shaking her head. I took her to one side and said, 'What's the matter?'

'He's probably gay,' she hissed. 'He's planning to seduce you with those bottles of wine.'

'Well, it's about time I did some experimenting,' I said, and pressed the copy of *A Rope from Hell* into her hands. 'Make sure that gets back to Tommy. And don't worry about me. I'm a big boy. I can look after myself.'

The anxiety written on her face suggested she was not reassured by these words, not even when I accompanied them with my most winning, devil-may-care smile. She continued to watch us, her forehead creased into a worried frown, as Peter Cockerill took me by the arm and I steered him, somewhat unsteadily, in the direction of Botley Staircase and Fellows' Guest Room 2.

X

The Writer who Sang in his Sleep (continued)

It was an impressive room. Even the undergraduate rooms on Kite's Court were known for their generous proportions, but this was something else. There was a double bed that could easily have accommodated half a dozen people, and it still left room for three sofas and four armchairs, two of which were placed on either side of the gigantic fireplace. No fire was burning, unfortunately, but Cockerill had left most of the standard lamps on while he was away, and the room looked fairly cosy as he led me into it.

'Well, here we are,' he said. 'I hope you realize there's no question of you leaving without joining me first in one of these bottles of wine. I must give you some recompense for the inconvenience.'

I'd been expecting this and, as I had intimated to Jo, I was well up for it.

'Are those Emeric's bottles?' I asked, settling myself in one of the fireside chairs.

'I don't know whose they are,' he answered. He went off into another room, which I deduced to be a kitchenette, and came back with a corkscrew. 'But I was offered no payment for addressing that roomful of yahoos back there, so I consider myself entitled to them.'

'Absolutely,' I agreed.

He poured two large glasses of red, and we ceremoniously clinked the cut-glass beakers. After drinking, we let out concurrent sighs of satisfaction.

'Well, I'm glad that's over,' he said. 'But I'm disappointed, I must say, not to have met the famous Professor Coutts.'

'Perhaps you could visit him in hospital tomorrow,' I suggested.

'Perhaps, perhaps.' He frowned. 'Tell me . . . tell me, erm . . .' Then, with a laugh, he admitted: 'Actually, I don't think I know your name.'

'Brian,' I said. 'Brian Collier.'

'And you're studying English, are you, Brian?'

'No, no, not at all. Medicine.'

'Medicine! Well, I would never have guessed, but there you go . . . A medic who reads modern fiction! Quite the *rara avis*.'

I laughed neutrally, not entirely sure that I understood his Latin.

'I think that, back in the salon, you were about to ask me a question about my novel?'

'Yes. Yes, I was.' I coughed and sat up straight. 'It was about the ending, really.'

'About the "almighty aposiopesis", you mean.'

'Yes.'

'What did you want to know? Wasn't it clear?'

'Well, I'd like to know what "aposiopesis" means, for a start.'

'Ah! Well. An aposiopesis is a literary device – a figure of speech – meaning that you break off in the middle of a sentence, and leave the rest to the reader's imagination. That's why, in this novel, I simply abandon the story in the middle of the final chapter, and say, "To hell with all this lying!" I'm coming clean with the reader. Telling him that everything up until that point has been a pack of lies.'

'But . . . but it hasn't been a pack of lies, has it? I mean, this is what really happened to you, and your family.'

'But it didn't happen the way I tell it in the book. I changed people's names, I changed significant events . . . I *fictionalized* it. And there came a point, during the writing process, when I started to feel disgusted with myself for having done that. It seemed . . . profoundly immoral.'

I thought about this. ' "Disgusted" is a pretty strong word,' I said.

'I chose it carefully.'

'But . . . "fictionalizing" things – isn't that what a novelist *does*?'

'It's not what I'm going to do, from now on. From now on, I shall tell only the truth. For instance, if ever I were to put this conversation we are having into a book, I should simply write it down exactly as it happened. So far as I could remember it.'

'Isn't that quite an eccentric way to go about writing a novel?'

'But I am eccentric. In the original sense of the word: outside the centre. I'm marginal. I'm an outlier. Look at all these new writers who are coming through at the moment – what are they called? – McEwan, Barnes, Rushdie. They're all ploughing the same furrow. Ironic, irreverent, left-wing. And *secular* – that's the main thing. Not a decent Christian among them. My moral philosophy is completely different from theirs, so my books should be completely different too. Don't you see?'

'But if you set yourself up as an outlier, isn't there a danger that people will just ignore you?'

'It's already happening. Every so often a piece appears in the newspapers about new trends in British writing. Am I ever mentioned? No. Do you know how many copies this novel has sold in hardback? Two hundred and seventy-two. Two hundred and seventy-two! I might as well be hawking it on street corners.'

'Doesn't that bother you?'

'It bothers me, yes.' He sipped on his wine and stared reflectively into the fireplace. 'It bothers me very much, as a matter of fact. If my work doesn't survive me, then . . . I will have failed. It will all have been for nothing. The whole struggle.'

'That's why you write? To get one over on your rivals?'

'No, not at all.' For the first time he seemed irritated by one of my questions. 'That has absolutely nothing to do with it. It's because . . .' He hesitated for a moment, and then asked me something very unexpected. 'Do you ever think about death?'

I shook my head. 'Not really.'

'No, of course not – why should you? You're twenty years old, twenty-one. It means nothing to you. I'm not so lucky, though. I think about it all the time – and have done, ever since I was a child.' He poured some more wine into his glass, which was almost empty, and also into mine, which was almost full. 'I would like to tell you that I'm a fearless man, Brian, but sadly I am not. The thought of death terrifies me.'

It occurred to me that if your earliest memory was of your mother leaning over your cot and singing a song about a man who has just been fatally poisoned, perhaps a lifelong fear of death was only to be expected. But I didn't say this.

'That,' Cockerill continued, with an emphasis I have never forgotten, 'is why I could never commit suicide. Never. Not because it's sinful. I simply wouldn't have the courage.'

'But look,' I said to him, 'I thought you were a Christian? How can you be afraid of death? Surely if you've lived a blameless life, you've got nothing to worry about. Paradise is waiting for you – for all eternity. Seems a pretty nice prospect, on the whole.'

'Nice for those who believe in it,' said Cockerill.

'You don't?' I was surprised.

'I believe,' he said, choosing his words very carefully now, 'in Christianity as an ethical system. A very profound and beautiful one. But a good deal of its . . . narrative content seems to me to fall into the category of mythology.' He drank some more wine. I noticed that he was getting through it pretty quickly now. 'And Christianity, after all, is rather a new religion. Long before the Romans got here, the English had their own belief systems.'

'Paganism, you mean.'

'Call it what you will. The ancient Celtic druids had a very different notion of what happened after death. They believed in the transmigration of souls. Once your body dies, your immortal soul simply finds another body to occupy.'

'Reincarnation, in other words.'

'Again, you may call it what you will. My own preferred term is "rebirth".'

'So you believe that after you die, you will be . . . reborn?'

'I believe that after I die, there will be a time when my books are forgotten. But then, they will come back.'

'That must be a comforting thought.'

'Oh, it's not enough just to *think* it. You would have to *make* it happen.'

His glass was empty, and so was the bottle. I reckoned that he had drunk about three-quarters of it. It was also starting to sound as though he was talking to himself, and not to me. I could see that his eyelids were drooping, and this seemed like my cue to rise from my seat.

'This has been fascinating,' I said. 'But I think it's time that I went. Do you mind if I use the loo?'

'Not at all,' he said. 'It's through that door. Be prepared for sub-Arctic temperatures.'

It was indeed freezing in there. Once again, the proportions of the room seemed to make no sense. The bath was vast. It would have taken hours to fill it. My bladder was full to bursting point by now. My piss came in a torrent, and seemed to go on for about five minutes. Afterwards I looked at myself in the mirror and grimaced. I splashed some cold water (ice-cold water) on my face, then sat on the toilet seat for a few more minutes, trying to sober up. After a while I realized that I too was falling asleep. I came round with a jolt and wondered how long I had been in the bathroom. Cockerill must be thinking that something strange was going on in here.

I needn't have worried on that score, however. When I went back into the sitting room I found that he was lying diagonally across the bed, fully clothed, and fast asleep. I retrieved a blanket from one of the dresser drawers and laid it over him. As I did so, a sound escaped from his lips. I thought he might be thanking me, in his unconscious state, but then the sound continued, and it didn't resemble speech any more. As I tucked the edges of the blanket around his recumbent body, I realized what was happening: he was *singing*. He was singing 'Lord Randall', and not in a drunken, tuneless sort of way, but in an immaculate, high-pitched, countertenor voice. He sang the melody perfectly and also seemed to remember all the words, although I'm not sure that he sang the verses in the right order. It was very quiet, of course – there was a hushed, breathy quality to his voice – but it was, nonetheless, a mesmerizing performance: one of the strangest and most haunting things I have ever heard. Nor was there any sign of it coming to an end. He was still singing 'Lord Randall' when I finished tucking him in, laid a farewell hand on his shoulder, tiptoed out of the room and closed the door behind me as softly as I could.

When I read the news of Peter Cockerill's suicide five years later I was surprised, of course. After all, had he not told me that night, candidly and unequivocally, that he would never kill himself, because the thought of death scared him too much? But people are unpredictable. People are complicated. (I worked for almost forty years as a psychiatrist, remember. I trust you can see my professional expertise shining through.) And he was a good deal more complicated than most. Obviously the demons that drove him – whatever they were – were too powerful to resist in the end, and somehow, from somewhere, he found the reserves of courage that he'd told me he lacked. The news shocked me, at any rate, but I was young and callow and the feeling faded almost as quickly as the newspapers' interest in the circumstances of his death. It happened at his cottage in the New Forest, apparently, which was burned to the ground in the process. He set fire to the house, to all the manuscripts and notebooks and paperwork that it contained, and to his own self into the bargain. And in case anyone should be in any doubt, he left a suicide note, not in the form of a few words scribbled on a sheet of paper, but in the form of an entire novel, which he called *My Innocence*, and which was published posthumously a few months later. His death prompted a paragraph or two in the broadsheets, a handful of obituaries, and after that he was forgotten. The revival in his reputation that he had predicted didn't start for a few years after that. I'm glad that it continues, even though I must admit that his books never appealed to me all that much. I prefer to remember him, not as the author of those cruel, neurotic, self-absorbed novels, but as the quietly melancholy young man who passed out after drinking three-quarters of a bottle of red wine, and sang 'Lord Randall' to me as I tucked a heavy woollen blanket around the curves of his sleeping body.

XI
The Chamber

Following her performance at her father's most recent salon, the rumour mill around Lavinia Coutts began to go into overdrive.

I'm not sure where the stories about witchcraft started to come from. I first heard them from Chris, who I think had heard them from Tommy, who had heard them from . . . well, who knows? Anyway, by the end of the Michaelmas term, 1982, they were being shared in every bar, common room and dining hall in the college.

It all stemmed from the time someone glimpsed her coming out of a shop in London. That, I suppose, and the incident of her cat and Professor Marshall's tomato plants.

Briefly, the story was this. Lavinia had a cat, or rather a kitten. The kitten's name was Jinx. Lavinia was devoted to her cat, and the feeling was fully reciprocated. Lavinia lived with her father in his college rooms, and in the rooms above her father's, at the very top of Kite's Court, lived Professor Marshall. He was a professor of pure maths, he was single, he was elderly, he was very quiet and reclusive, he had lived in the college for at least the last forty years, and he never bothered anybody. Professor Marshall had a tiny terrace on the roof overlooking the courtyard, and this was where he grew his tomatoes.

Somehow or other, Jinx found a route that would take her up to Professor Marshall's terrace. She developed an interest in his tomato plants. More specifically, she developed an interest in peeing on his tomato plants. His tomato plants did not take kindly to this treatment. They died. Professor Marshall, it is safe to conclude, was not happy about this. The story took a dark turn. A week or two later, the kitten's dead body was found in the stairwell outside Emeric's rooms. It seemed that she had eaten rat poison. Lavinia stormed upstairs and accused Professor Marshall of poisoning her pet. He denied the charge in the manner in which people are always said to deny such charges – categorically. Lavinia was not satisfied.

At this point, the sequence of events begins to get a little hazy. Someone – nobody knows who – who had been down in London for the day claimed to have spotted Lavinia there. She was seen disappearing into a bookshop situated in some obscure alley off the Gray's Inn Road. The name of the bookshop was Beltane Books. It specialized in works devoted to the esoteric and the occult. The window displayed several items purporting to be books of spells and incantations. After about twenty minutes, Lavinia emerged from the bookshop. She was said to be clutching a book in a brown paper bag.

Some days later, a second tragedy struck in Kite's Court. This time, the unfortunate victim was Professor Marshall. At ten o'clock one morning, an ambulance was seen driving into the courtyard. Paramedics jumped out, and shortly afterwards, a body was carried out on a stretcher from one of the staircases. It was the body of the Professor himself. At that stage it seemed that he was still alive, but he was pronounced dead on arrival at the A&E department of Addenbrooke's hospital. He had suffered a massive heart attack.

Now, it could be argued that a septuagenarian don who had never seemed to be in the best of health and was known to be partial to the odd decanter or three of the college sherry was already prime heart attack material. That would certainly be my own conclusion. But the theory started going around, inevitably, that Lavinia had taken revenge for the death of her cat by putting some sort of curse on the hapless Professor and bringing about his untimely demise. I didn't believe a word of it, of course, but I can't say that it did anything to diminish the fascination I felt for Emeric's daughter, who I have to confess had been pretty much the exclusive focus of my erotic imagination ever since I had witnessed her singing 'Lord Randall' that evening.

This is rather an embarrassing thing to admit, because I did, technically speaking, have another girlfriend by now. Her name was Jackie and she was a fellow medic who I'd met at one of the anatomy lectures I'd finally started to attend. She was a student at Clare College, rather than St Stephen's, so I'd taken to hanging out with her there and had made a few new friends as a result. One of them was a postgrad from America who had come across Lavinia at Princeton and reckoned that he knew all about her. And he gave me a very different perspective.

'I never spoke to her,' he told me, 'but everybody knew who she was. Partly because she stood out, with the black hair and the black clothes and everything else, but partly because of the company she kept – which was *not* what you would've expected. Her boyfriend at the time was a guy called Bill Silverman, and he ran the Princeton chapter of the Young Americans for Freedom. Never heard of those guys? Lucky you. Bunch of crew-cut free-market fetishists and libertarians. Started up in the sixties – you can imagine how popular they were on American campuses back then. Signing up with them was a pretty surefire way to get your head kicked in. But now the boot's on the other foot and they're the ones who are laughing. In fact half those 1960s guys are in the White House now that Reagan's president. Coutts was studying classics but she made a beeline for these right-wing weirdos and I think by the time she was doing her Master's she was practically running the show. I mean, literally, she and her nutjob boyfriend were taking flights to Washington every weekend and meeting with guys from the State Department and God knows what. So don't tell me that this girl is just some kind of pre-Raphaelite English rose with a sideline in black magic. Lavinia Coutts isn't a witch, I can tell you that for nothing. She's a fucking Nazi.'

My final visit to Emeric Coutts's rooms took place in February 1983.

The 1980s, remember, had not yet begun. Ernie Wise's mobile phone call was still almost two years away. And in St Stephen's College we were nicely cocooned from events in the outside world. Still, I was aware, more or less, that things were changing in Britain, and changing fairly rapidly. For one thing, we had been to war with Argentina, and won. Maybe none of us had known where the Falkland Islands were before this happened, but we had soon caught up, and thanks to the flag-waving triumphalism of the tabloids and the success of her own bellicose rhetoric, Mrs Thatcher had benefited enormously from the conflict. There would be a general election later in the year, and she was comfortably on course to win a second term.

One of the emerging features of her tenure as Prime Minister was the emphasis she placed on the 'special relationship' between Britain and America. Reagan was President now, and like most British people I didn't think about him much: I was happy to fall back on the lazy political jokes that I saw on television and in the newspapers, which portrayed him as a bumbling, incoherent cowboy figure, an actor speaking pre-scripted lines, full of folksy banalities and as fake as any Hollywood set. I realize now that I underestimated what his election meant in the long term: the beginning of a long, long era (we are still in the middle of it) in which his version of conservatism would set the tone of American politics, and have a lasting impact on the British version of it, too.

To give him credit, I knew at least one person who had already begun to suspect what was happening: Christopher Swann. And he's been following the story ever since. I know that a lot of people can be rather dismissive of Chris's blog, regarding it as a bit of a joke: personally, I find it impressive, not least because he does all the research unpaid and unassisted, while holding down a full-time job. Tireless is the word for it. Chris has been tirelessly pursuing the story of how hardcore conservatism has evolved and mutated, for almost forty years, on both sides of the Atlantic. And he started while he was at Cambridge. I know this for a fact, because one day, when I told him what my American friend had said to me about Lavinia, and asked him if he'd heard of the Young Americans for Freedom, he laughed disbelievingly and said:

'Have I heard of them? Have I *heard* of them? My God, Brian, you and Jackie really have been living on another planet for the last few weeks, haven't you? Of course I've heard of them. As I've told you countless times, I'm doing my dissertation on them!'

It was awkward to admit that I'd forgotten that – or rather, had never known it, because I obviously hadn't been listening on any of the occasions when Chris had told me. But he was forgiving about it, and invited me up to his room to share his research with me when he saw how interested I'd become.

'First of all,' he said, 'I really can't imagine that Lavinia has anything to do with these people. I thought everyone had decided that she was the Witch of Endor, or something, and spent her evenings throwing eye of toad and leg of newt into a big steaming cauldron in Emeric's kitchen?'

'I'm just going by what I've been told,' I insisted. 'Apparently when she was at Princeton she got very involved with this crowd.'

'OK then,' he said. 'This is what you need to know.'

So he began by telling me about the Sharon Statement, drafted at William F. Buckley's house in Sharon, Connecticut, in September 1960 and endorsed by the ninety or so students who were gathered there. The statement which declared that American conservatives should commit themselves to limited government and agree to the principle that 'the free market system is preferable over all others'. He told me how Ronald Reagan had joined the group's National Advisory Board in 1962 and still served as its honorary chairman. He told me about the organization's full-blooded support, in 1964, for Barry Goldwater in his bid to become US President, and the catastrophic failure of that campaign. He told me about the wilderness years of the late '60s and early '70s, when opposition to the Vietnam war was at its height and student activism on American campuses was dominated by the liberal Left. It was at around this time, he said, that the Young Americans for Freedom developed their fixation on one particular idea: that Middle America contained a conservative majority (also sometimes known as the silent majority) which resented the anti-war protests, the counterculture, the metropolitan newspapers and TV channels, the film industry, the Beautiful People – everything, in short, that could be described as the 'liberal establishment', as described by Kevin P. Phillips, a young lawyer in the Nixon administration, in his influential book *The Emerging Republican Majority*. The movement became increasingly disenchanted with President Nixon himself, whose opening-up of relations with the People's Republic of China was seen as a betrayal of conservative values (another of the Sharon Statement's five founding principles being 'Communism must be defeated, not contained'). Then came the founding, in 1974, of CPAC or the Conservative Political Action Conference (which remains the biggest annual rallying-point for global conservatism to this day). And finally there was the recent election of Reagan as President, which had carried the movement in triumph from the margins to the mainstream, with the result that many of its founders and leading figures had been given positions of power in the White House and were now engaged, not in mere activism, but in the actual business of government.

'If Lavinia had an older boyfriend,' Chris said, 'who had been involved with them in the 1970s, it's quite possible that he has friends who are now part of the Reagan administration. So, can I believe that they were flying down for meetings with them at the weekends? Yes, I can. Just about. Is she still in touch with this guy?'

I shrugged my shoulders. 'Don't ask me,' I said.

I had still never spoken to her.

Jo agreed to take me to one more salon, but for some reason she had to drop out at the last minute so I ended up going on my own. It took place on a frosty evening in mid-February 1983. It was a curious feeling, walking up that now-familiar staircase. I was no longer nervous about attending these events: in fact nothing about Cambridge made me nervous any more. Somehow in the last two and a half years that gauche, unworldly student from a comp in Middlesbrough had quietly vanished, his identity supplanted by that of a far more confident young man, who now felt perfectly at home amongst these ancient courtyards and cloisters – took them for granted just as he had once taken the streets of his council estate for granted. The provincial caterpillar had metamorphosed into the privileged butterfly without even noticing that it had happened.

I had no plan, that evening, but I did have an intention. The intention was to get into conversation with Lavinia Coutts; to discover, if I could, something about the years she had spent in America and also to discover (although this was a long shot) whether there was any truth to the rumour that there was a 'Shadow Chamber', a salon-within-the-salon, which took place some time after the main event.

How I was going to do any of this was not clear.

Well, I did get into conversation with Lavinia, but not in a very satisfactory way. As usual she had admirers buzzing around her like flies. I hovered on the edge of this crowd of Hooray Henrys, listening, as always, with appalled fascination to the inanely flirtatious remarks they made to her with such loud self-assurance. (I may have grown accustomed to most aspects of Cambridge life, but I would never get used to those braying voices.) By dint of perseverance and some dogged physical manoeuvring, I managed to get alongside her and – having had the foresight to pick up a bottle of Chardonnay on the way – I offered to refill her glass. She nodded her thanks and I used this as an opportunity to ask:

'Will you be singing for us tonight?'

To which she answered, 'No,' and moved over to another part of the room.

And that (let me put it on record) was the full extent of my interaction with Lavinia Coutts, then and subsequently.

Deflated, I started looking for somewhere to sit down. I wanted to be inconspicuous, but to have a good view of the whole room. Right at the back, in a far corner, there was a deep, cushioned windowsill which looked ideal for my purposes. I took my place there and quickly realized that it offered another advantage: it was right next to the door which led to the further, private recesses of Emeric's rooms, and through which the butler would periodically emerge carrying a tray of wine glasses and snacks. He would often leave the door slightly ajar when he did this, and so the opportunity to slip through the half-open doorway sometimes presented itself. I wondered if I would have the courage to take it, or would be able to do so unobserved.

The speaker this evening was a lecturer from another university – a *red-brick* university, no less – who was known for his uncompromising views. Presumably he had to moderate them a bit within the confines of his own lecture theatre but tonight he was off the leash and the title of his paper was 'Why the Power of the British Trades Unions Must be Broken for Good'. It was a talk which did, as they say, what it said on the tin, and it was warmly received. Most of the discussion that followed centred on the role of the National Union of Mineworkers, the union which had been instrumental in bringing down Edward Heath's Conservative government in 1974: a humiliation, some believed, from which the party was yet to fully recover. I could not help noticing that much of the debate had a bitter, vengeful tone which I did not normally associate with these salons (or indeed with the mild-mannered Professor Coutts himself).

As the discussion wound down, things started to go in my favour. The two people who had been sitting next to me on the windowsill got up and left, which meant that I now had this corner of the room to myself. The other guests stood up and began to rearrange themselves into small groups, talking among themselves. Lavinia was deep in conversation with a gallingly handsome history postgrad. My heart began to beat louder and faster as I realized that if I was going to do any espionage work, the time was now. And then, right on cue, the door next to me was pushed open, and the butler came through, his brow furrowed with concentration as he carried another fully laden drinks tray. Acting the part of the obliging guest, I held the door open for him, and he gave me a polite smile of thanks. As his back was turned, and before anyone could see me, I hurried through the gap in the doorway and closed the door carefully behind me.

I didn't have much time. Quickly I tiptoed down a short corridor, with doors leading off on either side. I opened the doors in rapid succession and saw Emeric's bedroom, then Lavinia's, then a bathroom, then a kitchen. Finally there was one more door. I turned the handle and found that it gave directly on to a short spiral staircase, leading upwards. I slipped through, climbed the stairs and came to another door at the top. I was nervous that there might be somebody on the other side, so I put my eye to the keyhole. This gave me a pretty clear view of a dimly lit room which at the moment appeared to be empty. Realizing that there was no going back now, I pushed the door open and went inside.

It was a spacious room, about as big as the one downstairs where the salons were usually held. The furniture in here, however, was sparse, consisting of little other than ten chairs arranged in a large circle. Within the circle formed by the chairs, on the parquet flooring, a simple pentagram had been painted in red. Immediately my imagination began to run riot, and I pictured Lavinia performing some sort of satanic dance in this space, culminating in her naked sacrifice to the goddess Hecate or some such lurid nonsense.

Looking around the room, there were very few clues as to what other purposes it could be designed for. There was no other furniture apart from a side table and a couple more chairs lined up against one wall. Another thing that I had noticed was that there was only one door – the one I had come through. I had no way of escaping except by the same route that had brought me here.

I was just starting to consider what this meant for my current situation when I heard footsteps on the staircase and voices on the other side of the door. I looked around in a panic. There was only one possible hiding place: the window bay at one end of the room, which was shielded by a heavy floor-length curtain. I dashed behind the curtain immediately and stood there, holding my breath, as the room began to fill up. Among the voices I recognized were Emeric's and Lavinia's. (Hers was the only female voice, in fact.) I heard the scraping back of chairs, the sound of people settling down. Paper rustling. Ballpoint pens being clicked. And then someone calling the meeting to order:

'Gentlemen. Welcome to the fifteenth meeting of the Shadow Chamber.'

Roger Wagstaff.

Yes, I would recognize that voice anywhere. Gently, very gently, by a fraction of a centimetre, I parted the velvet curtain in front of me and put my eye to the crack. He was sitting with his back to me, and Lavinia was in the chair next to him. She had some sheets of paper in front of her on a clipboard and seemed to be taking the minutes. I could see what she was writing fairly clearly. So far all she had written was 'MEETING NO. 15'.

I was hidden there for more than half an hour. It would be tedious to tell you everything I heard in detail, so I shall summarize. Half of the members of this exclusive group seemed to be of student age (including Roger Wagstaff and Lavinia). The other five members must have been dons from different colleges, whose chairs were placed at the five points of the pentagram. It was fairly clear, from early on in the meeting, that this was an influential, carefully selected caucus of academics who were collectively advising the government. Not just economists and political theorists: there were scientists and engineers there as well. Between them they seemed to have been preparing some sort of report. It had to do with energy supplies in a state of national emergency. A prolonged strike of some sort: 'between nine and twelve months', they said. The recommendations included building up maximum coal stocks in advance of the emergency, making contingency plans for the import of coal and introducing a system of dual coal- and oil-firing in all power stations as quickly as possible. This was all backed up with detailed figures based on a range of possible scenarios.

At the end of the meeting the report was approved and Emeric proposed that it should be delivered as soon as possible to 'a top-level contact'. The others agreed and when Emeric asked if 'the usual method' could be employed, Wagstaff nodded. In the minutes, Lavinia made a note: 'RW to deliver tomorrow by London train'.

The meeting dispersed, the lights were turned off and the room was emptied. As the last person left, I heard the door being locked behind them. I had escaped detection, miraculously. But I was trapped.

After a cursory exploration of the room I realized that the window was my only hope. I turned the wrought-iron handle and it opened creakily outwards. I stuck my head out into the cold night air and looked first down, then up. Neither view was especially heartening. I was peering out at a small and private internal courtyard. Downwards there was a drop of at least thirty feet and no obvious way of making the descent. Upwards looked slightly easier. Besides the drainpipe that ran next to the window there were some fairly solid-looking tendrils of ivy and one or two footholds where bricks were either protruding or had fallen out. It was not an appetizing prospect but I had no choice and I quickly decided that the sooner I got on with it, the better.

The climb probably only took three or four minutes but it seemed much, much longer than that. I tried to take my mind off it by focusing on other things, but all I could think of was the passage in *Titus Groan* that I'd read a couple of years earlier, when Steerpike had been locked in a room by Mr Flay but had managed to escape through the window and then climbed right up to the very rooftops of Gormenghast. I remembered the horrific, vertiginous details of the climb as he creeps up the 'swaying wall', sweating, bleeding, 'the hollow twilight at his shoulder-blades'. But when I reached the parapet and swung myself over it with relative ease, safe at last, I also remembered his sense of exhausted triumph on reaching the summit of the castle, and found myself feeling something similar. Here, of course, there was nothing to compare with Gormenghast's prodigious field of stone flagstones, spreading over many acres, which Steerpike had been the first person to glimpse for at least four hundred years. But in the clear light of the February half-moon I could see not just the tiled rooftops of St Stephen's College spread out all around me, as well as its clock tower and the distinctive spiky silhouette of its chapel, but most of Cambridge as well. A surprisingly modest grouping of colleges clustered along the Backs and fanning out around the market square, and then the lamplit sprawl of the town itself, most of it still unexplored and mysterious to me, the roads and the street lights dissolving in the distance into a cloudy, enveloping darkness which implied the bleak and windswept existence of the fens somewhere beyond it. Seeing all this laid out at my feet, I suddenly felt a dizzying sense of mastery and omnipotence, like Steerpike gazing down on the castle from his Olympian viewpoint, when 'only his hunger prevented him from leaning contentedly over the warming parapet and, with a hundred towers below him, planning for himself an incredible future'.

Well, I was not normally prone to delusions of grandeur, and this one did not last for long. I was no Steerpike. Even armed with my new information I was never going to mount a campaign of subversion that would bring Cambridge to its knees, as he had almost managed to destroy Gormenghast and all its occupants. I was motivated by a nagging, personal curiosity: that was all. And so tomorrow I would track Roger Wagstaff to London and attempt to discover the location of his secret rendezvous; but in the meantime, all I wanted to do was to find an open skylight, drop down into the safety of a college staircase and make my way back to the warmth of my bed as quickly as possible.

XII
The Shadow

Back in those days, most trains from Cambridge to London went to Liverpool Street station, not King's Cross. It was a boring journey, with stops at Audley End, Bishop's Stortford and Sawbridgeworth among many other places, and since I didn't know when the awful Wagstaff would be travelling I had to arrive at the station in time for the first train, which left at around five-thirty. No joke, on a cold and damp Friday morning in mid-February.

I spent a chilling ninety minutes sitting out on the platform before the station café deigned to open at seven o'clock. After that I could at least wait in warmth and comfort. I got through four coffees and a couple of bacon sandwiches before the need to go for a pee became irresistible.

It was almost nine o'clock by now and as I was walking back from the gents towards the café, I saw someone who looked vaguely familiar standing on the platform a few yards ahead of me. A young woman with a short-back-and-sides haircut who was carrying a shoulder bag which I could see contained a large manila envelope among other things. It took me a few moments to put a name to the face, but finally it came: of course, it was Rebecca, the object of one of poor old Tommy Cope's unrequited crushes a few months ago. He had written that terrible poem about her: *'If "meta" hides the meaning of my verse / It begs the question, what is "meta" for?'* I'd never forgotten that excruciating couplet. It did appear, however, that Rebecca had forgotten me, despite the fact that Chris had introduced us to each other at that Cambridge Union debate in our second year. She ignored my nod of greeting, and pointedly turned her face in the other direction after I had offered it. Fine. I was in no particular mood to talk to her. It was annoying enough that I had already encountered someone who knew me on what was supposed to be a covert mission. When the next Liverpool Street train drew into the platform, Rebecca stepped aboard, and I went back inside the café to resume my lookout.

I was just in the middle of ordering my fifth cup of coffee when the thought occurred to me. I had forgotten, completely forgotten, that her surname was Wood. Of course! How could I be sure that she wasn't the 'RW' whose initials Lavinia had written down in the minutes? After all, she and Wagstaff had been thick as thieves at that debate: she had sat there right next to him while he spoke, handing him pages of figures and quotations whenever he asked for them. And what was that manila envelope in her shoulder bag, if not a copy of the report from the Shadow Chamber? Should I risk it? Should I make that assumption, or should I carry on sitting in the café on the off chance that Roger Wagstaff himself arrived at the station?

The Liverpool Street train started to move. I cancelled my order, ran out onto the platform and managed to wrench open a door in the final carriage and jump on board with just a few seconds to spare.

The stations slipped by. Shelford. Whittlesford Parkway. Great Chesterford.

I debated with myself whether to walk further along the train, so that I could keep a closer eye on Rebecca. The danger was that she would see me again, and realize that she was being followed.

Audley End. Newport. Elsenham.

But why should she realize that she was being followed? I was just another student, taking a train to London for my own reasons. What if she did see me? How would it matter?

Bishop's Stortford. Sawbridgeworth. Harlow Mill.

I made my way through the carriages until I was about halfway along the train. And then I had a stroke of luck, because I could see Rebecca sitting in a double seat, facing the engine. She had her back to me, so there was no danger that she might have spotted me. I sat down about four seats behind her, on the other side of the carriage.

Harlow Town. Roydon. Broxbourne.

We started to enter the outskirts of London. A sense of unease began to grip me. Not because of the task I was engaged on: simply because the capital always had this effect on me. I may have grown used to Cambridge, but London still unsettled me, made me feel lost and vulnerable.

Cheshunt. Tottenham Hale. London Liverpool Street.

And here we were at last.

The figure sitting four seats ahead of me in the carriage got up, then turned sideways. At which point, I saw that it was in fact a man. A man in his early thirties. A complete stranger. I cursed myself for being so stupid, then ran forward and, pushing past him and the other people waiting to get out, stumbled down onto the platform. A stream of passengers was already heading for the ticket barrier. I jostled my way through them, unable to believe that I might already have lost my quarry. I scuttled through the ticket barrier myself, still without any glimpse of Rebecca. Then, in the distance, I saw someone who resembled her. She was heading off at speed for the escalators which led down to the Central line. I ran off in that direction.

Somehow I was able to keep the figure in sight, despite the hordes of people who separated me from her. I tried to elbow my way past as many of these people as possible, without annoying anyone too much. Eventually there were about six escalator steps between myself and the woman I was now certain was Rebecca. I recognized the shoulder bag if nothing else, and could see the manila envelope protruding from it.

Rebecca made for the westbound platform and took the first train that came in, disembarking at Holborn and then heading off in a north-easterly direction towards the Gray's Inn Road. I followed at a distance of about ten yards. She turned off the main street after six or seven minutes and ducked into a narrow and ancient mews, where the tall buildings on either side kept the street in permanent shadow. It looked at first as though this was a cul-de-sac, but in fact there was a tiny archway at the far end, which led into a still less promising thoroughfare. The streets became gloomier still, and narrower still. Rebecca knew exactly where she was going, but I didn't, so I had to keep a close eye on her – knowing, at the same time, that if she were to turn, just once, and look behind her, she would see me and the game would be up. By some miracle, it never happened. The buildings in this forlorn and shady part of the city were mainly residential, but there were also some boarded-up business premises and a handful of decrepit shopfronts. I was quite lost in the maze-like patchwork of mewses and alleyways.

Finally, making one last turn, Rebecca brought me into a slightly wider street in which one house, a little smaller and shabbier than the others, had been converted into a bookshop, its bay window offering a cluttered display of titles, with more books stacked in cardboard boxes and on trestle tables outside the front door. A fading, cunningly painted sign over the doorway advertised the name of the shop in Gothic lettering. It was called 'Beltane Books'. 'Specialists in Esoterica and the Occult' ran the legend across the top of the window.

Rebecca went directly inside. I ducked beneath a blackened archway which seemed to lead to somebody's garage, and lurked there for a couple of minutes, wondering what she was going to do next. But I didn't have to wait for long. She soon emerged and set off at a brisk pace in the direction from which she had come. I only received a brief glimpse of her shoulder bag but, so far as I could tell, it no longer contained the manila envelope. I didn't follow her this time. The question now was not where Rebecca was heading (back to Cambridge, I assumed) but what would happen next.

I stepped out into the street and looked to see if there was anywhere that I could take refuge. There seemed to be a sandwich bar about twenty yards further along the street, on the opposite side from the bookshop. I took a look through the window and quickly saw that it was an unwelcoming sort of place, but with a bit of effort I persuaded the owner, a laconic cockney with numerous tattoos on his impressively hairy forearms, to make me a cheese-and-onion sandwich and a black coffee. I kept an eye on the shopfront while he was doing this, but didn't see anyone coming or going. Then I took my position at the counter alongside the window overlooking the street, burned my tongue on the coffee at the first sip, and settled down for another long vigil.

Forty minutes passed before Beltane Books received a visit from another customer. At first glance, he didn't look much like the typical patron of a bookshop dedicated to the dark arts. Nor at second, nor at third. He was a squat, brown-haired man of about forty who wore a peaked cap and a light grey chauffeur's uniform. He was in the shop for less than thirty seconds and when he emerged he was carrying the envelope under his arm. I put my coffee to one side and said a garbled goodbye to my host, who seemed reasonably sanguine about the departure of his only customer. Rising to my feet, I winced sharply as I realized that my bladder was just as full as I'd feared it was. But still, I set off after the chauffeur, doing my best to ignore the pain between my legs. As he twisted and turned his way through the labyrinthine streets, I hobbled in pursuit at a safe distance. In about five minutes we had reached Theobalds Road.

There, a large black limousine was waiting for him, parked on a double yellow line. He got into the driver's seat and through the smoked glass of the windows I could see him handing the envelope to the passenger in the back. I could also see the face of this passenger, clearly enough to recognize him. It was, as I had expected, a well-known minister in Her Majesty's Government.

XIII
The End

So, my time is almost up. Since I wrote the last few pages, two weeks ago, things have got much worse. The pain in my stomach is terrible. And now I don't feel strong enough to write any more. I thought about dictating the remaining words to Jackie (yes, reader – I married her), but even my voice is weak these days. It hurts to say anything out loud. It hurts to talk, it hurts to move, it even hurts to breathe.

Besides, I have reached the end, more or less. What else is there to tell you? In a year's time the prolonged, bitter miners' strike would take place in the UK, and the Thatcher government would dig itself in for an extended war of attrition, armed with information about how the country could survive the disruption to its energy supplies. I might have proved, to my own satisfaction, that there was a direct line of communication between Emeric's salons and the government, but I didn't know what to do with the knowledge. Nobody was doing anything illegal. Nobody was even doing anything very surprising, when you thought about it. Chris certainly wasn't surprised when I told him what I'd discovered. 'Of course,' he said. 'Oxford and Cambridge are close to the centres of power. Very close. That's why they don't let people like you and me and Jo come here very often. They don't want too many of the plebs getting a glimpse of the machinery. But even when we do see how it works, what are we supposed to do about it?'

His own answer to that has been clear enough. He went to the States as a postgrad, carried on his research into the extremes of the conservative movement, got himself a university post, married a nice American called Elspeth, adopted a girl from Ethiopia, gave up academia, found a job in publishing instead. I don't know exactly how or why it all went pear-shaped for him, but a few years later he was back in the UK, divorced, and he took up the deputy editorship of a magazine called *History & Heritage*, and has been doing that ever since. Chris was always a brilliant student, and if he's settled for a deputy's job all these years (especially at a magazine that doesn't really deserve him), it's not through lack of ambition. His real life's work is his research. He has kept a close, watchful eye, for more than forty years, on those covert networks of power and how they operate. He's kept an eye on Roger Wagstaff in particular.

And Wagstaff has certainly been busy over the last few years. After a long time in the wilderness, the Processus Group (which was officially formed in the mid-1990s) has at last found its ideological soulmate in the post-Brexit government. Surely only a matter of time now before Roger makes it into the Lords. In fact I'm surprised it hasn't happened already.

Rebecca, as I understand it, has maintained her devotion to him, although I'm not sure it's ever been reciprocated in the way she would have liked. Emeric got his knighthood and still lives in Cambridge, though I think he's too old to teach any more. As for his daughter, the lovely Lavinia – she went back to the US, found herself a wealthy Republican husband, and the last I heard was advising Donald Trump on campaign strategy. She and her father are more or less estranged, sadly. I think she turned out to be too extreme even for him.

*

Popping the last chocolate into her mouth, and drinking down the final dregs of the cold, bitter coffee, DI Freeborne closed the ring binder and sat back in her chair. She put her hands together so that her fingers made an apex, which she rested against her mouth, and in this pensive attitude she remained for some time, thinking about what she had just read and listening to the first stirrings of birdsong outside the house, as cracks of grey daylight began to appear at the edges of the curtains. After about ten minutes she stirred herself, took a pen and paper from her briefcase, and wrote a short note to Joanna:

Dear Mrs Maidstone,

Thank you so much for giving me the opportunity to read Mr Collier's remarkable memoir. If you don't mind, I am going to take it away with me for a few days. I shall make a copy and return the original to you as soon as possible.

I have also borrowed the copy of Mr Cockerill's novel which was inscribed to your friend Thomas. Again, I shall return it as soon as I can. However, I think it may be of some evidential value.

I am most grateful for your hospitality yesterday evening and for your kindness in letting me stay overnight. This whole business must be unspeakably distressing for you and your family, but I have hopes that we can bring it to a speedy resolution.

I will be in touch very shortly. You may rest assured of that.

Sincerely and thankfully,
Pru Freeborne

PART THREE

Sorted

PROOF/REBORN
PROOF/
REBORN
An Essay in Autofiction

P.

So, we've decided to tell the rest of the story ourselves. We'll do our best to tell the truth, as we see it.

R.

Our truth, that is.

P.

My name's Phyl. Sometimes I'll be the one telling the story.

R.

And my name's Rash. Sometimes it will be me.

P./R.

And maybe, now and again, we'll try telling it together.

P./R.

It started in the same way, for both of us. It started at Heathrow Terminal 5.

The incident with the lifts/elevators.

It started with two guys (two different guys) who were convinced that they alone knew how to operate the lift/elevator doors. They were convinced that you could only open them by pushing the buttons, and that we were just helpless passive females waiting for them to come along and show us how to do things.

Both these incidents ended in the same way: with the men believing in their version of the truth (that they'd made the doors open) and us believing in ours (that the doors would've opened anyway). The only difference being that the men were delusional, and we were correct.

Not all truths are equal, however sincerely believed.

We both came away feeling angry and upset. We both came away wishing – in a spirit of *l'esprit de l'escalier* (*l'esprit de l'ascenseur*?) – that we'd had the guts and the patience to offer these mansplaining idiots some real proof as to how the doors were programmed to work. But we didn't. Instead we came home and complained about it to each other. And that was the start of the friendship between us. That was when we realized that we were on the same page.

Which would only have been a figure of speech, of course, until now. As of now, we are literally on the same page.

R.

I really liked the policeman lady. One of the things I liked about her was that she knew how to ask difficult questions in a tactful way. She wanted to find things out about my father's death but at the same time she knew that every mention of it would be painful to us.

Something she said over dinner that night has stayed with me. She said that everyone who gets to sixty has to learn how to deal with the death of their parents. It's just one of those nightmare things that no one can avoid once you reach that age. And honestly, from the way she was talking about it, she was every bit as affected by the death of her father – who died peacefully in a London hospital bed – as I was by the death of mine, even though the circumstances in his case were so sudden and so weird.

Of course I never really thought of him as my father. I never called him Dad, always Christopher or Chris. And once he'd split up with Elspeth, we didn't see much of each other. But that's not to say we weren't close in some ways. In the days since he died, I keep coming back to that summer I spent with him in England, when I must have been about eleven or twelve, and it was kind of awkward because we didn't really know how to relate to each other, so we spent pretty much the whole time watching *Friends*. I'm not sure he ever liked the show that much but it seems somehow typical of Chris that once he'd decided to commit himself to something, he'd never be satisfied until he became an expert on it. That was his Cambridge background, I suppose. Now that he's gone I do realize how much I respected that in him. If there's one way I can honour his memory I think it's by following that ethos. Don't be a dilettante. To understand a subject you have to know everything, you really have to fucking master it, whether it's episodes of *Friends* or the history of conservatism post-1979.

Since he died, there's one episode I've watched three or four times. A very early episode, actually: Season 1, Episode 8 – *The One Where Nana Dies Twice.* It's an unusual episode because Ross and Monica's grandmother dies and although to start with it's played for laughs – just when Ross thinks that his grandmother's dead, her eyes pop open and she comes back to life again – it's one of the few episodes – maybe the only one? – where you see any of the six main characters having to deal with grief. The funeral scene at the end is pretty touching, and the emotion feels genuine – it feels *earned* – because it's true that for most people in their twenties, dealing with the death of a grandparent is going to be their first and biggest experience of bereavement. Apart from Phoebe's mother dying a long time ago, when she was only ten – way before the time frame of the show begins – none of the characters in *Friends* ever has to come to terms with the death of a parent. That's another reason that kids and teenagers like the show, I guess, because it never deals with any of those massive adult crises and traumas that are waiting for all of us and we're never going to be able to avoid. Throughout the ten-year time span of the show, none of those six characters ever learns the thing that I have had to learn in the last few days: that whether you were close to them or not, when your mother or father dies, it shakes you to the core, and profoundly changes the way you see the world.

P.

When Cockerill's mother died, it shook him to the core, and profoundly changed the way he saw the world.

After reading this sentence (from Richard Wilkes's introduction to the reprinted edition of *My Innocence*) I picked up my yellow marker pen and highlighted it. I thought about the sentence and stared into space for a little while. Outside my window the overgrown jasmine plant, which my father had been talking about cutting back all summer, was tapping gently against the glass and creating pleasing, abstract patterns of light and shade on my bedroom wall.

We must remember that in a previous novel, A Rope from Hell, *he had fictionalized the story of his father's betrayal of his mother. If she herself had read the novel (and apparently she did) it seems reasonable to assume that it would have caused her considerable pain. Cockerill himself, surprisingly, had not foreseen this while he was writing it. However, the guilt he subsequently felt on this subject must have been one of the factors contributing to his growing unhappiness, which had turned into full-blown depression by the mid-1980s when he began work on* My Innocence. *In these circumstances, his mother's unexpected cancer diagnosis in the autumn of 1985 must have come as an even more terrible blow; and it was her death just a few months later which seems to have set him on the suicidal path that the book itself traces so dramatically.*

I turned from the introduction to the novel itself. I had read it twice over the last few days. It was a book in which Peter Cockerill had attempted to tell the story of his mother's early life: her childhood in the Scottish borders, her move to the English Midlands with her family in the 1930s, her courtship, engagement and marriage to Cockerill's father – this being a tragic mistake, he seemed to believe: the thing that had destroyed her. The book was part memoir and part essay: factual accounts of his mother's life, interspersed with authorial digressions about the impossibility of ever knowing the truth about your parents' past. There were also some passages set in the 1950s, in which Cockerill drew on his own earliest memories of childhood, and some which took place in the present – transcripts of conversations between him and his mother, when he was trying to draw recollections out of her. It was all very intense and moving, but there was also something cloying about it, something about the relationship between Cockerill and his mother that felt a little bit off. The most interesting (and, to me, paradoxically, the most honest-sounding) passage came on the very last page, when he cast a critical eye back over what he'd written. I'd read this page so often in the last few days that I almost knew it by heart. This is how Cockerill had finished the book, all those years ago:

But what have I learned, in the end, from this incursion into my late mother's years of youthful optimism? Has the real subject of this book been her innocence, or mine? I have tried to tell the truth: the truth as I remember it, as I have been told it, as I have been able to research it. In this way I hoped to do justice to her memory: to present nothing more ambitious, or more pretentious, than an honest and faithful account of her early life. But perhaps my very belief that this might be possible is, in itself, the purest demonstration of my own naivety. Any act of writing must also, by definition, be an act of selection; therefore distortion; and therefore invention. In this book I have skirted the rank dishonesty into which most writers are led by the siren call of 'fiction', and which so many needy and credulous readers appear to crave. But, at the same time, I realize that I have not hugged the truth's shoreline as closely as I hoped to do, and more importantly, the writing of this book has not brought me into the kind of closeness with my mother that I wanted. She is gone, and there is no bringing her back. Writing has turned out to be just another dead end: my words bring me no comfort, and my voice goes unheard. After this, I have nothing more to write. There will be no more writing. But without writing, can there be living? That is the question that confronts me now. And my answer? No, there cannot. It is impossible to carry on. Reaching this final page has proved to me one thing, and one thing only. It is time to give in, and bring this unhappy life to an end.

Phyl!

I heard my mother calling me. I ignored her, and read the last sentence again.

Phyl, are you coming down? The funeral's started!

The funeral. My parents were obsessed with this funeral. Christopher's funeral was still more than two weeks away but in the meantime this was the funeral everyone was talking about. The Queen. Did I really want to go downstairs and watch it? It was scheduled to go on for hours. History in the making, my parents kept telling me. I didn't know how they could bring themselves to be interested in it. Ten days earlier one of my mother's oldest friends had been stabbed to death. As far as I was concerned, that was way more historically significant. Especially now that a question had entered my head, and wouldn't go away.

How come Professor Richard Wilkes had been present in the hotel where the murder took place?

R.

On Wednesday morning, true to her promise, policeman lady returns the manuscript that she's borrowed. It comes in the post at about eleven-thirty. Phyl and I take it up to her bedroom and begin reading it immediately. We open up the ring binder and she passes the pages to me one by one as soon as she's finished reading them.

It takes us a couple of hours to read the whole thing, and after that we have questions. Lots of questions.

So first of all, I say, this is a man who swears that he's never going to commit suicide. And then a few years later, that's exactly what he does.

Phyl agrees, and says: Yeah, I find that really strange. And another thing that strikes me is when he says that he's desperate for his books to live on after he's died. 'If my work doesn't survive me, then I will have failed. It will all have been for nothing.'

Was he famous at the time?

No, not at all. He was never famous during his lifetime. He only became famous after he'd died and people began writing essays about him and teaching his books on university courses.

One of these people was this professor guy – Wilkes. Right?

Yep.

And what do we know about *him*?

I can tell you what we *don't* know, Phyl says. We don't know whether he and Peter Cockerill ever met.

And you think that's important?

I do. Very important. I found some old newspaper pieces by him online, from before 1987, all about the books scene of the time. But he doesn't mention Cockerill.

So, nothing to go on there.

Except . . . Except that would be the worst thing of all, wouldn't it? As far as Cockerill's concerned. To be completely ignored, passed over. As if you didn't exist.

We both sit there for a while, turning this situation over in our minds. I still can't get over how quiet it is in this house. At my place in Wanstead there's constant traffic noise, not to mention the music in the street and the sound of next door's TV. Here all you can hear is birds singing. I've never realized this before, but during the day, birds never stop singing. The little fuckers keep it up morning, noon and night. I've got to say, it's beginning to drive me slightly crazy.

So what's your theory? I ask, after I've had enough of the twittering of the blackbirds or the sparrows or whatever they are.

I don't have a theory, Phyl says. Not yet. But I have two hunches.

Come on then, I say after a while, when she fails to elaborate. Let's hear them.

One is that Peter Cockerill – perhaps even his suicide – has something to do with your dad's murder.

OK. With you on that one.

The second . . . Well, the second is a bit more off the wall.

She holds up her copy of the book – *My Innocence* – which has been practically glued to her fingers recently.

Let's not think of this as a novel for a moment, she says. Because it's also something else, right? It's a suicide note.

I nod.

But the thing is, it's a suicide note which might exist in two versions, do you see?

I shake my head.

Not really.

Well, there's the published version, the one we have here. But there was also the proof copy. Except nearly all of those seem to have mysteriously disappeared. But how do we know that the two copies were the same?

Well . . . they're bound to be, aren't they?

No – not at all. Authors make changes to their books when they're correcting the proofs. That's the whole point. So who's to say that Peter Cockerill didn't make changes to his suicide note?

I frown.

It's possible, I suppose. But what would it prove?

Well . . . Supposing – just supposing – Cockerill never *did* intend to kill himself. Supposing he was *murdered*?

By Wilkes?

Why not?

I think about this. It sounds crazy, but it's not outside the realms of possibility.

So what would that prove?

It wouldn't *prove* anything, Phyl says. But if he was prepared to do it once, thirty-five years ago . . . I don't know. Maybe he'd be prepared to do it again.

I feel like there should be some dramatic music playing after she's said these words. But there isn't. Just those birds. Twittering away.

P.

So how were we going to track down a proof copy of *My Innocence*? We only had one lead. My dad's friend Victor, who ran an antiquarian bookshop in London, had recently acquired a copy, and sold it on to someone for a vast sum of money.

He won't tell you who it was, my dad assured me.

OK, I said. That's fine. I wouldn't expect him to. But Rash and I are going into London on Friday, so there's no harm in dropping by his shop and asking him what he can remember about it, is there?

I suppose not. Wouldn't it be easier to call him on the phone?

We're going into London anyway, I said.

Fine, said my dad. Just don't pester him, that's all. Victor's a very busy man.

I didn't see how this could possibly be true, given the business he was in, but I let it pass.

On Friday, we took a mid-morning train to London. We had to change at Reading. On the second part of the journey, we sat opposite a couple of old guys, retired by the looks of it.

(By the way, Rash thinks I should be writing all of this in the present tense. She thinks it sounds much more immediate and authentic that way. To her the past tense is 'embarrassing' the same way that fiction is. If I were to take her advice, the last paragraph would have read like this: 'On Friday, we take a mid-morning train to London. We have to change at Reading. On the second part of the journey, we sit opposite a couple of old guys, retired by the looks of it.' Do you think it makes much difference? Personally, I don't think it does. I'm going to keep using the past tense. It feels more natural to me. After all, these things happened in the past. The present is just me sitting at my keyboard, now, typing these words.)

The old guys were discussing politics. That morning the new mini-budget had been announced and it sounded pretty wacky, with tax cuts being handed out left, right and centre. One of the guys was very agitated about this and kept saying it was crazy and irresponsible and everyone knew the economy was in a terrible state and had been ever since Brexit but nobody was prepared to admit that. The other guy was much more laid back and said everything in politics was cyclical and there would be a different party in power in a couple of years' time anyway and Brexit wasn't really that much of a big deal, the European Union was just a trading bloc and since when did people get so emotional about something like that? But they both seemed to agree Liz Truss was a wild card and they had a good old laugh about one of the newspapers which apparently was running daily photographs of a lettuce as it wilted and taking bets on which one would last longer, Liz Truss or the lettuce. I felt like telling them that people like me were sick of people like them treating politics as if it was all a big joke, but didn't. Maybe I was losing my sense of humour but something about their conversation was annoying me and for once it was a relief when the safety announcement came on and drowned out their voices:

If you see something that doesn't look right, speak to staff, or text British Transport Police on 61016.

We'll sort it.

See it. Say it. Sorted.

We reached Paddington and then we took the new Elizabeth line to Tottenham Court Road and then before we went to the bookshop we went for a coffee so that we could discuss strategy. We went to Starbucks even though neither of us particularly liked Starbucks. We just went because it was there.

The one thing I remember about Victor, I said, is that he really likes his lunches. And today's Friday so I reckon he'll be going for an especially big lunch, probably with one of his friends. So somehow I've got to try and persuade him to let me mind the shop while he's at lunch. I've met him quite a few times and he likes my dad so I think he'll trust me, and that way we can get a look at his customer account book. He's totally old school, he still keeps handwritten records.

Won't he just close the shop at lunchtime?

That's what he'd normally do, yes. But maybe we can find a special reason for him to keep it open.

Such as?

Well, you could pretend to be a wealthy customer. You tell him you're thinking of buying a really expensive edition but you haven't quite made up your mind and you'll come back in half an hour.

You want me to pretend to be a book collector? What kind of book am I going to buy?

Oh, I don't know. Anything, as long as it's expensive. A James Baldwin first edition, or something.

James Baldwin? So I only collect books by Black writers, because I'm Black?

No, of course not.

Good. Don't try to pigeonhole me, thanks very much. I'm quite capable of impersonating a connoisseur of Evelyn Waugh or Virginia Woolf.

OK, whatever. I'm sorry. I didn't mean to patronize you.

Anyway, I'm not sure I could carry it off. I don't look wealthy or middle-aged enough. Maybe I'll say that I'm doing it for someone else. A client.

A client? What sort of client?

I don't know. Don't worry, I'll think of something.

I wasn't sure about this, but on the whole I trusted Rash. We drank up and made our way to the bookshop, which was in Cecil Court. It was 12.45 when we arrived, the perfect timing. There were no other customers and Victor was sitting behind his little table drinking tea and listening to the radio. Some story about the budget again. I kept hearing Liz Truss's name, and Kwasi Kwarteng's. He didn't recognize me at first but when I told him I was Andrew Maidstone's daughter he became quite friendly. Then I introduced Rash and told him she was a friend of mine and she was here to hunt out rare editions for her wealthy client.

He told us to look around and I soon clocked an old copy of Radclyffe Hall's *The Well of Loneliness* in a locked cabinet.

Ask him about that one, I whispered to her.

Who's Radclyffe Hall? Rash asked.

She was around in the 1920s. Very controversial. It's considered a classic of lesbian writing.

Cool, she said, and then, turning round to Victor, she asked: How much is this copy of *The Well of Loneliness*? Is it a first edition?

It is, said Victor, getting up and unlocking the cabinet. Dust jacket in very good condition. Some minor foxing.

My client isn't too worried about foxing, Rash said. But he's very interested in lesbian writing. Something of a fetish of his.

I see.

How much is it?

One thousand five hundred pounds.

Rash drew in her breath.

A little steep – considering the foxing, I mean.

You don't find many first editions of *The Well of Loneliness*. In all my time in the business I've only ever encountered three.

Just three? Well, well, well.

It took both me and Victor a few moments to realize that Rash had just made a joke: whether it was intentional or not wasn't clear. We both laughed, somewhat nervously. I was nervous in case this charade was about to be seen through. Victor was nervous because he suddenly found himself on the brink of a big sale.

I think my client would be interested in this. It might be a good idea if I contacted him.

She looked at her watch.

He'll be in a meeting right now. I'll call him in half an hour.

Excellent. Unfortunately I was just about to close the shop for a couple of hours. I'm meeting a friend for lunch. Perhaps you could come back this afternoon, around three-thirty?

I'm afraid not. I'm booked on the Eurostar and have to be at St Pancras by two o'clock.

Ah. I suppose I could always—

I wouldn't like you to miss your lunch.

This was the point at which I intervened and offered to hold the fort while Victor was away. He was doubtful at first but the possibility of selling this copy was clearly too tempting for him. Rash departed in order to go back to her non-existent hotel and phone her non-existent client, and he quickly showed me how to operate the card reader and record the purchase in his ledger. Five minutes later I had the shop to myself. I put up the 'Closed' sign, locked the door, and settled down to study his list of recent sales and purchases. Before long, I had found both the names I was looking for.

*

We are very sorry to announce the death of Christopher Swann, who served as deputy editor of this magazine since 2012.

Born in Taunton, Somerset, in 1961, Christopher was a graduate of St Stephen's College, Cambridge. He pursued postgraduate studies at New York University, and lived in the United States for many years with his wife, Elspeth, and their adopted daughter.

Christopher joined our magazine on his return to the United Kingdom at the age of 50, and quickly became a popular and respected member of the *History & Heritage* team. He was known for being a rigorous fact-checker and a stickler for grammatical accuracy. He drew up a legendary style sheet which became the basis for all contributions to the magazine. Conforming to this style sheet – an absolute prerequisite for publication – became jokingly known in the office as 'doing it Swann's way'.

Christopher's fields of expertise were wide-ranging, and included the Hundred Years War, the Robert Walpole administration, and the dictatorship of António de Oliveira Salazar in Portugal. His main interest, however, was the development of conservative thought in America and the United Kingdom in the years following the Reagan/Thatcher 'special relationship'. Christopher made no secret of his personal politics but used to quip that 'some of my best friends are conservatives'. He had a generous respect for the intellectual foundations of conservatism but became increasingly concerned that the movement was being taken over by extremists on both sides of the Atlantic. In recent years, these concerns were expressed more and more often on his personal blog. (The content of which is independent from, and not endorsed by, *H&H* magazine itself.)

In his spare time, Christopher pursued some unexpected interests, and would sometimes surprise members of the *H&H* staff with his knowledge of fusion and jazz-funk albums of the 1970s, and his enthusiasm for American TV sitcoms which he described as 'the great underappreciated art form of our time'.

His funeral was held at Conway Hall in Red Lion Square, Bloomsbury, on Thursday 6th October this year. It was a humanist ceremony, attended by his sister, his former wife, his adopted daughter, and a large gathering of friends and work colleagues.

History & Heritage, December 2022

*

R.

The care home is in the middle of nowhere. We have to go to Waterloo station and take a southbound train which deposits us at a tiny station somewhere in the Surrey countryside. There, a car is waiting for us, with a woman in the driver's seat. This must be Helena. Helena Fezakery. She gets out of the car and introduces herself and shakes our hands, looking a little wary. Phyl takes the lead – she is always the politer one, of the two of us – and thanks her profusely and says that it's really kind of her to help us in this way.

Our escapade in the London bookshop was a great success. By the time I rejoined her, Phyl had found both the names she needed. We completed our little diversionary ruse by leaving a note on Victor's desk. *Sadly misunderstood my client's interest in lesbian classics. Only collects illustrated editions. Many apologies.* Then we left the shop and posted our spare set of keys through the letterbox. Back in Rookthorne, we set about googling the first of the names. Luckily it was a very unusual one: there only seemed to be one Helena Fezakery in existence, and she had a LinkedIn profile. This was the woman who had sold Victor the proof copy of *My Innocence*, as part of a job lot of about five hundred books.

We didn't contact her right away. In the meantime, we got another lucky break. A bit more online research told us that Cockerill's publisher, Newman & Fox, had been run by a guy called Charles Newman, who had written a memoir in the 1990s. I went down to London again and ordered it from the British Library in St Pancras and read it one morning. Pretty dry stuff, to be honest. A page and a half devoted to Cockerill and his novels, but surprisingly little information about his suicide: I got the impression the episode had been too painful for his editor to write about. There were, however, a couple of glowing references to Newman's loyal and long-standing secretary: Margaret Fezakery. It seemed a 100 per cent certainty that this would be Helena's mother. So, armed with that information, I phoned Helena and told her that I gathered her mother had worked for Newman & Fox and would it be possible for me to interview her for my PhD thesis on the publishing scene in the 1980s.

Helena is a brisk, no-nonsense woman, in her early fifties I'd guess. As she drives us rather too quickly along the narrow country lanes, she says:

I should warn you that my mother has dementia. But bizarrely it only seems to affect her short-term memory. She won't recognize me or have any idea who I am. But on the other hand she has perfect recall of everything that happened forty years ago. I think you'll probably find talking to her very helpful.

I'm really sorry to hear that, I tell her. But great that she might be able to help us.

Phyl remains silent. She looks anxious. I think I know what she is anxious about. She is feeling guilty that when Helena put her mother into a home, she parcelled up her collection of five hundred books and sold them to Victor as a job lot for around five hundred pounds without realizing that one of them was going to be sold on for a hundred times that amount. That's not our problem, I've been telling her. That's for Victor to have on his conscience. Not us. And if it's really bothering you, we can tell her when all this is over, but even then, what's she going to do about it?

We turn into a driveway and the care home looms into view. Avalon Rest Home, it's called. A sad old Victorian red-brick building at the end of a long avenue of trees. A big car park with only about half a dozen cars in it. When Helena turns off the engine and we get out of the car the silence is overwhelming. We're only about half an hour from London but this feels like the deep countryside. It's a breezy afternoon and the trees are starting to shed their autumn leaves. The sound of them pattering down onto the asphalt is the only sound in the whole world. The weather is definitely turning cold. This is a cheerless place. Helena is obviously used to it, and makes a beeline for the front door, with me and Phyl close behind, arm in arm, huddled together for warmth.

The entrance hallway is high-ceilinged and chilly and dark with a mild smell of damp. Helena goes over to say a few words to the receptionist and then leads us to the big central staircase and we follow her up first one flight of stairs, then another. She is fitter than either of us and by the time we reach the second floor we are both out of breath.

She leads us to a room towards the end of the corridor and ushers us inside. It is a dark and overheated bedroom and there is a very, very old woman sitting in an armchair next to the window, wearing a nightie and dressing gown. She has warm fluffy slippers on her feet, over a thick pair of surgical socks. She has a fine head of white hair which is pulled back into a severe bun. She looks at all three of us without recognition, but the appearance of three strangers in her room doesn't seem to alarm her. She turns to her daughter and says:

Have you brought me some visitors, sister? That's nice.

Hello, Mum, Helena says. It's me. Helena. Your daughter. Remember?

Margaret Fezakery looks intently into her daughter's eyes, searching, wondering. You can almost hear the cogs of her rusty memory straining into motion. The pain on her face, the sense of humiliation, is terrible to see.

Of course I remember, she says. (Although it's clear that she doesn't.) And who are these other people?

We introduce ourselves and as concisely as possible Helena tells her mother why we've come to see her. At the same time she fusses around the room, tidying things, throwing away used Kleenex and wet wipes, making the bed look a bit neater. Only after finishing this does she say hello to her mother properly, kissing her and folding her into a tight embrace. Her mother hugs her back, enjoying the human warmth even if she doesn't quite know who this person is.

So you're doing a PhD? Margaret says to me, when the introductions are over. She seems surprised. On publishing?

That's right. I'm writing a chapter of my thesis on the history of Newman and Fox.

A chance for you to talk about the old days, Helena says to her mother, nodding encouragingly as she sits down on the bed. There is only one other chair in the room. I take that, while Phyl places herself on the bed next to Helena.

Well, of course, I'll be very happy to tell you everything I can, Margaret says. I never thought that one day somebody would want to use me as a . . . as a historical source! What would you like to know?

This is a promising start, but things are not that simple. I don't like to cut straight to the chase so I ask her some general questions about Newman & Fox and their place in the British publishing scene of the 1980s and that sends us off on all sorts of tangents and diversions. She starts talking about some old writer called Beryl Bainbridge and how they wanted to 'poach' her from another publisher, which would no doubt have been very interesting if I had ever heard of Beryl Bainbridge, but I haven't, but never mind, that doesn't deter Margaret, who launches into a long story about how she once had lunch with Beryl Bainbridge which was clearly one of the highlights of her life (Margaret's, that is, not Beryl Bainbridge's). With some difficulty I steer her around to the subject of some of the authors that Charles Newman actually did publish, and she tells us what a lovely and gentle man he was and how all his writers adored him even though he never paid them enough money. For ten minutes or more we discuss a whole lot of unfamiliar and irrelevant names (with Phyl pretending to write them down in her notebook, on the pretext of being – what? my assistant? – we never discussed this) before I feel ready to get down to the real business of this afternoon by asking:

And what about Peter Cockerill? Wasn't he one of Charles's authors as well?

Margaret's manner changes when this name is mentioned. A hint of sadness comes over her, and a hint of animosity as well.

Oh, yes, she says. Charles was very impressed by Peter Cockerill. He considered him one of the most important writers on our list. I could never quite see why.

Didn't something happen to him in the end? Something tragic?

Yes, indeed. Poor Peter took his own life. The whole affair threw us into turmoil for quite some time.

I think . . . I think I read that it happened around the time that his final book was published?

A few months before that, I believe. The proofs had just come in. I remember that distinctly.

It was called *My Innocence*, wasn't it? A sort of autobiographical novel.

I don't know how you'd describe it. I only read a few pages. As I said, Peter wasn't really my cup of tea at all.

Can you tell me what happened? Anything you can remember about that . . . shocking episode, really. That's if you can remember anything about it at all.

Oh, I remember those few days *quite* distinctly. Of that I can assure you.

We sit and wait while she composes herself and takes a sip of water from the beaker at her side.

Well, she begins. It was a Friday, and the proofs of that book had just come in – about one hundred of them – and they were sitting in a corner of the office, in three big cardboard boxes. Only the top box had been opened, just so that Charles could see what they looked like. He wasn't going to send them out yet because he and Peter Cockerill had decided that Peter should write reviewers a letter about the book, which was going to be sent out with every proof copy. A foolish idea, if you ask me. But anyway, he was waiting for that to come in from Peter.

So the weekend went by, and then it was Tuesday morning. The post came in and it included a letter from Peter so I gave it to Charles to read. I didn't look at it myself. A few minutes after reading it he came out and walked past my desk looking as white as a sheet. He went out into the garden at the back of the office to smoke a cigarette and, I suppose, to think for a moment. After that he spent the rest of the morning trying to contact Peter on the telephone, but he couldn't get through. The phone wasn't engaged, it was actually out of order. And then early in the afternoon he told me that he was going out for the rest of the day. I didn't know where he was going. Only later did I find out that he'd driven down to Hampshire, where Peter lived by himself in a little cottage in the New Forest. When he got there the fire brigade were putting out what was left of the blaze and the place was swarming with policemen, and of course Peter's body was inside.

She falls silent, and in fact nobody speaks for a little while until Phyl gently prompts:

Do you know what happened to those proof copies?

They sat there in the office for a few more days, Margaret says, and then they disappeared. It was only years later that I learned Charles had taken them back to his own house and destroyed them all.

How did you find that out? I ask.

Margaret doesn't answer for a while. It's as if she's lost in some private train of thought, staring out of the window. Then her eyes come back into focus and she turns to us and says:

Oh, that was Howard.

Howard?

Howard, yes. Charles's partner.

You mean his business partner? Phyl asks. Howard was the Fox in Newman and Fox?

Oh, no, no. That was Nicholas Fox. He left the company years before all this happened. No, this was Charles's *romantic* partner. Howard Beddoes.

Phyl writes this down. The name is obviously new to her, but not to me. 'Howard' is mentioned on almost every page of Newman's memoir.

Howard was Charles's rock, Margaret continued. They were together for more than thirty years. I can't think what he would have done without him. After what happened with Peter, you see, Charles was never quite the same again. He didn't go to pieces, quite, but it did affect him very badly, and his drinking, which had always been heavy, got much worse. He was barely sixty when he died, poor soul. Heart attack. All those cigarettes and whiskies.

She pauses and draws breath, inhaling with a prolonged wheeze.

Speaking personally, I never really took to Howard. His politics were rather extreme, for one thing. I mean, he was always very reactionary, but Charles had held him in check, to a certain extent. I was quite shocked to hear, a few years ago, that he was standing as a councillor for the BNP or whatever they were called. But still, I was grateful to him for keeping Charles more or less on the straight and narrow for all those years, and we did try to stay in touch for a while after Charles had died. We even went out for dinner together once. I can't say it was a very successful occasion. He got rather drunk and rather maudlin and that was when he told me the full story of that week – the week of Peter Cockerill's suicide. I'd never known, you see, exactly what was in the letter that Charles read that morning. I never asked, and he never told me.

She falls silent again. Just at the most crucial point. Phyl and I are on the edges of our seats and for a terrible moment it seems that she might not be able to remember any more. She is frowning, looking worried. Finally she leans forward and says, in a whisper:

You know, I'm not sure I should be telling you all this in front of *her.* In front of a nurse.

She points her finger in the direction of Helena, who says:

Mum, I'm not a nurse. I'm your daughter. Your daughter, Helena.

Margaret stares at her daughter, uncomprehending. It's as if the words are meaningless to her. A terrible silence starts to descend. I'm desperate to break it before it becomes unbreakable.

And what *was* in it? I ask, looking directly at Margaret and speaking loudly, as if I'm addressing a halfwit.

What was in it? What was in what?

The letter.

Oh, the letter! Yes, of course. Well, it seems that Peter was asking for all the proof copies of *My Innocence* to be destroyed. And at the same time, he asked for some corrections to be made to the page proofs.

Phyl is looking animated.

So the published version, in the end, was *not* the same as the proof version? she asks.

No, I suppose not.

And do you know what the changes were?

Margaret shakes her head.

I do know that Charles carried out Peter's instructions. A few days later the three cardboard boxes disappeared from the office. Howard said that Charles brought them home with him one evening in a taxi and the next day they incinerated them. 'I was there when it happened,' he told me. 'I was there when it happened. Tears were streaming down Charles's face. But you can't ignore a dead man's wishes, can you? We did it together. We burned them. Every last one of them.' And that was when I said to him, 'But you know, that isn't *quite* true,' and you should have seen his face! 'What on earth do you mean?' he said. And I told him: '*I've* got one of those proof copies somewhere. I took one home with me, the weekend they came in, and started reading it. I never finished it, mind you. Self-indulgent drivel, I thought it was. All that drooling over his mother.' And Howard was looking at me with his mouth wide open, and then he said: 'So you have a proof of *My Innocence*, in your house?' And I nodded and said, 'Certainly I have. Somewhere or other. If I can find it, in all the mess.' But do you know what? I *couldn't* find it, in all the mess. I mean, I was never a tidy person. And I didn't look for it for very long, because I couldn't really see what all the fuss was about. Who knows what happened to it? Maybe it got thrown out with the rubbish, or I gave it to Oxfam, or something. Anyway, I couldn't find it. But I did have one, once.

Helena looks thoughtful, and says:

Do you know, Mum, when I packed all your books up and sold them I've got a feeling I saw it. I think it was one of the ones I sold. It was in one of the boxes in the attic.

Margaret leans towards me with an air of complicity and, jerking her thumb in Helena's direction, she loudly whispers:

Who *is* this woman? Do I know her?

I'm not sure how to answer, so I pretend that the question hasn't been asked.

And what was he like as a person, Peter Cockerill? Did you get on with him?

Well, Margaret says, I don't think these are very *academic* questions, if I may say so. But since you ask, I did find him rather difficult. He was a rather . . . now, what's the word? Well, he was a rather *angry* person, that's really the only way of putting it.

Angry? What was he angry about?

Oh, the same thing that all writers are angry about, I suppose. Lack of recognition. But it seemed to matter to him more than to most people, I don't know why.

Can you give an example?

Well, as I said, I didn't know him well. Didn't know him well at all. I do remember he was in the office one day and he was in a *furious* temper, over some article that had just been published in the newspaper.

This article said something about him? Something he didn't like?

Margaret laughs and shakes her head.

Oh, no. That was the whole point! It was much worse than that. The worst thing you can imagine – it didn't mention him at all. Two whole pages on the most important young writers in the country and his name didn't appear anywhere!

The thought of it seems to amuse her greatly. As, I suspect, it did at the time. And then Phyl asks:

I don't suppose you can remember the name of whoever wrote that piece?

Margaret shakes her head.

It wasn't a writer called Richard Wilkes, by any chance?

I've really no idea. It was such a long time ago . . .

Phyl and I exchange glances. It's frustrating not to have our suspicions confirmed. Meanwhile, Margaret is talking, but not to us any more. She now seems to be talking only to herself.

. . . yes, he was full of anger, Peter. As was Howard. Both of them, calm and quiet one minute, loud and angry the next. Both of them always losing their tempers. Angry men. It seems, in a way, to have been the story of my life. David, my husband, was the same. Angry men. I don't know what they're so angry *about*, because they seem to have things their own way, most of the time. And yet, all our lives, we just seem to be surrounded by angry men . . .

Phyl puts her notebook away. Margaret's quiet, inward-looking monologue continues even as we say thank you and stand up. Helena takes my place in the seat next to her mother, and we leave them to spend a few minutes alone together. I glance back at them as we leave. They look as close to each other as a mother and daughter could possibly be. And, at the same time, as distant from each other as two perfect strangers.

P.

Salmon inari taco. Beef teriyaki. Chicken teriyaki. Hoisin duck roll.

Sometimes the motion of the conveyor belt mesmerized me. I would stare at it and my mind would go blank and it would feel as if time was standing still.

Dorayaki pancakes. Prawn katsu. Tuna sashimi.

Other times, the movement of the belt seemed to *help* me to think. I would focus on one dish and watch its winding, circuitous progress around the whole restaurant.

Kaiso seaweed. Kaiso seaweed. Kaiso seaweed.

Today, it felt as if I was alternating between both of these states. I would pick out one detail of the mystery, follow it in my mind, round and round, and then, just when I felt that I was getting somewhere, I would realize that I had come back to the starting point again.

There were one or two certainties: Peter Cockerill had wanted all the proof copies of *My Innocence* destroyed. The weekend of his suicide, he had changed his mind about something, and written to his editor, asking him to make amendments to the text. A few years earlier, he had told Brian Collier that he would never have the courage to kill himself.

Chicken teriyaki. Prawn katsu. Mixed maki. Kimchi chicken.

And there was one big unknown: did this – did *any* of this – have the slightest bearing on the death of Chris at Wetherby Hall thirty-five years later? Had Rash and I become fixated on this idea to the exclusion of all others, quite forgetting that, according to DI Freeborne, there were numerous other suspects, all of whom might have had much more solid motives than Richard Wilkes for committing the crime?

Never mind that, Rash had said to me. We've started now, so we've got to see this thing through. We *have* to find out what's different about the proof copy. Which means we're going to have to go there. Come on, let's book the flights.

'There' was Monaco, on the Côte d'Azur. Because the second of the names I had learned in Victor's bookshop was Sir Leslie Kavanagh, the fabulously wealthy British entrepreneur whose address was simply *Arzachel*, Port Hercule, Monaco. *Arzachel* being the name of his yacht; Port Hercule being its permanent berth, and Sir Leslie's place of residence for tax purposes. Rash found a drooling article about him in the *Sunday Times* online, which confirmed that 'he is an avid collector of rare books, and is said to have one of the most expensive collections in the world, most of it housed in the spectacular study-cum-library on his luxury, five-bedroom yacht'.

By now Hey! Teriyaki owed me four days' holiday, and I'd also managed to save up a few hundred pounds: enough for two budget flights to Nice. We didn't want to reveal the purpose of the trip to my parents, so we sold it to them as a much-needed autumn break. 'What a lovely idea,' my mum said. 'It will help Rash take her mind off things.' 'Just what the doctor ordered,' my dad said. 'I know this place has been driving you crazy.' We booked the flights on Friday 14th October, the same day Kwasi Kwarteng resigned as Chancellor of the Exchequer. It seemed that 'the markets' (I'm never quite sure what is meant by 'the markets') had reacted very badly to his mini-budget. What's more the IMF (I'm not entirely certain what the IMF is) had issued an unprecedented (I couldn't tell you what was unprecedented about it) criticism of the budget a few days earlier. All in all, it seemed that he had screwed up big time, and managed to lose more of the country's money in a couple of weeks than most politicians are able to do in their entire careers. Three days later, on Monday 17th October, there was a new Chancellor in place and he seemed to be busy reversing almost every measure that his predecessor had introduced.

Two days later, Rash and I were at Gatwick airport by nine o'clock in the morning, and before our flight was called we decided to snatch ourselves something to eat. I couldn't believe the place she insisted on going to. It was the same place I was already spending most of my life.

Salmon inari taco. Beef teriyaki. Chicken teriyaki. Hoisin duck roll.

Do you have any idea how tired I am of this food? I asked.

I love Hey! Teriyaki. Their chicken katsu is the best.

Also, this branch is being run really badly. Look at this. Eighty seats and only two people preparing the food. The ratio's supposed to be twelve to one, not forty.

Aren't you going to eat anything? This tuna tataki is amazing.

I didn't answer. I was angry with her. Instead I eavesdropped on the conversation that was taking place between two young women at the table opposite ours.

So you know Ethan, right? one of them was saying.

The two women were about the same age as me and Rash, perhaps a little bit older. I guessed that Ethan was a friend of theirs, someone they didn't know especially well by the sound of it.

Yes, I know Ethan, the other woman said. What do you think of him? her friend asked. What do I think of him? He's nice. Cute. I don't have a problem with Ethan. Why, do you have a problem with him? I think he's kind of weird, her friend said. A bit neurotic. Why, what's he done? the other woman asked, and then her friend explained: Well, the other night, we were in the pub together, just the two of us, and we were having a drink, and it was all nice and friendly, perfectly normal, and then he asked me a question. A really weird question. What sort of question? the other woman asked, and her friend said: Well, I know this sounds kind of crazy, but he told me that he was going to have a wank later that night, and he wanted to know if it was all right if he thought about me while he was doing it. He wanted to know *what*? the other woman said, and her friend said, Like I told you, he was asking my permission. He wanted to know if it was OK to think about me while he was wanking. The other woman sat back and thought about this and looked a bit shocked and didn't seem to know what to say for a while. You haven't slept with him or anything? she asked eventually. No, of course not, said her friend, I'd never sleep with Ethan. I don't fancy him. Does he fancy you? the other woman asked, and her friend said: Well, apparently he does. Then the other woman asked: So why didn't he just ask you to go out with him? I don't know, her friend said. Maybe because he thought I'd probably say no. But what about the question he *did* ask you? the other woman asked. Did you give your permission? I didn't know what to say, her friend admitted. I was gobsmacked. At first I asked him, Do you always ask permission for something like that? And he said, Usually, yes. And

I said, Well, what if it's someone you don't know, like a celebrity or something? I mean, you can hardly call up Sydney Sweeney and ask her permission, can you? I suppose you could send her a message on Instagram but I don't think she'd reply, and he said, Well, that's not really a problem, because I don't fancy Sydney Sweeney anyway, which I thought was kind of missing the point, but anyway, never mind that, I was just about to ask him what he and I were going to be doing in this fantasy of his, whether it was just regular stuff, and then I suddenly thought, Oh my God, supposing it *isn't* just regular stuff, I mean, supposing he told me— Well, I didn't want to think about it, to be honest, and that was the moment when I realized how I felt about it, and told him, OK, since you ask, I'm *not* OK with you putting me inside your creepy little head and doing all sorts of weird stuff with me, I mean, if you'd never mentioned it I would never have known about it and you could just have gone ahead and done it, but since for some weird reason you decided to ask me— But he interrupted me, then, and said, It's *not* a weird reason, actually, I did it because I respect you and I didn't want to presume on our friendship, and I didn't know what the fuck I was supposed to say to that, so after that we just finished our drinks as quickly as we could and got the hell out of there. Come on, the gate's come up – Gate 564. Shall we split the bill?

Five minutes later our gate was announced as well. It was about ten minutes' walk away, and I was still trying to process the conversation by the time we got there.

R.

I've been wondering what the weather will be like on the Côte d'Azur at this time of year. To which the answer is: it's gorgeous. As the train carries us along the coast, I can't take my eyes off the flawless, fathomless blue sky and the sunlight as it glints off the turquoise water. Phyl is still a little bit angry with me for making her eat at that place, so we're not talking much. There's no need anyway. We're just sitting side by side on the top deck of the train now, admiring the view.

It's only a thirty-minute ride from Nice to Monaco. So far I've heard some French being spoken, and some Italian, but mostly English. Sitting behind us is a young American couple on some sort of backpacking holiday. He is excited to be travelling this close to the sea but for some reason she seems quite jaded about it and is ignoring the landscape and watching something on her phone instead. She has earphones in so I can't hear what it is, but when her boyfriend interrupts her and they start arguing I realize that it's an episode of *Friends*. In fact it's one of the most controversial episodes: *The One Where Joey Speaks French*, from the final season, Season 10, by which time – in the opinion of many fans – the quality of the show had taken a nosedive. I can't believe you're watching that shitty episode, of all things, he says, when you could be looking at this view. Shut the fuck up, she says, I'll watch whatever I like. It's such a lame fucking episode, he says. They've started to write Joey like he was some sort of imbecile. A nine-year-old kid could speak French better than he does. It's not supposed to be realistic, she says. It's meant to be a comedy show. Even a comedy show has to have some sort of grounding in reality, he says, and she answers: But *Friends* isn't reality, that's what's so great about it. That's exactly why I watch it – because it's an escape from reality. You want to escape from this reality? he says, incredulous. (I imagine him gesturing at the window.) We spent thousands of dollars so that we could come and see this reality. It's fucking beautiful. How can you have a problem with this? Reality isn't what you see out of the window, she answers. It's what's inside your head. That's the only reality that matters, isn't it? Spoken like a true narcissist, her boyfriend answers. Up until this point I've been thinking that the argument is quite good-natured, but this seems to be a sincerely nasty remark. She doesn't take it lying down. Are you calling me a narcissist? she asks. Are you calling me a fucking narcissist, because I'd rather watch a TV show than look out of the window at the sea? It's not even like it's a good TV show, he says. You're watching one of the crappiest episodes of one of the crappiest shows ever made. Oh, OK, I get it, she says. So it would be fine if I was watching *Curb* or *The Sopranos*, would it, or one of the other shows that gets the masculine seal of approval? Look, he says, I just figured we've come thousands of miles to see the Mediterranean, and the least you could do is pay some attention to it. I don't know what's going on in your head that's so terrible you have to escape from it with a storyline about a man who's so stupid that he can't learn a few words of French. Exactly! his girlfriend says. You don't know, do you? You don't know what's going on in my head. *Because you're not in there*. And I don't know what's going on in yours, either. All of us have our own realities and we're stuck with them. And one of the only ways you can get out of them for a while is by watching a film or reading a book or watching a TV show. So why don't you just let me do it, why don't you just let me do what I want, why don't you just . . . *leave me alone*?

I can tell that she is getting up from her seat at this point, and storming out of the carriage in tears, so I turn round to watch her do it. At the same time I catch a glimpse of her boyfriend, who is sitting back with his eyes closed, worn out by the argument, worn out by the effort of trying to deal with this woman, just as she is probably worn out by the effort of trying to deal with him. By and large my sympathies are with her, I have to say, because he does sound like a total asshole. But I happen to agree with him about that particular episode. It's one of the stupidest they ever made.

P.

The train stopped about seven or eight times on the journey from Nice. Usually in some tiny coastal town, each one more picturesque than the last. I couldn't resist taking photos of them all. (What is the word 'Instagrammable', after all, if not today's version of 'picturesque'?) Things changed fairly drastically when we reached Monaco-Monte-Carlo itself, though. At that point, the train entered a gigantic tunnel and pulled to a halt in a cavernous, ultra-modern underground station, and when we emerged into the daylight – after walking down a series of long subterranean passageways, all white tiles and automatic doors and escalators – we found that we were not in some quaint French fishing village, but in a dense conurbation, brutally packed with tower blocks which might have been the height of modernistic chic back in the sixties or seventies or eighties but were now beginning to show their age. Mostly these blocks were arranged in a vast semicircle around a harbour which we soon realized was the very one we were looking for – Port Hercule. There were a few small boats dotted around the water but mostly it was wall-to-wall superyachts – probably more than a hundred of them, most of them substantially bigger than the average family house on dry land. It was immediately apparent that we had found ourselves in a corner of Europe where the cost-of-living crisis, the subject of so much discussion back home, was not really making itself felt. Easy to be dazzled by the gleaming hulls of these monster vessels as they reflected the sunlight, but there was something oppressive, even saddening, about them too. I felt at once that I was in a place that I didn't understand, and in which I didn't belong. On the waterfront, behind the main road, was a gigantic hoarding advertising an estate agent, for which the slogan was *Considering Wealth Not as a Point of Arrival but as a Starting Point*. I stared at it for some time, trying to make sense of the words. Behind them were many assumptions: the first and biggest, I suppose, being that almost everyone who read them would be wealthy, to some degree or another. Otherwise, what were they doing here?

What *are* we doing here? I said, turning to Rash and speaking the final part of my train of thought out loud.

She didn't answer: she was sizing up the passers-by and choosing which one to waylay. Finally settling on a friendly-looking middle-aged man with a weatherbeaten face and a vaguely nautical costume, she caught his attention and said, in her passable French: *Excusez-moi, savez-vous où nous pouvons trouver un yacht qui s'appelle* Arzachel?

Yes, of course, it's the big black one. Over there, on the far side of the port.

Obviously he would speak perfect English. Everybody here would speak perfect English. We thanked him (in English) and then walked around the curve of the harbour until we were only about one hundred metres away from this grotesque, matt-black, monolithic five-storey boat, which towered over the yachts on either side. A metal walkway led right up to the rear of the boat itself. There didn't seem to be any signs forbidding us from using it. When we were about three-quarters of the way along, Rash stopped me by putting a hand on my arm and saying:

OK, here's what we're going to do.

There were two uniformed crew members at the back end of the boat: one of them was cleaning the deck with a bucket and mop, the other was going around polishing various fixtures and fittings. Both of them were muscular and handsome, but the one with the bucket and the mop especially so.

Don't tell me, I said. We're going to chat up those guys and get onto the boat.

No, said Rash. *That's* the guy we're going to chat up.

She drew my attention to another man, this one wearing a peaked cap as part of his uniform, who was standing on an upper deck, two floors above the other two men, leaning on the railing and looking down on them as they worked.

Those guys won't be able to get us where we want to go, said Rash. He will.

Who is he?

I'd say he was the chief stew.

I looked at her in surprise, not having expected her to be so well acquainted with yachting terminology. As it happened (and as she told me afterwards) Rash was a fan of a reality TV show which focused on this milieu in some depth. A guilty pleasure, up until now, it had also given her some knowledge that was about to prove useful.

OK, she said, you're a nerd, right? You're shy, you're awkward, you're crazy about books.

It took me a moment to realize that she was assigning me a role to play, rather than offering an assessment of my real-life character.

Here, put these on.

She fished in her bag and handed me her glasses. Rash wore glasses, I didn't. But today she had her contacts in. I took the glasses and put them on. The lenses were pretty thick and immediately the whole world went radically out of focus.

Are you going to be OK wearing those? she asked.

I guess, I said, doubtfully.

Come on then, let's go.

It was three-thirty in the afternoon. Only about eight hours since our Uber had arrived to pick us up from Rookthorne. A short space of time, really. And yet it seemed a long, long journey from there to here: from the gloom of an English October morning to the brilliance of Monaco's autumn sunlight, with Rash striding confidently down the walkway, shielding her eyes against the glare with one hand, while waving up at the chief steward with the other and greeting him with a cheery shout of 'Ahoy there!'

R.

Phyl is playing her part well, I have to admit. To perfection, one might almost say.

We have made it into the library now. It's been quite a journey.

The chief stew's name is Adam. He seems a nice guy. Australian. It only took ten minutes or so to get him to invite us on board. This is what I like about men. They're simple creatures. If a woman is reasonably young, reasonably pretty, talks to them in a friendly way and has one or two buttons on her blouse artfully undone, there's very little they won't do for her.

I tell him that we're only in Monaco for a day or two, and we've got nothing much planned for the next few hours. Of course I'm the one he wants to get talking to, but I make it clear that nerdy Phyl is part of the package.

He's proud of the boat: almost as proud as if he owned it himself. I suppose there is a professional pride in keeping it looking as good as it does. Sir Leslie is away. (Excellent.) Adam doesn't know where, he only spends a few weeks every year aboard the *Arzachel* anyway. Where do we want to start? Why don't we make ourselves comfortable on the aft deck and he'll fix us a couple of drinks. Normally the bar steward would do it but he's on shore today. We nod politely and ask for a couple of Aperol spritzes. While he's away preparing them, we spread ourselves out on the cream-coloured sofas that surround the swimming pool on three sides. I intend to sample this pool before too long. It will give me something to do while Phyl is busy with the book.

Not bad, is it? I say, dipping my fingers into the water and finding it a very acceptable temperature. I could get used to this lifestyle. All I need is a Sugar Daddy like Sir Leslie.

When the spritzes arrive, we sit drinking them with Adam for a few minutes. He tells us his life story, or most of it: childhood in Sydney, two years spent backpacking around the States, ending up in Florida somehow where it finally occurred to him that working on board these superyachts was as good a way as any of seeing the world in style. We pretend to be fascinated and ask him a bunch of naive and silly questions like, Is this a typical yacht? At which he laughs and tells us that this is one of the biggest and most expensive yachts in the world and we wouldn't believe what Sir Leslie has got on board here. Which is our cue for the grand tour.

And, in fact, the things that Leslie has on board are not especially surprising. Once you've adjusted to the scale and the revolting opulence of it all, it's exactly what you would expect. The grand salon with the twenty-seater dining table, the gym full of bikes and rowing machines and treadmills, the sauna, the cinema room with the multiplex-size screen, the games room with the full-size billiard table, the hull full of speed boats and jet skis and other executive toys. I think that's everything, Adam says, as he shows us the master bedroom suite with the jacuzzi and the wet room, and drinks in our coos of excitement. Apart from the library, I suppose. At which Phyl, in response to a nudge from me, lets out an especially enthusiastic gasp and says:

There's a *library* on board?

I laugh and josh her playfully. Classic Phyl! I say. All this amazing gear and all she really wants to see are a load of books.

It's not very exciting, to be honest, Adam insists. Like you say, it's just a load of books.

I'd *love* to see it, Phyl says.

She does love a good library, I tell him, and then I add, by way of extra inducement: Once she gets her nose inside a few books, you don't hear a peep out of her for hours.

Adam likes the sound of this, and takes the hint.

Come on then – it's on the second floor.

We follow him into the elevator and ride up together. Then he leads us down a long corridor and opens a room on the left-hand side (or do I mean the port side) by putting a six-digit code into a keypad.

This is the room he keeps locked? I say, in mock-surprise.

You'll understand why in a minute, says Adam. Or at least (gesturing at Phyl) she probably will.

The library is very big, and very beautiful. There's a leather-topped desk and a couple of leather armchairs and shelves of books from floor to ceiling. Even through the tinted glass of its three panoramic windows, the afternoon sunlight dances and shimmers. Phyl is having a good wander around and occasionally lifting up my glasses so that she can get a better look at everything. Adam notices this and says:

Are you long-sighted, or short-sighted, Phyl?

She laughs nervously.

Long, short and everything in between! she says, and then zooms in on a glass cabinet at the centre of one of the walls.

Gosh, some of these must be very rare. I can see a copy of *To the Lighthouse* there. Is it a first edition?

Adam laughs. I wouldn't know, love. I do know that collecting books is Sir Leslie's passion.

No, it couldn't possibly be a first edition, Phyl says. That would be worth a fortune.

I don't know if you've noticed, Adam says, but he isn't exactly on skid row.

He takes a bunch of keys from his trouser pocket and unlocks the cabinet.

What are you doing? Phyl asks.

Take a look. See if it's a . . . first edition, or whatever you call it.

He takes the book carefully from the shelf and hands it to her. She squints at the title page and the page opposite, unable to make out a thing with those glasses on.

It *is*, she exclaims. My God, this is incredible!

She pushes the glasses up so that they're resting on the top of her head and, able to see clearly now, she takes a closer squint at the other books in the glass cabinet. Adam is watching her, but not too closely. I think he could be easily distracted.

I think he has stuff by Shakespeare and all sorts, he says. Shakespeare, Dickens, Dan Brown. You name it.

Phyl is reaching out, however, for a small, unimpressive-looking paperback with a pale blue cover, sitting in between a Hemingway first edition and what looks like a very old copy of *Gulliver's Travels*. As she takes it from the shelf I can see that her hand is shaking. This is the book that she is holding:

This is the moment at which I lower my voice and say to Adam:

I don't suppose there's any chance of me having a dip in the pool?

Sure. Of course. Go for it.

Phyl has dropped the book unobtrusively onto one of the armchairs.

Trouble is, I say, I didn't bring a costume with me.

Oh, well that's no problem. We've got dozens. There's bound to be one in your size.

Phyl has covered the book with a cushion, and has now gone back to looking inside the cabinet again, running her eyes over what seems to be a complete set of James Bond first editions. Adam turns to her and says:

What about you, Phyl? Do you fancy a swim?

She moves away from the cabinet to an open shelf, presumably full of less valuable books. She takes down a nice illustrated edition of *The Wind in the Willows.*

What I would really love, she says, is to spend a bit more time in here. This is one of my favourite books.

Do you want to bring it up to the pool?

But it's so lovely in here, Phyl says. She is peering at him through my glasses again now and looks every inch the incorrigible bookworm.

What did I tell you? I say to Adam, triumphantly. She really is a hopeless case.

Well, whatever, he says.

He closes the glass cabinet and locks it. You didn't want to see any of the stuff in there again, did you?

Phyl shakes her head. He hasn't noticed that the proof has been removed and hidden beneath the cushion.

I just want to sit here for an hour or two with Mole, Ratty and Toad, she says. My idea of absolute heaven.

Adam laughs.

To each their own, he says, mildly incredulous.

I make for the door, flashing Phyl a look which is meant to convey a warning that she shouldn't take too long if she can help it. Meanwhile Adam looks very pleased with himself and puts his hand in the small of my back as he says:

Come on, let's go and find you that costume.

P.

We had agreed that we weren't going to steal the book. We weren't even going to remove it from the yacht. My task was simply to photograph every page, as quickly as I could.

It was a fiddly job. *My Innocence* is a short book – only one hundred and fifty-three pages – but I didn't want to damage this precious (probably unique) copy, and at the same time it was important to make sure that I didn't miss a single word. Fortunately the light in the room was good, but it was awkward holding the book open with one hand while I angled my phone with the other. I wasn't convinced that the glue holding the pages together was especially strong, and I was worried that the spine was going to crack at any moment. Nonetheless, I managed to get into a rhythm, and after a while I was capturing a page every ten seconds or so. Within half an hour the job was complete, and I had one hundred and fifty-three new images on my phone.

I could have gone up onto the aft deck at this point and saved Rash from the task of keeping Adam entertained for any longer than was necessary, but I knew that if anyone could look after herself, she could. He had seemed like a nice guy to me, someone who enjoyed the opportunity to flirt and who understood boundaries. Besides, there were lots of other crew members on board. Another few minutes would do no harm. I was desperate to satisfy my curiosity, right away, by comparing this proof copy with the published version that I'd brought with me in my tote bag.

I sat down at Sir Leslie's desk with both books in front of me. My gut feeling was that the crucial change, if Peter Cockerill had made it, would come on the final page. That, after all, was where the book turned aside from its narrative trajectory, and became a statement of intent.

. . . *I realize*, he had written, in reflective mode at the very end of the book, *that I have not hugged the truth's shoreline as closely as I hoped to do, and more importantly, the writing of this book has not brought me into the kind of closeness with my mother that I wanted. She is gone, and there is no bringing her back.*

The proof copy contained these same sentences, word for word.

Writing has turned out to be just another dead end: my words bring me no comfort, and my voice goes unheard.

Again: the copies were identical.

After this, I have nothing more to write. There will be no more writing. But without writing, can there be living? That is the question that confronts me now. And my answer?

I bent more closely over the two books, and looked even more intently at their closing lines. My heart was beating fast. What if the two versions were actually no different at all?

And then:

No, there cannot. (So said the published version.)

Yes, there can. (So said the proof.)

It is impossible to carry on. (Read the published version.)

It is possible to carry on. (Read the proof.)

Reaching this final page has proved to me one thing, and one thing only. It is time to give in, and bring this unhappy life to an end.

That was the last sentence of the novel, as it had been published in 1987. But the earlier version, which had survived only in this one proof copy?

Reaching this final page has proved to me one thing, and one thing only. It is time to move on, and bring this unhappy story to an end.

I sat back and stared into space, stunned by the implication of these words.

Not *to give in*, but *to move on*.

Not to *bring this life to an end*, but simply to *bring this story to an end*.

Which meant that Peter Cockerill's famous, public and emphatic declaration that he proposed to end his own life was never, in its original version, meant to be anything of the sort.

In other words: this novel was no suicide note.

R.

So how did it work out? Phyl asks.

How did what work out?

Your swim with Adam.

We've climbed the steep incline that leads away from Port Hercule, and have walked almost all the way to the casino. Now we are sitting in the Casino Garden, looking across the square towards this legendary building, this temple to the gods of money and chance. It's early evening and the sun is low in the sky, but it's still warm here, and the square is crowded, washed in a mellow, golden light.

Well, it was fine to start with, I say. What I hadn't counted on was the possibility that you wouldn't show up for nearly an hour.

Phyl has the decency to look embarrassed, at least.

Yeah, sorry about that. He did . . . behave himself, didn't he?

He got a bit handsy towards the end, that's all. If only he'd known that he was wasting his time.

I don't expect her to understand this, and sure enough, she doesn't.

What do you mean?

I mean . . .

I figure that it's about time I let Phyl in on this secret. We've come a long way together, and got to know each other pretty well in the last few weeks. So I might as well tell her.

What it is . . .

It's never easy to put this into words.

It's just that the whole sex thing . . . It's not really for me.

She looks baffled, as people always do.

You know, the whole inserting body parts, exchanging fluids business. It's not my bag.

Still nothing. Maybe some more clinical language is called for. So I tell her:

I'm what is officially known as a member of the asexual community.

Phyl's silence continues for a moment longer. Until:

Oh, she says, finally. And then, more emphatically: *Oh.*

She looks concerned, as if I've told her that I have some terrible disease and have only got a few months to live.

It's not an affliction, I say. It's not something I need to go into therapy for. It's just how I am. You know all about this stuff, don't you?

Phyl nods. She seems unhappy for me, I don't really know why. I steer the conversation back to the subject of Adam.

So yeah, I could have told him that, but there's no way he would've believed me. Men never do. They always think you're just saying it to get rid of them. So I thanked him for being so nice to us and said it would be great to see him again. Apparently they're all coming on shore tonight and going to some bar at ten-thirty.

You didn't say we'd join them, did you? Phyl asks – a look of panic crossing her face – and half-teasing her I say:

Might as well, unless you've got a better idea. I hate to remind you, but we still haven't got anywhere to sleep tonight.

A couple walk past us, with a cute little miniature dog trotting along behind them on a lead. All the women here seem to have miniature dogs, walking at their heels or being carried under their arms or with their little heads poking out of their handbags.

I mean, admit it, the bedrooms on that yacht looked pretty nice.

I'm not going back there, Phyl says, adamantly.

I shrug.

Whatever.

I take out my phone and open one of the booking apps. A few minutes' scrolling does nothing but depress me.

Jesus Christ. Everything here is so fucking *expensive.*

I've been trying to impress upon Phyl the urgency of this particular situation, but to tell the truth, it's hard to get her to focus on anything apart from what she has found in that book. I'm not even sure what she thinks she's proved. But since she won't really talk about anything else, I might as well ask her again.

So look . . . I'm still not sure that I get it. What are you telling me about this guy, exactly?

I'm telling you . . . (She leans forward, and lowers her voice.) I'm telling you that I don't believe Peter Cockerill ever intended to commit suicide.

All right. Yes. I see that.

But we do know, Phyl continues, that he died a violent death.

Which could easily have been an accident . . .

. . . Or it could have been murder.

Once again, this word hangs in the air between us after she has spoken it. After a few moments, though, I let out a sigh. I'm beginning to have the distinct feeling that we're on a wild goose chase.

We're supposed to be trying to find out who killed Chris. Are we really going to start investigating a thirty-five-year-old murder case instead?

I think the one might explain the other, Phyl says. And we already have a working hypothesis. A theory.

We do?

Yes. At least I do.

What's that, then?

That Richard Wilkes murdered Peter Cockerill.

I frown. This doesn't make much sense to me. And it turns out that I'm not the only one who feels this way. Because from behind us, we hear a voice saying:

Interesting. Very interesting. However, other theories are available.

We turn around. The smiling, ruddy-cheeked, white-haired woman behind us, dressed from head to toe in black, is immediately recognizable. It's a surprise – but, I have to say, a very pleasant one – to find that we are in the presence of Detective Inspector Prudence Freeborne. It's the policeman lady!

P.

Villefranche-sur-Mer is a fifteen-minute train journey from Monaco, back into France, in the direction of Nice. This was where Prudence had booked a hotel for the night, and where she generously suggested that we join her – at her own expense. Given our situation, we were hardly going to turn that offer down.

Not only did she find a room for us at her hotel and pay for it, but she took us out to dinner as well. She took us to a seafood restaurant that had tables positioned between the little main road and the waterfront, right on the edge of the sea, and ordered a couple of bottles of wine and an enormous platter of *fruits de mer* for us all to share.

I was so excited to find her there: not just because it was nice to see a friendly and familiar face, but because it showed that we were all following the same line of inquiry, and that Rash and I weren't going mad after all. Of course, Pru hadn't managed to get on board the *Arzachel* yet, and examine the proof copy, so we were ahead of her in that respect. I couldn't wait to tell her what we had discovered and to hear her take on it. The words came pouring out of me in an unstoppable flow.

So it's pretty clear to us that back in 1987 a murder took place. My guess is that Richard Wilkes killed Peter Cockerill, for some reason or other. After killing him he forged a letter to Cockerill's editor, telling him to destroy all the proof copies of his book and make changes to it so that the whole thing looked like a suicide note. You see, this woman, Margaret Fezakery, who used to work for Newman, saw him open the letter that morning and said he went as white as a sheet, and he would hardly have done that if it had just been a normal letter asking for normal changes – he must have thought that Cockerill had done something terrible, or was intending to do, so that afternoon he drove down to the New Forest . . .

Pru held up her hand.

Wait a minute, she said.

We were halfway through the plate of *fruits de mer*, and I have to say she was making a much better job of it than either Rash or me. Laid out before us on the table was an array of utensils which looked to me like the most terrifying selection of gynaecological instruments. The purpose of these utensils was to carve up lobsters, to disembowel prawns, to gouge the innards out of langoustines and to pull crabs apart limb by limb, but I didn't have a clue how to use them. My hands, mouth and chin were already covered with oil, lemon juice and fishy substances and even though in front of me was a plate piled high with the mutilated remains of unlucky denizens of the deep, it felt as though, in terms of flesh consumed, I had hardly managed to eat more than the equivalent of a fish finger. Pru, on the other hand, seemed to know exactly which tools to use, how to hold them, where to put them, what to do with them and why she had been given them. Furthermore, if she ever found it difficult to separate flesh from shell or flesh from bone, her solution seemed to be simply to bite off the relevant body part, crack the lot between her teeth and masticate the result until she was able to swallow it whole. In this way, entire lobster claws and crayfish torsos had been disappearing into her mouth, and overall she seemed to be very satisfied with her progress, judging from the big, serene smile of contentment that had started spreading across her face in the last few minutes.

Now she said:

Did you actually go and interview this woman?

Margaret Fezakery? Yes.

Well, you've certainly been very thorough, she said. I must admit that I'm impressed.

Rash didn't really seem to be listening. She looked tired, or perhaps she was just feeling a little bit tipsy and relaxed. She was staring out across the water to the headland on the other side, the gentle contours and twinkling lights of Cap Ferrat. Meanwhile I burbled on.

Of course we haven't managed to establish yet whether Peter and Richard knew each other or even whether they'd ever met. But it just seems way too much of a coincidence that Christopher was asking my mother to send him pages of stuff about Peter Cockerill and *the very next day* he's killed by someone who's spent his whole life giving lectures and writing books about him. Chris *must* have discovered something and when he confronted Wilkes about it the next morning . . . I mean, that has to be how it happened, right? You do agree with us about that? What I read on the boat this afternoon proves that—

Pru held up her hand again.

Forgive the pun, she said, but the proof *proves* nothing. In fact, at the moment I can't see any connection whatsoever between these two crimes. Or these two deaths, to be more precise.

She snapped a lobster's claw in half, put one end into her mouth and sucked a juicy gobbet of flesh from its interior. I have to say that I was disappointed, not to mention baffled, by her response.

But . . . if you think the proof has nothing to do with Chris's death, why did you come to Monaco to look at it?

I didn't come to Monaco to look at it, she said, casually dismembering a crab. I didn't have the slightest idea that it was here.

Then . . . What? You're here on holiday, or something?

No, I'm not here on holiday. I'm here as part of my investigation.

She put down her cutlery for a moment, folded her arms and composed herself before saying:

I've been in the police force for more than forty years. I've worked on hundreds, possibly thousands, of murder cases. And I can say categorically, without any hesitation whatsoever, that no matter what you read in detective novels, most crimes are about money, first and foremost. Money is the motive. Almost invariably. One of the suspects in this case has run up spectacular gambling debts. Where? At the casino in Monte Carlo. He's there at this very moment, in fact. And tomorrow morning, I have a meeting with the casino management to discuss his situation. That's why I'm here.

She drained her glass of wine, and refilled all three glasses from the second bottle.

Furthermore, two of the other suspects in this case are involved with a political organization which Mr Swann had been looking into for some time. It seems that he was about to publish his findings and again, when you look at the things that he was about to reveal, you can see that large amounts of money are at stake. That's what it usually comes down to. Money. Everyone talks a lot about values, these days, and culture wars, but in my experience people rarely kill each other because of anything to do with values or culture. They kill each other because of money. Human beings are primitive creatures, really.

She took a generous knob of butter from the little saucer in front of her and spread it thickly onto a slice of bread.

Now, I don't deny that there is something strange going on, with Professor Richard Wilkes and the suicide or non-suicide of Peter Cockerill all those years ago. There is definitely something amiss there and perhaps, when I'm finally allowed to retire, I shall look into it. Since we were talking about theories, I will admit to you that I have a theory of my own about that affair, but it isn't the same as yours. In fact, it is the exact opposite. And by the way – this rare copy of the book that you were looking at today: I don't suppose it was signed? Or there was any inscription? Or any handwritten corrections?

No, I said. Nothing like that.

Pity.

Why do you ask?

Well, I'd like to see some more examples of Cockerill's handwriting. Surely he must have left behind some papers – some letters, some manuscripts? He was a writer, after all.

They're all gone, I told her. According to the newspaper reports at the time, everything was destroyed in the fire that burned his house down when he killed himself. Everything.

Prudence gave a private smile.

Well, that's very convenient, I must say. Apparently, he visited Wetherby Hall himself at some time in the 1980s – another suggestive detail, by the way – and wrote quite a long message in the visitors' book there. It might be worth going back to have a look at that . . .

I wasn't sure whether the last words were intended for us, or whether she was talking to herself. After a reflective pause she continued:

Anyway – my point is that I'm not at all convinced that this has anything to do with the death of Mr Swann. There's nothing to connect the two events, as far as I can see. And there are various things which seem to point in a different direction entirely. If Richard Wilkes was the killer, for instance, what was Christopher trying to say when he left that clue?

Clue?

Rash looked towards us, turning her back on the water, and became alert for the first time. The word had caught my attention too. This was the first that either of us had heard about a clue.

Yes. In the few seconds before he died, he managed to write a message. Rather a cryptic one, I must say. Here, let me show you.

Pru took out her phone, and scrolled to a photo which looked like this:

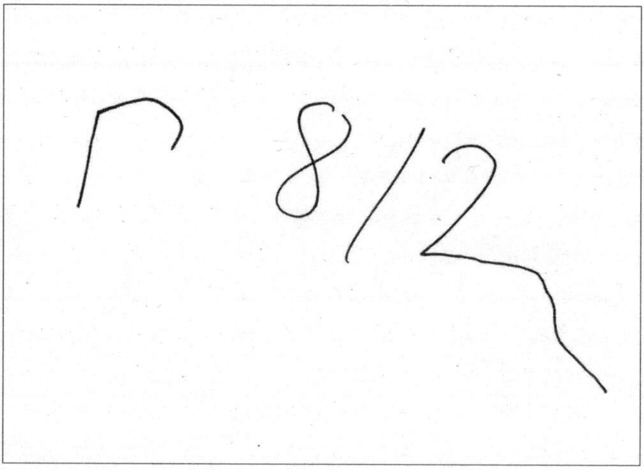

She held it up so that both of us could look at it. I examined it closely for a few seconds, but then Rash – acting rather strangely, moving in a trance-like sort of way – took the phone from Pru's hand and gazed at the image on the screen for a long time, for more than a minute at least.

What does it mean? I asked the detective.

Well, I only wish that I could tell you that. First of all he seems to have been trying to write a letter – possibly the letter R. But then he stopped midway and wrote these numbers instead.

Eight/two.

Eight/two. Any idea what it might signify?

I frowned, and tried to turn my mind to the conundrum, but no solution presented itself. Meanwhile Rash was still staring at the image on the screen. Her deep brown eyes were covered with a film of tears. Gently, Prudence took the phone back from her and said:

I'm so sorry. Of course, that must be a very upsetting thing for you to see. How thoughtless of me.

She poured some more wine for us both. Rash picked up her glass, turned away from the table again, and took several long sips while looking out to sea. I focused my attention on the lobster on my plate, making one last, futile attempt to extract some meat from its claws. Prudence caught the waiter's eye and asked for some coffee. For a long while none of us spoke. We listened to the gentle breaking of the water against the sea wall, the buzz and hum of multilingual conversation at the tables all around us, and thought, I suppose, about Christopher and what the last moments of his life might have been like.

Unexpectedly, Rash was the first one to speak. What she said was unexpected, too.

When I was little, Chris and I used to play puzzle games.

Prudence looked across at her keenly.

Go on.

Games with numbers and letters. He used to make up codes, things like that.

Codes?

The simplest one was when you substitute numbers for letters. Going through the alphabet. So A would be one, B would be two, and so on. All the way to twenty-six for Z.

I see, said Prudence, counting on her fingers. In which case, eight/two would represent . . . H and B.

We pondered this suggestion for a while, but nobody came up with any ideas. Prudence was given her coffee, to which she added three lumps of sugar and a good deal of cream. Rash sank back into her mournful silence. I felt terrible for her: I think seeing Christopher's scrawl on that piece of paper had been the first thing that had truly brought home to her the fact of his murder. The first time it had seemed real.

Then:

Wait a minute, I said. There *is* an H. B.

There is? Prudence said.

Howard Beddoes.

Howard Beddoes? Who on earth's that?

He was Charles Newman's partner.

Charles Newman?

Peter Cockerill's editor.

DI Freeborne smiled indulgently and said:

Well, that seems a bit tenuous, if you don't mind me saying so.

But his initials are H. B., I insisted. My heart was racing and suddenly I felt that we were on the verge of a breakthrough.

And . . . ?

I began to improvise wildly.

Margaret told us that Charles Newman was practically destroyed by Cockerill's suicide. After it happened, he started drinking heavily. Now, supposing Wilkes *did* murder Cockerill? Howard knows it, but he's never been able to prove it. But he's always hated him for it. So then when Wilkes comes to speak at the conference—

But nobody knew he was going to speak at the conference. His lecture wasn't in the programme. He was a last-minute replacement.

Ah. Yes. Well, OK, maybe it was just a coincidence. Howard *didn't* know that Wilkes was going to be speaking. He just happened to be at the conference anyway.

Why?

I fell silent. But after a few seconds, it was Rash who spoke up.

Don't you remember? She told us that he became a councillor for the BNP. Always a conservative, she said, but more and more extreme in his old age. Just the sort of person who'd go.

I turned to Prudence in triumph.

So there you are! That letter was never meant to be an R. It was going to be a B – for Beddoes.

But H would have worked perfectly well, Prudence countered. And anyway, aren't you forgetting something? Wilkes wasn't the one who was stabbed. It was Mr Swann.

So Howard went into the wrong room, I said. It was a simple mistake.

Prudence laughed, finished the last of her coffee, and stood up.

Come on, you two, she said. I think it's time we all went to bed.

We walked together along the seafront. It was only a few yards to our hotel. Prudence stopped to tilt back her face and take in a generous draught of sea air. She looked very pleased with life after her meal and her wine. Meanwhile, I was torn between enthusiasm for our new theory and frustration that she wasn't taking it seriously.

I'll tell you what, she said. When I get back home, I shall look through the list of conference delegates and see if there was one called Howard Beddoes. That should settle it once and for all, yes?

We nodded.

But I don't think there will be, somehow.

What *do* you think? I asked, insistently.

Prudence turned towards us. The half-moon above the water shone down on her white hair and gave her an almost divine, angelic appearance.

I think . . . she said. I think that Mr Swann saw something – or heard something – the night before he was killed, that put his life in danger. I also think that he was a careful, methodical man, and whatever it was that he saw, or heard, he would have kept some record of it. A photograph, perhaps, or a sound recording. That was what he had on his phone, and that was why the murderer went to the trouble of taking the phone and throwing it into the lake. I also think that, as a careful, methodical man, he would have made a backup, and sent it to someone. Maybe as an email. Probably to your mother: except that he knew that her email address wasn't working that day, unfortunately. So he might have sent it to one of you. Are you *sure* you never received anything?

We both shook our heads.

Ah, well. Talking of phones . . .

She looked at the screen of her own telephone and shook her head sadly.

Talking of phones, you two go inside. I have to call my husband. We have a slight medical emergency to deal with.

Oh, I'm sorry, Rash said. Nothing serious, is it?

Well, said Prudence. Several months ago, my husband became aware of a small lump in his neck. He made an appointment to have it diagnosed, but . . . What with one thing and another . . . You see, everything that could have gone wrong with the system, went wrong. There was an online form to fill in, and he's not very good at that sort of thing, so he made some mistakes, which delayed things . . . Then there were so many patients waiting to be seen on the day of his first appointment that it had to be postponed . . . In the middle of all this the surgery he was registered with was sold to a private company, and there was a delay while everything was transferred, and actually a lot of the patients' records got lost in the process . . . Then he was passed on to a new consultant who didn't know anything about his case . . . Anyway, finally, *finally* he got to see the right person and got a proper diagnosis but by then it had progressed, he was on to Stage Four . . . And now, just two days ago, he was meant to have an operation but again it was cancelled for some reason, nobody seems to know why, and since then he's spent most of his time on the phone trying to find out what's going on . . . It's all a mess. A big, ugly mess . . .

She tailed off. Rash gave her a sorrowful smile and I touched her arm but neither of us said anything.

Prudence sniffed, then blew her nose on a lace handkerchief and said:

Well. There we are. I'm sure Mr Swann would have had something to say about this situation. As would my mother. But, sadly, neither of them is around to say it any more.

R.

Phyl wakes me up at 6.30 the next morning. I've had a terrible night's sleep. I have a hangover, and all that seafood is playing havoc with my stomach and my bowels. Sunlight is flooding our bedroom and outside the sea is a gorgeous blue-green. All I want to do is pull the bedclothes over my head and go back to sleep.

Get up, she says. We're going to Venice today.

P.

It turned out that it was not difficult to travel from Villefranche-sur-Mer to Venice by train. I got no sleep that night and booked our tickets on my phone as I sat out on the balcony at five in the morning, watching the sun rise over the Mediterranean. The train I booked was scheduled to leave at eight. I tried to persuade Rash to come downstairs for some breakfast but she was feeling too ill. After breakfast, though, I somehow managed to get her out of bed and walked her to the station with me, and then I bundled her onto the train while she was still half-asleep. For the first part of the journey she sat huddled up in the corner, trying to snooze and occasionally getting up to use the toilet.

As for me, despite my lack of sleep I felt wide awake. My mind was racing. The last few weeks had given me a lot to process and it was time to organize my thoughts. I opened the Notes app on my phone and started tapping on the screen.

Key to the mystery lies in the proof of My Innocence
A writer forgotten, then reborn
Proof/Reborn
Pru Freeborne

I pondered this for a few moments and added:

Pru Freeborne thinks that most crimes are committed for reasons of MONEY not values/feelings.

This is why she thinks that the murder must have been committed by one of the other suspects. Richard Wilkes had no financial motive for killing Christopher. (So far as anyone knows.)

Having written this, I sat back and looked out of the train window, allowing my thoughts to drift for a while. The railway line was still hugging the shore, offering up absurdly beautiful views of the sea and the coast. We had already travelled back through Monaco and entered Italy. It was weird how, in the rest of Europe, you could just slide from one country to another without noticing it, no borders to pass through, no one checking your passport. Everyone here just seemed to take that idea for granted. The British, I realized, had never really been on board with it.

MONEY

I wrote the word again, in block capitals. And then strangely, I found my mind returning not to the murder case, but to something I had read in Brian Collier's memoir of his time at Cambridge.

One of Brian's most vivid memories: something he was told in the tea shop, by the guy who was chatting up (?) my Mum. (Name? – Nigel?)

He asked Brian whether his parents had ever given him 'the talk' and this turned out to be a talk about money, not sex.

His father had explained to him that the whole purpose of life is to make money. Everything else is just sentimental. You have to make it, and then you have to make sure that you hang on to it. Nothing else matters. Or rather, everything else (happiness??) will follow from that.

Something I understand, now, from reading Brian's memoir and Christopher's blog: forty years ago (twenty years before I was born!) Britain changed. What we had before then: consensus – more or less. What came after: libertarianism/individualism. Every man and woman for his/her self. Survival of the fittest. A system devised for and by the Roger Wagstaffs of this world.

How is someone like me supposed to survive in a world like this? Everything that defines me is unsuited for it. My passivity. My idealism. My innocence. I just don't have what it takes.

Our first change was at a place called Ventimiglia. We had about twenty-five minutes between trains. I took Rash to the station café and force-fed her a couple of espressos. However, when we got on the next train (destination Milan) she fell asleep again almost at once. I watched her for a while as her breathing became slower and more regular, her mouth half-open, her head resting against the window. I have to say that she looked very beautiful in repose.

Rash is convinced that the older generation, the Boomers, hate us. They hate us and they want to punish us. Snowflakes. That would be their word for someone like me. Hopeless and over-sensitive. I need toughening up. They can't make me do National Service but they can give me Liz Truss as Prime Minister instead.

Not sure this is true.

Rash woke up not long before we reached Milan, early in the afternoon. At Milano Centrale, in the hour before our next train, we had coffee and *tramezzini* at one of the cafés, and discussed our plans for when we arrived in Venice. Our conclusion was that we didn't have any plans, short of walking into the university and demanding to see Professor Wilkes.

Then what?

The Venice train was almost full. We were lucky, I realized, to have got two seats together. By now Rash had regained full consciousness and rejoined the civilized world. She was the one who was all bright-eyed, and I was the one who was beginning to flag. I kept tapping away on my Notes app, but my thoughts were beginning to wander.

The thing Rash said once about how angry the older generation seemed: the sort of people who would have gone to this conference, anyway. For forty years the country's been shaped in their image and now they look around and they don't even like what they see.

The world they see and the world that Rash and I see bear no relation to each other. We see different worlds.

Most of the other passengers were wearing masks. We'd both forgotten to bring ours. It hasn't occurred to us to bring them, in fact. People in Britain seemed to have given up wearing masks on public transport. Last time I'd worn one, on the bus home from a Hey! Teriyaki shift, an anti-masker had told me to take it off. He said they carried germs and wearing them was more dangerous than not wearing them.

Opposing realities. I'd only been at uni a few months when the pandemic happened and I had to come home, and a few weeks after that Dad got

Covid and he was sick, really sick. Mum had to take him to A & E one evening and we were so scared for him. But there are people who say that the whole thing was a hoax, there is no proof that it ever happened. The scamdemic.

What can we all agree on? What is our common ground?
PROOF/REALITY

An announcement came over the speaker system. My Italian wasn't good enough to understand it. Something to do with the train running a few minutes late, I think. I realized that there was something weird about this train, something that was part of the background noise on British trains, but not here. You didn't hear the words '*See it. Say it. Sorted*' every few minutes.

I closed my eyes and felt the rhythm of the wheels on the track beneath me. It fell in with the rhythm of that phrase when it popped into my mind again and wouldn't go away.

See it. Say it. Sorted. See it. Say it. Sorted.

When everyone sees the world so differently, how do you <u>find</u> the truth?
SEE IT.

How do you <u>tell</u> the truth?
SAY IT.

How do you <u>agree</u> on what's true and what isn't?
SORTED.

I thought back to the conversation we'd overheard on the train to Monaco yesterday. (Was it only yesterday? It felt like ages ago.) The young American couple who were clearly on the verge of splitting up. You don't know what's going on in my head, she had told him. *Because you're not in there.* And I don't know what's going on in yours, either. All of us have our own realities and we're stuck with them.

Was that how it was going to be, from now on? We'd all have our own realities, and nobody would agree whether the pandemic was real or if it was a hoax, whether climate change was happening or not, whether the earth was flat or the earth was round. What was the point of writing a book in a world like that?

How do you write the truth?

PC found his own solution: abandon fiction. From now on tell 'the truth in the form of a novel'.

What does that even mean?

A theory: even if he had lived, PC would have written no more books after My Innocence. *By renouncing fiction, he murdered his own talent. Silenced his own voice.*

And he knew this.

I tried to look out of the window as the landscape shifted. Were those fields or vineyards stretching out, blue-grey, into the distance? Or a body of water, maybe? I had it in mind that we were somewhere near Lake Garda. It was hard to see anything clearly because the windows were so dirty. I turned to ask Rash if she thought we were going past Lake Garda but she had her AirPods in, and was nodding her head in time to some music. Lost in her own rhythm. Inside her own head, where I would never be able to go.

Rash thinks fiction is 'fake' and 'embarrassing'. Is she right?

Alternative viewpoint: in a world where all efforts to tell the truth in words or images are compromised, contaminated, there's something unique about fiction. Something authentic, something you can depend on.

PURE/RELIABLE

After that, I could feel my eyelids beginning to droop. I think I began writing my last note somewhere between Brescia and Verona, and dozed off in the middle of it.

PC's obsession with the idea of rebirth.

Perhaps he hoped that by turning his back on one sort of writing (his death as one kind of author) he would discover a new sort (be reborn as another). But what if he did it, and then realized that it hadn't worked? What options would be open to him then?

Pru said that her theory about PC's death was 'the exact opposite' of mine.

My theory is that RW murdered PC.

The exact opposite of that would be

And that, I guess, was when I fell asleep at last. I don't know how long it was for. Anyway, Rash woke me by nudging me in the ribs. She was reading the news on her phone.

Guess what? she said.

I don't know, I said. What?

You'll never guess, she said.

If I'll never guess, you'd better tell me, I said.

Liz Truss has resigned, she said.

And in the distance, the skyline of Venice rose into view.

Poor Phyl. She's completely out of it. She was so tired I don't think she even remembers finding this hotel and coming up to this room. She's been sleeping for ten hours straight. She's lying close beside me but her breathing is so quiet and slow that I can barely hear it, not even in the almost-silence of this room, where the only sound is the occasional lapping of canal water against our hotel wall. There is no traffic noise in this strange, watery city.

I've been sleeping, too, but at four in the morning I've woken up with a start. It's one of those moments. One of those moments when you wake out of a deep sleep and something that's been bothering you for weeks is suddenly crystal clear. You've been lost for a solution all this time and now it's staring you in the face. It's amazing how this happens sometimes. Sleep is a miraculous thing.

I sit up in bed. After a few moments I reach over and touch Phyl on the shoulder. I shake her gently until she stirs and turns towards me and her eyes flicker open. She looks at me, a question in her face. I feel cruel for having woken her.

Mm? she says.

I just thought of something, I tell her.

She sits up too. She can hear the urgency in my voice.

What is it?

You know I told you that I got another notification? About someone sending me a sound file? And I assumed it was that creepy guy again? Well, supposing it wasn't from him? Supposing it was from Chris?

She is wide awake at once.

When did it come?

The night before he died.

Have you listened to it?

I'm finding it now.

I've put the email into my trash folder but it hasn't been deleted permanently. It contains a link to a sound file but there is no message with it, nothing to say who it's from. All the email tells me is that the file was sent at 2:45 a.m. on the 9th of September.

I glance at Phyl one more time and then, my fingers trembling slightly, I click on the link. I hold up the phone between us so that we can listen together. We both crane in towards it, our heads almost touching.

This is what we hear.

Silence for the first few seconds. Then some distorted noise, as if the phone being used for the recording is picked up or moved, scraped across a surface. Then three dull taps, as if someone is checking that the microphone is working. And then . . .

. . . Chris's voice.

It's so weird to hear it again. Like a voice from beyond the grave. He is speaking in a low, murmurous undertone, almost a whisper, with his mouth very close to the microphone.

'This,' he says, 'is Christopher Swann speaking.'

A chill comes over my whole body. A convulsive shudder. Phyl puts her hand on my arm and rubs it tenderly. We move in even closer to listen.

There is a very long pause. Then we can hear Chris drawing in a slow, cautious breath, and saying:

'I am in room seven of Wetherby Hall hotel, in the Cotswolds. It is two o'clock, on the morning of Friday the ninth of September 2022. The other person in the room with me is a man who calls himself Professor Richard Wilkes. He is currently asleep. I am now walking over to his bed, and putting this recorder close to his face.'

Throughout this speech, another sound has been dimly audible in the background. A tune. A tune that I've never heard before, although now that I hear it, it seems all too familiar: somehow melancholy and sinister at the same time.

Phyl's hand grips my arm more tightly and she says:

That's the song. The one I heard on the radio. It's 'Lord Randall'.

The melody is quite distinct now. The singing has been subdued, at first, the phrasing tentative and fragile. It has become louder as the recording goes on, and louder still when Chris must have placed the microphone close to its source, close to the lips of the sleeping man.

And now it's quite clear what Chris has been recording, and what we are listening to in the eerie stillness of this Venetian hotel room, in the hour before dawn. We're listening to an elderly man, singing. He's singing a song that he's known all his life. In a high voice – almost a countertenor – the man who goes by the name of Richard Wilkes is singing to himself, softly, softly, softly, in his sleep.

P.

That song is implanted in my memory, Peter/Richard was telling us. It lives in my subconscious, and has done ever since I was a tiny boy, when my mother used to sing it to me as a lullaby. I had no idea that I sang it in my sleep, until Christopher Swann told me, the morning that I killed him. But when he did tell me, I can't say that I was surprised. It made perfect sense, in a way.

As soon as he said those words, 'the morning that I killed him', I felt Rash stiffening in her chair beside me. I looked at her face, but it was a perfect blank. I didn't know whether to admire her composure or to be scared by it. I'd offered to meet Peter/Richard by myself. I'd told her to stay away if she didn't think she could handle it. But she'd been determined to come with me, and it seemed now that she was determined to hear his story.

We were sitting on the terrace of a restaurant overlooking some canal. I couldn't say exactly which one, although I know it wasn't the Grand Canal. Coming to this restaurant had been Peter/Richard's idea. It was late afternoon, and the restaurant was closed, but he seemed to know the owners, and had persuaded them to let us sit out on this terrace. We were the only people there. He'd chosen a table in a shady corner. The afternoon sunlight was bright, and was shining full on our faces, but his face was in deep shadow. We could barely see him. I suspect that this was intentional.

So, there we were, the three of us. A rectangular table, in a shady corner of the terrace. On one side of the table: Phyl/Rash, family friend and adopted daughter of the dead man. On the other side: Peter/Richard, his murderer.

And that was how Chris identified you? I asked.

Yes, it was. He knew that there couldn't be many people in the world who knew that song, and only one person who had ever been known to sing it in his sleep. A friend of his, apparently, had heard me do it at Cambridge forty years ago, and had mentioned it in some sort of memoir that he was writing. Unlucky for me, I must say! But that, you see, is the power of the written word. It means that nothing is ever forgotten. Nothing is ever lost. Writing halts the passage of time. That's the only reason anybody does it, in the end. Isn't it?

It was the next morning, while I was out having a walk in the kitchen garden, that Swann came out to confront me, and to tell me that he'd guessed who I really was. And of course, as soon as he told me that, I knew what I would have to do. He told me that not only had he heard me singing 'Lord Randall' in my sleep the night before, but he'd made a recording of it on his phone. So I knew that the phone would have to go as well.

Fortunately, I was familiar with the layout of the hotel. Many years earlier – decades earlier – when I was still known as Peter Cockerill, I had stayed there, and the owner had been good enough to give me a thorough guided tour. He had shown me the hidden passage that connected the four rooms on the first floor. So I knew that I already had easy access to Mr Swann's room, and of course I'd noticed the collection of knives in the cabinet downstairs. I wrapped my hands in a scarf so as to leave no fingerprints, and got on with the job. It was not a pleasant business, by any means, but it was quickly done. Too quickly, in fact. In my haste I hadn't realized that he would still have enough strength to go to the desk and leave a dying message. Apparently he wrote the numbers eight/two on a piece of paper. I have no idea what he meant by that, or what the relevance of those numbers might be to myself. Anyway, I was concentrating on the final phase of my mission, which was to dispose of his mobile phone as quickly as possible. The best I could think of was to run down to the end of the passage and throw it as far out into the ornamental lake as I could manage.

Peter/Richard paused, and drank from the wine glass in front of him. The owner of the restaurant had furnished us with a bottle of white wine and some bowls of crackers and olives. It's as well to be refreshed, I suppose, while listening to a murder confession. And while making one.

Anyway, Peter/Richard said, I suppose what you really want to hear is the story *behind* the secret that Swann uncovered. The death of Richard Wilkes, and how I came to assume his identity for more than thirty years.

Well.

Where to begin, with that one?

Richard Wilkes was a name that I knew, nothing more. It was a name that quite a few people knew, if they were in the publishing world in the 1980s. He had made a modest reputation for himself, writing reviews and articles. Contemporary British fiction was his speciality. And yet the strange thing was, very few people seemed to have met him. I had never met him. He never seemed to go to launch parties, or bookshop events. He filed his copy by post and when he interviewed writers, he did it over the telephone. Everyone assumed that he was just a shy person, a recluse. People said that he'd held down the occasional academic post for a year or two – perhaps he still had one – but that was all that anyone seemed to know.

One day – I think it was when I was in the closing stages of writing *My Innocence* – he came out with an article in the *Guardian* that really enraged me. Martin Amis had just published his novel *Money* at this point, and that was the focus of the piece, but it was more wide-ranging than that. It set out to be a survey of the entire British literary scene at that moment, and every single writer he talked about was, in my opinion, worthless. I was so indignant, in fact, that I wrote him a letter about it. I told him, straight out, that the qualities he seemed to value most highly in a work were the very qualities that I detested. Irony, insincerity, self-awareness – *unseriousness* would sum it all up, I suppose. All of the writers that he mentioned were left-wing, and Godless, but they also had something else in common: a spurious internationalism, which deprived their work of all character. Where were the authors, I wanted to know, who had something to say on the subject of *England*? Where were the authors who valued its heritage, who understood its culture, whose work was deeply rooted in its lore and history? Was he not aware (well, obviously he wasn't, or he would have referred to it) of my novel *Motet in Four Parts*, which drew parallels between Thomas Tallis, the great composer of High Renaissance choral music, and a fictional twentieth-century namesake? Had he not read *A Rope from*

Hell, which specifically addressed the theme of how our great English traditions were being corrupted by socialist fantasies and spurious concepts of progress?

To give Wilkes credit, he wrote back to me, and engaged with some of the issues I had raised. It was painfully clear, though, that he had not read my books, and had no intention of doing so. Well, I refused to let this lie, and a lengthy correspondence ensued. It went on for several weeks, and during that time the tone of our letters began to change somewhat. What had started as a hostile, even rather abusive, exchange, morphed into something politer, more civilized. We started to look for areas of common ground rather than division. A note of affection even began to creep in. We still disagreed with each other profoundly, but I began to feel a sort of grudging respect for his position, and he for mine, I believe.

Finally I proposed a course of action which had probably been inevitable from the very start. I suggested that we should meet.

At this time I was leading a very solitary life, living alone in an old gamekeeper's cottage in one of the remotest corners of the New Forest. I had withdrawn there after my mother's death, and indeed I had bought it with the modest sum which was all that she had been able to leave me. Her death had flattened me. Not least because she had read my last book, *A Rope from Hell*, and it had upset her very much. Considering the way that it mixed fictional elements with real episodes taken from her own unhappy marriage, this was not surprising, and I was mortified that I hadn't foreseen it. So I was feeling a terrible mixture of grief and guilt, compounded by the fact that, most days, I never saw or spoke to another living soul. I had no friends, and no neighbours.

It was with some excitement, therefore, that I received Wilkes's letter, in which he accepted my invitation to come down and visit for a few days.

He arrived by train on Thursday afternoon. I picked him up from the station, which was a good twenty minutes' drive from my cottage, and I can remember, even now, how awkwardly he stood and watched me as I made coffee for us both in the tiny kitchen upon his arrival there. We were shy and combative with each other to start with. However, that would change rapidly in the next forty-eight hours, as a measure of understanding and indeed intimacy began to flower between us.

Wilkes was withdrawn, pale, somewhat delicate in build and rather diffident in manner. I suspected at once that he had not led a particularly happy life and this turned out to be the case. Over the next two days we would spend a good deal of time in conversation, as we took long walks in the forest and explored the coastline together. I learned everything about his early years. His mother had died in childbirth and he had been given up for adoption. After ten years, however, his adoptive parents had separated and he had acquired a new stepfather, with whom he had a very difficult and uncomfortable relationship. In the middle of the 1960s, when Wilkes was just fourteen, this new father-figure made a big decision on behalf of his family, and the ill-matched threesome emigrated to Australia, where Wilkes would spend the next ten years of his life. Deeply unsuited to the ways of that country, he became quiet and introspective, spending more and more of his time absorbed in the world of literature. He studied English at the University of Melbourne and even completed a PhD there, on the early poems of Alexander Pope. But he could not wait to leave, and to come back to England. When he said goodbye to his adoptive parents, he said it for ever, and by the sound of it there was little regret on either side. He arrived back in England in the mid-1970s, completely alone.

In the next few years he had held two minor teaching posts at British universities: one at Lancaster and one at Queen's University, Belfast. He also began to submit short reviews and articles to the British newspapers. Like many people who are uncertain of themselves in person, he was extremely forthright in print, and of course editors are very drawn to this. His articles were provocations, and as such were very welcome in the British media. He had not enjoyed teaching and gave it up as soon as possible, believing – naively – that he could make a living as a freelance literary journalist. However, despite the name he had started making for himself, he was earning very little money, and when I met him he had just accepted another teaching job, this one at the University of Aberdeen. In the meantime he was living alone in a small flat in the most anonymous of

English cities, Peterborough. 'If I died,' he said to me at one point, 'nobody would miss me. Nobody at all.' It was a remark that would come back to me before the weekend was over.

During all of the two days in which I learned Wilkes's story, as we became more and more closely acquainted with each other, a shadow hung between us. An elephant in the room, as I believe the expression is. More than a week earlier, I had posted him the manuscript of my new novel, *My Innocence*. I knew that he had read it, and of course, I was desperate to know what he had made of it, not least because this book was a new departure for me: the book in which I had turned away from the whole dishonest business of fictionalizing one's own experience, and attempted to tell only the literal truth as I saw it. I believed – in fact I knew – that I had written an important and indeed revolutionary book. However, Wilkes said nothing about it. Every time I dropped a gentle hint that we might start discussing it, he changed the subject. We talked about some of my other books. We talked – a lot – about other writers. (He came back again and again, at wearisome length, to Martin Amis and his novel *Money*, which he seemed to consider the great literary achievement of our time.) But of my own new work, my *magnum opus*, as I had started to think of it, he said not a word.

Not a word, that is, until the Saturday evening of his visit.

The Killing

In the many years since all of this took place I have, as you can well imagine, gone over the sequence of events countless times in my mind, and in the process I have created a narrative around them. A true narrative, I might say, but one which also has a kind of structure and logic to it. It is divided into four parts – I think of them as the movements of a symphony – which I refer to as *The Killing*, *The Reflection*, *The Course of Action* and *The Aftermath*.

I choose the title of the first part very carefully, and I refer to it as *The Killing* because I am unable to decide, even to this day, whether I really murdered Richard Wilkes or not.

Anyway.

The Saturday of his visit was marked by particularly dreadful weather. The month was April. All day rain had been pouring down and a bitterly cold wind had been blowing through the forest. In the late afternoon we had taken advantage of a break in the rain to go for one of our long walks, but even then we misjudged the weather and soon found ourselves caught in a torrential downpour. When we got back to the cottage, Wilkes immediately went upstairs to run himself a hot bath. He was up there for quite some time, during which I laid a fire in the hearth, and prepared some supper for us. After supper, I too had a bath. Wilkes had borrowed my dressing gown – the only one in the house – so after bathing I put on my flannel nightshirt and went downstairs to join him by the fire, for whisky and conversation.

This was the moment at which he decided, no doubt after much deliberation on his part, to tell me exactly what he thought of my new book. The whisky bottle, I noticed, was significantly emptier than before, and I'm sure this played its part as well. In any case, his verdict was scathing. Clearly he considered the book to be a failure on every level: aesthetic, structural, stylistic and moral. 'Sadly, Peter,' he said, 'you have no idea. No idea about the contemporary world or how it operates or how it feels, and no idea how to represent this in a work of literature.' At first I was merely speechless. But my indignation grew when I realized that he was talking not just about this book, but about my work as a whole. 'You are laughably out of date,' he told me. 'You're using modernist techniques which may have been current in the 1920s, but they have no relevance at all to the ways in which novels should be written sixty years later. What's more, by renouncing fiction so publicly and committing yourself to a desperately narrow vision of "the truth" you have driven yourself headlong into a cul-de-sac from which there is no possible way out.' Once I'd recovered my powers of speech I started to defend myself, and decided that the best way to do it was by going on the attack. Bearing in mind his wild over-enthusiasm for certain other fashionable contemporary writers, I accused him of being shallow and easily impressed. 'As a reader, or as a person?' he asked, to which I answered: 'Both, of course. A man's qualities as a reader cannot be separated from his personal qualities.' 'The same is true – even more so – of a man's qualities as a writer,' he replied. 'And that makes you a pompous, ineffectual, deluded reactionary.' It was amazing how quickly the argument escalated from simply discussing the merits of a book to mercilessly anatomizing each other's defects and failures as human beings. Within a few minutes, fuelled by whisky, we were staring at each other with unalloyed hatred. But it got worse. Based, he said, on what he had read in the book, he proceeded to make a comment – more than a comment, a vile and unrepeatable slur – on my mother's character, and on my own relationship with her. 'Take that back,' I said to him, and when he wouldn't, I rose to my feet, and pulled him bodily from his chair.

From then on, no more words were exchanged. Our conflict took on an entirely physical form. In front of the blazing log fire, we wrestled with each other. His dressing gown fell open, my nightshirt rose up around my waist, and before either of us realized it, we were both naked. (At least, that is how I remember it now. The entire episode, of course, has become very blurred in my mind.) Our muscles strained and our bodies glistened with sweat. I put my fingers around his throat and tried to throttle him. He heaved me away, his hands pushing against my shoulders. He lay on top of me and twisted my ears, his face close to mine, his teeth bared and locked into a rictus grin. I kneed him in the groin, feeling the impact of my knee against the semi-hardened tissue of his penis, while he grabbed my testicles and squeezed them until I howled with pain. His fingers raked down my back, leaving bloody scratches. I pinned him to the floor and punched him again and again in the face. Finally, as he struggled out from underneath me and tried to raise himself into a sitting position, I once again thrust him to the ground, but this time I pushed harder, and his skull made brutal contact with the tiled edge of the hearth. There was a sickening crack, and all at once he was still. Quite still.

I struggled to my feet, and looked down at him, panting heavily. The room suddenly seemed very quiet, apart from my breathing and the occasional popping of the fire. Wilkes stared back at me from his place on the floor, his eyes wide open, unseeing. A pool of blood was already beginning to form around his head.

A feeling of preternatural calm descended on me. After resting in an armchair for a few minutes and contemplating Wilkes's body, I went upstairs, cleaned my teeth, climbed into bed and slept for eight hours. When I came downstairs the next morning, I covered his body with a blanket, then made myself coffee and sat in the same armchair, drinking the coffee and listening to the rain pattering against the cottage windows.

There seemed no point in hurrying to do anything.

I was very far from being in a state of panic. In fact, as the hours went by, I felt myself ascending to an almost Olympian perspective, watching from on high, looking down on this little front parlour with its artfully arranged tableau of a man sitting in an armchair, absorbed in leisurely thought while a prostrate and lifeless body lay at his feet.

I soon came to realize that, while what had happened was obviously a disaster, it could also be reconfigured as a possibility.

'If I died,' Richard had told me, 'nobody would miss me. Nobody at all.'

Well, presumably some members of the English department at Aberdeen University would miss him, because he was expected to take up a post there in September that year. But none of them had met him. His interview for the job, he'd said, had been conducted in London by a member of staff who was leaving the department in the summer.

Presumably some literary editors would miss him, if they asked him to review books for them and he never replied. But perhaps someone could reply in his name – and write the reviews too, while they were at it?

Curiously, as the day went on (a day in which I never moved from that armchair) I remembered more and more of the appalling, hurtful things we had said to each other during last night's argument. Every insult, every vituperation, every swear word came back to me with a bright and terrible clarity. I realized, too, that a lot of what Richard had said had hurt me so much, pierced me so deeply, only because it was true. For instance, his comment about the cul-de-sac

I had driven myself into confirmed an intuition that had been building within me for many weeks: that *My Innocence* was the last book I would ever write. I had nothing more to say, and had left myself no voice in which to say it. My work as a novelist was done.

But . . . but . . .

How do writers survive? I don't mean, How do they make a living? I mean, How do their works survive, after they have gone?

They rarely survive unassisted. They survive because people find them. People are directed towards them. Readers read them. Enthusiasts proselytize for them. Critics discuss them. Teachers teach them.

The objective had always been for my books to outlive me. I had completed the first phase of this project, by writing them. Now, perhaps, was it time to embark upon the second phase?

The Course of Action

If I were to walk away from this house as Richard Wilkes, I decided, then I must leave all trace of Peter Cockerill behind. *Destroy* all trace of him, in fact. Destroy everything about him except those things which must, and would, survive him: his books.

The idea of a conflagration quickly presented itself. It offered two particular attractions: it would do away with all of Peter Cockerill's paperwork, and it stood a good chance of making the body of Richard Wilkes impossible to identify.

I had no doubt that people would assume I had committed suicide. I had talked about it, occasionally, to my few acquaintances in London, including my editor, Charles Newman. Charles had read the manuscript of *My Innocence* and while he had admired it, he described it as the work of a deeply unhappy person. The last page of the book offered a tentative note of optimism, but this, he said, did not materially alter the reader's perception of the novel: that it was, in essence, a howl of despair.

I had spoken about killing myself, but I had always known that I would not have the courage to go through with it. And yet here, unexpectedly, I had been given the opportunity to present the illusion of suicide, while evading the act itself. All that was needed, to complete the illusion, was some sort of farewell message to the world. It didn't take me long to decide what form that should take.

Richard had enraged me by (among other things) enthusing at length about Martin Amis and his novel *Money*: a book which I had disliked intensely, and for which I felt the strongest contempt. One of the things that irked me about it, in particular, was that it bore the subtitle 'A Suicide Note'. Like everything else in the book, this struck me as a gimmick, nothing more: a symptom of the author's callous flippancy and insincerity. A writer should, if nothing else, be sincere. But in *my* novel, it occurred to me, I had the chance to offer a perfect, devastating riposte. The whole of *My Innocence* could be read as a long and genuine suicide note. The only thing that ran counter to this reading was the hint of optimism on the final page – something which its most sympathetic reader, Charles Newman, had in any case found unconvincing. And that could easily and quickly be changed. I'd been told that the bound proofs of the novel had already arrived in the offices of Newman & Fox. That was unfortunate. They would all have to be destroyed. But the amendment to the text itself would simply be a question of changing a few words.

When I finally stirred myself from the armchair, in the late evening of that wet and windy Sunday, I wrote a letter to Charles Newman, instructing him to destroy the proofs and to make three small changes to the novel's final page. The next morning I posted that letter in the nearest village, and also stopped by the local garage to buy some cans of petrol.

My cottage had two bedrooms, the second of which I used as a study. It was full of a lifetime's worth of papers: letters, notes, manuscripts and much more besides. All would have to be destroyed – not least because I wanted to remove as many traces of my own handwriting as possible. I found it a hugely liberating and exhilarating prospect. Late on Monday afternoon, I dragged Richard's body up the stairs into this room – with great difficulty, I must say – and this was the first object that I doused in fuel. From the pocket of his coat, which was still hanging downstairs, I had already taken his wallet and keys. Then I emptied the remainder of the cans, making sure that some petrol at least had been deposited in every room in the house. Finally, I went out into the little back garden, stood next to the open window of the kitchen, struck a match and tossed it inside.

As soon as I saw the flames rising and spreading, and was satisfied that my preparations had been sufficient, I ran into the depths of the forest as fast as I could, and never looked back.

The Aftermath

In September 1987, I presented myself at the University of Aberdeen, claiming to be Richard Wilkes, a claim that was accepted at once.

I had spent most of the summer at Wilkes's flat in Peterborough, where he seemed to have been as unknown to his neighbours as he had been to the rest of the world. In order to more closely resemble him I had grown my hair and grown a beard (which I have to this day, and which I have always hated). I had read my own perfunctory obituaries in the newspapers, and also read the posthumous reviews of *My Innocence*, which were just as crass and wrong-headed as I might have expected. Now I was rather looking forward to my new career as a lecturer in English. On the whole, the relief of not having to be Peter Cockerill any more was immense.

To revive my own reputation as a novelist, I decided that I needed to play a long game. Tremendous patience was required. After a year or two, I began to drop the name of Peter Cockerill into some of the reviews that I was writing in the guise of Richard Wilkes. I would drop in occasional remarks about a forgotten genius, a great writer who had somehow been allowed to slip through the net. I publicly shamed myself for having underrated him, to the point of not even mentioning him in any of my earlier surveys of contemporary British fiction. At the university, I would privately press copies of *Motet in Four Parts* and *A Rope from Hell* into the hands of favourite students, but it was not until about five or six years had passed that I felt able to start including him in my modules on 'Creative Memoir' and 'Post-War Fictional Experiment'. Shortly after that, I published my first major article on him in the *Modern Language Review*. It aroused considerable interest.

There was always a danger, of course – although a very slight one, as it would turn out – that some former academic colleague or personal acquaintance of Wilkes would encounter me and become suspicious. Therefore, I was always on the lookout for academic opportunities abroad, and when the University of Ca' Foscari in Venice advertised for a Senior Lecturer in English Literature, I applied for the post and obtained it. They were looking for an anglophone lecturer to teach international students, but my application was strengthened by the fact that I already had decent Italian, and since then I've become fluent. Early in the 2000s, after I'd been here for a few years, they offered me the chance to organize a conference. 'Peter Cockerill and the Conservative Literary Movement' was the subject I chose, and that event – which attracted scholars from all over the world – was really the start of the serious revival of my literary fortunes. The proceedings were published in a book of essays (which I edited), which in turn prompted a number of similarly themed conferences throughout the following decade in locations as far-flung as Singapore, Prague, Adelaide and Austin, Texas. Most gratifying of all was a letter from the editor of Penguin Modern Classics in 2013, proposing that *A Rope from Hell* be included in that prestigious series, in an edition introduced and annotated (naturally) by myself.

A modern classic at last! Well, I deserved nothing less.

Of course, there is still a good deal of work to be done. Like everything else in life, maintaining one's own literary reputation is a perpetual struggle, and one can never relax one's vigilance. Enemies are everywhere. The writers who were allowed to overshadow me during my lifetime are still in the ascendant, and still have their acolytes. Until the whole world can see that what I was doing was right, and what they were doing was wrong, the battle will never be over. Peter Cockerill has still not had the recognition that he always knew to be his destiny, as well as his due.

But I have made a start, anyway. Out of catastrophe, I created at least the *possibility* of triumph. And in the midst of death, I found a kind of rebirth.

P.

It had taken Peter / Richard a long time to tell us all this. The sun had moved westward, and now the whole table was in shadow, not just his face. A chill breeze was blowing off the canal, its waters stirring and churning. The wine bottle on our table was empty, and so were the bowls of snacks. A sense of desperate melancholy, as well as anger and hatred, had stolen over me.

I said:

How tragic, that after everything you did, you still feel that you've failed.

Failed?

Yes, failed. You murdered a man to get what you wanted. You murdered another man in order to keep your secret safe. And yet the good fortune that it's brought you still isn't enough. You remind me of the people at that conference. Remaking the world in their own image, and then still not liking what they see. You'll never be satisfied, any of you. People like you never are.

Peter / Richard rose to his feet.

Well, I've already told you quite enough.

He was about to leave, when he paused and said:

You know, I suppose I ought to thank you.

Why's that, then? Rash asked.

Because . . . Well . . .

He sat down opposite us again.

I've come to realize, in the last few years, that I was born with a compulsion – a need – to tell stories. And turning my back on that, all those years ago, was in a way a repudiation of my own nature. A very foolish, self-destructive thing to do. And of course, *this* story – the one I've just told you – is the one I've been wanting to tell for years. Decades. Ever since it happened. Well, now you've given me the opportunity. Really, the way you just turned up here, and presented yourselves . . . It's been perfect. You've been my perfect audience. Not least because I know that if you tell anybody else this story, they won't believe you. They won't believe any of it. Who's going to take the word of two silly young women over mine? You'd have nothing to back up your version of things. No proof.

Rash and I looked at each other, exchanging a knowing, conspiratorial glance. Lying between the three of us on the table was my phone. I'd been recording everything.

I actually feel a huge sense of . . . unburdening. I actually feel lighter – physically lighter – than I've felt in a long time. Because I think, in a way, that this was *the* story. The one I was put on this earth to tell. Do you know what I mean? And it's such a good one, isn't it? Beautifully shaped. Everything ties up perfectly. No loose ends.

Oh, there are plenty of loose ends, said Rash.

Really? said Peter/Richard, switching at once from a tone of immense self-satisfaction to one of quick, subdued hostility. For instance?

For instance – you didn't destroy every example of your handwriting.

He waved his hands airily.

Oh, yes, there are a few signed copies floating around. There wasn't much I could do about that, apart from buying them up whenever I found them.

Nothing else? I asked him. You don't remember, for instance, writing in the visitors' book at Wetherby Hall, the first time you visited?

A distant, thoughtful look came into his eyes.

No, I hadn't remembered. Although, now that you mention it . . .

Quite a long entry, by all accounts, Rash added.

Well then, maybe I shall have to do something about that.

With these words, he stood up again, and held out his hand. Obviously neither of us shook it. We glared after him as he wove his way out through the tables in the restaurant's dark interior.

Are we just going to let him go? Rash asked, indignant.

Don't worry, I said. It's all over for him now. Pru will get him, as soon as she hears.

Peter/Richard had emerged from the restaurant, and was walking away from us down the narrow path that led alongside the canal. The sight of this baleful, scuttling figure in his distinctive red jumper, ducking between pillars and in and out of courtyards as they grew shady in the Venetian dusk, triggered a cinematic memory.

Look at him, I said, as he paused at the midpoint of an ancient little bridge spanning the canal. He's like something out of *Don't Look Now*.

What's that? Rash asked.

Oh, it's just one of those old films my dad's always going on about.

We watched him for a little longer. I had the sense that he was aware of us looking at him. And then, not wanting to pay him the compliment of our attention any more, we turned our backs on him in contempt.

We didn't say anything until suddenly, right next to our terrace, there was a loud splash in the water behind us. We both wheeled around again.

Did you hear that? Rash said.

A fish jumping? Are there any fish in this canal?

I don't think so. Where's your phone?

We both stared in horror at the table. There was no phone lying between us any more.

The bastard! I said. He's done it again.

We looked towards the bridge. The figure leaning against the parapet waved cheerfully at us. And then Peter/Richard, too, was gone.

R.

She doesn't believe us. This is crazy to me, but the policeman lady doesn't believe us.

He confessed, we say to her. He confessed to everything.

Yes, but you have no record of that. No proof. It's just your word against his.

Phyl says: He's going to come back to this country. He's going to come back and go up to Wetherby Hall to destroy that old entry in the visitors' book. He said as much. You have to arrest him when he does it.

I could arrest him any time, and anywhere, policeman lady answers.

Then why don't you?

Because I don't know for certain whether he killed your father or not.

What about the recording? I say. You've just heard it. He was singing in his sleep. Richard Wilkes is not really Richard Wilkes. He's Peter Cockerill.

Yes, policeman lady says patiently. I know that. But I'm afraid that my point still stands.

This is incredible. How much more evidence does she want? We are sitting in her office in the Oxfordshire constabulary headquarters. A shabby little room at the corner of the building, where the shelves and cupboards are almost empty. She had already cleared them out before this case started, apparently. She is supposed to have retired by now. I can't understand why she doesn't want to bring this whole business to a conclusion as quickly as possible.

What happened to your other theory? she asks.

What other theory?

I thought you'd decided that the murder was committed, in error, by Howard Beddoes, Charles Newman's partner?

Oh, that.

I suppose we look a bit embarrassed. It had seemed like a good solution at the time – a possible explanation for the clue that Chris had left behind.

As a matter of fact, policeman lady says, I checked the list of conference delegates, and there *was* one called Howard.

Phyl sits forward, suddenly interested.

There was?

His name was . . . (She looks through a few sheets of paper on her desk.) Howard Fitch. Forty-three years old. Conservative Party councillor from Ludlow in Shropshire.

She looks at us with the smug, know-it-all smile that is starting to irritate me.

Not our man, I'm afraid.

I stand up.

Come on, Phyl. We're wasting our time here.

Don't worry, policeman lady says. We'll be watching the airports. And the Eurostar terminal. If Wilkes comes into the country, we'll know about it.

This promise does nothing to reassure us, or to quell the tide of anger and frustration that I can feel growing inside me.

Out in the corridor, Phyl says:

Can you wait here a minute, Rash? I need the loo.

While she goes into the ladies' toilet, I stand with my back to the wall, leaning against it, thinking about the conversation we have just had. I'm not happy about it. The more I think about it, the less happy I am. And I'm using the word 'happy' literally. Ever since our meeting with Peter/Richard in Venice last week, I've been feeling flattened. Flattened by sadness: the sadness of what that little piece of shit has taken away from me.

I push away from the wall and begin to walk slowly back towards policeman lady's office. The walk takes me through the incident room which is currently empty. It is late in the afternoon of Monday 24th October. A television screen is mounted on the wall of the room, broadcasting a news channel with the sound muted. From the corner of my eye, I half-read a ticker-tape announcement as it scrolls across the bottom of the screen: 'Rishi Sunak, new Conservative leader, to become Britain's first Asian PM.'

I walk back into her office and say:

Please find him.

She looks up.

Find him?

Or her. Whoever it is.

I find myself sitting at her desk again. I find myself sitting opposite her. I look across the desk at her and now, for the first time, I notice what a sympathetic face she has. On the surface her manner remains brisk and professional but when I look directly into her eyes I can see warmth and sympathy there. It's enough to make me feel that I can talk to her. Make one last appeal.

So I say:

I need you to get this done. Really. I'm not sure I can carry on otherwise. I mean, I know you've handled hundreds of cases like this. To you it's just another puzzle. But Chris was more than that to me. He was my father. He was my fucking *dad* . . .

I can feel the tears beginning to sting as the distant memories return to me and the words come tumbling out:

He was a human being, you know? Just another human being, with all the usual contradictions. And I wouldn't be the person I am without him. I wouldn't be the person I am without my dad. He was generous and he was loving and he never stopped . . . He could never do enough for me. He used to wash my hair in the bath when I was tiny, and get upset when I cried because the shampoo had got in my eyes. He used to read to me at bedtime. Sometimes he'd read the books he'd loved when he was a kid and try not to look hurt when I didn't like them. He taught me to roller-skate. He taught me to ride a bike. He taught me to play tennis. He taught me how to do long division when the teachers at school just confused me. He invented puzzles for me, and games with numbers and code words. I made him watch Disney cartoons that he really, really hated but he sat through them with me because he knew that I loved them. He had beliefs and values and ideals but he never tried to impose them on me. He always let me be who I wanted to be. He put up with my mom for way longer than he should have done because he didn't want to lose me. After he left he sent me letters and drew little cartoons in them, really terrible cartoons. He couldn't draw to save his life. He tried to be an optimist but he often got depressed and when he got depressed he'd watch Laurel and Hardy and the Marx Brothers and then he would cheer up. He called himself a socialist but some of his best friends were conservatives. He hated social media but he couldn't stop blogging. He liked jazz-funk but he always listened to it on headphones because he was embarrassed about it. He loved cheddar-cheese-and-pickle sandwiches and beans on toast and fish and chips. He supported Bristol Rovers, not Bristol City. He had an encyclopaedic knowledge of *Friends* episodes. He loved the countryside but he never knew the names of the trees or the flowers. He loved reading. He loved history. He liked watching quiz shows on TV and shouting out the answers. He wanted to lose weight but he never could . . .

I fall silent. There is so much more that I could say, but I'm too tired to go on. The grief has exhausted me.

On the surface, Pru Freeborne's expression has not changed. She still looks calm and professional. But I know that my words have made a difference, and I trust her now. I trust her to get this thing finished.

She says:

Wilkes landed at Luton airport fifteen minutes ago. He's booked a hotel for the night near Paddington station. I'll be there, tomorrow morning. I'll be there to meet him.

I nod and I thank her and I get up to leave. In a daze, not really sure where I am any more, I pass through the incident room and back into the corridor, where Phyl is waiting for me. I'm so glad to see her. So glad she's there. Her friendship has been the only good thing to come out of this nightmare. She holds out her arms and I find myself falling into them and hugging her as if neither of us will ever let go.

P.

Rash doesn't like books that are full of made-up things. She thinks it is fake and embarrassing to write about invented people, to put imaginary words and thoughts into their mouths and heads. She thinks that you should write only about your own interior life, candidly, without filtering, with present-tense immediacy, because this is the only reality that we can know. Around forty years ago, the writer Peter Cockerill arrived at the same conclusion.

My own belief? I can't quite share the purity of their convictions. I think back, quite often, to that conversation I overheard at the airport. Do you have to get permission to put someone inside your head and make them do anything you want them to do? Do you need to obtain their consent?

No, I don't think so.

The inside of your head is your own space. You are the queen of that castle.

There are times when you have something to say, and you can't say it in your own voice, or from your own point of view. So, should you remain silent?

No, I don't think so.

Here's an example. You've read this far. You only have a few pages left to read. Presumably you would like to know how this story ends. But neither Rash nor I were present when DI Prudence Freeborne finally confronted Peter Cockerill and arrested him. We can't know for sure how it happened. So how can I tell you?

Here's how. I'm going to have to use that most maligned and embattled of human faculties: the imagination.

Let me sit back in this chair, close my eyes, put my hands behind my head, and try to picture the scene.

It could have happened . . .

It might have happened . . .

It would have happened like this:

Prudence would have made her way to Paddington station and soon spotted Peter Cockerill on the concourse as he waited for his train to Moreton-in-Marsh. As always, he would have stood out from the crowd, on account of the vivid red jumper he sported beneath his tweed jacket. She would have boarded the same train as him, and found herself a seat in the carriage next to his. She would not have arrested him immediately. For most of the journey, she would have sat and run over the details of the case in her mind. Unfortunately her thoughts would be interrupted, at regular intervals, by the endless safety announcements.

> *If you see something that doesn't look right, speak to staff, or text British Transport Police on 61016.*
>
> *We'll sort it.*
>
> *See it. Say it. Sorted.*

Several things would have suggested to her that Peter Cockerill was the murderer. From his visit to Wetherby Hall many years earlier, he knew the layout of the house and he knew of the existence of the secret passage: therefore he had the means, as well as the opportunity. Did he have the motive? According to Phyl and Rash, he did. He had a guilty secret, which Christopher Swann had uncovered. Christopher had made a recording of Cockerill singing in his sleep. Singing the song 'Lord Randall'. They had brought it into her office, and she had listened to it. But that still wouldn't have been enough. She would still only have their word for it that Cockerill had actually confessed to murdering Richard Wilkes all those years ago, and stealing his identity. The recorded evidence of that confession had been destroyed: if it had ever existed. Could their story be trusted, or was it just the feverish speculation of two over-imaginative young women with too much time on their hands?

Her hunch would have been that they were right. After all, she herself had already concluded that Richard Wilkes must be dead, and that Peter Cockerill had been living under his name. This would have been her conviction from very early in the investigation: ever since she had closely examined the text of Wilkes's lecture to the TrueCon conference, and had seen that it began with a handwritten reminder on its first page: *Insert quotation from Edward Thomas, etc.* Shortly afterwards, on the night of her dinner in Rookthorne,

Andrew Maidstone had shown her his copy of *A Rope from Hell*, which had been inscribed on the title page. Inscribed, by a lucky coincidence, to an old friend of his wife's, called Thomas. Today she would retrieve the printouts of both pages from her briefcase, and lay them side by side on the table in front of her. Once again, she would note the striking similarity between the two samples of handwriting. In fact, when it came to the name 'Thomas', there was more than a similarity. The writing was identical.

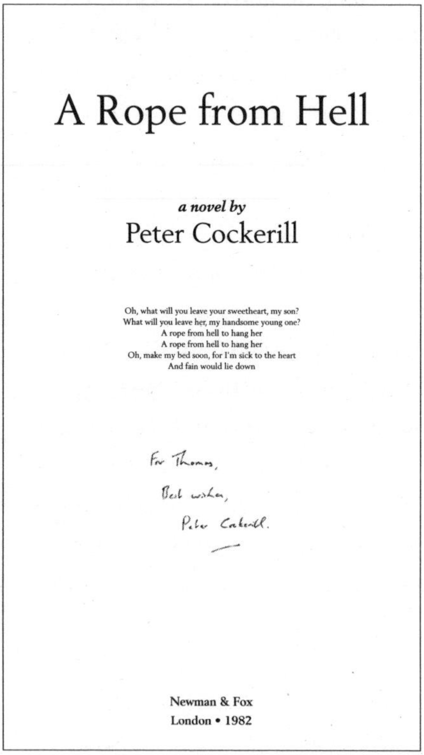

A Rope from Hell

a novel by
Peter Cockerill

Oh, what will you leave your sweetheart, my son?
What will you leave her, my handsome young one?
A rope from hell to hang her
A rope from hell to hang her
Oh, make my bed soon, for I'm sick to the heart
And fain would lie down

For Thomas,
Best wishes,
Peter Cockerill.

Newman & Fox
London • 1982

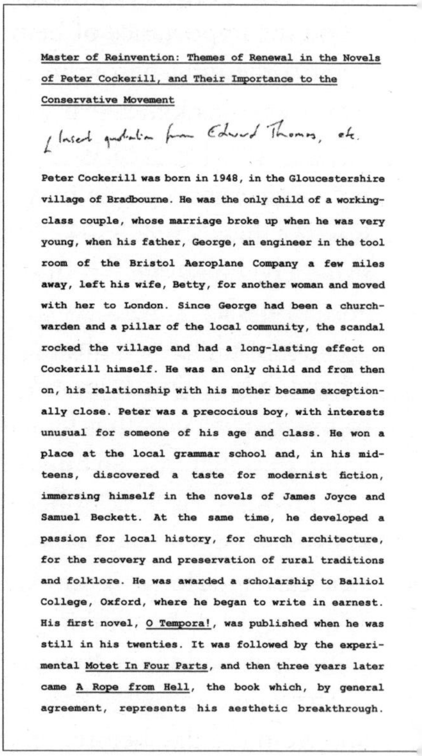

Master of Reinvention: Themes of Renewal in the Novels of Peter Cockerill, and Their Importance to the Conservative Movement

[Insert quotation from Edward Thomas, etc.

Peter Cockerill was born in 1948, in the Gloucestershire village of Bradbourne. He was the only child of a working-class couple, whose marriage broke up when he was very young, when his father, George, an engineer in the tool room of the Bristol Aeroplane Company a few miles away, left his wife, Betty, for another woman and moved with her to London. Since George had been a church-warden and a pillar of the local community, the scandal rocked the village and had a long-lasting effect on Cockerill himself. He was an only child and from then on, his relationship with his mother became exception-ally close. Peter was a precocious boy, with interests unusual for someone of his age and class. He won a place at the local grammar school and, in his mid-teens, discovered a taste for modernist fiction, immersing himself in the novels of James Joyce and Samuel Beckett. At the same time, he developed a passion for local history, for church architecture, for the recovery and preservation of rural traditions and folklore. He was awarded a scholarship to Balliol College, Oxford, where he began to write in earnest. His first novel, O Tempora!, was published when he was still in his twenties. It was followed by the experi-mental Motet In Four Parts, and then three years later came A Rope from Hell, the book which, by general agreement, represents his aesthetic breakthrough.

That in itself would have been enough to convince DI Freeborne, beyond a reasonable doubt, that Peter Cockerill and Richard Wilkes were one and the same person. But even so, even now, that would not necessarily prove that he was guilty of the murder at Wetherby Hall.

If you see something that doesn't look right, speak to staff, or text British Transport Police on 61016.

We'll sort it.
See it. Say it. Sorted.

Prudence Freeborne is a conscientious detective. Her brain is forensic, methodical. And there would still be an element of lingering doubt in her mind. There would still be one element of the puzzle that hadn't fallen into place: the clue.

In the course of this investigation, she has developed a considerable respect for the murder victim. Christopher Swann had possessed a formidable intellect, and like Pru herself, he had understood the importance of being thorough, clear, precise. There had been something heroic in his dying attempt to leave a message identifying his killer. Pru would have concluded, by now, that the single letter he tried to write on that piece of paper was never meant to be an R, let alone a B. He had begun to write a P for Peter; but had then realized that, since he was the only person who knew Peter's real identity, the clue would have meant nothing to anyone who found it.

So instead, Christopher had written the numbers 8/2. Numbers which, in his mind at least, were sufficient to point unambiguously to one figure. Was that figure Peter Cockerill? Was there anything about him that singled him out from the other three suspects?

Pru would sit back in her carriage and look out of the window, watching the Berkshire countryside roll by in the autumn sunshine. One carriage along, Peter Cockerill might be doing the same thing. What might he be thinking?

What would *she* be thinking?

She would think back to the conversation she had had with Phyl and Rash the day before. She would think back to the unexpected passion with which Christopher's adopted daughter had listed his qualities. All the small, idiosyncratic things which had made him admirable, and lovable. Some of them Pru had known already; some of them had been a surprise.

One detail would suddenly come back to her. What was the phrase Rashida had used? 'Encyclopaedic knowledge.'

Prudence would take out her phone and open the Wikipedia app. She would navigate to a page called 'List of *Friends* Episodes'. She would scroll down until she found the one she was looking for. Season 8, Episode 2.

The One with the Red Sweater.

Detective Inspector Prudence Freeborne would nod to herself, and give a little smile of satisfaction. She would then stand up and make her way into the next carriage, her body swaying with the motion of the train.

Soon she would be standing over the suspect. Peter Cockerill would not in fact be watching the passing landscape through the train window. He would be gazing instead at the screen of his phone: at a live broadcast from the steps of Number 10 Downing Street. Becoming aware of her presence, he would look up, and she would see the flame of recognition rising slowly in his eyes. She would speak his full name and say, 'I am arresting you for the murder of—' before once again being interrupted.

If you see something that doesn't look right, speak to staff, or text British Transport Police on 61016.

We'll sort it.

See it. Say it. Sorted.

Meanwhile, on the phone screen, Liz Truss would be making her farewell speech to the British people.

From my time as Prime Minister, I am more convinced than ever we need to be bold and confront the challenges that we face. As the Roman philosopher Seneca wrote: 'It is not because things are difficult that we do not dare. It is because we do not dare that they are difficult.'

Peter Cockerill would look up from the screen again and say to DI Freeborne:

How appropriate. Then he would add, ruefully: Well, at least I dared.

You did indeed, she would answer.

I'm not sure it was ever meant to end like this, he would say.

Like this?

I don't mean my sorry little story. That was never going to end well. I mean the experiment that we started, back in the 1980s.

We need to take advantage of our Brexit freedoms to do things differently.

This means delivering more freedom for our own citizens and restoring power to democratic institutions.

It means lower taxes, so people keep more of the money they earn.

We really thought – some of us really thought – that the country was changing for the better back then. Somewhere along the line, it seems to have gone horribly wrong.

DI Freeborne would say: Perhaps some enterprises just have the seeds of their own failure planted in them.

Perhaps, Peter Cockerill would say.

And he would return to looking at his phone screen, just as the resigning Prime Minister spoke her final words, and just as the safety announcement was heard one last time:

I look forward to spending more time in my constituency.

If you see something that doesn't look right, speak to staff, or text British Transport Police on 61016.

Our country continues to battle through a storm.

We'll sort it.

But I believe in Britain.

See it.

I believe in the British people.

Say it.

And I know that brighter days lie ahead.

Sorted.

EPILOGUE

27th February 2024

Joanna surprised herself by wanting to attend Emeric's memorial. She surprised herself by being upset at the news of his death. She supposed that, with Brian gone, and Christopher gone, he had, after all, represented the last living point of contact with her student self. And, whatever reservations Christopher may have had about Emeric and his influence on public life, she had always felt a residual fondness for him, and could not remember him treating her with anything other than decency. Now he was gone too. When she read in her alumni newsletter that there was going to be a memorial service at the end of February, she knew that she would have to make the effort to be there.

The complicated journey from Rookthorne to Cambridge went smoothly enough, and Joanna arrived with half an hour to spare. A tangled cluster of feelings gripped her as she entered the main courtyard of her old college. It was the middle of the Lent term and there were a lot of students around. As they passed among these gaunt, impressive buildings in groups and in pairs, she thought that they looked perhaps not so different from how she, Christopher and Brian must have looked more than forty years ago. Carefree and preoccupied; confident and shy; but on the whole very much at home here, just as she and her friends had (eventually, fleetingly) come to feel at home. Today, however, Joanna felt herself to be a perfect stranger. A few icy raindrops began to fall as she made her way across the courtyard, past the central fountain from which water was spilling onto the flagstones as the spray was caught by gusts of bleak easterly wind. She pulled her coat tightly around herself and leaned into the wind, battling against it, as she headed for the sanctuary of the chapel doorway and the vestibule.

The service would not start for another twenty minutes, but already the pews were filling up. Joanna looked around for familiar faces, but most of the congregation seemed to be either much older or much younger than her. She glanced through the order of service and saw that the main eulogy would be delivered by Lord Wagstaff of Bishop's Stortford (just as she had expected) but he didn't seem to have arrived yet. She was just resigning herself to spending the next hour in her own company when a balding, corpulent man wearing an old-fashioned tweed overcoat eased himself into the pew beside her and said, 'Do you mind awfully if I sit here?'

'Not at all,' Joanna said, shifting slightly to make more room for him.

The man got himself settled. Despite the cold weather he was sweating slightly and dabbed at his forehead with a handkerchief.

'Unless I'm much mistaken,' he said, turning to look at her, 'we do know each other. Joanna Reeves, isn't it?'

'Goodness! Yes, it is. Joanna Maidstone these days. But I'm not sure I remember . . .'

'I know. I've changed. Changed terribly. It's all happened in the last five years. The belly's expanded and the hair's fallen out. There's nothing I can do about it. Same thing happened to my father. At exactly the same age.' He held out his hand. 'John Poole. We sat through many a Coutts supervision together in silent terror.'

'John! Yes, of course, of course.' She smiled warmly at him. John Poole had been a dull sort of person, an unremarkable student who had plodded his way through a philosophy degree and emerged with a middling 2.2, and she hadn't given him a moment's thought in the last four decades. But she was pleased to see him now.

'Good turnout,' he said. 'Have you come far?'

'We live in Berkshire,' Joanna said. 'Not far from Ascot. What about you?'

'Evesham.'

'Oh, very nice.'

'And obviously you're married. Children?'

'One daughter. Phyllida.'

'And what does she do?'

Which gave Joanna the opportunity to say, with a flood of maternal pride: 'Well, since you ask – she's just published her first novel, as it happens.'

'Really? That's wonderful. Congratulations!'

'There's an interview with her in the paper only today.'

'Splendid. I'll be sure to look out for it.'

The conversation dried up, momentarily. Joanna would normally have gone on to ask him some polite, innocuous question, but she had the strong sense that he wanted to say something to her, and was finding it difficult. She let him have time to find the words, and waited patiently for the confession or question or whatever it was. When it came, she knew at once that she might have predicted it.

'Actually,' he said, 'now that I've retired, I'm thinking of writing a novel myself.'

'Really?' said Joanna, her heart sinking.

'They say that everyone has a book in them, don't they?'

'Do they?' And then, out of a reluctant sense of duty: 'Did you have anything in mind?'

'I thought I might try my hand at a murder mystery,' he answered, in a complacent tone of voice, as if no one had ever thought of this before.

Joanna couldn't bring herself to congratulate him on the originality of this notion, so instead, to fill the silence, she found herself saying: 'Funnily enough, that was what my daughter started writing.'

'Oh, really? And she got it published?'

'Well, no . . . She's rather a quiet and secretive person, so I don't know the whole story, but I believe she tried writing something along those lines, and experimented with different styles – three different styles, I think she told me – but she wasn't happy with the result. So then she wrote something different. Quite different.'

'Ah. I see,' said John Poole, although it wasn't at all clear that he did. In any case, Joanna now saw an opportunity to change the subject, because she noticed some new arrivals making their way up the nave.

'Here comes Roger Wagstaff, then. That is him, isn't it?'

'I believe so, yes.'

Roger was flanked by two women, both taller than him, both dressed in black. One of them Joanna recognized immediately: the ever-faithful, ever-present Rebecca Wood. The other she didn't know. But John Poole was able to help her out.

'Well, well,' he said. 'And that must be Emeric's daughter.'

'Lavinia! Good grief.'

Joanna cast her mind back to the woman who, in their last year at Cambridge, had lived in Emeric's rooms and adorned his salons with her singing and her limpid, elfin beauty. Slender, seductive, blessed with an almost other-worldly charisma: eldritch, she had been called, by the more poetic amongst them. She was not unrecognizable now, exactly, but there was certainly none of that other-worldliness about her. She looked like a driven, hard-living sixty-year-old who had been Botoxed and facelifted to within an inch of her life.

'Well, this all takes me back, I must say.' John Poole's face was wearing a happy, far-off smile of reminiscence. 'Those salons! Do you remember? With all those visiting VIPs, and the music students playing Bach on the harpsichord.'

'I always thought it was a clavichord,' said Joanna.

Lord Wagstaff, Lavinia and Rebecca had found their reserved places in the pews at the far end of the nave, close to the pulpit from which Roger would shortly be addressing the assembly. Seated at his instrument on the western side of the chapel, an organist had started to play soft, meditative music.

'I suppose they must have flown in from America yesterday,' John Poole said.

'America? Why, what's been happening there?'

'CPAC,' he explained. 'The Conservative Political Action Conference. Biggest event of the year, for those of their particular . . . persuasion.' He reflected on his choice of word, decided that he was satisfied with it, and went on: 'Haven't you been following His Lordship's political career?'

'Well, yes, I suppose I have. From a distance.'

'I always knew he'd end up in the Lords. The whole system stinks, doesn't it?'

'Yes. I'm rather afraid that it does.'

'I used to keep track of his progress,' John said, 'by reading Christopher Swann's blog. I miss looking at that, I must say. Fascinating stuff. I was sorry to hear he'd passed on.' He glanced at Joanna, and could see that she was affected by the mention of this name. 'You and he were quite friendly, back in the day, weren't you?'

'Very much so. We stayed friends afterwards, as well. Poor Christopher. I still miss him.'

'I'm so sorry. I hope it wasn't . . . I mean, I hope he didn't suffer too much, or anything like that.'

'No,' said Joanna. 'He died very suddenly. It was a car crash. He was on his way to a conference.' A thought occurred to her now. 'Actually, if you're in Evesham, you probably know where it happened. Do you know Fish Hill?'

'Oh, good Lord, yes. Everybody knows Fish Hill. Very dangerous stretch of road, that. I'm amazed there aren't more accidents there.'

Joanna said, in a more introspective tone: 'It was all rather odd. Christopher was a good driver. And it was broad daylight, in the middle of the morning. Perhaps he was just going too fast . . .'

The nature of the organ music changed, quite abruptly: from meditative to martial. The congregation turned in expectation, looking towards the chapel's narthex. It seemed that the college chaplain and her deputies had arrived, and were waiting to make their procession towards the altar. The service was about to begin.

One hour later, Joanna said goodbye to John Poole beneath the archway of the college's great gate as they sheltered from the last remnants of rain. He asked her what she was doing for the rest of the afternoon, and offered to take her out to lunch at the Ivy, but she invented a little white lie and told him that she had work to do, and would need to get home as soon as possible. They shook hands before kissing awkwardly on the cheek as they parted.

Once he was safely out of the way, Joanna began to wander aimlessly along Trinity Street.

The rain was over and the sharp easterly wind had died down. Joanna walked slowly, taking in the mixture of familiar and unfamiliar landmarks, the new shops and businesses that had taken up residence in the old, well-loved buildings. She thought about Emeric's memorial. She thought about Roger Wagstaff's eulogy and how alien she had found it, with its relentless emphasis on politics; how distant a relation it seemed to bear to the bumbling, diffident figure of the old don she had carried in her memory. She wished that Christopher and Brian had been there to talk about it.

Why had she declined John Poole's offer of lunch? Had she just been put off by the thought of making polite conversation for an hour and a half, nodding along as he outlined the plot of his murder mystery step by step? No, it was not only that. In the absence of her close friends it was solitude that she craved now, not company. She needed time to reflect.

Turning the corner from St John's Street into Bridge Street, she took what was, for her, a bold decision, and walked into the Mitre, where she found a corner table and ordered herself a bowl of salad and a half-pint of lager. Alcohol at lunchtime! Whatever was she thinking? It was years, she realized, since she had last been to a pub by herself. In fact had she *ever* done it, in all her years of married life? How timid she had become, how circumspect, since marrying Andrew. Not his fault, of course. They were happy in most respects, and if the spice had gone out of the marriage, that was just what happened to every couple at some point. But their world had really shrunk in the last few years: neither of them ventured far outside the parish these days, and it had taken Phyl's homecoming after university, her growing impatience with the confines of Rookthorne and the dreariness of vicarage life, to make Joanna see how narrow their horizons had become.

If all went well, if there were no medical disasters, they should both have another twenty years left to spend together. How should they use them?

Without answering this question, Joanna left the pub and strolled back along Trinity Street, her mind a prey to conflicting, ambivalent thoughts, teetering somewhere between regret and fragile optimism. Right now she wanted to take one final look at her old college, to walk down to the Backs and stand on the bridge and watch the grey waters of the Cam pass beneath her feet, just as she used to do so often when she was a young and hopeful student. Passing through the college gateway again, she nodded a greeting to the porter who was on visitor duty – a female porter, how things had changed! – and skirted the great courtyard along its northern and western sides. She was just passing by the door to the Fellows' Parlour when her telephone rang. It was Phyl.

'Hello, love – is everything OK?'

⋆

Phyl had begun her working day in the same way that she began all her working days: by chopping vegetables and slicing fish.

Vegetables first: using the *hangetsu-giri* technique she spent thirty minutes cutting carrots, cucumbers and aubergines into half-moon shapes. Then she took the ginger, garlic and green onions she had bought fresh from the market that morning, and cut them into thin, round slices using the *usu-giri* method. With the salmon fillets that had just been delivered, she sharpened her *yanagiba* knife and began to slice them into ever thinner and thinner pieces. The work was soothing, hypnotic. In a way it was no different from the work she had done in her old job at Heathrow airport, but here there was a crucial difference: she was working for herself – or at least herself and Rashida – and it was amazing how much more fulfilling these routine preparations felt as a result.

Rash arrived late this morning, at about eleven-thirty, and was brimming with excitement. She had a copy of the newspaper with her and pulled it out of her briefcase with a flourish.

'I've already read it online,' she said, 'but we've got to have a copy of the print edition, haven't we? Such a gorgeous photo. Are you happy with it?'

She held up the paper and Phyl looked at the portrait for as long as she could bear, which was about three seconds.

'I look like some middle-aged schoolteacher from one of my dad's old black-and-white films,' she said.

'Bullshit. What did you think of the piece, anyway?'

'I haven't read it.'

'Oh, for fuck's sake, Phyl. Put that knife away and sit down for a minute, will you?'

They sat opposite each other at the chopping table and Rash started to read out the whole thing, although after a few sentences she relented – in the face of Phyl's objections – to the extent of saying:

'Well, the first few paragraphs are just him banging on about what a genius you are, anyway. You don't need to hear any of that. Here, this – *this* is the bit I wanted to ask you about. *Maidstone's book was the result of much experimenting and many false starts. An almost pathologically modest interviewee* – ha! He's got you there. Spot on – *she would much rather talk about the failure of her early attempts than her final success. She began writing, she says, in response to a tragic accident – the death of a close family friend in a car crash. "I couldn't bear the thought that this was just some random, pointless event. So I attempted to build a story around it. Partly to give his death more meaning, but also to try and give myself closure on it. Detective stories are famous for providing neat, tidy solutions, so I thought that was the way to go."'*

Rashida put the newspaper down and looked at Phyl intently, her brown eyes unwavering.

'I hadn't realized that you'd tried to do that,' she said. 'Why didn't you tell me?'

'I suppose I'm telling you now,' Phyl said. 'Indirectly.'

It took her friend a few moments to absorb this answer before continuing to read aloud: '*She quickly came up against the limits of genre writing, but pressed on with the same story while working in a more confessional mode. "My friend Rash"* – thanks for the namecheck, by the way – *encouraged me to use a more subjective, immediate style."'* Once again, she lowered the newspaper. 'I did?'

'Yes. It was one of the first conversations we had, in my bedroom at home. I drew up a list of three different kinds of writing. Three possible ways to go. Don't you remember?'

Rashida frowned. 'Vaguely. Hang on, what's this? *"I even started to write some of the sections in her voice."* Wow, I'm certainly finding out a lot today. *"But that didn't seem to work either. In the end I had to try something completely different."'*

'Actually, I said quite a bit more than that,' Phyl insisted. 'He's taken a chunk of the interview that was about ten minutes long and—'

'Well, that's his job, isn't it? You should practise the answers in advance next time. Make them a bit more concise.'

Phyl took the advice on board and nodded. Then she said: 'Look, you're not angry with me, are you?'

'Angry? Why?'

'Because I started off making up a story about Chris's death. It was really . . . It was just my way of trying to come to terms with it.'

Her friend leaned across the table, took both of her hands in both of her own, and squeezed them fiercely. 'I am so proud of you,' she said. 'So, so proud. Look what you've achieved. You just did whatever it took to get there. I'm not going to get mad at you for that.' Seeing the gratitude well up in Phyl's eyes, she picked up the newspaper and hurried on: 'Anyway, check this out – there's a nice plug for the restaurant. *The "Rash" in question is her friend and business partner Rasheeda Swan* – shit, they've spelt both of my names wrong, the sloppy fuckers – *with whom she has recently opened a pop-up Japanese restaurant in Dalston. The stated ambition of the restaurant is "to bring out the spiritual dimension of Japanese food"* – sounds pretentious like that, doesn't it, I knew we shouldn't have put it in the business plan – *which might explain the name that Maidstone, with her love of language games and word play, has chosen for it: My Inner Sense.*'

'Hang on – we chose that name together. They can't give me the credit for thinking of that all by myself.'

'Just chill. This is PR gold. You can't buy this kind of publicity. Anyway, did you read what he said about your book in the end?'

'I told you. I didn't read any of it.'

'*It's hard to believe Maidstone will be chopping vegetables for much longer.* Well, I'll be the arbiter of that, thank you very much. *After her unsuccessful experiments with genre, she has created a work that is* – listen to this – *breathtaking in its sheer originality, and entirely* sui generis. *Reviewers are already talking about it as a future classic, a book that will be read and remembered for generations to come.*'

While Phyl was pondering this phrase and wondering why it sounded familiar and made her feel vaguely uneasy, Rash's telephone rang. She didn't recognize the number.

'Hang on, I'll take this next door.' She grabbed her phone and headed out in the direction of the restaurant itself, pausing in the doorway only to give Phyl one last look, and one last smile. 'Superstar,' she said. Then answered the call.

Rashida had left the newspaper lying on top of the chopping table, but Phyl still couldn't bring herself to look at the interview. Instead her eyes drifted across to the opposite page, where she noticed a dramatic headline:

Britain's 'deep state' thwarted my plans, Liz Truss tells US far-right summit.

Curious, she picked up the newspaper and started to read.

Liz Truss, the former British prime minister, was among the headline speakers at this week's Conservative Political Action Conference at the National Harbor in Maryland. CPAC is billed as the biggest annual gathering of conservatives in the US but has in recent years embraced Donald Trump's brand of nativist populism.

A moderator at the summit introduced Truss by saying after her election in Britain 'there was a collective cheer in the conservative movement in the United States saying, wow, Margaret Thatcher is back!'

Reflecting on her 50 days in office as Prime Minister, Truss claimed that her attempts at radical reform were thwarted by vested interests embedded deep within Britain's state institutions.

'I became Prime Minister because I believed our country needed to be turned around. And I put forward a range of policies, and those policies got support from our party members, from our base. The policies were cutting taxes, cutting the size of government and reining in the administrative state.

'I believe that if all of those policies had been implemented, Britain would be stronger and we'd be in a better position now.

'I'm not saying I'm a perfect person or that I did everything exactly right, but I faced the most almighty backlash to those conservative policies, from the usual suspects in the media and in the corporate world. Even the IMF intervened.

'So these are the lessons I've learned: it's not enough to have the right policies. It's not even enough to get the position of power that you need to deliver those policies, because conservatives are now operating in a hostile environment.

'We have to understand how deep the vested interests of the establishment are, how hard they will fight and how unfairly they will fight in order to get their way.

'And it's ultimately conservatives being in power that will save the West. We will not save the West without that.'

Phyl put the newspaper down, confused by what she had just read. She felt a powerful wave of regret break over her, wishing that Christopher was still here. If anyone could have helped her to understand any of this, it was him. All she really remembered about that time, the fifty days of Truss's premiership, was that they had begun with Chris's death and after that, for a few weeks the whole family had felt lost, untethered from reality. The shock of the accident happening so soon after his visit, so soon after she had got to know him. Those were the days in which she had started writing, and her friendship with Rash had started to blossom and deepen. It had been a strange, volatile moment. Incomprehensible, in some ways. She'd used this word to her father, and he had replied that there was nothing incomprehensible about the financial measures introduced during that brief episode of political madness. Ask any pension funds manager, he had said: they would tell you that billions had been wiped off their balance sheets as a result of those fifty days. To which Phyl had answered that that wasn't what she was talking about, and besides, figures didn't really tell you anything. Someone else would come up with a different set of figures that showed the opposite. People lived in opposing realities and there was nothing you could do about it. The events of September and October 2022 showed that, if nothing else. All she could really say about that time was that it was hard to look back on it now and be sure that any of it had really happened: and if Liz Truss herself was choosing to weave conspiracy theories in order to make sense of it all, Phyl was hardly in a position to blame her. Everyone had to find their own kind of meaning, their own kind of closure.

She rose to her feet, picked up her *usuba* knife, and went back to work.

A few seconds later Rash came back into the kitchen. She looked shell-shocked.

'What's the matter?' Phyl asked.

'That phone call . . .'

She sat down at the table and stared ahead of her, unseeing. When her eyes came back into focus again, she looked up and said to Phyl:

'It was the police.'

'The police?'

'In Oxfordshire. Calling about my dad. It seems there's been . . . a development.'

*

After speaking to her daughter on the telephone, Joanna stood motionless for a while, stunned, trying to digest the news she had just heard. Then at last, when she felt capable of movement again, she stirred herself and cut through the passageway that led past the college's dining hall and connected the largest courtyard to its smaller, more elegant counterpart beside the river. Here, in the colonnade beneath the old library, there were stone benches ranged against the wall, and she was able to sit in relative peace for some time, breathing heavily and trying to decide on her next move.

She had been there for ten minutes or more when, amidst the groups of students drifting this way and that, on their way to the library or the college bar, she spotted the very two people who had been occupying her turbulent thoughts.

Roger Wagstaff and Rebecca Wood were heading in the direction of the college's newest court, built in the early nineteenth century: the same court in which Emeric used to have his rooms and had hosted his famous salons. It abutted the river, and was also the only court in which cars could be parked. Joanna followed them at a distance and caught up with them as they were packing their coats and briefcases into the boot of a bottle-green Tesla Model S, registration number RW I.

Coming to a halt within a few feet of them, she took a deep breath and said:

'Mr Wagstaff?'

Roger turned around, in the act of opening the front passenger door of the car. He neither confirmed nor denied his identity. However his companion, who was opening the driver's door, said:

'It's *Lord* Wagstaff, actually.'

'Hello, Rebecca,' Joanna said. 'You probably don't remember me. Joanna Reeves. We were students here at the same time. I came up for Emeric's memorial.'

'Yes. Joanna. Of course.' Her tone was so frosty it was impossible to tell whether she remembered or not.

'I listened to your eulogy,' Joanna said to Roger.

He waited patiently for a compliment. When there was no sign of it coming, he made as if to get into the car again.

'Well, we must be moving along.'

'Actually,' Joanna said, 'I wanted to talk to you about Christopher Swann.'

He looked at her sharply as soon as he heard this name, a shadow crossing his face.

'Who?'

'I think you know exactly who I mean,' she said. 'Christopher was also a student here. He died the year before last.'

'Oh yes, of course. Swann the blogger. How could I forget? Well? What was it you wanted to say? We're on a fairly tight schedule.'

'You know how he died, I assume? His car came off the road, on a hairpin bend, halfway up a steep hill.'

Again, Roger would neither confirm nor deny whether he was aware of this or not.

'He was on his way to a conference. The one you organized, in fact – in Chipping Campden.'

'Sounds like a very nasty accident,' said Roger. 'Now please come to the point, if you have one.'

'I've just had a phone call from my daughter. She was talking to Christopher's daughter, Rashida. Rashida has been talking to the police.'

Joanna paused. It seemed that neither of them was going to respond.

'A new witness has come forward. A white-van driver. And now it appears . . . It looks possible that it wasn't an accident at all.'

Rebecca made a show of consulting her watch, and said:

'Come on, Roger. We really must be going.'

'Apparently his car was forced off the road. The witness saw the whole thing.'

In spite of Rebecca's impatience, and her clear wish to curtail this encounter, Roger could not help asking: 'And why has this person only come forward now? I thought you said this happened the year before last.'

'He had his reasons,' Joanna said. 'His ownership of this van was not . . . strictly legal.'

Rebecca scoffed.

'He said there were two people in the car. He couldn't be sure if it was two men, or a man and a woman. He said that from behind, it was impossible to tell.'

Now Roger laughed – a hollow, insincere laugh – and said: 'A man in a stolen vehicle, who couldn't even see the driver in front of him properly?'

Joanna looked him in the eye. 'In some ways he was a very reliable witness. He remembered the make of the car, and the registration number. It was a bottle-green Tesla Model S. Registration RW 1.'

Roger finally opened the passenger door. 'OK, I've heard quite enough of this.'

'What does the RW stand for?'

Rebecca got into the driver's seat, and turned on the engine.

'Is this your car, or Rebecca's?' Joanna asked, her voice rising, her breath quickening.

Roger slid into his seat, closed the door, then opened his passenger window for just long enough to say: 'Madam, I simply have no idea what you are raving on about.' He pushed the window button again and added in a clipped voice, one moment before it closed:

'This conversation is at an end.'

On which note, Rebecca reversed the car swiftly; so swiftly that Joanna had to jump out of the way before she was knocked down. And then, with a derisive scrunch of gravel, Roger and Rebecca drove out through the archway, and sped across the little sandstone bridge that crossed the river. Their car was last seen disappearing from view between the rows of tall, impervious linden trees keeping watch on either side of the Avenue.

Thanks to all of the early readers of this book whose comments helped to improve it or give me confidence in it: Janine McKeown, Matilda Coe, Ralph Pite, Charlotte Stretch, Ian Higgins, Paul Daintry, Philippe Auclair and Tony Peake. Thanks also – for diverse and various reasons – to Madeline Coe, Michele O'Leary, Adrian Poole, Joanna Cooney and Vittoria Coffrini dell'Orto.

In addition, I must pay tribute to my copy-editor Mary Chamberlain, to Richard Bravery and Anna Hoyle for their wonderful visuals, to my agent Caroline Wood and above all to my brilliant editor at Viking, Isabel Wall.

J.C.